Love Loss and Little White Lies

love, loss

and little

white lies

INDIA RIGG

HODDER studio

First published in Great Britain in 2022 by Hodder Studio
An Imprint of Hodder & Stoughton
An Hachette UK company

1

A CIP catalogue record for this title is available from the British Library

Paperback ISBN 9 781 529 38265 5
eBook ISBN 9 781 529 38263 1

Typeset in Plantin by Manipal Technologies Limited

Printed and bound in Great Britain by Clays Ltd, Elcograf S.p.A

Hodder & Stoughton policy is to use papers that are natural, renewable
and recyclable products and made from wood grown in sustainable forests.
The logging and manufacturing processes are expected to conform to the
environmental regulations of the country of origin.

Hodder & Stoughton Ltd
Carmelite House
50 Victoria Embankment
London EC4Y 0DZ

For my mum,
Thank you for reading, re-reading and re-reading

I

'Come here often?' the man next to me turns and asks. With his jet-black hair and the immaculately manicured edge to his stubble, he looks like he works as a budget Craig David in Norfolk look-a-like contests. I could flatter him by pointing out that the contrast of his dark hair pigment and pale skin tone is perfect for laser hair removal, but I feel like he may not appreciate it as much as a twenty-eight-year-old woman who's been waiting all her life to have skin like an amoeba.

My eyes sting as I look up from my glaring phone. Infuriating, as I turned the brightness down for exactly that reason.

I hesitate – it's kind of an odd question to ask. If I answer yes, then obviously that implies that I am super hairy somewhere on my body, which is a gross mental image to give someone, and if I answer no, he may wonder why I suddenly care about personal hygiene. Not that it really matters; I'm not trying to feign attractiveness.

'Not really,' I respond. I mean, how often can you physically come to a laser clinic? Your body only has so much surface area. Not wanting to sound rude, I decide to offer him a question next. 'So . . . what are you getting removed?' It spurts out of my mouth with the jarring awkwardness of letting out a silent fart at your work desk. (I haven't been in company for a long time – forgive me.)

There's a time and place for icebreakers with strangers and laser-hair-removal clinics come in the same bracket as the doctor's surgery – not a social affair. My chances of making love to Mr David by Wednesday are well and truly scuppered, as he appears to be having heart palpitations.

Clearly, it's inappropriate to ask someone what treatment they're getting in a hair-removal place. People go all twitchy and mutter under their breath, just like when you ask for the morning-after pill at the chemist.

Before I'd been interrupted, I was engrossed in @JemimaIsADuck's latest holiday in Greece. Bronzed, candidly smiling girls with tassels on their skirts and tousles in their hair. I shut my eyes and imagine what it would be like there: the warm rays on my face, the beats from Greece's latest restaurateur-turned-DJ, waking up to the Sahara Desert in my mouth and a gorilla hacking away at my brain with a pickaxe. Horrible. That's why I didn't go, I tell myself, not because I wasn't invited. Can I send these photos to Florry? Or would pretending I've been on holiday for a week be a bit much?

I click off Instagram and put my phone in my pocket as the platinum-blonde, blue-eyed beautician sings my name.

I bash away the tendrils of thought that I could have been on holiday with a group of girls with whom I no longer have synced periods with and walk towards a Harley Quinn impersonator, who's going to blast my pubes off instead.

'Hello,' she says. 'Have you been here before?'

'No, I haven't.' I dart my eyes round the room, the lights burning my pupils. The tiny box we've just walked into is painted white; it's clinical but without the stark cleanliness of a hospital. That eery smell of sanitisation – it should feel like home to me.

'No problem. Take off your skirt and underwear and put this towel over you, I will be back in a second.' I lack dating experience, but I assume this kind of request is only acceptable in a hair-removal haven.

I chase away the memories of endless corridors, bleach and beeping machines and get to the practical task of undressing myself in front of a stranger.

As if she is trying to tease me, the girl comes back in, lifts the towel and looks a little surprised. *Peekaboo*. It's not doing anything for my anxiety. Is there something wrong with my vagina? Adam never seemed to have a problem with it.

'Oh, erm. Did you not shave before?'

'What?' Now, I'm really confused. 'I called up the front desk last week and asked if it was like waxing, and she said yes, so I assumed that meant that I needed to keep the hair.' That was the entire point of my call. The whole reason for having a receptionist is to book appointments and accurately respond to enquiries about pubic hair length.

'Hmm, no, you need to be fully shaved and then I run the laser gun over it to kill the hair follicle.' She says it as if I had asked some inane question like, *What will happen if I try to hold my breath for more than ten minutes?* 'Maybe she thought you meant would the hair grow back in the same time as waxing?'

If I had wanted to know that I would have specified, I want to say, but I can't be sarcastic. I'm lying on a bed, with my pants down, with six weeks of pubic hair growth and a lady holding a gun. Vulnerable doesn't even cut it.

'Oh my God, I'm so sorry. This is embarrassing. What should I do?' I look like I'm auditioning for a seventies porno. I haven't shaved for weeks; I've had no reason to until now. I've enjoyed role playing Indiana Jones in the bedroom, allowing my victims to traipse through the untamed jungle, beating away nature's creatures before they arrive at the jewel in the ancient tomb. That's a joke, obviously. There have been no serpents in that jungle for fucking months. There's about as much life in there as a morgue.

I already know that I won't sleep with Kevin tonight, but my vagina has been known to have a mind of its own. Lasered back to its birthday suit, it might suddenly be desperate to party.

'Well, you're here now, and I have another appointment in thirty minutes, so I will have to shave you.' She says it so bluntly I'm almost unaware of the harrowing activity she's about to pursue.

'Err, OK then. I guess you'll have to,' I reply nonchalantly, as if she's offered to make me a cup of tea.

I didn't really think about it, but having someone shave your vagina is *incredibly* embarrassing. I don't think anyone has ever shaved me before. I feel like I'm having a very intense sexual experience without the sexual part. I can't even look at my vagina in the mirror. Now I've got a lady carefully shaving every minutiae of it. Every clump of black pubes, disgustingly shaken off with a cheap Bic razor into the bin.

I'm given a pair of oversized sunglasses, which I'm pretty sure are part of Kanye's latest Yeezy collection, and the laser starts. This is what it must feel like if you are a freshly plucked chicken, ready to be made into a KFC bargain bucket, having an elastic band repeatedly pinged all over your tender skin.

I can't even make the standard, polite 'Going anywhere nice this year?' conversation during the treatment, as I'm mortified by the whole experience. Whichever receptionist took my phone call was a sneaky little bitch. I bet this poor girl didn't think she was going to spend ten minutes shaving a girl's vagina when she woke up this morning. I'm sure it's a fetish somewhere, ready to be made into a documentary. Louis Theroux, thank me later.

Finally, *fucking* finally, she puts the gun down, and inspects my vagina again, running her cold hand over my raw skin. Note to self: next time I'm going through a dry spell, come to a laser appointment; there's so much action here, I think Noah's ark might set sail again.

'OK, don't do any exercise or have a hot shower for at least twenty-four hours. But it looks like you have taken well to the laser.'

Hmm, is that a compliment? I guess so.

'Great, thanks.' I step into my pants, covering my red and traumatised vagina, pull my skirt back on, say the customary 'See you again soon' and get the fuck out of what I can only describe as one of the most embarrassing experiences of my life.

I walk to the nearest café, I need a coffee and a sit-down. That was very traumatic and something which, in isolation, I never want to experience again. Though I will, of course, relive it a few dozen times more for my friends and followers – this is content gold. Vagina shaving can go on the list of the worst jobs in the world.

Sipping my oat milk flat white, I relay the whole ordeal on the WhatsApp group to my home girls, appropriately named 'Homies & Hoes'. They are dying with laughter at my embarrassment.

Julia: OMFG, Milly, what were you thinking? You are so cringe sometimes.
Nicky: I find it quite hot when a guy shaves me.

Maybe if things go well with Kevin, I'll shave his balls and let him touch my new dolphin-skin vagina.

Their amusement helps ease my mortification until I'm smiling too. It's nice to be the funny one again. It used to be my role: I'm the social one. The one organised enough to plan the nights out, but still fun enough to be the one making everyone laugh. I am the girl always at the end of the phone, the person people confide in. Julia brings trainers on a night out to walk home in; Nicky walks home the next day with stilettos in one hand and a McDonald's in the other; while I throw up in the toilets and am first on the phone the next day to hear Nicky's tales of sexual proclivity and to find out from Julia how I got home. Or I used to be. That was when I went out. When I had someone to come home to.

I hesitate, wondering if the smoothness of my genitals is too much information for an Instagram story. I mean, is there even such a thing as TMI in 2019? It does make a pleasant change to share something while smiling rather than broadcasting out happy photos of my face or commenting with laughing emojis as I sit at home in my pants sobbing or scoffing crisps.

@FashHun1991 OMG hilarious Mills!
@JemimaIsADuck Would only happen to you!
@ItsMiaBabes I would literally DIE!

People like to engage with me through the barrier of the screen but not in person, for fear they will catch whatever it is that I have – a deep-rooted sadness? The black cloak of darkness only a widow can wear? It's OK, I've heard happiness is contagious, so I can understand them thinking sadness might be too. I respond with the classic, no thought required and extremely inappropriate, '*get the defibrillator* literally dead!' and go back to scrolling. It's a pastime that I hate to love. I genuinely feel like I've been at Ava's birthday brunch #27YearsYoung, I can imagine the sweat pouring off me after a forty-five-minute morning session at Psycle and I mentally salivate over Arabella's perfect poachies on rye, all without moving a muscle – well, apart from my extremely toned right thumb. Sometimes, I contemplate deleting the app to improve my mental state, get my hippocampus back in gear, as opposed to glassily staring at a screen, not taking anything in. But then I really would be alone. No pretend friends and no real ones either.

My vagina might appear party ready, but as usual, my mind is still wearing a dressing gown and slippers. Small talk and Kevin are at the very bottom of my to-do list. I can't even feign interest in the fact that he used to play rugby union. He's fit but looks aren't personality. He's trying to be funny, but I don't find jokes about fat people amusing and I hate *How I Met Your Mother*. Luckily for me, Adam didn't subject me to his TV rubbish, but he did have a soft spot for the odd trashy romance. Although maybe he was just humouring me – I'll never know. What can I even say to Kevin to make the time pass quicker and go home? If only I was into mindfulness, then I could transport myself to pastures lush and green like a Buddhist monk. I can feel my eyes glazing over and I've already hit the ice in my gin and tonic, my straw slurping and rattling around as I try for the last drops of the delicious on-the-spot anaesthetic which is imperative for a conversation with Kevin.

'Excuse me, I need to use the bathroom.'

Stacey's a dirty slag!

Whoever decided to pen that on the cubicle door must have been clutching at straws – did they not know being called a slag is a compliment in the twenty-first century?

I pull down my knickers and sit on the cold, hard seat where a thousand dirty bums have sat before. I would have worn a thong, but my vagina is smarting from my earlier ordeal and I couldn't deal with chafing; these are my Marks and Spencer period pants – calling them *knickers* is a compliment.

Flirting with my own underwear, now that's a new low.

I have a small scroll. It's a force of habit now. When I wake up, when I pull down my pants, when I get into bed. I pause at Julia's latest photo, a candid one taken by someone else – *jealous*

– of her holding hands with James on the beach. I *wish* I was her. It was always Julia and I, in our long-term relationships, and dear old Nicky, who we lived through vicariously. I DM her:

Stop being so greedy with your two Instahusbands.

I click to add that overused emoji, a round yellow circle, with two black dots for eyes and a flaccid penis for a tongue to show I'm not being serious. Even though I am.

Finally, a little tinkle. I find urinating relaxing; an emotional release of sorts. I should probably go back; Kevin will be wondering where I've got to. I fumble in my pocket as I flush the chain. Oh well, another one bites the dust.

'I was starting to worry that you had done a runner!' he says as I return to the table.

'Ha. No. Erm, shall we get another drink?' The words fall clumsily out of my mouth. I put my hand up to my head, brushing the hair behind my ear. I hope I don't regret this.

'What is that?' Kevin points to my hand, where the diamonds caught the light. I pretend that I hadn't intentionally planted an obvious marital symbol on my left hand. 'Are you fucking married?' He spits the words, angry and baffled. 'Why would your sister set me up with someone who is married? Are you fucking pranking me? I knew I shouldn't have ghosted her friend that time. You girls are fucking nuts.' He's gone balls-to-the-wall crazy, as expected.

'I'm sorry. Sometimes my fiancé and I like to go on dates to liven things up a bit. Being strictly monogamous is so, I don't know. . .' I reach in the air for the word before landing on it. '2008.'

'What the fuck? Do you think it's funny?'

'Not really, but I do find if you tell your date that you're already engaged, it ruins the whole experience. I would never have heard you repeat jokes from Marshall in *How I Met Your Mother* season one, and then where would we be?'

'You're nuts. Don't think I'm getting the bill and *don't* tell anyone that I rejected a threesome or whatever it is you were offering; the lads will think I'm a right prude.'

Good inference of the situation, Kevin. I'm not sure I mentioned stepping out of my pants and into bed with you and my imaginary fiancé, but boys will be boys.

He gets up to leave, then puts twenty pounds on the table. His mother taught him well.

I feel bad. Sort of. It's a small price to pay. Kevin would much prefer that I pulled the old fiancé card out, or rather – the very literal engagement ring – than go on multiple dates with me, only to find out that I'm an emotional train wreck. You can't fuck with crazy.

I call Florry.

'We need to talk about Kevin.'

'What the fuck have you done now, Milly? Tell me you didn't pull that heinous wedding ring prank again.'

'It was like watching paint dry and he's obnoxious. Have you ever met an obnoxious can of paint? Why did you even bother introducing us? Did you really think he was good for me?' I fire questions at her like a machine gun.

'Milly, right now, you're not one to judge. Beggars can't be choosers.'

'Beggars?! I'm not a beggar. I'm not begging for someone to love me.' My voice quavers.

'I didn't mean what I said. But. . . he wasn't exactly my first choice more. . . my last hope. I've run out of options.'

That's it. Me, done. I'm like a pack of five-per-cent-meat ham on the reduced shelf in Lidl, destined for the bin. Thank you, wheel of fortune, for spinning me this sublime turn of events.

20 April 2011

The smell of summer. You can taste the heat in the air, sun cream on skin, grass that's just been mowed. Everyone's happy. They can't help it – the sun releases endorphins. Fact. Unless you have hay fever, then you may as well live in a cave.

Exam season is here, and we've all been inside for days, revising. It doesn't matter, as it's been raining – April-showers. Adam and I have been binge-watching *Gossip Girl* in the evenings, but in the day, we've barely seen each other. I hate exams; I get stressed. Bright-red-rash, hyperventilating stress. My beige walls have been replaced with hundreds of colourful mind maps, I recite the process of DNA's transcription and translation in my dreams and I colour code flash cards at every given second. Adam doesn't get stressed until the very last minute. I walk around in a daze, bumping into tables because my vision's been replaced with the scribbles of charts and my usual fluid conversation substituted with the Latin terms for animals and body parts. Adam sits around eating pizza and playing PlayStation. He crams everything in at the last minute and still gets a first. *Boys.*

Anyway, today we woke up, saw the sun and the exam season stress just wafted away. Adam BBM'd me, and here we are, having a gorgeous picnic in the park. As much as I'd like to kid myself that I'm the idyllic sort of girlfriend who's been up all night making tiny little sandwiches and baking scones, with flour dusted compellingly across my cheeks, we're students. That means the picnic consists of – Thai sweet chilli Kettle Chips (don't know why, but they're the perfect hangover food – not that we were drinking last night, but you know), hummus (university staple – made of chick-peas so it's basically a vegetable), two BLT sandwiches from

Tesco (because bacon), a pack of strawberries (I'm not feral) and two bottles of cava (one's never enough, and I'm not one to turn down a deal).

'I can't wait until exams are over,' I say, basking in the sun. 'We can do this every day.'

'I know, me neither.' Adam turns his face towards mine, smiling, stretching his hairy legs out further on the rug. Sometimes I can't help but stare at him. He has piercing blue eyes, a smile that lights up his whole face and scruffy dark hair that is the superb combination of just-got-out-of-bed and trying-to-be-effortless-on-purpose. He also has perfect legs, in proportion to his top half, not like Thomas the Coat Hanger. I'm forever thankful.

'You haven't even done any revision yet!'

'Yes, but I will do eventually, and I don't want it hanging over me, the stress is ruining my game of *Call of Duty*,' he jokes and fills up our plastic flutes with more cava.

'I wish I didn't get stressed, like you. If only I could, I dunno, play *The Sims* all day and then get a first, I'd be happy. What's your secret?'

'It's all in the mind,' Adam mocks, pointing his forefingers to his temples. 'Why don't you come to Charlie's birthday drinks tomorrow night? Probably be good to relax a bit – exams aren't for a few weeks anyway.'

'I can't. I'll be way too stressed! I've got a million organism names and life cycles to learn, and the only way I even have a chance of passing these stupid tests is if I start early. I barely have time to catch up on *The Only Way Is Essex*.'

'What will ITV be doing without your viewing figures?!' Adam chortles. 'You wanted to know my secret?'

I nod.

'I wear a little daffodil in my hair for good luck.' And he plucks one from the grass and pops it behind my ear. '*Ma petite jonquille.*'

I snort with laughter but kiss him all the same. 'You better be wearing a flower crown to your exams, or I'll know you're lying.'

'You might mistake me for Titania from *A Midsummer Night's Dream*.' Adam is a voracious reader of anything literary although he has a passion for historical fiction, but he's aware that often his references have the ability to fly straight over my head. However, we've had this discussion before, and I read *A Midsummer Night's Dream* for my GCSEs.

'I won't be looking so glamorous, I can guarantee that. I'll be shaking from a Pro Plus overdose.'

'You'll still be my little daffy.' Is that his nickname for me? It seems cringe and cute at the same time. I like it – it's endearing.

That's why I love him. He allows me to be me. I don't need to get up extra early to do my make-up, blow dry my hair or shave every minutiae of my body so I can be the vision of a woman that exists only in porn. He even holds my hair back while I'm sick from kebabs and Jägermeister. That's true love.

Adam starts picking the tomato out of his BLT.

'Why are you doing that? You like tomatoes.'

'I hate them in sandwiches – they make the bread all soggy. Do you want them?' He points to the limp-looking slices of tomato strewn on the grass.

'Erm, no. Rats would have been weeing on that grass, and then I might get sick before my exams.'

'No more exam chat!' Adam exclaims. 'I'm making a new rule: we can't talk about exams' – he checks his watch – 'after two p.m.'

'That's basically the whole day!'

'Exactly. What are our summer plans then?'

'*Our* plans?' Almost questioning his togetherness.

'Yes, I was thinking I could come to Norfolk for the summer and stay with you for a bit. Maybe get a job in a pub or something. We could even go away somewhere super chic like the Canary Islands.' He winks.

'I'd love that!' My cheeks ache almost instantaneously from the grandeur of my smile.

We kiss and Adam puts his arm around me. We sit basking our faces in the sun, sipping our cava.

I take a deep breath. 'Well, now I've decided to let you spend your summer with me, I have a question for you. Don't laugh, and I know you're not big on social media, but . . . can we be Facebook official?'

'I mean Facebook official? Phwoar, that's about as important as marriage, isn't it?'

I laugh. Adam is like a grandad on Facebook. His profile picture is a pug dressed as Luke Skywalker. He always laughs at me when I come running into his room, shouting about the next couple to become Facebook official who have been together for at least six months already. He uses Facebook for the photo albums and having lame back-and-forths with his friends about games and drunken debauchery. He'll say something like, 'Why do you need to tell everyone about your relationship status? Do people comment "Fingers crossed for this one" when you're entering your fifth Facebook relationship of the year?'

'I'm proposing to you via Facebook. Everyone knows it has to be Facebook official to be *official* official.'

'If that makes you happy, Mills, then yes. I'll tell everyone who already knows that we're together that we're together again, and I'll await the floods of messages, cards and gifts.'

I go on Facebook and tag Adam in my post.

'Are you ready?'

'I'm ready.'

Milly Dayton is in a relationship with Adam Hadfield.

'We're basically married now.'

'Married at university? Who'd have thought it?'

'Don't say it.'

'I came, I saw, I conquered.'

'I knew it. Now, let's get drunk. I've got some exams to forget about.'

'Shot!' Adams shouts, as childish as ever. 'You said *exam*!'

2

4 February 2019

Another fucking Monday. Another week that'll be a car-
bon copy of the last. I'll wake up at the same time, go to
bed at the same time, travel to work along the same line and
see the same people waiting for the Tube at 8.46 a.m., with
their headphones in, looking bored out of their blank minds.
The gentleman who always eats a ham-and-cheese croissant
from Gail's Bakery; the elegant blonde lady with the insane
designer bag collection; the young mousey-brown-haired girl
who recently got engaged. Her rock of a ring nearly knocked
me out one morning. I didn't offer her any congratulations
because even though we see each other nearly every day, we
don't speak. This is London. It's illegal to make eye contact.

I wonder what they all think when they see me every
morning? Their fellow commuter, pal of the Underground,
the silent friend hiding in the shadows of the Central line. I'm
a nuclear twenty-eight-year-old. I was born, grew up, went
to school, college and finally finished my education with the
admirable university degree. I moved to London to make my
riches six years ago and am still trying. I'm five foot three
and a half (basically five foot four), have brown hair, blue
eyes, wear Fucci belts and Yves Saint Faurent bags. I spend
my days watching people through a screen, living lives that I
thought only existed in movies, and wondering why I never
got picked to be a Disney princess. Real people are boring
anyway.

Today, like every other day, I wake to the annoying iPhone jingle that signifies another day of monotony and open my favourite app, Instagram, for some pre-morning-routine scrolling and, of course, #inspiration from my life gurus. I don't need to wake up in the warm arms of someone I love. I can wake in the soulful eyes of thousands. I'm greeted by inspirational #MondayMantras, wardrobes of beautiful clothes and the hilarity of memes, not a judgemental comment about morning breath, night fidgeting or sleep burps.

Ping. Notification. *Ping.* Notification.

I'm lucky to scrape double-digit likes on an immaculately edited photo of my own face when @TongueWateringly-Jemma can easily hit the thousands with a subpar photo of yesterday's cacao nib porridge with tomato-seed-milk-hand-squashed-by-orphans.

I see Olivia's been out to brunch again, to that place where your food is served on a palm leaf. I comment:

OMG Jellllll <3

She likes it almost instantly. I haven't seen Olivia in person for about eighteen months; since the funeral, our relationship consists of comments with hidden meanings and colourful emoticons. I angrily post superlative comments on inane photos while she massages her own ego. It's a win-win.

It's not because Olivia has done anything wrong. Nothing worse than Arabella, Mia, Jemima, Emily, Ava and the rest of the uni lot, anyway. I haven't singled any of them out; they all get the same treatment. Ironically, that day, I could barely look at any of their faces, as all I could see was my own grief. Now, all I do is sit and stare at the contours.

Amanda's posted too. A photo of their Yorkshire terrier, Tank. Adam chose the name, as he thought it was funny for such a small dog to have such a large name. I would unfollow her, save myself the heartache of the memories that she might post; baby photos of Adam, or snaps of us at the house at Christmas, but she mainly posts the classic country-mum-on-social-media shots, like a blurry cup of tea or a new pair of Dubarrys. Occasionally, Amanda posts something that causes a stab in the gut, but it's usually limited to his birthday, or the anniversary of his death, and we text then anyway. It used to be more frequent, but now it's only on the days where grief overrides all feelings – *Thinking of you x* – because we don't have much in common apart from a missing piece of our hearts.

I like the photo and keep scrolling.

The whole point of social media is being a time saver. It's much easier for me to like a photo from someone that I haven't seen in two years while putting haemorrhoid cream on my face or watching reality TV than organising after-work drinks. To be honest, real people can be annoying, asking too many questions about how you're feeling and offering advice about things they can never dream of understanding. It's also much harder to hide emotions in person – I don't like confrontation.

I've also found that Instagram's great for private messaging and stalking in secret, but irritating in that the first thing any stalker sees when they click onto your profile is how unpopular you are – the exact number of friends you have. What's wrong with my profile? Is it the filter? The combination of food shots, scenery and candid body shots? I can fix those if someone just lets me know. Or is it something entirely unfixable, like my eye-to-nose ratio or my blackened past? At least Adam liked me for who I was; he didn't even seem to mind that shaving my legs coincided with my monthly period. I should be grateful; if Instagram showcased the number of my *actual* friends, then I'd probably be in the negative.

It's annoying that everyone's success in the twenty-first century is defined by how many followers they have on Instagram.

It means that even though, deep down, I know I've been mildly successful, working for one of the top healthcare PR companies in the UK, it just doesn't fill me with joy. If I was able to flick onto Instagram one morning and be greeted with a post that went viral and thousands of new followers, I think I'd scream. And even I know that's sad. Sometimes, I do think I look like an addict; I really should take more pride in my appearance. I wake up every morning with black bags under my eyes from scrolling into the early hours. I have marks all over my arms where my phone has imprinted during my slumber. I'm constantly filled with anxiety about when I'll get my next high – who is going to like my #ThrowbackThursday post of dolphins at Disneyland Florida when I was ten? Will it be worth it? Should I have used the Mayfair filter rather than Amaro? It's all starting to sound pretty sombre.

Florry thinks I'm addicted to social media, and I quote, 'Milly, I really think you should see someone. Social media has the same addictive tendencies as cocaine, and as much as you annoy me, I don't want you dying an early death or degrading your septum.' I couldn't be bothered to explain to her that it isn't really cocaine, so it would be pretty hard for my iPhone to degrade away my septum unless I started rubbing the electronic rectangle on it every morning and night, but the sarcasm would probably have washed over her head. It also clearly doesn't have the same high, otherwise you would see people drooling over their notifications on a Saturday night at Phoenix, and you don't see addicts in the street screaming in agony every time someone walks past scrolling through their newsfeed.

Florry's my three-year-older-yet none-the-wiser sister. Those extra three years without internet means that although her knowledge of the menstrual cycle and taxes is A*, her knowledge of technology is well, grade E, at best. Basically, she's still trying to upload her selfies to a floppy disk using a Nokia 3310.

Anyway, as much as I disagree with Florry, she then spoke to Mum about it, who spoke to Dad, who called me to discuss the probability that I was indeed an Instagram addict, which is ironic considering they don't even know what Instagram is. They probably still think it's a planet somewhere after Uranus. I'm not addicted to social media, it's just more fun living in the make-believe, but I don't expect people over the age of thirty to understand that.

I'm bored of upsetting people and have decided it's much easier to placate them instead, so I've decided to give it a whirl and visit Violet, the social media addiction counsellor, for her take on the dark side of those adorable little red hearts.

I say that as if I made the decision to visit Violet myself, which isn't quite true. Florry mentioned me seeing a social media counsellor a few months ago, and I disregarded it because I'm an adult and am totally fine with how I choose to live my life. It went something like this:

'A social media counsellor?' I scoffed. 'Per-lease, who will I be seeing next? A ghost hunter? Normal people don't do that kind of thing.'

'And what is *normal* to you? It doesn't mean anything,' Florry said, looking at me quizzically, as if trying to mentally undress me.

'It's just . . . normal, you know.' I try to shrug the question off.

'You shouldn't look down on other people because *you*'ve decided a version of normal. What is it then? Two and a half kids, a dog and a house in suburbia?'

'That sounds like your ideal life.' I scoff. 'No, normal, is just being yourself – a normal person, doing normal things.'

'Do you think normal is spending your whole time on social media and never going out? That's not "normal" as you put it, unless you're defining normal as a shut-in.'

'Yes, all right!' I snap. 'I do think normal is living in a nice house, with a nice husband and nice kids, and no, that isn't me, but I don't need to see some stupid counsellor.'

'But you think that you won't ever be happy until you have that, until you fit into that societal mould, and that's not true. That's why you need to go and see someone.'

I stormed off after that and we pretended the conversation never happened. But then Florry found out that I'd been lying not only to her, but to my parents too, and seeing a counsellor became less of a choice and more of an obligation.

What was I supposed to do? They would have been unbearable if they knew I hadn't been out with Julia or Nicky or Ava, or whoever else for months, so I sent my parents and Florry carefully cropped photos from other people's Instagram accounts to prove I was out brunching with friends, keeping myself active and occupied. It wasn't until one fateful day, when I was being a bit lapse, and Florry found one of my edited photos of the perfect brunch on the *Daily Mail* website taken by @EtherealEats. I think Florry always had an idea of what I was doing but she was just waiting for proof. The realisation that I had become the person who catfishes anyone with a pulse hit home, and I felt really fucking shit. And so here we are. Florry tattletaled on me, and now I am losing my therapy virginity, which I should probably have lost years ago.

Instagram exhausted, I contemplate getting out of bed, ready for another day at the PR grindstone, before remembering I haven't checked WhatsApp and revel in the opportunity to stay under my duvet for another five minutes. Realistically, any messages could only be from one of about five people, but more often than not, they're from Julia. There's nothing nicer than being greeted by a selection of little green messages; it's like rubbing Aladdin's lamp and a friendly genie popping out. Julia and I have always texted, but on the day my heart severed in two, Julia started messaging me every day and she's kept it up. I'm not sure if that says more about me or her – she's a good friend, but am I also still tragic?

Julia's been my best friend since we were ten. We attended the same shit school in the depths of north Norfolk and we became friends, because luckily, like me, she was one of the few to have ten toes, eight fingers and two thumbs. Though we may both have the correct number of digits, Julia's cooler (she eloped and got married in Vegas) and more sensible than me (she did it to save money for a house deposit). Julia's beautiful and seems to have everything that I ever wanted – a husband, a nice house, a good job, fantastic nose, not a care in the world. I don't have many friends, but I'd like to think that the ones I do have are good ones. You shouldn't really have more than five good friends; it's too hard to keep track of their lives otherwise or read their WhatsApps.

> **Julia:** Saw this in *Time Out* and thought of you.
> **Julia:** Nostalgic – "someone who seeks comfort in nostalgia, such as buying canned spaghetti after a break-up." Lol.
> **Me:** Dafuq?! I'd NEVER define myself as that!
> **Julia:** Hahahaha, I would. Remember when you broke up with your first ever boyfriend and you wanted to eat ice cream on the sofa like they do in the movies, but instead you bought a jar of gherkins?

Pickles. Adam loved pickles. Once, when we were drunk in McDonald's, Adam asked a stranger if he could eat his left-over pickle. Don't worry, I didn't kiss him after. Although I'd kiss him now if he ate ten strangers' pickles.

> **Me:** Whatever. You're just jealous. Pickles are low in carbs as well as having probiotic powers. They are also

a good source of electrolytes and hydration, so they
helped replenish my tears.

I know I said I didn't want to wake up in the warm arms of
someone I love, but that's just something I tell myself. In reality, I'm not very good on my own. I need reassurance from
someone, otherwise how do I know if I'm doing a good job at
this thing called life? It's much easier to pretend you don't like
having loads of friends, or a life partner, than to admit that you
must be the only twenty-eight-year-old in the world who feels
lonely. It's not normal for young people to feel alone, especially
when we are the most connected generation to ever exist.

Ping.

Your friendiversary with Adam Hadfield. Eight years
ago today, you and Adam Hadfield became friends on
Facebook. We've made you this video to celebrate your
friendship. To many more years!

I take a quick snap of the sun on my street for my Instagram
story on my way to work, complete with #earlybirdcatches-
theworm and #worthitformorningslikethis – it isn't but no
one wants to see negativity on their feed. I should at least get
a sympathy like from Olivia at any rate – she owes me.

'The usual?'

'Yes, please! Oh, and this.'

I keep meaning not to get a Starbucks every morning, but
I can't help it. It's the only warmth I get to experience at the
moment; almost as good as human contact but not quite.
At least coffee doesn't contain the same complications
as relationships do. According to her Instagram (I found
her by going on the Starbucks Croydon location tag – you
won't believe me but it's a hub of activity), the girl who is

serving me, @ILikeMyMenHotAndBlack, and I, are quite similar. She likes going out on a Friday and Saturday night and loves David Attenborough. So does everyone, I guess. We could probably hang out together, but I can see what she's doing through Instagram anyway and she probably has enough friends.

'Cool shoes! I wanted some but they had all sold out.'

We even have the same fashion sense. I look down at my size-four feet and feel proud that I had taken the plunge as soon as the powers that be had shoved at least five bloggers wearing them in my face on Instagram. Adam loved his trainers, but he would have hated these – *You look like a chihuahua in platforms* – I bought him some new trainers for *up there* because he was worried that his old ones might be a bit scruffy for eternity.

'Thanks, I was really lucky to get them.'

I sit down and rest the Marmite-and-cheese roll in front of my right Fila Disruptor and take a snap. And another and another. There, perfect. The light is coming through Starbucks's window and reflecting off the bright white of my plastic shoe. I add the hashtag #MarmiteMondays on the off chance they are looking for a new ambassador.

I work in healthcare PR at one of those offices where you can wear anything you want. Apart from when the boss decides that you can't. It's quite likely that if I wear anything 'young', he will comment on it.

If you're ever really stuck for what to wear, I've found that wearing ripped jeans works wonders. At least one person over fifty will comment that time-honoured joke that 'work must not be paying you enough', which, thank you for pointing out, they don't.

My boss is called Mark and is at that age where he's young enough to join in Friday drinks but old enough to still be cringe while doing it. He says things that he thinks are funny and a sign of being 'down with the kids', but actually what he says borders on inappropriate.

'How many whales did you kill to get those shoes, Milly?' Mark jeers as I walk in. I've learned nothing will stop some people making terrible jokes, not even my being a grieving widow.

'Fuck off, Mark. Bollocks, I didn't mean to say that. Fuck.' I said it again. 'Sorry.'

You could have heard a pin drop, and I can feel the heat rising from my whale shoes all the way up to my sweaty five-head. It looks like I forgot to reset my work boundaries.

'Milly, maybe tone the language down?' Mark says with a smile so that I can't understand if he's joking or being serious.

'Sorry, Mark, I didn't realise who you were.' Not that I should be telling anyone to 'fuck off' in the office. Or ever, my mum would say.

'Maybe I should start reminding you who the boss is then, hey?'

Right, I'm the one who's unprofessional.

I shuffle coyly into my seat next to Marjorie.

Peter pipes up. 'I find it really inappropriate that people even buy plastic shoes in this current climate. It's like shouting about how many turtles you have single-handedly slaughtered.'

What would you know about climate change, fuckwit?

I manage not to actually say it this time.

Peter's one of those smarmy guys that clearly got bullied at school. He's managed to quickly climb the rungs at work because he's a boy and doesn't have any friends. Now, he takes out all his anger from his past life on anyone who resembles the kind of person who would have laughed at him at school. Obviously, one of the ringleaders was a five-foot-three-and-a-half girl with brown hair called Milly. Ironically, I don't have many friends either, but I don't have a dick that

I like to spend half the day scratching, so I hold the ladder while Peter climbs up it.

When someone dies, everyone is always super nice to you at first; they can't give you more love, more sympathy, more presents or more time (well, no more than the three weeks' grievance leave tops). That's until death isn't paramount any more, and something more important comes along, like a friend's break-up or the government questioning the exact sugar content of a doughnut. Then, despite it only being three weeks post-traumatic-death-incident, you have to pull your socks up, slap that smile back on and remember to laugh in all the right places at boring jokes so you aren't a downer on society any more. Three weeks is ages anyway. A lifetime, in fact, in the world of healthcare PR.

Marjorie pretends that she is ferociously working but she's clearly been listening to every word. She's another one of those people that was nice when Adam died and is now back to being fucking annoying. One of those women who takes her job super seriously but to no avail, and she's also *terrible* at technology. It really winds me up. Marjorie doesn't get me and I don't get her. Marjorie has hobbies like Zumba and flower arranging. Do people have hobbies any more? Or do they repeatedly do things they enjoy but aren't regimented about them?

I could be working on PR campaigns for Coca-Cola in Amsterdam right now, smoking weed and dipping chips in that really nice mayonnaise you only get on holiday, but I turned it down. More fool me. Instead, I sit here every day, working out how to make a chronic disease have sex appeal.

Scroll. Blast away stubborn belly fat with celebrities' favourite Boo Boo Tea. Scroll. Unboxing! Latest Dior hand-bag and why I fell in love with the sales assistant. Scroll. More free trips to Dubai featuring girls with bodies that don't exist. This isn't what I yearn to see in my scrolling. I want brunches, lunches, parties and holidays with my friends. I want to create stories in my head, close my eyes and transport myself back to the time when I too had a seat at the table. I wish I could sit and continuously scroll through the good years of my life and all the bad stuff would be magically filtered away, like a spot on FaceTune.

Fuming at the turn of events, pre-10 a.m., I start the wearisome process of turning my computer off standby.

I click onto Facebook and the video pops up again. I may as well watch it. Adam and I with turkey hats on our heads at our first Christmas together – was that seven years ago now? Adam holding my legs up into a handstand on the common outside our university halls. Adam and I kissing on a balcony in Seville. I close my eyes and remember when life was good. I can almost taste the salt on his lips from that incredible bruschetta we had. Fresh tomatoes, crisp sea salt and a squeeze of sun-ripened lime.

I open my eyes. Marjorie is staring at me; she's totally ruined that bruschetta.

'Morning.' I smile sweetly while my eyes are glaring – if they were lasers, she would be a pile of floury dust.

'Can you do the agenda for this afternoon's meeting?'

'Yes, I can, once my computer has turned on.'

'Well, maybe instead of scrolling on Instagram, you could think of some ideas now. I find social media such a time waster.'

Scrolling on Instagram?! How would you feel if the usually placid outlet you liked to confide in had kindly decided to make you a video of your dead husband before 9 a.m. on a Monday? As if there wasn't enough salt in the wound.

'I'll do the agenda for you, Marjorie, once my Outlook has opened,' I repeat firmly. I turn, put my headphones in and continue to scroll on Instagram. I feel as if I'm always miserable. Surely that can't be right. It's not even because I am a twenty-eight-year-old widow. Everywhere I look, I see a timely reminder of where I am not. Sitting in a freezing-cold, grey office, worrying about how many carbs were in my Marmite-and-cheese roll while absent-mindedly watching playful stories of Lola Lo and her boyfriend frolic in the white sandy beaches of the Bahamas, coyly drinking fresh watermelon juice.

I decide against sharing the Facebook video – it will only entice an onslaught of people commenting streams of red hearts, crying faces and kiss emojis. It might even entice a couple of strays to drop me a 'Milly! We must go for a drink soon' texts, which they won't follow up. I've come to learn that people think death is contagious, like a horrific game of dominoes. Everything I touch will fall down in blackened ash. Keep your loved ones locked up in case Milly Dayton gets her hellish limbs, grasping like a noose, around their necks.

Florry: Hey, shithead, are you going to see that counsellor tonight then?

Me: Morning to you too! Yes, I am. That OK with you?

Florry: Honestly, I can't believe that the world is in such a state of disarray that my baby sister has to go and see a professional about a communication device. You are not out shagging robots as well, are you?

Me: If only. Would be about as much action as I can get at the moment.

Florry: What's happening with that guy, Tom?

Me: It was Jacob, but nothing.

Florry: Why not, I thought he was nice?

Me: Nice? I'm not a charity case. I don't need a 'nice' boy, I need someone to challenge me. So vanilla. Stick a flake in me, I'm done.

Florry: I thought you wanted a nice boy after the Kevin fiasco? I can't keep up. Call me after your sesh, k?

12 January 2015

'How did it go?'

'Let me put my bag down, and can you make me a drink?' I respond, rushing into the flat as if I have somewhere important to get to. 'Maybe two gin and tonics. I need one to take the edge off and one to savour.'

I look around the bright white room of our home while Adam fixes me a drink. It's a tiny flat, a one-bed in one of those new-build tower blocks where every room looks exactly the same, as if it's part of a computer game. All the appliances are sparkling new, and the built-in features are MDF-covered-in-vinyl shiny but everything else is second-hand – bright orange pine, or dark chipped wooden furniture decorated with vases from John Lewis and faux plants from Marks and Spencer. It looks as if someone's bought all the furniture from the sixties into a lab to study it. We're between flat-shares with friends, but I quite like living alone, just the two of us.

Adam fixes us each a gin and tonic in the fancy glasses his mum bought us for Christmas. They're one of the things I own that makes me feel so adult. Special glasses to drink gin in, not a chipped mug that says *I should have been in Gryffindor*.

'How grown-up is this?' I say as I take a long sip, the ice clinking in the glass, swilling the bitter taste of juniper berries around my mouth. It's instantly soothing. Medication for the over-eighteens. 'You making me a drink after work – I feel positively middle-aged—'

'Come on, Milly, what did they say?!' Adam interrupts me.

'They said . . . I've got the job.'

'That's brilliant news! Why didn't you tell me that as soon as you came in? I'm so proud of you!' He rushes to clink our glasses in a congratulatory cheer.

'Well, I did get the job, but not the one in London . . .' I pause. 'The one in Amsterdam.'

'That's amazing.' It doesn't seem to faze Adam. 'My girl-friend a jet-setter, so continental.'

'It's not *amazing*, Adam, because I want to be here with you, so I'm turning it down.'

'You can't turn down your dream job because of me. We'll make it work.'

'It won't, though. You hear all the time about long-distance relationships being tricky. Your job is here in London and I can find another one, here with you.'

'Of course it would work. It would be tough, but Amsterdam isn't that far away.'

'It doesn't matter how far away it is, because it's still far. I feel settled here. I want to be with you. I don't want to leave London without you. I can't be bothered to make friends alone, go out to clubs, FaceTime you every day, sleep alone – it'll be like being single again and I have you.'

'It wouldn't be like that at all, and I would come visit at weekends, and you can come here to see me and our friends.'

'Yes, I *could* do, but I don't *want* to. Why does life have to be so difficult? I've been offered my dream job and I have my dream boyfriend, but they are hundreds of miles apart . . .' I pause, trying to picture Amsterdam on a map. '. . . If not thousands.' I pause again before concluding. 'I have no idea how far away Amsterdam is.'

Adam smiles before reaching for me.

'No, geography has never been your strong point.' He looks me straight in the eyes. 'I don't want to be the reason you turn down this job. I don't want to be the person that goes stamping on your dreams – you'll end up resenting me.'

I look straight into his piercing blue eyes. 'I promise I won't resent you.' I take both his hands in mine. 'It's just one of those annoying things that happens in life. There'll be other opportunities for me. This isn't the only one, just the first one that's come my way. I wouldn't be happy in the job anyway, as you wouldn't be there. Besides, do you want me hanging round the red-light district by myself on a Friday night?' I hold out my glass for another G and T. 'Another please, sir, I did request two, I believe.'

Adam takes my glass and takes a couple of strides into the kitchen area.

'Milly, you get scared being alone in the flat – I know you wouldn't hang round a red-light district.'

'True.'

'What if I got a job in Rome?' Adam asks me in between slicing and eating cucumber.

'A barman never eats his garnish on the job,' I point out. 'That's different, as you've wanted to work in Rome since you were six.'

'Ahh, my Augustus phase. I believe it was age eight that my true love for Julius Caesar took hold.'

'Stop being a nerd and get back to talking about me.' I grin childishly. 'Anyway, I haven't wanted to work in Amsterdam since I was six, so I can just as well stay in London.'

'It's your decision, but of course, I'd welcome you back to London with open arms.'

'I haven't left yet. Besides, I'm getting used to this life of luxury – my boyfriend making me drinks after work – who would give this up?' And I recline further on the sofa, feet in the air as Adam throws a slice of cucumber in my direction. 'Sackable offence!' I laugh.

3

After an extremely slow nine-hour day of tap-tap-tapping away at a keyboard, punching out passive aggressive lines of 'Thank you, I'd love to add this really boring project of filing all of your emails to my already overflowing list of to-dos', it's finally time for vivacious Violet to tell me my fate, and whether I should, in fact, start snorting lines of cocaine because it would be better for my health than scrolling through pornographic photos of beaches and betches through a glass screen.

I pop to the bathroom to quickly top up my make-up so I don't look the colour of full-fat milk, courtesy of being trapped inside a boring grey box with no sunlight for days on end. I order myself an Uber, as Mum said she would pay for it (and I think she should, as I was basically forced against my will to attend this session). I told them I already had a shrink – @SocialShrink91 – but Florry said that was a class A explanation as to why I needed to go and see Violet. Normal people don't rely on friends they don't know, apparently.

I'm not in the mood for chatting, as I'll probably be doing a hell of a lot of it in twenty minutes. I know it's rude, but I can't be bothered to tell the driver my whole life story today or hear about how busy he has been since he clocked on to his shift. I can vouch for the fact that Uber drivers are the best shrinks – when I was returning home from one of Adam's hospital visits, squealing like a hysterical pig after seeing his face change from normal human skin colour to out-of-date-sausage overnight, the nice driver waived the charge and gave me a chocolate bar – but I don't want that now.

I scroll on my phone instead; school friends are going out for drinks and sushi and I'm on the way to a counselling session. What a juxtaposition my life has become. I click onto his profile; I didn't use to go on it so much, but then I thought, why not? After he died, I avoided it like the plague. I had people constantly comforting me, for a few weeks anyway. Then everyone moved on and I was left very much alone, and I realised that it's nice to live back in those days, months and years, next to Adam, before my whole world got turned upside down. I like reading all the latest comments, not in a sadistic way but I find it comforting, remembering when everyone cared. On the first anniversary and first missed birthday, there was a flurry of:

Gone too soon.
Happy Birthday angel.
Sleep tight up there.

We don't really get much activity now. I imagine I'm the sole watcher of his timeline, which was populated on a semi-regular basis and then suddenly reached a dramatic end, like the battery on the recording device ran out. Or someone took it upon themselves to stamp on it so there was no chance of it working ever again.

The scrolling combined with the movement of the car starts to make me feel sick, so I spend the rest of the journey staring into the London abyss, watching everyone scurry around as fast as their legs will carry them. It isn't often that I sit and watch the world go by. On Instagram, everyone's always preaching about taking time out of their day to practise some sort of meditation, but I can't think of anything worse than sitting and thinking about things. I enjoy being busy. The last thing I need is more time with my thoughts.

I had everything primed for a successful life and I feel like as soon as I left university, it all came crashing down. If Adam hadn't gone and died on me and I hadn't turn into a widow at twenty-six, then maybe, just maybe, my life would be on track.

That's exactly why I don't like sitting and thinking about things. Silence allows the mind to wander, and I need mine to be distracted.

Ooh, a Facebook message from Mia. What does she want?

Gyals, Jemima is getting married! We can't believe it! Our little chicken is finally flying the nest. We want it to be EPIC. Please all transfer £350 into my bank account – this will cover the entire weekend apart from the dinner on the Friday night, drinks on the Saturday and maybe a roast on Sunday. We've managed to find a beautiful house in the Cotswolds for all thirty of us, complete with a hot tub – bring your cozzies (phit ones, we are vetoing anything branded by Speedo). We won't all be able to use the hot tub at the same time, so we will have to do shifts. (Just remember to have a shower before your turn as we don't want anyone to catch anything!) We wanted to have a good theme, so we looked up what 'Flake' meant, and it means 'shark often used for meat', so we will be dressing up as sharks for the night on Saturday. Sexy sharks, though, obvs, and don't worry, dick straws will be plentiful – why do you think we need £350? Jokes!

Apart from the shark-themed night out, Jemima wants the colour scheme to be white and gold, so please only wear these colours, and if you bring any props, they too must be white and gold. We're sorry, but if you do end up wearing something in a different colour, you won't

be allowed in. YOU HAVE BEEN WARNED! We don't
want to lose anyone, so will be making tags for us all to
wear on the Saturday night with my name and number
on, as I'm the organiser and therefore, chief hen. Finally,
we want you all to have a great time but there is a sick
fine, so please make sure you are all sick in the loos or
if you do accidentally do it in the house, just make sure
you cover it up. Ellie knows one of the Dream Boys from
work, so she is sorting the stripper, but if anyone else
wants to book one too, feel free – you can't have too
many naked guys on a hen, can you?

Love youuuus, Mia X

Oh Mia, still as irritating as ever. She doesn't even know she's
doing it, that's just her. One of those people that you need a
McDonald's-sized vat of salt to carry around with you, seasoning every word she says.

She couldn't even tone it down for the funeral. Though,
to be fair to her, I was annoyed by everyone that day. All I
wanted was to be left alone, but I suppose I can't fault people
for wanting to share their grief.

I know I've only been invited as a charity case. The token
widow – a diversity invite. The friend you barely remember from uni but invite anyway to beef up numbers. I don't
think it even warrants a reply. I'm 100 per cent not going.
End of.

I send a filtered snap to Homies & Hoes of me with a muzzle
on and some dog ears.

Me: I'm off to find out my fate, girllls – if you don't hear
from me, my phone's taken me hostage.

Nicky: I am going to start dangling my phone in front of you to make you run faster.

Julia: It would be a good way to lose weight if you had to run after your phone every time you want a scroll. I spent three hours on Instagram yesterday according to Screen Time.

I switch to Famalam:

Me: Your socially damaged daughter/sibling is off to discuss her Instagram track marks.

Mum: GOOD LUCK DARLING. YOU WILL BE FINE! LUV MUM X

Dad: Thinking of you, Amelia. Lots of love, Dad xxx

Florry: Make sure you explain that none of your friends are real and the last person that you slept with was an iPhone 8.

Nice to see that this is as much a joke to everyone else as it is to me.

'Thank you,' I say as the Uber pulls to a stop.

'Five stars, yeah? You'll give me a five-star rating?'

'Oh, err, yes, of course. Great driving.' I give him a thumbs up. I wish I could get constant gratification for simply doing my job. I'm lucky if I'm allowed to work flexitime.

We've pulled up in front of a Victorian townhouse-esque building in Shoreditch – exactly where you would imagine someone who analyses media moguls and the bearded elite to reside. A little gold plaque on the door reads *Dr Violet Redfern – Social Media Expert*. It's all starting to feel a bit serious.

I press the doorbell and get buzzed inside to a waiting room, where I give the receptionist my name and take a seat on one of the leather chairs. The girl next to me smiles gingerly and continues to rock back and forth, her bright bottle-dyed purple hair catching the sunlight with each move. There's a boy the other side of the waiting room who looks pretty normal apart from the fact that he keeps taking his phone out of his pocket, looking at it, saying 'No!' really aggressively and putting it back in his pocket. On repeat. I feel a flash of memories from my conversation with Florry about what 'normal' really means, if anything. Is it a townhouse with two and a half kids, or is it following other people's lives on social media because you can't face your own? Who am I to judge? I just know I'm not anything like these people.

I rewatch the video that Facebook kindly created for us. I can't even remember who added who. It's the sort of question that I would ask Adam. He would think about it and come up with a highly plausible answer, which we would then debate, before deciding that I probably did it because he hated social media – *'I don't need 'likes' from people I don't even know to prove that I'm living my life'* – that's the sort of thing he would say when I tagged him in statuses or locations of nights out. He did say he loved me first, but he also died first, so with only my memory to rely on, I suppose I'll never know.

How many times have I watched that video now? It only lasts a day on Facebook, and then it will vanish. I'll have to hope that the Facebook algorithm still works in the same way and they send me the video again next year. May as well make the most of it, allow myself to get lost in my past happiness.

What am I doing here? I'm not addicted to social media any more than I'm addicted to caffeine. This is so stupid. I stand up, ready to leave. What a waste of time—

'Milly Dayton?' Too late now, I guess. 'Milly . . . ?' A lady with a scarlet bird's nest where her hair should be, a sharp jawline and an aura of kindness in her eyes visible through heavy-rimmed, dark green glasses smiles at me.

I take a deep breath and walk towards someone who gets paid triple my salary to read tea leaves for a living.

I squirm awkwardly on the outlandishly extravagant velvet chaise lounge. I feel uncomfortably hot. If this session has plunged me into early menopause, Florry's going to be paying for it.

This is my idea of hell. I hate talking about my feelings, about myself – in person, anyway. I don't like being analysed; I like being the analyser. I spent *weeks* on end telling everyone about my feelings two years ago. As soon as I entered a room, everyone would be on high alert. Although I quickly learned that I shouldn't be too honest when they asked me how I felt. Nothing that might require a response beyond a maximum three-second hug. I was upset, of course I was. Well, more like distraught. I thought I'd be hanging on the railings wailing for days on end, seeking the comfort of others, but mostly I wanted to be alone and scream into one of the Adam-scented-pillows I kept.

My friends and family were so worried that I'd want to be tucked in next to the dust that remained of him, but of course, I didn't. Just because I didn't know how to go on living without him didn't mean I didn't want to. I may have just looked on the verge of death – though that's no surprise. That's what a diet of white wine, cigarettes and cocaine does to you. It's not known for glowing skin and nice nails.

Everyone wants to be the one to *cure you*, the new twenty-first-century miracle man. But some things take time and *shockingly* can't be cured by a cup of tea and a pat on the shoulder. Despite what they may have thought, I've never wanted to join him. The truth is that I'm scared of death, now more than ever. I'm desperate to be able to live again, join in with the life I'm glued to online, but I don't know how. I spend my days living vicariously through celebrities, chefs, fitness gurus and fashion models who don't even know I exist. I like to live in the world of make-believe that Adam and I used to flit in and out of on occasion; it made life more fun.

'So, Milly. What brings you here today?' Violet asks me inquisitively, not looking up from her furry pink notepad. I'm starting to feel dizzy from the obsession with hot pink and fire red. The satanic millennial underworld. Maybe I really am on drugs?

'Well, I, err.' I'm stumbling over my words, feeling awkward and embarrassed. My hands are clammy. Why did I wear a grey T-shirt today? Come the fuck on, Milly! Who cares what you say, you never have to see her again, just put a face on – you're good at doing that.

'My sister, Florry, seems to think I'm addicted to social media slash my phone in general. Which, of course, I'm not. I've seen the people outside in the waiting room, I'm nothing like them. She seems to think that being addicted to an inanimate object is the same as being addicted to cocaine. I've never heard anything more absurd!'

Absurd. That's what our landlady said when we requested putting a hot tub outside on the terrace. Adam scrunched his head into his shoulders and screamed it from his gullet. 'Absurd said the bird!' mocking her as I laughed and filled the bath with bubbles to create a pauper's tub instead. Is it crazy that even a word can remind you of someone?

'It's probably hard to get your head around.' Violet moves her head up and down like one of those nodding pugs on car dashboards. 'Does being addicted to social media seem silly to you?' Clearly Violet doesn't see the insanity in the situation. Two and a half years ago, I was in a stable relationship with the love of my life. We used to go out dancing with friends on Saturdays, hungover beers on Sundays and get pizzas on Mondays. We didn't have any worries because life seemed endless. Now, my husband is dead, and I'm being told I have a social media addiction. Oh world, throw me a fucking bone, will you?

'I mean, yes. My friends and I joke about it, and I find memes about phone addicts funny, but I don't actually think I am one! Even if I was, I'm not popping pills or injecting myself every day, so how's it even bad?'

'Being an addict doesn't mean that it is always visible to the outside world. There is a lot of stigma surrounding addiction and you should be very careful who you judge. Social media addiction can often be described as an innate reaction to things. People can become addicted without even realising it. They stop engaging with things outside the screen of their phone.' Violet must be a magician; she can talk and write at the same time – there's a chance that she is a robot.

'Why's that a problem? Real life isn't always that fun unless it's engineered.'

'Do any of these ring true to you, Milly? Switching on the television and then sitting scrolling. Going to bed in the early hours, just to get a last-minute scroll in. Meeting friends for coffee but both of you spending the majority of the time communicating through a screen even though you are right in front of each other? Wishing your parents happy birthday on Facebook even though they don't have an account?'

'Look, I'm not going to lie and sit here and pretend I don't do those things, as we both know I do. But *everyone* does them! Your phone is your companion, the port key to all your friends – who wouldn't be on it all the time? Most of the time it is more exciting than my actual life, so of course, I want to spend all my time on it.' I feel almost breathless. Would anyone else like to stand up and vividly explain to me how much of a twenty-eight-year-old turd my life has become?

Violet strums her pen on her book. Every so often, the pen catches one of her acrylics. Not in a gross way. I think her nails are one of the things I admire about her. Perfect, plastic points.

'Just because everyone does it, doesn't mean it's right. It isn't that scrolling on Instagram is bad – we all do it. It's about the effect it has on your body, your mind, your relationships. I often find that millennials – your generation – find it extremely difficult to connect with people physically. Virtually, of course, that is no problem. I am sure you have thousands of Facebook and Instagram friends. I am sure you send messages to a handful of them on a daily basis. I am also sure you wouldn't be phased to "slide into someone's DMs". But what about going up to someone in the street and saying hello, would you do that?'

'It's not the same. Going up to someone in the street and saying "hey" is weird. People will think you are going to mug them or something. You don't say to people in the street what you say in a DM. Imagine if you were walking around and then a guy came up and shoved a dick pic in your face!' The thought of it makes me chuckle.

'If you wouldn't say it in person, then should you say it at all?'

Hmm, she does have a point. There are a lot of dicks that I don't want to ever see in person. I mean, I never asked to see them in 2D, but I can only imagine the perpetrators in 3D.

'It's different, it's always been different. I used to call my friends up on the house phone to say things I was embarrassed about in person.'

'Do you think that the phone is a barrier to your emotions, then? Is it a safeguard?'

You might be about to overstep the mark now, Violet.

'I honestly don't know. I've never given my phone this much thought before.' And neither should anyone else. Surely there are way more important things to think about other than the latest iPhone. Violet should be the first to know that.

'There are many theories as to why we are all so obsessed with social media. It isn't necessarily bad, but it is about managing your feelings. It's not uncommon for people of your generation to feel misjudged and left to pick up the pieces from other generations. Older generations, the baby boomers as you might know them, were able to get the buzz of achievement from things like career progression and buying houses. They were able to do this in a way that your generation can't. Often people fill this void with social media and directly correlate feelings of gratification and self-worth with the receiving of likes and virtual interaction. Each time you see that colourful notification, it releases dopamine in your brain, similar to what happens when someone takes some cocaine. And just like cocaine, it compels us to repeat the experience. Social media is a way of feeding an ego; it doesn't require any talent to post a photo of your face or your dinner but it rewards. You are able to easily feel achievement and success in a way that is not available in the real world.'

Violet seems to know a lot about cocaine. I am not sure how I feel taking advice about addiction from a suspected addict . . .

'God. I didn't realise that people have done so much research into something that is supposed to be just a bit of fun! I just don't think people think about it that much. I get that we all spend far too much time online, everyone knows that, but I really wouldn't say I turn to social media because I'm embroiled in some sort of political turmoil.'

If I really wanted to, I could let Violet know that I'm a widow. Maybe this might help her analyse my case, but I don't want to tell my whole life story to someone who I barely know. This is real life, not Instagram.

'I know it is hard to understand, but that's OK. A lot of things we do in life, we have no idea why we do them, and when we think about it, the reasoning behind it seems silly and inaccurate. I want you to try a few things for me and write down how you feel. These are for your own personal benefit, so if you never want to see me again, that is totally fine. Turn your phone off at nine p.m. every night for a week and write down how you feel. Do you feel tired, energised, anxious, relaxed? Choose a series to watch and put your phone on the other side of the room. Try not to scroll when you are watching TV. Limit yourself to thirty minutes a day on social media for a week. When you go for coffee with a friend, keep your phone in your bag, don't write notes, don't message that person about that thing that can't wait. Leave it. I want you to write down how you feel. Be in tune with your surroundings once more. Allow yourself to feel something rather than the numbness of waiting for the next hit.'

Rude.

'OK, fine, I'll write it down, but I doubt it will be that different.' I say shaking my head.

'Great. Now, Milly, before you go, I would like you to fill in this form, and if you do decide to see me again, you can see how things have changed, if at all.'

Violet passes me a questionnaire. Bloody hell, this is intense – who knew a phone could be so dark.

How often do you lose track of time when surfing the web?

Have you ever felt ashamed about how much time you have spent on your phone?

Do you wake frequently to check your phone?

Do you find yourself upset when others seek your attention when you are online?

Do you ever find yourself using the internet in inappropriate situations?

How can a normal person answer these without looking like a complete freak?

'Do I really need to answer all of them?'

'Look, no one is going to judge you, Milly. These are for your own personal gain. You didn't have to come here today, you chose to. All you need to do is think about some of the things I have said today and think how you can improve your happiness in life. You must be feeling an element of unhappiness or you wouldn't have shown up here today.'

'Look, Violet, I came here today because my sister made me. I totally appreciate everything you have said to me, I understand it. It does make sense, but that isn't me. It isn't what I do. I'm in tune with my surroundings. I do spend time on my phone but I don't do it to fill a void, I do it to connect with my friends and share all the good things that are going on in my life, just like everyone else. I'm really sorry if you feel that I've wasted your time.'

I stand up and muster a smile at Violet. I cannot believe that she gets paid for this. Do you think she studied Instagram at university? I thrust my hand out and into hers. I don't want to leave on bad terms. My karma can't take another knock.

'OK, well, thank you, Milly. I am sure we will bump into each other again.'

The difference in temperature between our hands is ridiculous – Violet's cool, calm and collected, and mine, hot, clammy and agitated. I don't know why, but she's really riled me.

If everyone who spent more than two hours on social media a day was accused of being an addict, we would have no one left. Violet's one of those people who makes money out of making people feel like they need help when they don't. Like those people who run ayahuasca retreats. Why do you suddenly need to travel to Peru, take a load of LSD, shit yourself, puke and spout about how good you feel? You don't. It's one of those twenty-first century jobs that prays on the fact that people have money and don't know how to spend it.

2 November 2010

Adam and I lay on the bed in silence, where we've been for the last half a day, trying to decide if this is what death really feels like.

'God, I feel soooo hungover. I think I might be dead,' Adam says, still with his eyes shut.

We went pretty hard last night – Tinie Tempah was bringing the beats and the drinks were flowing freely. Easy when it's one pound fifty for a double.

'I still feel pretty shit too. I think it was the Jäger – I can still taste it. The thought of drinking it again tonight is making me gag. You were burping it in your sleep. And I swear I could smell it sweating out of your pores. Absolute filth,' I say, half laughing.

'I don't think it's possible to burp in your sleep.' Adam hasn't moved an eyelid, unphased by my comment.

We continue to lie in isolation from one another, feeling too ill to even touch. I love these days. Hungover at university, not a care in the world, no itinerary, just each other.

'Of course it is! People sleepwalk, -talk, -hiccup – 100 per cent you can sleep-burp.'

'I'd google it, but I can't be bothered to type.' Adam puts his hand to his forehead, exaggerating his sickness.

'I should know. Trust me, I'm a scientist.'

'Not until you graduate.'

'Which I'll do in a couple of years. I might even become a professional burping professor – discover a cure for the infamous sleep-burpers.'

'Shut up!' He playfully nudges me. 'How is it three p.m.? All we've done is lay here, crammed together in this tiny bed like two sardines. I think I could eat.' It's mental to think that we get on so well after such a short amount of time. I have to pinch myself that it's real.

'Now you say! We could have gone down to the Thai place with Emmy and the girls when they knocked!'

'Coulda, woulda, shoulda. I prefer it when it's just us two, anyway. I reckon we've spent the last three weeks in this bed.' His eyes are now open, not quite the piercing blue of normal; more the French tricolour, with the added bleariness of the red, mixed with the white.

'I know, it's actually disgusting. I need to change the sheets; I'm turning into a festering animal. What do you fancy – Pizza Hut?' There's something so comforting about being able to be your weirdest, most disgusting version of yourself with someone. I don't have to pretend to be anyone else with Adam. I don't need to put on an accent or try my hand at sophistication. I can be plain, hungover Milly, who's probably still got morning breath.

'Only if it's Hawaiian? Please don't say you hate people who like fruit on their pizzas.'

'Do you know what? It's my favourite! Let's play a game. What's your favourite ice cream?' I love being childish – it's a release from the strains of adulthood.

'You are such a child sometimes. But probably mint choc chip.'

'Are you kidding? That's also mine! I hope you're not secretly my brother or something. That kind of thing does happen in Norfolk.'

Adam pulls me in for a hug. 'I love you,' he whispers.

I sit bolt upright, laughing.

'You just said you love me!'

'No, I didn't!'

'Yes, you did. I heard it.'

'OK, fine, whatever, I did say it.'

I feel panicked. What am I doing? I'm only a fresher. I have all the time in the world to fall in love. But I do kind of love him. Or is it the leftover Jäger talking?

'It's OK, Mills, you don't have to say it back.' He turns over.

'I love you too,' I blurt out. I don't want Adam to be annoyed at me.

'You don't have to say it just because I did.'

'No, I do. You surprised me, that's all. I don't think anyone's ever said that to me before. Is it normal to love someone this early?'

'There's nothing normal about you.'

'I'm just glad you said it first, otherwise you might have thought I was weird and clingy.' I know I do mean it; I felt it last night when he was pretending to slut drop on the dancefloor – I wanted him to be all for me and no one else.

I turn over from my isolated lying position and rest my head on his chest so I can hear his beating heart.

4

I want to go home, but Mum said she'd only pay for the Uber one way. I wish I could click my chihuahua platforms together and be magicked back into my flat, like Dorothy clicked her sparkly red shoes to dance down the yellow brick road home.

I share a quick meme where someone has smashed their phone with a sledgehammer and is trying to snort it. I have a scroll through Adam's profile and telepathically recite the idiocy of my recent meeting. I used to enjoy tagging him in memes and funny videos on Facebook. To be honest, I did it recently, but it came up on Julia's newsfeed and I had to pretend I'd done it by accident. Adam would have laughed anyway.

I open up Homies & Hoes and start frantically messaging my girl gang instead, as they are very much alive and kicking, thus able to respond.

Me: Girls, honestly, that meeting was a total farce. I don't know how she makes so much money by making social media into a drug metaphor.
Julia: Ha ha ha ha. WTF happened?! Tell me all. Did she check you for track lines?

Julia always knows how to cheer me up. I plug my headphones in and blast James Brown through my pods. I need some sixties vibing and jibing.

Me: Yeah, she made me take a breatha—

SMACK! Screeeeeeeeeeeeeeeeechhhhhhhhh.

'Hello? Darling? Come on, open your eyes. That's it, you're all right. You're in safe hands.'

'Is she OK? Is she OK? What the actual fuck. She just came out of nowhere. Didn't look where she was going. On her bloody phone, wasn't she? God. I'm glad she is OK. Fucking hell. What a shock.'

I open my eyes very slowly; I have a girl on one side of me, a shouty man on the other, an ambulance, and I'm lying on the pavement. The coldness of the concrete is seeping into my bum, making it feel numb. It's light outside and I'm not drunk. Tragic.

'There we go, sweetie. That's it. Sit up slowly. You're OK, but you've been hit by a car. That's quite a tumble you had.' The female paramedic holds my arm gently.

I've been hit by a fucking car, love, not tumbling around the soft-play area with a couple of tots.

The owner of the silver bullet on wheels looks anxious and angry at the same time. Wringing his hands while shaking his head.

'Where's my phone?' I say, in a trance. The girls are going to wonder why I haven't replied. It'll make a great Insta story. I go to stand up. *'What the fuck!'* I scream. Pain's suddenly soaring up my leg. Tears are pricking in my eyes. Now I really need my phone. I need my mum. I need Adam. Why, oh, why is this happening to me?

'I wouldn't do that, love; I *think* you've broken your ankle.'

I look down to the tree trunk that's replaced my lower leg – a slightly inobservant comment from the second paramedic who has just appeared. I used to be quite proud of my delicate ankles and now I've got the world's biggest cankle. I *think* by my non-medical observation that my ankle is well and truly fucked.

Please tell me this is not a real day and I'm having a night terror.

The paramedic puts a hand on my shoulder.

'There, there, love. It will be OK.'

My hysterical pig snorts are starting to attract attention, and a group of teenagers are standing on the other side of the pavement, observing what happens when a farmyard animal is let loose in central London.

'My phone.' I sob and snort. 'My phone, I need my phone.'

'Looking for this, darling? Think it's seen better days! Probably could do with a break from it, as I think it was this little demon that caused you to be lying on the side of the pavement!'

Better days? It looks like it's been thrown against a brick wall repeatedly and then used as target practice by a firing squad. The owner of the four-wheeled silver bullet is starting to get on my tits. Who's he to know how important my phone is? Does he not have a daughter?

I wonder if anyone will even care where I am. I could be stuck in the hospital for days with no method of communication. There'll be photos of me broadcast over the news – probably no reward offered, as I've been such a sapper on society. If Adam were here, this would never happen. He'd never stop searching for me. @ILikeMy-MenHotAndBlack will be devastated – that's sad, isn't it? That my barista might be the only person to notice my absence.

Fuck, the last photo of my face on Instagram was a highly edited one with dog ears and a cartoon tie. The BBC are going to broadcast that photo out in my missing persons case. I will become a laughing stock. My mum will be doing her nut – she's probably sick with worry already.

'Come on then, darling, off we go.'

I clutch my broken lifeline in my right hand and sob into my neck as the two paramedics lift me onto a stretcher and into the back of an ambulance. Happy fucking Monday.

The adrenaline has worn off and everything's starting to become a whole lot more real. I hope the nurse has studied dendrology; she's going to need a degree in tree surgery to get this wooden block of a leg back to normal.

My conifer leg is throbbing, and when I reach the hospital, all I can do is lie there looking up at the blank ceiling, thinking about the last few hours. Why aren't there TVs in here? A and E is notoriously slow and everyone in here is in *pain* – at least make it more bearable. I wish someone would spike the water machine.

I don't want to complain about the NHS, as it's a free service, and if I'd been hit by a car in America, I'd probably have to crawl to the hospital because my salary wouldn't even cover the cost of a nurse's pinkie. But, what would you give a traumatised car crash victim with whiplash symptoms, a broken ankle and half the skin ripped off her lower leg? A couple of paracetamol tablets, that's right. They don't even get rid of a hangover. I need my blood to be replaced with morphine.

As I lie on a stretcher, waiting for the two little white pills to kick in even the tiniest bit, I'm starting to feel distressed. I don't know if I'm more upset about breaking my phone or breaking my ankle. . . What's been more supportive over the last twenty-four months?

Is it OK to feel distraught at losing your little electronic sidekick? It's been with me every day since the last iPhone upgrade. It knows me better than I know myself. It's seen me looking my best and my absolute worst.

Some of my old friends may have finally decided to message me and now I'll never know. What about all my photos? All those snapshots into a happy past that I never look at. Gone forever. A past I'll never be able to recreate.

Oh fuck. All the photos of Adam I have. I knew I should have printed them.

I feel a tear in my right eye. Don't cry, don't cry, don't cry. It's only a phone. You can easily get another. The cloud will have the pictures, right? You're always crying – grow up, Milly! Life's shit for everyone!

I'm going to read a silent eulogy for my phone and mourn in silence. After all, as Florry pointed out, it was the last person that I slept with.

Dear phone, thank you for being with me through the good times and the bad. For never judging me. For fuelling my alcoholic call marathons and never asking questions. For bouncing back when I throw you in a rage. For comforting me as I drip tears onto your screen. For only giving me minor facial bruises when I drop you onto my face in bed. Thank you for being the only constant in my life.

After my silent funeral for an emotionless robot, I'm wheeled out to the waiting room, where the nurse registers me in a wheelchair. This ankle is really hurting now; I feel like it might even have to be chopped off. If I lose my leg, I honestly don't know what I will do. Maybe it's karma for dating other boys. Part of Adam's black humour.

'Can I get you anything?' the nurse asks me. 'We're going to put you in a bed soon, just waiting for one to free up. Then you'll have an X-ray and we can get that old thing all plastered up!'

Hospitals make me feel sick. It's like some twisted drama school where everyone walks around with a smile painted on their face while giving out horrendous news – 'You're going to die today, poppet. Happy Christmas!'

'Can I have some painkillers, please? Maybe some codeine or something?'

'Darling, we just gave you paracetamol in the ambulance. You can only have two every six hours.'

'Can't I have some codeine or something a little stronger? Please, I'm in agony. Honestly, I eat paracetamol like sweets when I'm hungover – my liver's absolutely fine.' I've been hit by a car! What does a girl have to do to get some of the good stuff?

'It's against hospital policy for us to give you anything other than paracetamol until the doctor's seen you and we can assess exactly what's wrong. And I wouldn't go around telling everyone you eat paracetamols like bonbons – they might send you off to an addiction centre.'

At least I'd get given something stronger there. It would be a cruel twist of fate to send me there after spending the afternoon shouting that I'm not an addict. What a waste of money that session with Violet was. My phone's been destroyed already. Maybe that was all part of the master phone-rehab plan.

'Please, I'll do anything. My ankle has quadrupled in size and I can't walk on it. Pretty sure it's broken. Can I at least make a call? Is there some sort of hospital landline? I really need to call my mum – she might think I'm dead.'

The nurse wheels me out to the payphone in the corridor. Normally, I'd have a lot to say about a phone attached to a wall, but in this situation, it is a total necessity. I might even have to retract all future negative comments about landlines.

The only number I know off by heart is my mum and dad's house phone.

'Hello?'

'Mum, it's me.'

'Oh, hi, darling, everything OK? I can't be long – I've got my evening Zumba class.'

So much for being worried sick . . .

'I've been hit by a car.'

'What?!'

'I've been hit by a car, but I'm fine. Well, kind of. I've broken my leg and broken my phone, that's why I'm calling you on the hospital phone.'

'Oh, darling. Oh my gosh! I am so glad you are OK! You didn't run in front of the car, did you? We've been so worried since Adam . . . '

I burst into tears.

'Darling, don't cry, come on. I didn't mean to upset you. I will get Florry to come and get you and take you home immediately. Which hospital are you at?'

'I'm at the Royal London. Love you, thanks, Mum.'

'Love you, darling, but I really must dash, as I have Zumba. Call you later, OK?'

'You can't call me because—'

She's gone. Great.

You can't call me because my phone is broken! I might as well be Tom Hanks in *Cast Away*.

My eyes overflow with tears. This is all too much. If Adam were here, this would never have happened. Firstly, I wouldn't have been at a social media addiction counselling session (which he would have rolled his eyes at – *Something else for yuppies to spend their cash on*, he would have said). Secondly, we messaged all the time, so he would have known instantly that something had happened. Being alone is terrible.

Finally, God takes some notice of my cries for help and I get taken for a scan. I pull myself together and try to interact with someone in real life.

'Oh my God, those cardboard booties are so cute! Do babies need to wear them to have an X-ray?' I ask the radiographer inquisitively.

'Those?' She points to a shelf of what I thought were cardboard baby booties and laughs. 'They aren't for babies. They are for men to pee in.'

'Oh right. God, I'm so stupid.' I was trying to make conversation but looks like I've forgotten how to be normal after living in silo for so long.

'Hahaha! No, you're not – you just obviously don't spend most evenings frequenting hospitals. What happened then?' She doesn't know that hanging out in hospitals was my past life. I wince at the memory of my darling Adam with his eyes closed on the bed. The final goodbye.

'I got hit by a car. Pretty stupid,' I add because it *was* particularly brainless of me.

'Not ideal,' she exclaims, taking a pen from the top pocket of her white jacket. 'But at least you're still alive – things could have been much worse.' And much better, thank you very much. She studies the X-rays of my leg, ankle and foot – first time someone's taken a photo of me for a long while – before speaking. 'OK, you've broken your ankle . . .'

'Nooooo!' I drone, smacking my head back down on the bed. 'Please don't say I have to wear one of those big, grey moon boots.' To be fair, they look like something that could be next on the Balenciaga designers' hit list and they could do with an upgrade.

'Luckily for you, it's not a major break – it's a fracture at the end of your tibia. It will be sore, you won't be able to bear weight on it for at least three weeks and I'm sorry but you will have to wear a boot.' I put my hands over my eyes, wishing for a whole host of reasons that I'd looked where I was fucking walking. She continues, 'Your cuts look pretty sore too. Has anyone cleaned them yet?'

'No, so far I've been here several hours, taken two paracetamol and basically had a photo taken.' I can feel my eyes prickling with tears. 'Sorry, I don't mean to come across as rude, it just really hurts.'

The radiographer pats me on the shoulder and gives me an apologetic smile, the one where both your lips fold in on each other and your head cocks to one side. 'It'll be OK, we're doing everything we can.' I know they are, but sometimes I feel like I can't express myself any more. They were amazing for Adam, even if they couldn't cure him.

I'm wheeled back out to the waiting room and finally called back in to the doctor. She cleans my leg with a salt wash – probably one of the most painful experiences that has ever existed – then proceeds to jab something in my arm, which is in fact a tetanus injection. The mascara all over my face must make them think I have rabies. London can be pretty scummy, so maybe they just give anyone with the slightest bit of saliva showing a jab as a precaution.

I also have a doctor's note – no work for a few weeks for me – yippee. There are some silver linings to being hit by a car and smashing your bone and phone to smithereens, no matter how threadbare thin they are.

After a lesson on how to use my two new metal legs, I'm back out in the waiting room.

I must be hallucinating, as it appears an angry middle-class woman, who can only be described as a 'Karen', seems to be shouting at me. Oh no, it's just my embarrassing older sister.

'Oh my God, Milly! Mum called me and told me what happened. I've been worried sick!' Florry shouts as she marches across the waiting room towards me. At least I know she cares about me. It's not often she shows that kind of love – it's usually portrayed in some sort of shit sandwich.

'Sorry.' I always feel so insignificant around Florry. She has the perfect life; she has *my* life. Or the life I was supposed to have, at least. Living in a suburb with more grass than chicken shops and a husband who's still breathing.

'If you were on that fucking phone when you got hit, I swear to God. Honestly. I can't believe it. At least you're OK. Your ankle looks fucking awful, by the way. You've gained about twenty pounds just on one leg. At least it confirms that you wouldn't look good if you got fat.'

'Err, thanks, Florry. Can we just go home? I've had a pretty long and intense day and I'm kind of ready for bed.'

'Come on then. The car park is free for another fifteen minutes, so I need you to start speeding up on those crutches. Imagine someone has stolen your phone.' She gives me a hug and a kiss on the head. I know she loves me; this is just all part of the older-sister act. Teasing, my dad would call it.

I limp awkwardly across the sanitised corridors and then the dirty car park, cigarettes and plastic bottles strewn. Florry chats mindlessly, five steps in front carrying my medication. It's a relief to finally sit in the car – crutches are exhausting.

'What's wrong with you, Milly? You've been dead quiet.'

'I've told you not to use that word as a descriptor before. I'm still very much alive – thanks.' She squirms at my comment. I continue, 'Do you mean aside from the fact that I got knocked down by a car?! It's making me feel nervous seeing all these people walking around not paying attention. I just want to scream out the window – look at me!'

'Show them your boot and maybe they'll be more cautious – it's enough to even turn a Lothario inside out.' She chuckles at her own joke while I pretend to grab the steering wheel from her, adding to the danger. 'Milly! Fuck's sake,' she shouts before continuing with the classic conceited sister-abuse tirade. 'You *were* on your phone, then! I knew it! Bloody hell, Milly, did you tell Mum and Dad? Do you think it was a coincidence that you went to see a shrink about a social media addiction and then got hit by a car because of your social media addiction? How was it anyway?'

'Oh my God, Florry! It doesn't matter what the circumstances are, I was still knocked down by a one-tonne vehicle. All accidents happen because someone isn't quite in the zone. It was fine. I mean, she spoke a lot of shit, but whatever. I don't want to talk about it any more.' I fold my arms and look out the window.

'OK, I'm sorry.' She knows she's taken it one step too far. Normally, I can give as good as I get, but not today. 'I got you a present – look in the back' I turn and see a wad of magazines, a tub of grapes and a family-size bag of Haribo.

Tiny hairs prick on the back of my neck. I bought Adam Haribo when he was in hospital; he loved sweets, and he said, '*When in Rome?*' And winked at me. '*Why would you bother trying to be healthy when you're about to die?*' He had a point.

'Thanks, Florry. That's really sweet.' When your relationship is based on one-upmanship, it takes swallowing a lot of pride to be thoughtful.

We eventually make it across London to Croydon. I don't think I've ever been so happy to see the Saffron Square Tower and Chick'n Box. I even cheerily waved at the drunk guy who told me to 'Fuck off, you slag' through the window – basically a compliment.

'Why don't you move back to Clapham? Croydon is such a shithole.'

I don't know how to explain to her that I can't afford it on my salary alone, that I didn't move out after Adam died out of choice, so instead I make a quip about a famous rapper.

'Stormzy was born here? Don't ever tarnish his birthplace with such crass talk again.'

'I'm not going to reel off the list of A-list celebs who live in Clapham, but whatever – you've had a tough day.' Stormzy is to rap what Shakespeare is to poetry, so I'm not sure where Florry was going with that one.

After an extremely long and tiring hike up the stairs – Florry's aggressive arm manoeuvres made me think I was grappling with a bear on Everest at some points – I finally make it into my tiny little one-bed.

I call my flat a shoebox, however, Leafed Estate Agents called it 'a modern studio apartment with fantastic access to local amenities', and with my measly budget, I was 'extremely lucky to have found such a gem on the market'. In my opinion, estate agents would sell cyanide to a child if they thought they could take a cut from it. I live alone because, apart from the fact that I am now a widow, most of my friends have partners, husbands, boyfriends or in some infuriating cases a 'better half'. My usual bed partner is a slightly grubby but extremely cuddly bear, with the insightful nickname, Bear-Bear.

Florry helped me in and said her pleasantries but then she 'really had to go' – says anyone who finds themselves trapped in a room with a sick/upset person for more than five minutes. Except, I didn't; I used to sit with Adam for hours, days, sometimes. He would have done the same for me.

When you've experienced some kind of trauma, home, however shit it normally appears to be, is always where the heart is. There is just something about that I've-been-out-for-the-day-but-now-I'm-back smell, the way you can carefully prise your one shoe off without a care in the world and cry uncontrollably as if no one apart from a nosy pigeon is watching.

Today has been long, very long, and disturbing. I switch on *Come Dine with Me: Couples Edition* and fall asleep on the sofa as soon as Tia and her husband, from Birmingham, have reheated mac 'n' cheese and served it on top of a piece of ham in the shape of a smiling teddy bear.

8 May 2017

'Wait there. Are you OK to stand by yourself for a minute?' I say, slightly concerned, leaving Adam propping himself up slightly by the wall. His complexion is pale, like it always is after the chemo, but compared to the other days, I swear I see some colour in his cheeks.

I rush into the living room and check the day's handiwork. It looks perfect. I pour two glasses of Merlot and put the two cups of popcorn in the centre of the table. A small bunch of daffodils from the florist at the market – 'They are out of season now, miss. This is the last bunch you're gonna get. Someone must love the ol' daffs!' The little wooden table that usually looks a bit tired has been given a new lease of life with a red-and-white checked tablecloth I bought a few days ago on Amazon. I even purchased a couple of crystal wine glasses from the local charity shop and placed two blush-pink tapered candles in some empty wine bottles to give the whole place that French bistro feel. I sync my iPhone to the Sonos and open the door to collect my date.

'Good evening, sir. May I take your jacket? Your table awaits.' I swing a tea towel over my right arm for dramatic effect.

'Why, thank you, madam. What a wonderful establishment you have here. And what a glorious evening it is too.' My eyes light up at the smile on his face. I know he's in pain, I can feel it myself, but he's still Adam. He still loves make-believe, jokes and eating in restaurants, even if he can't physically go out any more – well, not much anyway.

'Here you go, sir.' I say in the plummiest of voices, pulling out the chair and gently sitting him down. 'Are you waiting for someone?'

'Yes, my fiancée. She shouldn't be long – let her loose on Oxford Street with my credit card, didn't I?' He rolls his eyes the way I've seen rich men do in Selfridges as they pretend to themselves that their wives aren't with them just for the money. 'May I ask what the cuisine is this evening?'

'Of course, sir, it's European.' I cough, wondering if my choice of cooking is in fact European or Argentinian but whatever, this is just a game. 'Steak, to be precise.' I look at Adam, who's nodding.

'Wonderful – my favourite.'

I throw my tea towel into the kitchen and re-enter the room.

'Darling, how are you?' I lean over and give him the biggest kiss on the lips. One of those kisses that I see the wives giving their husbands after they've bought them the 'it' bag of the season.

'And what was the damage on my card this evening, sweetie?' He knows I hate that phrase – *What's the damage?* But tonight, it just makes it even more endearing that he remembers. It reminds me of how much we know about each other. How long it's been.

'I barely touched the sides. Just a couple of Guccis and maybe a Cartier bangle. Nothing much.' I grin at him, stuffing my face with the popcorn. 'Sorry, I must dash to the bathroom.'

I run into the kitchen, grab my tea towel and check on the chips. I fry off the steaks and give the creamed spinach a quick stir.

I pop open the daily dose of pills and pop them on a side plate. At least the injections have stopped for a while. I'm squeamish – I hate blood, guts, gore, the smell of hospitals – but I try my hardest for him. He mustn't know anything about how hard I find it, because he needs to enjoy every minute he has left.

I walk to the table, resuming my role as waitress.

'Here you go, sir. Take these, they enhance the flavour of the steak.' Adam swallows them with a glass of water, grimacing slightly, but quickly covering the distaste with a fresh smile. Nothing's changed, yet everything has. He's still him, just thinner and sadder. I still love him, more than ever.

I follow up with the two plates of medium-rare steak, creamed spinach and fries.

'I believe this is your favourite?' I say, laying the masterpiece in front of him.

'How did you know?' It used to be an at least weekly affair, going out for dinner, and nearly always Adam had a steak because – *you can't cook it at home*. 'Flat Iron inspired?'

'I called them, and they sent me the steaks and gave me the ingredients for the creamed spinach, so it *is* Flat Iron, your favourite restaurant.'

'Thanks, Mills.' Adam smiles at me sincerely, both of us slipping out of character for a mere second.

We continue to act out our scene; living in make-believe is the only real way we can live in the moment right now.

There's nothing in the present that is worth talking about. I think we both like pretending that life is normal, fun almost, like it used to be.

5

5 February 2019

'Hit me, baby, one more time!'

What. The. Fuck? Why is Britney Spears in my bed? My eyes are glued shut as I try to prise them open with both fingers. God, I feel awful. Did I get drunk last night?

'Oh, baby, baby. The reason I breathe is you.'

I've come to the realisation that, of course, my nineties idol is not in central Croydon surprising me, but my phone is on loud. I must have never switched the ringtone from when Julia changed it as a joke to embarrass me when I was seeing a production of *The Vagina Monologues* at the theatre – to subtly prove that even though I'm widowed, I still have a vagina and it has needs.

Why's work calling me, anyway? It's Fee. (It turns out my severely smashed phone does receive phone calls, even if I can't do anything else on it.) Fee's the receptionist at work, she lives in Marlow with her parents and basically works at SugarPharmers so she can meet eligible bachelors on a Thursday and Friday night and finally move out of her childhood home.

'Oh, hey, Milly.'

I can tell that phone voice anywhere. I remember when they broadcast the job spec – 'You are the door to the company: our multimillion-dollar ticket to success; the wrapper on a packet of biscuits, the smiling kid eating an ice cream on TV prime time; the three-generations playing PlayStation in their immaculate home. Your voice should entice the client, soothe them, relax them, excite them. Make them feel at ease and confident with using us for their healthcare PR.' I don't know how you can do all that in a simple 'hello', but I guess you've either got it or you haven't.

'Err, hey, Fee. You OK?'

'Yeah, fine. Marjorie asked me to call you. It's nine forty-five. Where are you?' Fee continues before I can answer. 'She said you have a meeting at ten and she needs the agenda. You'll never make it in now – sounds like you've just woken up – I can make up an excuse for you if you want?'

'Well, the thing is, Fee, I don't need a fake excuse. I was hit by a car last night and have broken my ankle, so I won't be in work for a few weeks. To be honest, you're lucky you're not attending my funeral today.'

'Oh. My. Fucking. God. Milly! I'm so sorry. You poor thing! Don't worry at all, I'll tell the team.'

'OK, well, thanks, Fee. Appreciate it.'

'Get well soon!' She hangs up. How many times over the next few weeks am I going to hear those three patronising words?

I try to make myself some breakfast, but I don't have any food in the fridge, obviously. I resort to eating handfuls of the grapes that Florry bought me and drinking instant coffee through a straw (I recently had my teeth whitened).

Florry's gifts include a copy of *Glamour* magazine – a paper guide on how to give your hair that perfect shine, make your pores disappear in three steps and get your pins ready for summer in just *two weeks*! I haven't read this or anything for years! Why is everything about hair, make-up and beauty? I want to learn how to do micro-plaits again, like Florry used to do in my hair, and build a palace out of Lego. *Cosmopolitan*, again similar; there's the odd raunchy article on how to have an orgasm, but that's about it.

No wonder people don't read magazines any more – they're so boring and fake. Not everyone's worried about the size of their pores or having shiny legs for summer; some people have real issues to talk about. They want advice about the mundane – mortgages when the deposit is more than your salary and student debt that's higher than the deposit; the sorrow that creeps up with age – caring for ageing parents; not the inane issues that only the fortunate have time to ponder – the hottest beach clubs to visit in Europe this summer, or how to make a Chanel bag work ten different ways.

> *Dear Tanya,*
> *My husband died, now I'm a widow at twenty-eight years old and sometimes I wonder if anyone even cares about me any more. Help!*

Maybe that's too depressing. Wouldn't want my grief repellent to remove any more people from my life.

When I was growing up in the nineties, my life gurus came in the form of a couple of handy manuals called *Mizz* and *Shout*. I need them back. These pink glossies contained highly influential quizzes that were *life*. They helped me decide, at the grand old age of thirteen, whether I was a party girl or a *ubi vermis liber* (book worm for those lucky enough not to be forced to take an A level in Latin), whether I should get with a jock or a computer nerd. I really miss those little directional quizzes. Every Tuesday a new instalment would pop into my Norfolk letter box, and I'd run downstairs to remove the package from the little plastic sheath, get reading, try out my new lip gloss, see which version of me I was going to be this week or how many yeses I needed to make out with Ronan Keating.

Now, I don't even need to get out of bed in the morning to get my fix; I just pull my thumb out of my mouth and sit and scroll. The problem with Instagram, unlike my old pink glossies, is that no one is honest on it – that immaculately curated, colourful grid is no place for thrush.

Before, you never needed to ask those embarrassing questions such as:

I fancy my teacher, what do I do?
I don't know how to put a tampon in.
My best friend keeps copying me, what should I do?

Because all the answers were included in a detailed format in the magazine. You didn't even need to write in with those questions yourself, as it appeared that every other thirteen-year-old in the country was having the same problem.

Instead of memes, you had the 'cringe' page, filled with embarrassing stories from your peer group, which you could handily cut out and share in the playground.

There was also the boy section where they were categorised as a 'minger', 'lush lad' or even 'your dad'. You didn't need to wait for them to ghost you on Tinder to find out they were a lads lad. There was a special 'Tricky Talks' section where you could ask advice from some kind old soul and she would help you out, from explaining why you shouldn't snog your teacher to how to shave your legs. And pull-out posters of all your hot crushes – probably Ronan from Boyzone, Brian from Westlife or Abz from Five. Free lip gloss, plus a lesson on how to wear it and not get your hair stuck to your lips as you do a sassy Britney flick by the goalposts. Flow-chart quizzes that would tell you what type of person you were even if you didn't know yourself and what job you should have – jobs that no one actually has, like a dog-scarf knitter or a cat cuddler. Any profession whose job it was to advise individuals as they navigated tender tweenhood was redundant, as these magazines were the ultimate shrinks. I guess, like

Violet in paper form. Why did I never listen to these quizzes? I'd give my right arm for someone to be on hand now.

I need to get a new phone, particularly if I'm going to be trapped inside for weeks on end. I'm a prisoner in my own home! Before I log in to the cloud – literally, I've never known a name more apt; so ambiguous, no one even knows what it means – I head to Instagram.com on my iPad. Lame, I know, but what's a girl to do?

Adam bought me my iPad. After his diagnosis, I lay awake all night for days on end, worrying, crying, screaming. He said it would be good if I watched something to fall asleep to, take my mind off things. We'd lie next to each other watching *Gossip Girl* like we did at university. I'd ask him if he wanted to watch something else, but he said, '*What's the point in starting a series? I might never make it to the end. At least now I know who Gossip Girl is, thank fuck. I couldn't enter the pearly gates without knowing – it would be* agony!' If I'm having a bad day, I like to cuddle up in his sweatshirt and watch the rerun.

I pick up the tablet, feel a pang of sadness at the screen-saver I haven't changed – Adam and I smiling in Seville – and suddenly feel connected to the real world again. I used to expand my mind by reading books. Now I just look at pictures. My once literary-rich mind has redigressed to that of a five-year-old.

Scroll. Jemima's having a barbecue with all the other home girls, sipping gin and pink lemonade. Scroll. Harley's having a spa day with Jade at the place we once went to for Nicky's birthday. Scroll. More fun, more friends, more activities that involve everyone else but me.

Maybe I'm just jealous. I shouldn't worry about what other people are doing, Adam always told me that. I do still have friends; I have Julia and Nicky. It's just much more of a tight-knit circle now than it used to be.

Scroll. Stupid DMs I haven't read from boys I've flirted with when I've been in need of a pick-me-up. I like flirting with the idea of flirting, but it's just way too traumatic. I cannot deal with any more pictures of penises; they're giving me nightmares.

I go on Facebook instead and have a little scroll through his photos. I smile at the time we all went to the pub and our friend Charlie was sick after doing too many flaming sambucas. Adam with his arm around Chris, pretending to give him a kiss. Photos of our friends laughing and joking. Photos of Layla and I. I feel a little pang in my heart at lost friendships, lost life, but I've seen it all before. I don't need to dawdle; I was there, they were my experiences too. I just like to make sure I remember them, so I know what it's like to be happy.

I go back to Instagram and scroll through some photos of my fake friends to make me feel *even* better. I'm glad the Instagram algorithm only works based on what you physically look at and not on your mental state. Sadness doesn't exist in the imagination.

At least *Mizz* didn't make you depressed. It wasn't about bragging or pretending. It was about your real life. Even if your own life was depressing, you felt better because you shared and other people seemed to care. It gave you the answers to questions you didn't know you'd asked.

Adam never had Instagram. He said it was a time waster and he much rather enjoyed heading to Instagram.com/milly. dayton24 in secret to see what I had been up to. Facebook's for memories; Instagram's for living.

I usually relish the thought of having a sick day, but it is not even lunchtime on my first day of a three-week slog and I'm already bored. Usually, when I'm sitting at my desk scrolling through ASOS, LADbible videos and my virtual friend's lunchboxes, curling up in front of the television in my duvet is my dream, but now it's my life.

I should probably tell the few followers I have that I'm currently out for the count and will be missing all future social engagements. Not that I really have many or that anyone would care.

People may feel nervous talking to me in person, but they don't have any guards up online. They are freer than a married man in a strip club. The one thing I've learned over the last two years is, in person, grief is a conversation stopper but online, if I post about feeling sad, my feed will be flooded with fake niceties – death is a virtual magnet. If I didn't have my online platforms, what would I have?

On the off chance that there's an invitation to a bottomless brunch flying to my inbox that I'll have to regretfully decline, I start snapping on my gigantic iPad – I look like a tourist in my own home. I upload a photo of my ugly tree-trunk leg, with my succulent on the left to add a bit of texture to the photo, and cover it all with a grainy reusable camera filter – make it edgy.

See, I know how to take a good photo. Just because I have sub-one thousand Insta followers doesn't mean that I couldn't get more; I only struggle with content as my life is so monotonous, although there's been a slight uplift over the last twenty-four hours.

I've done a lot of Instagram research ready for when I eventually become an influential blogger. I know how to do it; I just need more content and I can't get that if I work every hour of every day. I've analysed @TongueWateringlyJemma's photos down to a T; I know that G7 filter from VSCO like the back of my hand.

The photo: Tilt your head down and to one side, pop your leg out at a slight angle. Be tanned, contoured and elegant. When you pose, think *jealousy*.

Inspirational caption: Doesn't need to relate to the photo, something along the lines of: 'Integrity is everything.

Life is a blank canvas, and you need to throw all the paint on it you can'. The photo could be you eating a burger, it really doesn't matter, but the caption has to be whimsical yet poignant.

The outfit: A designer bag is needed somewhere – I guess I could always borrow someone's purely for the shot, if necessary. Black-and-gold Ray-Bans are a must.

Finally, the filter: Remember all those blurry, lined photos you have from old disposable cameras in the nineties, where it looks like you hang out with a squad of thumbs? Yes, the filter needs to look exactly like that.

See, I know exactly how to take the perfect photo. So why am I not gaining thousands of followers? Once I have a thousand followers, maybe I'll finally be happy.

Ping. Notification. *Ping.* Notification. *Ping.*

Woah, I think this is the most notifications I've EVER received. It must be stressful being a blogger. Everyone seems to want to send their well wishes.

> @AvaGirl OMG, Milly, that must have been SOOOO scary.
>
> @CharlieChap You poor thing. We need to go for a drink when you are better.
>
> @TaurusWins Hey Milly, remember me? We went to school together. So sorry to hear about your accident, get better soon!
>
> @Lad1993 I'd still fuck you.

After scrolling through the torrents of niceties and a few people with fetishes for trunk legs who have slid into my DMs from nowhere, I finally find the messages I want from my real friends.

@JuliaKnight Oh. My. Fucking. God. Are you kidding me?!?! You got hit by a fricking car? I don't know whether to laugh or cry. Why haven't you been replying to me?

@NickerBockerGlory Babes. That looks soooo sore, like really, fucking, super sore. What are you going to do? Like, how are you going to wash and stuff? Shit the bed, you are not going to be able to come to that party with me now, are you?

Well, no Nicky, not unless I want all future suitors to recoil in disgust at my mutated drumstick of a leg.

Good job I'm not looking for sympathy. Why aren't people rushing to my door with flowers and a freshly made cake? Why, for once in my life, can't the multiple virtual messages I've received cheer me up? I've dreamt of being sent fifty DMs ever since I realised that curating a public photo album of yourself could be a sustainable source of income. I should be jumping or hopping for joy. Maybe Violet was right. Was that really only yesterday? It seems like years ago.

Why has everyone been messaging me, but no one wants to see me? Does no one like me? Just like after Adam died, everyone is super busy with their own lives and sitting with someone miserable is not high on their list of priorities. They want to look like they care, but it's another to actually follow through.

At least he's always there, virtually. I look at photos of him most days and read posts that he wrote on my wall, back when writing on people's walls was cool. I don't think about the process of him dying, that's usually buried away, under molten lava, in the centre of the Earth's core. Since I saw Violet, or maybe it's the car accident, it's been bubbling up to the surface again. I can feel it, and that surely can't be a good sign after eighteen months of being burned.

'Milly! I wasn't expecting to hear from you so soon after our first meeting.' Violet peers with one eye into the laptop camera. It's the classic old-people-with-technology stereotype. Us 'young 'uns' spend ages moving the laptop around the kitchen in order to capture the best light, sit side on to make our jawline slimmer, whereas people over the age of forty take this as an opportunity to give their eyes a close-up, as if they want to show off their world-renowned impression of a cyclops.

'Well, I got hit by a car straight after our meeting and I have nothing better to do.' My sarcasm seeps through the screen and I want to shake myself. I'm acting as if I don't want to speak to Violet, though I obviously do, given I'm the one who requested the Zoom call. I'm well aware that I'm putting on a display more childish than a toddler requesting an ice lolly then screaming because it's too cold. I just don't know how to stop.

What I should tell Violet – what I *want* to tell Violet – is that I'm feeling lonely. That the grief is resurfacing and I'm not entirely sure whether being hit by a car is what's triggered it.

I should tell her about Adam. But that relationship was everything to me, and when all I have left of him are memories, I don't want a therapist poring through them, dissecting them and tearing them apart. It's too special.

So, instead of asking for help, as usual, I shut down.

'Gosh, Milly, that sounds dreadful!' She shakes her head. 'I am so sorry, poor, poor, poppet. I'm so glad you are OK.' She puts her hand on heart, shaking her head some more. 'Is that the reason you're calling? I'd love to chat but I have another appointment in five minutes – can we arrange a proper session for another day?'

Another fucking person who doesn't have time for me.

I slam my laptop shut.

I'm alone in this world.

15 December 2018

My sweatshirt and trackies are all hard and bobbly; they could have done with a wash about two weeks ago. I sniff my armpit, so could I. There are plastic trays and paper bags on the side in the kitchen, creating momentary wafts of stale curry and noodles in the air. Wine bottles and Diet Coke cans lie scattered around the pre-decorated faux tree my mum bought me, ready for an alcoholic's Christmas. My face is all puffy from crying, but I don't dare catch myself in the mirror for fear I'll hate what I've become. I know that I'm living in squalor, but I don't care.

Ping.

Ava: Babes! Who's free next Thursday? I've booked the Red Room (Don't worry, I'm not going to go all Mr Grey on your arses) at Soho House. Tons of bloggers will be there, and there'll be free food and cocktails to celebrate Higgy P's new bralette line with boytears.com. Let me know if you can make it! Mwah xoxo

Let me check my blank calendar to see if I have any other pressing engagements.

I watch the stream of messages populate my phone.

Can't wait! X
Higgy P – OMG – count me in! x
Wouldn't miss this for the world! X

Do I really want to spend my Thursday drinking expensive cocktails from Marie Antoinette glasses, gossiping with my friends and eating delicately battered squid covered in exquisite Bloody Mary dressing?

No, no I don't.

Even if I wanted to, there's no way my friends would have the time or patience for me in this state. I'm aware that after a while, people get bored with the person sapping out the fun. I'd just ruin everyone else's night.

Me: Sorry, Ava, I'm busy.

I turn my phone over, slump back on the sofa and continue shoving the remains of a family packet of crisps in my mouth.

6

@FlorryMarie: Get out of bed, bitch.

There are nicer ways to wake up, I'll give you that. Florry knows too well that there's no way I'd be up before noon in my current state. I scroll on Instagram every morning as usual, just on my iPad rather than my poor dead phone.

I reply to her DM:

Me: I'm SICKKKKK. It's the one time you're supposed to stay in bed.
@FlorryMarie: You're supposed to wash though, otherwise you'll get bedbugs.

I sigh and lug my heavy body the metre across my bedroom to the bathroom and then into the kitchen. I'll give Leafed Estate Agents their due – this is the perfect flat for someone who has an impaired limb.

After having at least ten cups of tea, because filling up the kettle and turning it on is something to do, I've had a little think. Maybe there's hope for me yet. I've been gifted by God three weeks of no work. Three weeks of a chance to change my subpar, depressing life for the better. I can't always be thinking that the world is out to get me – it's no way to live, and I was a total, entitled bitch to Violet. Maybe getting hit by a car while messaging on my phone, post-social media addiction consultation was finally a sign from the big man himself? I've been told the world moves in mysterious ways. I'm always complaining that I can't be a blogger because I spend too much time working, and now, I'm unemployed and have nowhere to go.

What if I shared things to make people laugh, not things that make them feel depressed or anxious? Not everyone's a confident size six with Chris Hemsworth for a husband. What if I shared things that people don't have to buy or have an intense social life to enjoy? I already know people love oversharing. Maybe I can turn my relationship with social media on its head. Can I even provide the answers to the questions no one knew they had?

Let's have a little look and see what's out there.

My horoscope for today on @MakeYourOwnFate is:

Get physical. Go for a run, a walk, even head to the gym to clear your head and really grab hold of today. The planets are circling; earth, wind and fire are uniting. Intertwine yourself mentally and physically for the upmost in wellness.

Nothing out of the ordinary there, your classic all-rounder, multifaceted horoscope. Applies to most people, can be read in a way that relates to anyone *apart* from someone who can't do anything physical except put a biscuit in a cup of tea, take it out and cram it into their mouth.

I've found most things on social media don't apply to me, because content is created for young, fun-loving, exceptional women. However, I'm a widow, an outcast of the digital world, and seeing photos of twenty girls laughing at brunch doesn't make me get straight on the blower for next Saturday's reservation; it makes me feel like curling up in a ball.

I need to stop rooting around for sympathy and expecting people I know only from a like on a photo of some bacon and avocado on sourdough to pop round with a bunch of flowers – I need to grab the bull by the horns.

I continue to scroll. More jokes and comedy accounts about mothering your boyfriend. None of this relates to your average Joe. Where are all the people like me? All the girls who were worried about starting their period in front of their crush, or who interchanged the words *snog* and *shag* as if they meant the same? I need those people back in my life. Where are you now, girls?

The magazines we read in the early noughties, the way they united all the teenage girls in the country, stopped us from embarrassing ourselves knowingly in front of our peers and presented us all as a united front. I think that's what the world is missing. An upgraded adulting handbook for everyone who doesn't really know how to deal with life any more. The millions of unanswered questions that we have every day and epiphanies about the world need to be shared. They need a voice. They need a Mizzennial.

Mizzennial (n.) *A person who, as a teenager, had an additional parent in the form of a handy little magazine called Mizz and is waiting for the new adulting instalment.*

A world where we read magazines and spoke to people face to face rather than thumb to thumb. If other people knew what I knew, maybe they wouldn't care so much about the latest Gucci handbag, or going for brunch every day. I haven't really got anything to lose. I'm trapped in this flat for a few weeks as it is. I want to make people seem real again – including myself.

Maybe that's where I'll find all the other girls like me, who seemed to have got lost in the upgrade from print to phone but haven't found someone to help them understand it yet.

What do you think, Adam? Or is this one of my many ideas that will never get off the ground? I sigh, cramming my fourth biscuit of the morning into my mouth. Adam used to love biscuits; he had that classic male metabolism where he would eat a whole packet of Bourbons and grow another ab, while I would eat one and wonder why I had a new Bourbon-shaped piece of fat on my inner thigh.

'Hello again, Milly.'

Violet's eyes are magnified tenfold through her thick glasses and then the screen, her voice soft and inviting. Regardless of how I acted on the last call, Violet must be there for me because I'm paying her. Luckily for me, that means I have someone to talk to, as my friendship circle is looking particularly thin, and beggars can't be choosers – thanks, Florry for reminding me.

'Hi, Violet. Thanks for speaking with me again. Err, sorry about last time.' I recoil slightly. Even I know how childish I was.

'No problem at all, Milly. We all have bad days.' Everything about her voice exudes friendliness. (Maybe that's the secret – paying people to be your friend.) 'It's nice to hear from you again.'

I pause before divulging. I need Violet as a sounding board for my big idea. 'Do you think that social media can be used in a positive way?'

'Of course!' Violet gets straight into it, probably pleased not to have too much awkward back-and-forth. 'I wasn't saying that social media is the root of all evil – too much of anything is bad.'

How can too much lettuce be bad? Whatever, I'm not paid to advise.

'Hmm.' I'm just going to jump in again. 'Do you think that social media can be used to help with, I don't know, trauma?'

'Trauma? Is there something you would like to talk about, Milly? I'm always here to chat.'

Could I tell her about Adam? I mean, this is her job, to advise. Otherwise, what am I even paying her for?

'You know I came in to talk about social media. Well, that's what my sister and parents wanted me to talk about. But I don't think that's really the problem.'

'Oh, and why's that, Milly?' Her voice softens further than I thought was possible and feels like caramel oozing through the tinny speaker on my laptop.

'I'm not really very happy at the moment.' I feel my breath quicken and my diaphragm starts pumping ten to the dozen, like a grandad blowing up a balloon.

Violet stays silent.

'I had a husband and he, well, he died. And now I'm sad, really sad.' I seem to have digressed back into a five-year-old who wishes for nothing more than a hot chocolate and a cuddle from her mum.

'I'm sorry, Milly. That must be devastating. It can take a lifetime to come to terms with grief.'

'Thank you, Violet.' My face feels hot and prickly, but I smile as I say it because I mean it. 'It feels good to talk.'

I Facebook Julia, as I don't have WhatsApp on my iPad:

What are you doing? Do you want to come over? I'm really bored and depressed.

That should make her feel bad and want to visit me. You can't leave a 'depressed' friend in need – it's not socially acceptable.

Depressed is the term most people use for feeling *ultra-sad*, in a sarcastic Starbucks-ran-out-of-almond-milk-and-I've-had-to-have-coconut kind of way. If you are feeling really depressed, the likelihood is you won't ever tell anyone because everyone will run away from you. However, people can't question what type of depressed you're feeling, even besties.

As soon as Julia arrives, we crack open a bottle of rosé. The pale pink nectar fills our glasses, and the clink of the ice immediately relaxes me. Pure bliss.

I can't help but marvel at how sophisticated Julia and I are and how far we have come since our youth. We are sitting here, having wine, with no intention of going out. When we were younger, we used to tell our parents that we were going to the cinema but sneak into town instead. Unbeknown to them, we would be hanging out on the corner of Tesco, pushing our tits out in a training bra, begging for some guy to buy us a bottle of Smirnoff.

'God, I love wine.'

'Me too.'

'I honestly can't believe you were hit by a car. It looks fucking awful. Like so, so, so, so, so, bad.' Julia's mouth looks like one of those Punch and Judy puppets, going up and down with the emphasis on how bad I look.

'I rather like my new look,' I respond with the same sincerity as someone sliding into your DMs trying to recruit you for a pyramid scheme.

'If anyone can pull off a car crash, it's you.' Julia grins. 'What are you going to do with all your time off? At least you'll have loads of visitors, cards and presents and stuff!'

'Yeah, I guess.'

'What do you mean, "I guess". Come on, cheer up, Milly!'

'People don't seem to send cards any more, more a few DMs on Instagram and that's that.'

'Well, maybe you should start reaching out to people and you might get some back. Did you send Ava a card for her birthday or Jemima one for getting engaged?'

I shrink into myself, knowing that Julia's right. She's always right.

'Maybe I could print all my DMs out and post them on my wall instead.' I joke not wanting to address the real situation.

'That's the spirit!' Julia laughs, knowing me well enough not to keep pressing. 'Are you going to Jemima's hen, by the way?'

'Oh, erm, no,' I answer with the least amount of conviction.

'Why not?'

'I'm busy that weekend.'

Julia almost spits out her wine. 'Sorry, Milly, I love you, but I know you're not. You know that watching reruns of American teenage series and eating out of packets doesn't count as busy?'

'It does keep me entertained, but obviously, no, you're right, I'm not busy.' I sigh. Why bother lying? 'I don't feel like they would want me there, anyway. I'm boring now, and what if I cry or something horrendous like that?'

Julia shakes her head. 'Milly.' She looks at me sternly and holds up a finger. 'You need to stop this. Do you know how hard it is making the cut for a hen party? If they didn't want you, they wouldn't invite you. Second' – she holds up a second finger – 'you need to stop making excuses. It doesn't matter if you cry – no one cares! I love you, but you're acting like a twat.'

I look down at the floor as if I've just been told off by my mother. 'I'll think about it then.' Right again, Julia.

She beams at me. 'Great! Now, would you rather get eaten by a snake and be alive in its stomach for fifteen hours, or be snapped up by a crocodile in teeny-weeny chunks?'

Julia starts it, but we always play it. I'm pleased that we don't have to keep talking about the hen situation, because the whole 'going out, friends and parties' thing makes me feel anxious.

'Mmmm, I think eaten by a snake, as it would be less painful.'

'Really?!' Julia sounds shocked. 'You'd just be swimming in the inside of a snake with all its organs for ages. Rank!' She gulps her wine enthusiastically to help her deal with my 'shocking' answer.

'You would rather die by losing one limb at a time?' This is a game of opinions not fact, however, all players take Would You Rather extremely seriously, as if these are life-or-death questions. And while they may in fact not be life-or-death questions, trust me, they're questions that can be asked on your deathbed to lighten the mood – '*Would you rather a human body and a toucan head, or a toucan body with a human head?*' It wasn't even that funny, but the combination of tiredness, sadness and hysteria had us in fits.

'You'd die from the loss of blood pretty quickly.' Always the voice of reason, Julia says.

'Well, you didn't say that. My turn. Would you rather see your parents have sex once, or hear them having sex every night for the rest of your life?'

'See them once for sure,' Julia answers monosyllabically, as if this is the fact I was looking for.

'But it would be graphic sex, so bad you could never get it out of your mind. You would be having dinner and it would just be there, in your mind's eye.'

'I still think I would rather see it once.'

'OK, me again.'

'Would you rather your house burned down or lose all your Instagram followers?'

'Lose my house, if I had one.'

'No, you wouldn't!' Julia exclaims, spilling wine down her front.

'Yes, I would. Your followers are your life status. If you were a blogger and you lost all your followers, you'd basically be back to being a nobody again.' Do I believe this? I am a nobody, with or without my 559 followers.

Julia laughs. 'Maybe, but you have about five hundred followers. I bet a handful are your friends, some are people from school who you don't even speak to any more – cue hen-party-gate – and the rest are fake or paedophiles. It wouldn't be a mammoth task for you to recoup your followers.'

'So? I'll have more one day. I'm going to start a blog and soon I'll be getting paid five hundred quid for a close-up of my right incisor. You have to start somewhere. If I lost all my followers, no one would know who I was.'

'Yes, they would. You don't walk around with a sign above your head. Everyone knows you for you, not because of your Instagram.'

'I'd be unidentifiable. Like we always say, not having social media is like saying you were born without a name. Literally a ghost of society.'

'To be honest, I'd be scared to delete my Instagram,' Julia admits. 'I don't have time to chat to every single person every day. I can stalk them online and see what they are doing, so even if I don't see them for months, when I finally do, I can act as if I know what is going on in their life. It is your pre-coffee homework: quick catch-up on their virtual life and make sure you have liked at least half of their recent photos.'

'Exactly! Sometimes, I feel like I've spoken to you, but I've been tagging you in memes or watching your date nights with James on Insta Story. Virtually third-wheeling your romantic nights in.'

Julia twiddles her fingers. I know she gets awkward every time I mention James and her because she feels bad about Adam. It wasn't her fault he got cancer, but I'd feel the same if it was James. Julia can't help it that her life has exploded with an exponential rise of happiness and mine has sunk into the ground.

'I love Instagram,' she says, 'but it's a bit weird. I feel like I'm so much more up-to-date with everyone's lives but sometimes I think I actually know people even less.'

'It's like when people DM'd me when I was in Thailand – "Wow, Milly, looks like you are having a great time." And I replied, "Yeah, amazing." You were the only one that actually knew that I got mugged and had been stealing salad from the hot dog bar in 7-Eleven until my parents transferred me some money.' I slept on the beach for five nights and mated with sandflies.

'Ha, yes, I remember! You don't know how people are feeling. I mean, I know everything about you, Milly, because you're my bestie, but I feel like I know some people I follow because I watch their every move, but I don't actually know how they feel. Surely, no one can be that happy all the time? Remember when we were teenagers and used to call each other every night? On a landline! Does anyone even have a landline any more? "Hi, can I speak to Milly please?"'

Does Julia still know everything about me? Does anyone?

'Sometimes I feel like I need a social media break,' I admit.

'I know, me too. But I don't think I'm ready to have a purely offline presence. What would I do in my spare time? Anyway, have you seen Natalie's new boyfriend? He works in investment banking – he must be mega rich.'

We sit scrolling on Instagram, stalking Natalie from school and her new 'supposedly' rich boyfriend, who appears to work in investment banking at Merrill Lynch, but for all we know he could just hand out sandwiches in the canteen.

It's only 9 p.m., but time for Julia to go home. Those antibiotics are making me feel exhausted – mentally and physically.

I lie in bed on my iPad, have a quick look on Instagram before I go to sleep, but I'm starting to think it's filled with lies and trash:

@SocialShrink91 CUPCAKES ARE MERELY MUFFINS THAT BELIEVED IN MIRACLES!

Hey, Social Shrinkers! What a day. Bet you couldn't get out of bed this morning? Days are what you make them. Why can't all days be a fun day like Sunday? Set your alarm for 5 a.m. (I love catching the sunrise on my balcony), go on a beach run, grab yourself a bullet coffee or a mean green smoothie and start your day off right! We create the world around us! Remember, if you do have a cupcake, make sure it is gluten- and lactose-free, otherwise it might make you feel sluggish and bloated!

I decide to listen to a motivational TED Talk on YouTube instead; maybe it'll fill my mind with motivation and inspiration instead of wondering whether I can turn into a sponge cake.

I think about what I said to Julia. Would I really rather my house burned down than lose my Instagram followers? A house provides warmth and comfort; my Instagram is filled with people who believe that cupcakes are on par with Jesus.

After a traumatic birth, lots of screaming due to misspellings and Instagram malfunctions, @Mizzennial has finally been born. Hurrah!

I've got the Instagram handle and the blog page – two blank canvasses that I need to start filling. I made a snazzy pink logo using a twenty-first-century form of WordArt bubble writing and a free PowerPoint package.

FYI, if you want something to be cool, it *has* to be in pink. Not candy pink, bubblegum pink or pig pink – Millennial pink only. This new millennial pink isn't associated with pigtails and Barbies, which is what everyone associated pink with when we were five, it is gender-neutral. The more testosterone a guy has, the more pink they wear – the rise of the metrosexual male. Millennial pink is about as standard in the modern-day colour palette as beige was in the 1950s.

Now I'm stuck between these four walls, it's made it even more blindingly obvious how horrible it is having hundreds of people a day gloat about how fantastic their life is. It's great to have thirty likes on a photo but wouldn't it be even greater if I had thirty people checking if I was OK? It can't only be me who doesn't have a list of friends the length of the Magna Carta.

I don't want Mizzennial to be about boasting and making people feel lonelier. I want it to bring people together, exactly like my old teenage guides. You read advice that you didn't know you needed, but it made you feel like you had a place in the world. Turns out, everyone had the same problems – first kisses, periods, school exams. Now, it might be all bitchy bosses, ghosting and Generation Rent, but it's still the same, we've just graduated to the next level.

Most importantly, above all, I must remain anonymous, for now, at least. If people know I'm a widow, they'll probably unfollow me. It's better I just stay known as Mizzennial.

@Mizzennial Welcome to Mizzennial – the page for the nineties qween! Remember when reading magazines was the ultimate thing to do in your girl gang? When your shrink came in the form of a What-length-skirt-should-you-wear-to-school quiz? When you lived for your horoscope to tell you to kiss the boy in class? Well, it's back, but with a modern-day millennial makeover. Get your tissues ready for a heavy dose of nostalgia and twenty-first century truths coming your way!

I've had to cut a photo of *Mizz* issue number 456 for my first post, but whatever, I'm sure I'll find some original content soon.

After all, I need my content to be engaging. And funny. When I was at the height of my mourning, I used to enjoy having the odd laugh at LADbible videos between tears. Laughter's a wonder medicine.

I used to be a fun person. Maybe I can be again. Arabella used to say I made her laugh all the time, and Adam . . . he used to share jokes with me too. I was funny – I had Adam creasing with hysteria in the darkest of situations, where laughter is sacred.

I already have five likes on my post! I literally feel like every time I receive a like, an extra endorphin is released. It's the most excitement I have going on in my life right now. I should sit down. According to Violet, that's five bumps of cocaine I've just had.

Oh-my-fricking-Gooooddd! I have my first comment!

@HilaryisBuff @FizzyMcGuire I used to LIVE for those quizzes #DidYouGetMainlyABOrCs?

That endorphin release was short-lived.

I can't stop clicking on my Mizzennial page to see if I have any notifications. It's just like after Adam died, when I couldn't stop clicking on his Facebook. As if the more I looked, the more likely he was to come back.

7 September 2015

I love that early-morning haze as the frost evaporates into the fresh autumn air. It's like a sea of mist beneath our knees. I think this is my favourite time of day. Crunching through the crisp grass, holding hands with my life partner.

It's Saturday. We wake up super early to seize the day and make the most of the weekend. I throw on some old gym wear and a hoodie; Adam does the same. We spend nearly an hour crunching round the common, holding hands, our noses pink from the morning chill. Every so often, Adam grabs my hands and blows into them to keep them warm.

We stop at our favourite coffee shop – a farm deli with wooden slatted tables and Campbell soup cans filled with cutlery. Condensation covers the windows, the stark contrast between the heat of beating human hearts and nature's chill. It's not until we open the door and feel the rush of heat on our faces that we realise anyone's in there.

Adam picks up the menu on the counter and calls to me as I grab us a table. 'The usual, Mills?'

I nod, Adam orders, comes back to the table and picks up his latest novel, *The Russian Spy*, and is instantly absorbed, telling me facts about the KGB and how brave he thought the unnamed American was. Adam's an avid reader. Historical fiction is his kryptonite – he has the entire Bernard Cornwell collection pride of place in his bedroom. I WhatsApp the uni group, arranging our pub drinks for the afternoon.

'Are Charlie and Leo coming later, Mills?' Adam looks up from his book.

'Yes, they are. You're in the group!'

'I know, but I can't keep up and you *love* organising.' I know he's pandering to me, sucking up so that I continue doing the organisation. I won't let him know, but I do love a good plan.

'It's not the 1950s, and I'm not your mother! You should at least know what we're doing!'

'Ha! Well, I have organised something. I forgot to add it to the calendar – don't hate me.' He quickly adds, knowing how much it annoys me when he double-books himself with my plans. 'I'm watching the Ryder Cup with the boys in a couple of weekends' time. Why don't you invite the girls round and we can make a night of it?'

'Bloody golf.' I smile, secretly pleased that, for once, he has managed to round the troops. 'OK, I'll make the drinks!'

Ten minutes later, rich-yellow fluffy scrambled eggs on sourdough and an almond-milk latte arrive in front of us both. We have the same taste buds, so we often end up eating the same thing. Apart from coffee. Adam likes his milk from cows, and I prefer squeezing the life out of nuts.

'Why is this always so good?' Adam exclaims, his mouth full to the brim, every word emphasised purely by the amount of food he has stuffed in there.

'I know. Your scrambled eggs are good, but they aren't this good.'

'I'll have you know I am a cordon bleu scrambled egg chef! They are great, though. And this coffee! Heaven!'

'Adam? You know, this is my favourite thing to do.'

'What is?'

'Walking round the common and then having our breakfast. It's our thing now, a tradition. When we're married and have children, we'll be holding their hands as we walk and feeding them eggs on sourdough. I love you so much.' I'm feeling soppy today.

'I love you too, my little daff. And the eggs, I love the eggs.' He grins at me with his mouth full to the brim.

'What are we doing next Saturday?'

'It's unlike you to not know the plan.' Adam smiles at me. 'Walking round the common, eating eggs and drinking coffee?'

'That sounds perfect to me. I'll put it in my diary.'

'Do you have to put everything in that bloody diary of yours? I've never known anyone to write as many lists and plans and actions as you, Mills.'

'I just like to know what I'm doing you know. And this might not seem an important thing to you, but it is to me. It holds the same weight as going for brunch at Zingos, if not even more.'

'It is important to me. The most important. Can you pass me the pepper? If I'm being really honest, I think my eggs might need a tad more seasoning'

'Shut up, master chef.' I smile and pass him the pepper pot.

7

I've woken up to a blue sky, birds tweeting and a tracking email to say my brand-new glitzy iPhone is on its way to Croydon via special delivery. Life's good.

What more could I ask for? Only fifty new followers and thirty likes on my latest Mizzennial post! I mean, it was a good one: a graphic on how you know if you're about to roll your *R*s, extend your *A*s and change your name to *Allegra* based on how much you spend at Wholefoods. That's right, *fifty new followers*! Someone even commented: 'This is f**king hilarious!' Am I going viral?

Even though I'm probably the happiest I've ever been, I'm starting to feel a little nervous. What if I can't keep this up? What if my comedic value runs out after one post? What if, what if, what if? The only saving grace is no one knows that their comedic online pal is being catfished by a twenty-eight-year-old widow.

I think Adam would laugh at me right now. We always shared the same humour. He was also always super proud of me and everything I did; he would tell me to come out of anonymous mode and show the world who I am – but he isn't here to pick up the pieces when, inevitably, it all goes wrong. He is playing PlayStation and eating pizza in the clouds right now, teaching Julius Caesar about *Call of Duty* and learning every fact about Ancient Rome he could wish for, having the best time. He has his feet up on the sofa and a cushion in the gap where I'd normally sit. That's what I hope for him anyway.

'Violet, can I be honest with you?'

'Always, Milly.'

'I've started my own sort of blog thing. Do you remember that magazine, *Mizz*? Exactly like that, but comedy, if @FatMartha did blogs.'

'Wow, Milly, that sounds great. How are you finding it? Giving you something to do, being stuck inside? @FatMartha sounds a little, I don't know . . . fatphobic?'

'It's not, because she said it about herself. Self-deprecating – it's all the rage nowadays. I love it! I love being silly, but . . .'

'But what?'

'I'm lying to everyone. I'm pretending to be a fun-loving, joking twenty-eight-year-old, and that is the opposite of who I am. I'd love to be honest on Mizzennial, but I'm scared.'

'Good things are never easy, Milly, otherwise everyone would do them. You told me about your husband in our last session and you felt good, didn't you?' I did. There was something warm in my heart when I opened up to Violet. 'You don't have to tell everyone everything, but people have secrets. You are not alone, Milly.'

Everyone always says that, but I don't see people flocking towards me with open arms and open ears. I see people through screens who are preoccupied leading their busy lives. They need to cut themselves free from me so they can stop feeling guilty about enjoying themselves.

'It's not that I'm trying to be secretive . . .' I stop, thinking about why my mind has felt imprisoned over the last couple of years '. . . But I feel like I've kind of lost my identity.

Everyone I know sees me as "Milly the widow". Even I don't know who I am outside of that yet. I don't want my followers to know I'm a widow, but I don't want my friends and family to know that I'm behind the Mizzennial account either. It's like a space I can exist outside of all that.'

Violet nods and makes some notes. 'Why did you choose to start Mizzennial, Milly?' she asks. 'Is there something that triggered it?'

'I was talking to my friend, and I told her I would rather my house burned down than lose my Instagram followers, then I went on Instagram and realised there wasn't any comfort or warmth there like there would be in the home I metaphorically chose to burn down.'

'I see. And was that the only reason?'

'No.' I pause again. Violet's making me analyse my life and my actions more than I thought possible. 'I was thinking that if I loved reading those magazines and sharing real stories when I was younger, I'm sure other people did too. It's nice feeling part of something, especially when I can control the content. There must be so many people that are searching for more online than fancy restaurants, holidays and new bags – maybe I can bring the comfort and warmth back to the online portals we choose to live in instead of our own homes?' That's probably the truest thing I've said in a long time. 'And I've got a lot of time on my hands now, I might as well do something productive.'

'Well, I think it's an excellent idea, Milly. Well done.'

You've got to be kidding me.

Dear Ms Dayton,
Due to unforeseen circumstances, your SpkAnywhere delivery has been rescheduled for tomorrow. We apologise for the inconvenience.

In the meantime, see our latest deals, including the new
XX ODYSESSY with unlimited data for £30 a month, no
upfront fee.
Best wishes,
Your friendly customer service team

Does nobody vet these emails?

1. I hate it when anybody calls me Ms – it highlights the fact
   that I'm a widow. Not marriage material, so not Mrs, and
   not young enough to be called Miss. Why are men allowed
   to be all floozy and independent with their prefix, not telling anyone if they are married, single or widowed?
2. Tell me what the unforeseen circumstances are! I deserve
   to know. Was the driver embroiled in some sort of horrific
   accident? Did something awful happen? Was he arrested?
3. You don't know how desperate I am, so don't apologise for
   something you don't understand.
4. Why would I buy another phone from you, when I haven't
   got the one I asked for originally?
5. You should check that the offer you are trying to entice me
   with does not undercut the one I've literally just paid for.
   Dicks.

I'm so angry – now I actually have a positive use for my
phone, the delivery is delayed; I'll have to sit and absentmindedly watch TV again for the rest of the day and eat more food
that my inactive body doesn't need.

I miss everything about him, even the way we used to
bicker deciding what we watched on TV – the BBC's blockbuster new thriller, or some gory Tudor series, or historical
dramatisation of a ship that went missing in 1925. To be fair,
I've missed that for a while. Adam was still Adam right up
until the day he died, but every so often, a little bit of him

would depart early. I wanted him to be forthright and give me his one-minute spiel on why we should watch Sky's new Wild West drama, but he'd just pass me the remote and say, '*You choose Mills, I'm not bothered. I'll probably fall asleep.*' I'd put on something for the both of us anyway, and then I'd gently wake him, give him his medication and take him to bed.

I sigh. Everything reminds me of Adam, and I miss him all the time. When people say it gets easier, what do they mean? Do you just start forgetting about them, a tiny bit each day until you can barely remember the way their brow furrowed when they were concentrating, or how their bright blue eyes managed to catch the light in the darkest of rooms? I don't want to forget him; I just don't want grief to keep tripping me up all the time.

Anyway, even TV gets boring after a while, so I've been doing some research into magazines. Agony aunt pages, to be precise. People send in their *real* problems to be discussed, and they have been doing this since the beginning of time.

I found an extract from a 1972 *Jackie* online (we've basically had the same problems since the seventies, except now they involve more dicks, fuckboys and detectable STIs):

Dear Cathy and Claire, I am fifteen and have never been out with a boy. I've had various offers, but I've always said no because I don't know how to kiss. I'm terrified in case I make a fool of myself. I can see myself as an old maid in a garret, with a parrot and a cat for company, if I go on like this!

No one would dare say this now. They'd talk about anal in an orgy over a bacon sandwich and a cup of tea and no one would even splutter. What about the real millennial truths that we have that we never tell anyone?

I received an 'anonymous' text saying I have chlamydia. I had a year's dry spell so knew exactly who it was. He sits two desks away from me and always winks at me. Help, Tanya! or *Whenever I try and sleep, I imagine someone dragging me into a grave and gauging my eyes out. Help, Tanya!*

Is that too dramatic or have I been speaking to the wrong people?

How ironic that I told Julia I needed a social media break and now I've started a social media channel, even if it is for a good cause. I wonder how many other people feel like they need a break sometimes. Not just from social media, from *everything*.

@Mizzennial How many times have you said to yourself, 'I need a break from social media', and then gone on it absentmindedly for another four hours? I've literally just become the victim of my own woes. It's ironic because we all need a social media break; our generation has probably never needed anything more. Apart from oxygen, of course. I saw this 'Day In The Life' post from one of Instagram's top influencers. It involved personal trainers, nutritious smoothies and Dior bag hauls, so here's a more accurate version:

8 a.m.: Wake up to the classic iPhone jingle. Swear to myself that it's so early even though I get up at the same time every day and wish I hadn't spent that last hour last night online browsing things I 100 per cent don't need.

8.15 a.m.: Still scrolling on Instagram, wondering if there is a possibility I could become a blogger in the next fifteen minutes and quit work. Share any tier one BBC News stories with my friends, hoping I am first in a bid to look educated.

8.16 a.m.: Jump out of bed after realising the time, dry shampoo my hair, and if I am feeling really adventurous, make myself a smoothie.

8.45 a.m.: Face shoved into a man's armpit, coffee on my top. Probably been involved in some type of commuter brawl.

9.10 a.m.: At my desk, staring at my computer screen.

12 p.m.: Chef's chicken salad for lunch, or sushi if it is a Friday and I am feeling flush.

3 p.m.: Bored AF.

4 p.m.: Due to boredom have probably bought something inappropriate on ASOS by this point, like some hideously expensive accessory that I will never wear, or an alternative jumpsuit that will inevitably make me look like I am a child labourer not a lean, sexy model.

5.29 pm: Mouse poised on 'Shut down?', ready for the start of the end-of-day rat race.

5.31 pm: Repeat sweaty, angry commute home and await the greeting of a Tesco meal deal and the day's episode of *Homes under the Hammer*.

What about you guys?

@BallsyBladder Mine also involves going to the toilet at least 15 times to make the day go quicker. Sometimes I try and have a danger nap too.

@TinyTyson Don't forget holding yourself back from fighting your boss/checking your bank balance to find it's empty/clicking on and off WhatsApp waiting for a boy to message back.

It's been a lazy morning. I've been walking around the flat on tenterhooks hoping SpkAnywhere don't pull an out-of-the-box excuse as to why the delivery driver hasn't arrived. Got involved in a manic delivery driver car chase or a walrus fell out of the sky and ate him. You know the sort.

Buzz.

Finally.

'Hello, it's Steven from DHL. I've got a package you need to sign for?'

'Hello, Steven, if I buzz you in, could you come up?'

'Of course, darlin'. No worries.'

'Thank you so much! Third floor, I'll wait at the top.'

My mum would probably have a fit at the thought of me inviting a strange man up to my flat, but this is no time to be suspicious.

'Cor, long way up 'ere, darlin'.' It certainly felt a long way up. His heavy step and panting echoing up the stairwell lasted a lifetime, but his voice is kind, and I shouldn't judge. He nods towards my booted foot. 'Just sign your name, Milly, isn't it? What happened to you, then?'

'Nice to meet you, Steven. I was hit by a car. All my own fault, sadly, but still a bit of a shock.'

His eyes widen with shock, 'Well, you be careful next time!'

I take the box. An insignificant white rectangle to the naked eye. Inside holds my many digital masks; I can be whoever I want to be when I have that in my hand.

'Take care!' he calls as he walks back down the stairs. Knights in shining armour can come in many forms . . . even overweight DHL delivery drivers. Maybe I'm a princess after all, and my carriage is a yellow and red van.

I set up my new phone, re-logging into all my apps and making sure my favourites are pride of place on the screen, for the ultimate in thumb dexterity.

There's something I should probably do now I have my additional limb. Something I really need to know if I'm thinking about being honest on Mizzennial. What happened before when I exposed my feelings online? The most important share of my whole life.

I scroll down, fast, to the day that changed my world. Posts and pictures flash before my eyes. I stop.

@Milly.Dayton24 I've been dreading this day since I heard the news. Praying, wishing that the doctors had made a mistake and it wasn't true. We planned on spending the rest of our life together. I may not physically be able to hold your hand any more, but I'll always hold you in my heart. Thank you everyone for all your kind words and love — we appreciate it. Love, daff X

223 likes and 150 comments.

I shared and people cared, they just didn't follow through on the support part. Maybe they just didn't know how, or maybe I didn't ask?

Did I ask?

Eurgh.

I don't even know any more.

20 March 2016

'Fuck, we're old. Having takeaway and watching a movie on a Saturday night instead of downing Jäger bombs and twerking in the streets.'

'You're the twerker.' I laugh, remembering Adam grinding up against bins on a walk back to our university halls at 3 a.m. one night.

'True – you're the bomb maestro.' It's a compliment – I think I can do four in a row without being sick. I'd add it to my CV, but people don't appreciate it nowadays.

'It's cute though. As long as we don't do this every weekend. It reminds me of watching *Blind Date* and *Generation Game* with my parents, while not understanding why people needed to date through a screen or the fascination of a wooden man. Can you pass me the saag aloo, please?'

Adam passes me the remnants of the dish we've basically already devoured, and I scrape round the sides of the tinfoil, licking the spoon.

'What the fuck are we watching?' Adam pipes up as I scrape escapee bits of saag aloo from my T-shirt. 'This is so bad. Why did I let you choose this film? She isn't even acting, just speaking really loudly, wailing almost.'

'I like watching trash – it makes me feel happy. I find your movies make me really tense and stressed. I spend the whole time wishing it was over and would reach a happy ending, but in all your movies, the nice people always die.'

'You can give me a happy ending if you like.'

'Fuck off. I'd pay you to go to one of those masseuses for a night of peace.' I wink.

Adam nudges me coyly.

'On the count of three, let's both say our favourite movie. One, two, three!'

'*Parent Trap*!'

'*Pulp Fiction!*'

'I haven't even seen *Pulp Fiction*,' I say.

'Are you kidding me? To everything you've just said. Your favourite movie is *Parent Trap* and you've never seen *Pulp Fiction*. Have you been living under a rock?'

'I always wished I was a twin, *and* I think Lindsay Lohan really missed out on an Oscar for her performance. A-class acting.'

'I love you, but oh my God you are so uncultured sometimes.' Adam whips his phone out and starts frantically scrolling. 'OK, here is Rotten Tomatoes' list of ten films to see before you die: *Clockwork Orange*, *Pulp Fiction*, *The Godfather*, *Fight Club*, *Psycho*, *The Terminator*, *Some Like it Hot*, *Trainspotting*, *Breakfast Club*, *The Naked Gun*. But then we also have: *The Big Lebowski*, *Lethal Weapon*. How many of those have you seen?'

'Honestly?'

'Yes.'

'None.'

'Right, you are watching them. Turn this shit off right now. We'll start with *Pulp Fiction*.'

'OK, well if we're watching your list of films, then we'll also need to watch my top list, which is: *Matilda*, *Parent Trap* and *Drop Dead Fred*.'

'If you manage to make it through my list, which you need to purely from a cultural perspective, I'll watch your movies. Deal?'

'Deal. I'm not good with blood, though. You know that, right?'

The credits start rolling and I feel my whole body tense up. I just know it's going to be no *Legally Blonde*.

'Stop working yourself up. It's good, OK?' He holds my hand and swings my legs up on his. 'Also, no phones. You need to concentrate to get the whole Tarantino experience.'

'It's a Tarantino? Fuck.' There will be blood. 'I'll grab a sick bag.'

8

I'm editing a #cringe post for Mizzennial when the doorbell reverberates around my flat.

> **@Mizzennial** Went back to a guy's house, post-Infernos. He bought me a kebab, so what could I do? Was so drunk I went into his housemate's room and shagged him instead. #Cringe.

Thanks @AmyLowe8972 for sending that one in!

It's 9 a.m. Who needs to see anyone at 9 a.m.?

'Milly? Darling? It's Mum. Your dad and I have come to visit!'

You don't know how pleased I am to see a friendly couple of faces.

I'd say they came bounding up the stairs to greet me, but they're over sixty, so they walked as fast as they could.

They pull me in for a huge embrace. Ahh, physical love and contact – that's something that you can't get from social media or books. Mum strokes my hair and Dad gives me a kiss on the forehead. I'm back to being ten years old and protected by the barrier of my parents.

'Oh, Milly, darling. We are so happy to see you. How have you been? We had such a stress getting here.' The joys of retirement – they don't know what stress is.

'Did you not download Citymapper like I told you to before?' It's almost rhetorical, as I already know the answer.

'Oh, you know me, I just used my map.' Mum waves the ancient Ordnance Survey in her hand. 'Apps aren't as good as the real thing.' There's no point explaining the obvious ease of GPS – someone's already read the map, processed the information and is now purely directing you. Whatever, it's a waste of breath.

'Well, I'm glad you two intrepid explorers made it across London with nothing but a sheet of paper and long-distance eyesight. It's lovely to see you.' Sometimes I sound sarcastic, but I genuinely couldn't be happier to see my parents. They're two people that can't do enough for me and regardless of my anger, my tears, they still love me. They won't leave me. Willingly, anyway.

'Shall I put the kettle on? I think we could all do with a lovely cup of tea and a biscuit.' One of those little idiosyncratic comments that comes with all British people over the age of fifty.

She's right though, nothing beats it. Tea and biscuits – it's just *so* Adam.

As my mum bustles round in the three cupboards that I call a kitchen, I strike up a conversation with my father about his new hobbies.

'How are you, Dad?'

'Oh, fantastic, darling. I had fencing last night and gave the other guy a real thrashing – he was only ten,' he responds, suddenly animated.

I bought my dad fencing lessons for his birthday, and he has turned into some sort of dancing monkey pensioner – he even pliés on demand now.

'Wonderful! Did Mum cook you a nice dinner last night?'

'Yes, lovely, darling – we had liver, kidney, mash and gravy.' He's even more animated with this response.

'Gross!' I recoil. 'It's the twenty-first century, Dad. You don't need to eat organs any more. That's why the industrial revolution happened so we don't have to live in squalor and eat parts of the digestive system!' I'm sure Adam would have some historical quip he could add if he were here.

'Well, I find it rather tasty. I'll buy you a tin of Spam next time I see one.' He chortles, finding himself hilarious in the way that only dads can do. 'Did you know it is seen as a delicacy in Japan?'

Luckily, my mum holds the purse strings and buys all presents for Florry and myself, apart from when my dad sees something he can't resist, like a pair of binoculars for my eighteenth birthday, or a knitted mouse ornament for my twenty-fifth Christmas.

'We bought you a box of treats to cheer you up.'

I look inside. My parents know how to treat me. A packet of Super Sour Nerds, a thriller novel about a lady whose husband dies in a hit-and-run (very appropriate), chocolate digestives and my favourite Beanie Baby from home – a tiger called Jasmine.

I rip open the McVitie's and pass them round – I love the way the chocolate melts off in your hot hand and that comforting wheat taste. Every bite reminds me of picnics in the garden with Florry in the nineties and late-night trips to Asda with Adam in the noughties. We'd stock up on snacks for movie marathons – it's fun eating in front of an animated box when you're with someone, but it's borderline tragic when you're alone.

I've forgotten how much I used to love Beanie Babies. They remind me of saving my pocket money to buy the latest addition to the collection, how I used to make fortresses, jungles and plush polyester towns with Florry so they could reside in comfort. Those were the days. When we used our minds, not our thumbs, to escape the monotony of life. When all I worried about was what time dinner would be and which boy in my class was I going to declare my love to next through saucily written notes like, *Meet you by the jungle gym at first break X.* What I would do to rewind time fifteen years right now? Would I still have chosen Adam or would I have saved myself the heartache?

I never thought I'd be in this situation at twenty-eight. When you're waiting for your GCSE results, being in your late twenties seems like the ultimate adult age. I assumed I'd be married with three children, hosting dinner parties in my four-bedroom house. Let's see if the Instagram world feels the same as me – widow or not.

@Mizzennial
How did you meet your Prince Charming?
a.   Our eyes met over the bar in Chiltern Firehouse. He slid his number over on a piece of paper alongside a glass of champagne.
b.   On Bumble, like everyone does nowadays, but he was different. I sent him my favourite movie quote and he responded with the next line. It was fate.
c.   He sent me a dick pic on Tinder and it wasn't from an underneath angle.

How did you think you would act as an adult?
a.   Mashing avocado and toasting rye bread faster than you could say 'holy guacamole'.
b.   Watering my inside foliage, fluffing my designer pillows from Liberty and doing macramé for alternative wall art.
c.   Spending most Sunday mornings, stuck inside my duvet cover, deciding whether this life is really worth it and if I can sacrifice one night out a week to pay for a cleaner.

Where did you think you would live in your twenties?

a.   Exactly where I do now, in a converted warehouse just off London Bridge. Daddy paid for my deposit, while Mummy bought my sofa.

b.   In a cute little flat I have been saving for just outside London. It isn't much, but I really enjoy it because it is all mine.

c.   In a 'studio flat' above Chicken Village. There is nothing that gets me out of bed more than the smell of fried chicken. Have you heard of the expression living hand to mouth?

Just as I click 'upload' on to my new channel, the most hilarious meme pops up. You know the one of the two pugs with their chins showing, which exactly depicts your mum and dad on FaceTime? I show my parents, as some people say technology keeps them young.

'What is that again?' My mum looks more than confused. 'You said a *mem-a*. Is that right? A *memmmm-ay*. What is one of those? I assume it's a joke, but I'm not sure I understand.'

'It is called a meme. Siri, what's a meme?' I speak into my new phone, thankful to finally use Apple's most extraneous feature.

Mum and Dad look startled and amused at the same time as it appears I have captured an adult woman and imprisoned her in my phone and I'm not even subtle about it. What's the world coming to, eh?

Siri pipes up. 'A meme acts as a vessel for cultural ideas and allows them to be transmitted from one mind to another through different mediums, such as images, often with a comedic theme.'

'OK . . . but why is it funny?' Dad's eyebrows have knitted together.

'Because it is – two pugs on FaceTime, who look like you two when you FaceTime me.'

'But we are not dogs?' Well observed Mother.

'Yes, but it's a funny representation. Look, here's another one, maybe easier to understand.'

@Memeable's Instagram account. There's a picture of a baby's fine-haired head next to a kiwi, with the caption, *Don't talk to me or my son ever again.* That one.

'That one is funny. But we are not kiwis.'

Honestly, they must read too much. I've given up on memes and parents for now.

'Right, darling. We need to talk,' Mum says, putting down her tea on the kitchen counter. 'We've been worried about you for a while, and now you've been hit by a car, we are even more on edge. What will be next? You used to be such a social butterfly, and now you are, well, a cocooned caterpillar. You don't really see anyone any more. You seem to have a very small group of friends. You don't have a boy to look after you the way Adam used to.'

Tears are pricking in my eyes. My life is totally fucked. Thanks for highlighting, Mum. I could have launched into a ballad by Beyoncé to prove that I am an independent woman but the truth is, at the moment, I'm not. Alone? Yes. Independent? No.

'All we want is for you to be happy. Get yourself living in the moment more, to stop all this social media nonsense. Hiding away behind closed doors isn't going to ever bring Adam back. He would want you to be out meeting people, being your charismatic self again. Did seeing that counsellor help at all?'

'I can't really do anything at the moment.' I ignore the part about Violet. I haven't told them about our routine Zoom dates and I'm most definitely not telling them about Mizzennial. I know Violet said about opening up, but I don't think I'm ready to do it to people I'm close to yet. I've been pretending I'm fine for so long, it'd be embarrassing to admit I was lying.

'Well, we know that darling, but we just wanted to say our piece. We aren't trying to upset you. Let's get you out. Shall we go somewhere nice for lunch, OK?'

I know they're trying to be supportive, but it's never great having someone point out how terrible your life is.

I chose this really cute Turkish place for lunch for my parents and me. It's all over Instagram and looks the bomb! We all needed some substance after Mum and Dad had to help carry me down the stairs from my flat. I thought we were all going to die at some points. The last time my dad helped me on some stairs was when I was drunk – and I accidentally punched him and gave him a black eye. It was slightly more sophisticated this time, even if I was wearing a dress and my bare bum was being squashed against the walls at varying points.

I really wanted the open chicken kebab, but I remember putting on Instagram recently that I was giving up meat for a while, and I don't want to lose the few followers that I have. Instead, I opted for the halloumi and pomegranate, which is more photogenic anyway. Mum and Dad also chose a meat-free option, thank God. I didn't want to cause an upset when they had travelled all this way.

'Stop!'

'What?' Mum looks very confused. She's clearly not aware of dining etiquette.

'I need to take a photo.'

'Why?'

'Because I need to. There is no point in coming here for lunch if no one knows. What a waste of money.'

Truth is, I barely venture out for something as fancy as a meal I haven't purchased, cooked and served myself. I'd be a fool to pass on content falling into my lap like this.

Mum starts laughing. 'How many photos of food do you have on your phone? What are you going to do with them all? Sit and salivate over hundreds of meals, half of which aren't even yours?' How many photos do I have? Fifty? A hundred? A thousand? I have no idea; they serve no purpose. Oh well, that's for me to decide what I want them for.

'I really don't think you get it. Can you move your chair out slightly? Your skirt's getting in the way of the photo. Dad, I think maybe your head's blocking the light. That's better.'

'Who are you taking this photo for? Personally, I think it is a way of showing off to everyone. A boasting showreel.'

I wouldn't have sat and salivated over them – I would have posted the photos on Instagram with a GIF about food porn and people would respond with a tongue-out emoji even though they couldn't give a fuck what I'm eating, as they are probably out doing the exact same thing. Friends I haven't seen since the funeral might comment about how we should go for a lunch or a drink or even send a message again, but it won't happen. I sigh. Mum is a parrot for my inner conscience, telling me everything I already know. The whole reason I started Mizzennial was to stop the fakeness, the boasting, the showing off.

I started taking the photo before I even knew what I was doing. What would I have done with it, anyway? Probably spent ages adding a filter, cutting and cropping. Thinking of a caption that made people think I was out having fun, brunching with my many friends. What's the point of being a liar? I've stopped just pretending to everyone around me and started doing it to myself as well.

'Milly, I'm sorry, I didn't mean to upset you.'

I must have been silent for a long time.

'No, it's OK, Mum. You're right, I don't know why I need a photo of my food. If I want to see this plate again, I'll make a reservation for another day.'

'What have you done with my daughter? Reveal yourself, alien life form,' Mum jokes as she puts her hand on my fore-head, mock taking my temperature.

'Dad, get in and we'll ask the waitress to take a snap of us all.' I'm not ready to give up taking photos altogether. I know how important photographic memories are to me; I mean, I look at ones of Adam and I nearly every day.

The waitress comes over, asking how we are finding the food, but even if she had served us pig brain on a pile of dog shit, we would have still said, 'Great, thanks,' as we are British and that's what we do. She took about twenty snaps but there was only one where one of us didn't have our eyes closed or were baring all our teeth like a smiling chimpanzee. It turns out she's a wannabe author. Dad starts to tell her how I love creative writing – basically pimping me out, in a desperate attempt for me to have more friends. It's highly embarrassing. People don't make new friends past the age of twenty-five. Like it or lump it, once you get over the mid-twenties hill, no one has time to make new friends any more. The closest you are going to get is a twenty-minute friendship on a night out in the girls' toilets, where you feel her boobs and she offers you a free swipe of lip gloss in return.

Mum and Dad start talking about Florry and Chris, the happily married couple, and all the great things they've been doing together. All their new house-renovation projects, Chris' new promotion, blah, blah, blah. They don't mean to rub in the disparity between their offspring's lives. They are proud of Florry; I just wish they could be proud of me too.

Life's short and not very sweet at times. In another life, baby Ralf has started at preschool and I'm having a coffee with my new rich friends discussing how irritating it is that the cleaner for my second home is away for the next two weeks.

Maybe I *should* open up more. I should take Violet's advice and tell my parents what I've been up to, then I'll have to be accountable for my own improvements. That way, I limit the risk of falling back into my own ways, like taking silly photos of my food when I'm supposed to be improving my relationship with Instagram.

'Mum, you know I went to see that counsellor? Well . . .' I swallow. 'I've been speaking to her on Zoom too.'

'That's great news, Milly. We are really proud of you.' She smiles and squeezes my hand.

Dad continues eating his halloumi kebab. He's even worse at communicating than me.

I take a deep breath.

'I'm trying, you know, Mum. I know you worry about me, but I'm really trying. It's just so hard sometimes and it's easier to pretend everything's fine, but I'll be OK.'

'I know you will, Milly. You are very brave. Not everyone would be able to go through what you've been through.'

We all take a mouthful of our kebabs, silently eating, like three cows chewing the cud. There's not much more that needs to be said.

'How did your appointment go, babes?'

'Oh, absolutely fine, nothing to worry about! I can come and pick you up after work, if you like as I've taken the day off?'

'Yes, sounds wonderful! Maybe we can go out for dinner or something, make a night of it?'

'Yeah, sounds, err, great. And Milly, I love you.'

'Love you too.'

I run at him, and he swoops me up in his big arms, swinging me round. Gosh, maybe he is going to propose to me or something? Maybe in a French bistro restaurant over a bottle of wine and a medium-rare steak, and we'll start planning the most perfect day of our lives. A big party for all our friends and family, what we always wanted. A celebration of our love, of us, till death do us part.

'Shall we go for a drink then, milady?'

'Yes, sir, we shall.' And I do a little curtsey.

'Nothing like the crisp coldness of a pint of San Miguel.' I grin at him and clink my glass on his.

'Nothing.' He smiles in agreement back at me, but he looks strained. I can see it in his eyes – the sparkles in the sea have vanished – and the way his lips aren't curling up properly, his dimples barely present.

'Are you OK?' I shift nervously on the leather seat of the pub booth, my hands suddenly clammy and sticky.

'Milly, I don't really know how to say this. I don't think there is any right way, so I'm just going to come out with it.'

He puts his hand on mine. Fuck, is he going to break up with me? Has he met someone else? I feel the hairs on the back of my neck stand up and a ball of sick rises in my throat. I've got it all wrong, he wasn't going to propose after all. Stupid Milly.

'I've got cancer.' He pauses, although my ears have somehow managed to block out the surrounding clinks of glasses, laughing and mindless chitter chatter to create a deafening silence. 'Testicular cancer.'

Sometimes you know that something is up. Sometimes it hits you like a ten-tonne truck. This is a mixture of the two.

C-A-N-C-E-R. The six-letter word that stops time.

Everything's a blur, yet I'm alert. I feel like I don't know anything any more. I've suddenly been plunged into a nightmare. Adam, the love of my life is sitting statuesque right in front of me, but I feel so removed from him. People are laughing and joking around me as if they're in another world, while I sit here, unable to comprehend the gravity of what's just come out of Adam's mouth.

'What?' Tears are falling down my face without me even noticing. My emotions are ahead of my words.

Adam says something else, but I don't know what he's saying. Every syllable is pronounced to the point that it doesn't even make sense any more. He clasps his hands together and grabs mine.

'I'm so sorry, Mills.'

'But they can cure it, right?' I don't even wait for an answer but continue blindly. 'There are loads of treatments out there now. Everything's so advanced.' The words rush out of my mouth so optimistically I don't even have time to register what they are. My tongue feels dry even though streams of tears are falling out of my eyes and dribbling down my nose into my mouth. I wipe the snot on my right arm.

'No, they can't. It's stage four. They can only manage the symptoms, but they can't cure it.' He squeezes my hand tight, his eyes watery. 'I'm so sorry. I love you.'

Tears are falling down my face thick and fast. My breathing has become frantic.

I'm sure people around me must be staring, wondering what's going on, but I don't care.

My mind races and races. Cancer. Thoughts fling from left to right and back again. Cancer.

What does it mean? Cancer. Death. Alone. Pain. Cancer. Hurt. Gone. Forever.

Adam. I can't live without him. He's my whole world. He makes me, me. I planned my whole future with him. I can't do it alone. I'm not an independent person. I need him.

I thought I was entering a new chapter with him. My adult life beginning. New job, proposal, marriage, house, babies, weddings of friends, christenings, birthdays, parties, holidays. Love, life, laughter.

'Adam, I can't . . .' *Live without you*, I was going to say, but I run to the toilet instead.

I put the lid down, squeeze my knees into my chest and cry uncontrollably. How could he have cancer? He's twenty-six. The love of my life. Gone. There's no good news. No silver lining. No light at the end of the tunnel. Nothing. This really is the end.

I hit my head hard on the side of the cubicle to check I'm not having a nightmare. I'm not. I hit it again just to check. I want to hurt myself so I can't feel the pain on the inside. So, this is what heartbreak feels like. You find the perfect person, you live the perfect life, and then BAM! It's all ripped out from under your feet, as if the world was jealous of how much you were enjoying it all.

What on earth must Adam be going through? It isn't fair for me to be this upset. I'm such a fucking bitch. Why was he sorry? It isn't his fault he has cancer. Stop crying, Milly, think about someone else for once. You're so selfish, Milly. You need to be strong, to be there for Adam. You have all the time in the world to get over it. He doesn't.

Adam stands up as I walk back towards the pub table and pulls me in for the tightest hug in the world. I see a young couple staring at us over Adam's shoulder. The girl, who must be about my age, gives me a sympathetic smile. She probably thinks Adam's broken up with me, because people don't expect relationships in their twenties to end because one of you has a terminal illness. They expect them to end because you found someone else. But there'll never be someone else.

'I love you so much,' he whispers in my ear. My cheeks are wet, leaving an imprint on the shoulder of his shirt. I can feel the wetness of his own tears on the nape of my neck.

'It will be OK, Adam. I'll always be here for you.' I feel myself biting back more tears. Ignoring the stabbing pain in my chest and the wave of nausea rising from my stomach.

I lie because it hurts too much to tell the truth. It doesn't matter. White lies are good. I feel like I'll be lying a lot from now on.

Nothing will ever be OK again. How can it be?

The miracles that it takes to even exist – everything needing to be aligned, the perfect sperm, the perfect egg all at the perfect time – it's a wonder we even make it this far.

9

It's the middle of the night. Why can't I sleep? It's been ages since this happened. I'm a liar. I'm a fraud. I need to start speaking my truth. I've been thinking about the lunch date with my parents. Mum spoke my truth when I couldn't. Why do I care so much about what people think about me? Why do I pretend to be something I'm not? Why can't I own being a widow? I should be shouting it from the rooftops – like my mum said, I'm brave. Other people should know they're brave too. You don't have to be fighting lions with your bare hands, you can just be a survivor.

I've been sitting with my thumb poised over the 'share now' button for what seems like an eternity. I thought I'd be opening a bottle of champagne when I hit a thousand followers or having a fancy dinner when I hit three thousand, but it didn't seem right, because I wasn't doing what I came here to do – be honest. I'm not here to celebrate the four thousand five hundred followers I currently have, although it does seem like an achievement, I'm here to make people feel at home again. The number of followers doesn't matter, it's the real people that do, the ones that have feelings. Oh God, I don't know if I can do it. I guess it's the first step, anonymously post that the person behind this account is a widow, I don't need to tell anyone my name. No one needs to know that it's Milly Dayton, twenty-eight-year-old widow from Croydon. I can dip my toe in the water and see if it's cold. Maybe people will realise that widows can be funny too.

Come on, Milly, no one even knows it's you! Fuck it. Share now.

> @Mizzennial Someone close to me died and I can't stop thinking about it. It's been nearly two years now and I can't get over it. I can't move on. I can't sleep. I live in the world of make-believe. I'd just love someone to understand.

What would my former self reply to that message? What would my pre-widow advice be?

> 'Dear Milly, I'm sorry to hear that, it must be a very troubling time for you. Grief takes a long time and can come in many forms. Have you tried talking to a professional about it? I find listening to audiobooks helps me sleep. That said, unfortunately, time is the best healer, but it can be a long process to get there. Love, Tanya x'

Everyone used to ask me for advice. They used to like my balanced view on problems, but not since Adam died. Why would you ask a widow for love advice? It clearly hasn't worked out very well. Now, no one really asks me anything, scared that I might suddenly break down in tears, divulge thoughts that even a cup of tea can't cure and bring a storm of negativity down on their perfect little lives. To be fair to them, I'm not at one with my emotions right now, so I guess I can't blame them. No one tells me their problems, because how can any of their problems ever relate to my husband dying? But I don't want them to relate, I just want to have fun with them again.

Looks like the rest of the internet doesn't think along Tanya's wavelength.

A fight has broken out. A war among trolls.

Some BITCH, and I don't like to be a tattletale but @GoldieLookingMane is her Instagram handle commented:

@GoldieLookingMane Pipe down, Little Miss Moaner. People die all the time – there's no place for this on Instagram. Go to a counsellor if you want to chat.

Does she not know how much courage it took me to post that? She knows nothing, I repeat *nothing* about my life.

Luckily for me, before I almost expose myself very publicly online, an angel known as @ShelleyFarrell comments:

@ShelleyFarrell @GoldieLookingMane, do you not have anything better to do than troll people online? You are the reason why people have so many issues. Bullies only have a place in hell.

How can I have caused such a commotion? Little old Milly Dayton. I could have cried when I first read @GoldieLookingMane's message, but @ShelleyFarrell gave me some hope. At least, there are people that understand.

Oh, and I've received a private DM:

@ElephantsDon'tForget @Mizzennial Don't worry, I understand exactly what you mean. My best friend passed away and everything reminds me of her. Like literally everything. Jokes people say, TV shows, scents in the air. I keep trying to detach myself from what's happened, but then I come across a reminder, and it makes me start the grieving process all over again. X

Automatically, I start typing a response:

@Mizzennial @ElephantsDon'tForget Some reminders are good. It's perfectly normal and perfectly fine to smell your best friend's perfume and feel those pangs of sadness, and in time you will be pleased to have those reminders. They may even make you smile. Have you spoken to someone about how you feel? X

What am I doing?

How can I give advice to people that I don't take myself? Where did that version of Milly just appear from? The words just flowed out of my thumbs before my brain could catch up.

I delete the response and close Instagram.

'I did exactly what you told me to, Violet. I shared on my channel and then I got trolled.'

'Oh, Milly.' She looks saddened. 'Not everyone will agree with your opinion all the time. There are so many trolls online. They like to cause drama and say things that they would never say in person. They are probably jealous of you.'

Jealous? Of a depressed, one-legged widow. Come the fuck on, Violet.

'It's made me never want to tell anyone anything ever again. I'll resort to being a mute,' I respond stubbornly.

'It is good to share things, Milly. The more open you are with people, the more they will open up to you. You might surprise yourself. Remember what you said to me last time? You're gradually detaching from the identity you've created for yourself – you're not just Milly the widow. You're funny, clever, charismatic, but you had something horrendous happen to you. You're gradually shaping yourself into a new version of Milly.'

'I can't be dealing with anyone else's problems right now – I have enough of my own.' The words are flowing from my lips but I'm not sure if I totally agree with myself; it's an automated response. A guard.

'Anything I can help with?'

'No.' Not unless you are going to take me to a séance.

'Well, remember, Milly, any time you want to talk . . .'

'Thanks, bye!'

It feels good talking to Violet, but at the moment, it still feels better speaking to Adam. It's easy to talk about things but much harder to put your words into practice. It's all part of the process, I tell myself.

I remember what I typed out earlier to @ElephantsDon'tForget – reminders are good.

I shut my eyes and pretend he's next to me, sitting on the sofa wearing his favourite washed-blue Levi's with the rips and navy polo shirt. I can smell his aftershave in the air and feel the bristles already coming through from his morning shave.

'Why's it so hard to get people to care?'

'It's not that people don't care, Milly, it's that they don't always know what to say, so sometimes they say nothing.'

'Some people say nothing and everyone else says the wrong thing.'

'Yeah, well, you can always call people out. They probably don't realise the impact of what they're saying.'

I open my eyes and look at the stream of blue messages on Facebook Messenger.

What.

The.

Fuck.

Am.

I.

Doing.

23 May 2018

'Hey, Mum, everything OK?'

'Yes, darling, just calling for a chat, you know.'

'Great. How are things? Have you got photography today?'

'I'm leaving in about ten minutes. We're going to Holkham Beach to practise our nature shots. Your father has really got into his fencing – he has bruises all over his torso, looking super macho.' Rank.

'That sounds wonderful, Mum,' I say, scrolling absent-mindedly. Hmm, @FreyaDack's hair looks good blonde. 'I'm going out for a Thai with Julia and Nicky later. We found this kitsch place in Brick Lane. Looking forward to it.'

'That sounds wonderful, darling! I'm so happy that you're keeping yourself busy and back to your socialising self again. You know since everything with . . .'

'OK, got to go, Mum. Love you. Bye.'

I press the red button and put my phone down. Going out for dinner would be one of the last things I'd do. I haven't washed my hair in three days, and I'm wearing the same bob-bly university stash sweatshirt and unflattering leggings that cut me up in all the wrong places that I've been sporting all week. I was wearing one of Adam's sweatshirts that he saved for me, but it stopped smelling of him a while ago and desperately needs a wash.

Adam died nearly a year ago, August 8th, etched into my memory for eternity. I thought I'd be over this stage of grief. What's wrong with me?

I'm going through a bad patch again; I can feel it.

I've declined every invitation that's floated my way for drinks, dinner, gym classes, brunch, lunch, you-name-it, for weeks now. The effort it takes to smile and pretend I'm hav-ing a fucking fantastic time is too much. I desperately want to be back to normal: I want to research the latest avocado hotspot to launch in a dilapidated warehouse; I want to care about my body fat percentage; I even want to be complimented by random strangers who would do anything to fuck me, but I just don't care about anything any more.

I taunt myself online, peeking through a glass screen at all my friends' smiling faces. Ava and her pals at rooftop drinks, Florry and Chris out for their tenth dinner of the week. I pretend I'm there. I comment and like and message them all continuously, but the words are fake. I do want them to have a nice time, I do wish I was there, but at the same time I don't. That fake world of love, laughter, friends and activities keeps me going. It's an online storybook where I can be the main character when I want to and be cast out when I don't.

10

Happy Galentine's Day! Love you, sis! X

Florry can be nice.
  I reply:

Love you too x

It's sweet of Florry but it's no bouquet of red roses or making a picnic on the floor of the living room and watching some soppy chick flick with my sidekick.

To cheer me up on this *ultra*-depressing day, I'm going out for brunch with Julia. Well, it's actually a late lunch, but someone must have noticed that if you replace the letter *L* with *BR*, it starts to sound like you're made of money.

I throw my crutches to the bottom of the stairs and then slide down on my bum – like tobogganing but without the snow or toboggan. It reminds me of skiing when I was younger (what I called skiing but really was sliding down a hill near our house with Florry and Dad); a severe lack of snow, money and an immense amount of cold rain. That's why British people aren't as elegant as the Europeans on the slope; we spend our winters falling from the top to the bottom of the stairs while they ski round the Alps.

Anyway, after I elegantly descend the stairs, I order an Uber as clearly, I can't walk unaided yet.

I finish helping out a Mizzennial follower on a highly embarrassing situation when the Uber pulls to a stop.

@Mizzennial I came downstairs to my niece and my GRANDMOTHER playing with a new toy. On closer inspection, I realised that it was, in fact, my dildo. One has bad eyesight and the other can't speak but still #Cringe

'Babes!' Julia pulls me in for an embrace outside Tom Tom. It's this brunch place which serves tomato everything, including the oh-so-desirable Bloody Marys. I give her a tight hug and kiss on the cheek. Why does Julia always look so glam without trying? Her skin is dewy, her hair in waves, her jeans are tight without being stretched and her mid-length blazer grazes her hips, taking pounds off her.

My jeans are cutting into my stomach, my foundation is clumpy because I haven't been moisturising properly and my lipstick is clinging to the few remaining bits of dry skin on my chapped lips. I'm an extra from the *Rocky Horror Show*.

It must be happiness that gives her that eternally youthful glow.

'How are you, darling? You look great!' Julia's pleasantries make me feel almost human again until I realise that she has to say that because she is British: you say what should be said in society, not what you actually mean.

One of us walks and the other hops through the front door, which is shaped like a giant tomato with a green hedge sprouting out the top. A large vine runs through the restaurant with red, circular tables sprouting off it. Pretty cool.

'I don't, but thanks. How are you, anyway? You always have so much going on – your life is much more interesting than mine.' This isn't because I'm British – I mean it.

Julia makes a joke about her life being super boring – it's all broken-down washing machines and a bathroom pipe leak at the moment (it was a bit dull but it's more than I have going on) before launching into a story about her plumber leaving mid-job to go on a Tinder date/lunchtime quicky.

We sit down at one of the round, red tables and I rest my head at the top, to pretend I have a vine for a beard, while Julia takes a photo. After some procrastinating and ordering our red wedding breakfast, Julia pulls out the final knife.

'I do have something to tell you, Mills.' She pauses, twiddling a lock of hair around her finger. 'I'm pregnant!'

Silence.

'Milly, say something! You're sitting there in silence and your mouth has dropped open.'

'That's such great news, Julia! Sorry, you caught me off guard, I wasn't expecting it.' When your life comes to such a dramatic pause, it's easy to forget that other people's keeps moving forward.

'Are you happy for me?' She sounds annoyed and disheartened at the same time.

'Of course, I'm happy for you!' I reply quickly – the last thing I want to do is upset my best friend. 'I just can't believe it. It seems so far away from my life right now. I can't imagine growing another human inside me.' I'm happy for Julia, I just wish we could trade lives, I've always wanted children but I'm more likely to get impregnated by one of London's promiscuous pigeons before that happens.

'Don't tell anyone, though. I did one of those ultra-early pregnancy tests and I couldn't believe it when I saw positive! Don't worry, I didn't know when we drank all those bottles of rosé.'

I did half wonder if it was now acceptable to get drunk while procreating. Happiness is almost exploding from her face – if only I could steal some. Julia continues, unaware that her best friend is starting to become jealous of an emotion – which is beyond ridiculous.

'I know you shouldn't tell anyone until twelve weeks, but if anything does happen to the baby, I'll be severely depressed and be crying to you about it for the rest of my life, anyway. I can't believe I've been pregnant but had no idea! I was worried about all the nights out I have been on, but the doctor told me not to worry – most women don't know they are pregnant for ages.' She shakes her head in disbelief. 'Please don't ask me "Was it planned?" because my mother's already asked me that, and yes, it was sort of, we just didn't realise it would happen so soon!' Finally, she pauses, as I try to look as engaged as possible. 'When he slash she is born, I would love you to be the godmother.'

'Oh my God! I'll be a godmum? Oh, Julia, thank you, thank you, thank you!' I pull her in for a hug; it's like she is sharing her happiness with me. Something to give me purpose again. I can't yet be a real mum, but I can be something attributed to the big man himself. That should start to give me some luck.

'Of course, who else would it be?'

'Can I ask you a question I've always wanted to know?'

'Go on . . .'

'Can you and James still have sex?'

'Oh my God, Milly. Just because I'm pregnant doesn't mean I immediately turn into a nun. I'm still me.'

'I always wanted to know if you could. Or if you can feel the baby on the other end.'

'Gross. I am ten weeks pregnant. The baby is the size of a strawberry, so I don't think it can feel anything.'

'Good, as the godmother, I was worried about its welfare.'

'Well, that is exactly why I chose you – super sensible. Sorry, I have to go wee, honestly my bladder is so weak, feels like it is made from a muslin sack.'

Fuck.

Me.

Julia's having a baby. A real-life miniature version of her and James. Something that she has to put before Instagram, clothes and espresso martinis. I'd love to pretend that having a baby is not for me, but it is. For a while after Adam died, I used to pretend that I hated marriage and children and those nice family homes in the centre of Surrey. I don't, of course. My happiness is tinged with sadness. Adam would be so happy for Julia. We always used to dream about what life would be like when we all had children. Now I'll have no one to share this happy moment with. I guess I can talk to Violet about it . . .

We've been the same age our entire lives, at the same stage, and then suddenly, whoosh. I'm widowed and Julia's married and having a baby.

How will Julia know what to do with a baby? She's the same age as me and I wouldn't know what to do. I can barely look after myself. Maybe that's when you get given your 'How to Adult' handbook, as soon as you give birth. The millennial adulting gene gets passed onto your mini-me, like in a relay race. One out, one in.

It's such a whirlwind of emotions. You think you're about to catch up with everyone again, and then they hop into the fast lane for a quick life-stage upgrade. Like everyone's been playing *The Sims* and given the not-so-secret 'rosebud' password for all the new features, like houses, husbands and babies, but by the time you get there, it's stopped working.

Maybe it won't be so bad Julia having a baby. It can be a new member of our gang. I always wished that mine and Julia's children would be besties growing up, but there will probably be such a stark age gap, they'll be like parent and child.

Julia returns from the bathroom.

'I'm super proud of you, Julia. You're really smashing the back door out of life right now.' Don't think I'm being a back-stabber, there's no way I can reiterate the thoughts that have just been churning over in my black mind. I'm not two-faced, I'm grieving – no one understands.

'I know things have been tough, Milly, but they'll get better you know?' She plays with the napkins on the centre of the table. 'I'm not sure if this is going to be appropriate or inappropriate, but James and I did something for you.'

What did you do?!

'I know you've tried your hand at dating and stuff recently and it's not been going very well. And I can't imagine how hard that must be,' she quickly caveats, 'being slung back into a world where sparking up conversations offline just doesn't exist any more – Lord knows what I would do in that situation. I just wanted to give you a helping hand.'

Tell me what you did! I want to shout, but I continue sitting patiently, my eyes blinking provocatively.

'Anyway, James and I filled in an application for you to be on that new dating show, *Swipe Right,* and you've been put forward! Can you believe it?'

No. I can't fucking believe it. If I had a pound for the amount of helping hands I've received over the years, I would be dishing out the help. I wish Adam were here so I could do funny things to my friends with my sidekick.

'I don't really know what to say.' I look up to the ceiling of vines – Help me, Adam. The last thing in the world I want to do is date anyone else, but I know I can't hide at home forever.

'You're mad at me, aren't you? Fuck. I'm so sorry.' She bites her bottom lip.

'No, I'm not. *Shocked* is more the word.' I rest my chin on my thumb and flick my nose with my index finger, thinking. 'Well, I wasn't expecting you to say that . . .' I think about

Mizzennial, Violet and all the new things I'm trying. Now's as good a time as any. 'Maybe I'll give it a go. My life can't get any worse right now, surely.'

'Great!' Julia smiles at me. I know how good it makes everyone feel thinking they've helped a friend in need.

I twist the diamond ring around my sweaty finger. I hope you forgive me, Adam. If I want that family home in Surrey and a baby to match Julia, I better start finding suitors.

'One Virgin and one Bloody Scotch Mary?' The waitress calls over.

I take a sip of mine, start coughing dramatically as the spice hits my tongue. Fuck, she must have meant Scotch bonnet. I thought it was a joke about Mary Queen of Scots – she had tomato-red hair, didn't she? I'm dying.

There's been dates since Adam, and they've all been a disaster. I seem to have lost my ability to attract anyone normal, become the antithesis of who I once was. Forgotten all social etiquette – it's like I've spent eighteen months under a rock, not glued to a communication device.

I'm at a loss. How will I ever be comfortable with someone else again? I want to go out, get too drunk and shove a doner kebab smothered with garlic sauce into my chops, and I want him to want to see me again. What was it that attracted Adam to me? I wish I'd asked him so I knew how to find another mate. I have a whole list of questions I wish I'd asked.

I'm sure loads of other people must feel the same as me.

@Mizzennial Why is it that when you are low, the world has to make sure you are really feeling it? I'm already feeling like everyone is streaks ahead of me in the race of life, and then my bestie tells me she is pregnant! I'm happy, but I can't help but feel a bit gutted at the same time. Anyone else feel like that?

@PhishingforPhitties Urgh. Tell me about. Half my friends are pregnant and the other half are engaged. My boyfriend of seven years broke up with me and I'm living back at home. #ImSingleGetMeOuttaHere

@OptimisticOrange Don't feel pressured. Everyone has their own timeline. Things happen when you least expect them to.

@PhishingforPhitties   @OptimisticOrange   Yeah like getting dumped on Valentine's Day. #SometimesLifeisShit

I accompany this with a joke post to lighten the mood – I'm sure people can relate to this too. I feel so far behind with dating, like I've been transported straight from the nineteenth century in a petticoat and taken to Ann Summers. It's easier to own being a widow, or tell people 'I'm a widow', than it is to share all the feelings and comorbidities that come along with it.

People say things like 'God, you poor thing', 'I'm sorry that must be so awful for you', 'I can't imagine what you're going through'. They don't think further into the situation, like how on earth do you ever date anyone again, or how do you know what to say, or how do you have sex again without thinking about the person you used to make love to, or, or, or? That's the stuff that's harder to acknowledge. That's the stuff that's embarrassing to share and even harder to admit.

@Mizzennial My friends said they were going out sharking at the weekend. I thought, great, I love dressing up, particularly as a shark! I found the ultimate Great White outfit – complete with a dismembered arm coming out of the mouth – and headed out to meet them. When I arrived, they were all wearing miniskirts and heels – I looked a bit out of place. Turns out 'sharking' is a term to hunt out the opposite sex, for well, sex. Sad to say that on a Wednesday night, at a city function, I didn't pull. #Cringe

That sounds like the sort of thing I'd do at Jemima's hen party. I know Julia's going to make me go. She's right, I should go – considering all the engagements, hen parties and weddings I've missed, it's an honour they still invited me. I know why I didn't go before; I wanted to pretend that everyone's life had stopped like mine had, but that's all I was doing – pretending. Just because I don't attend, doesn't mean they don't go ahead; it's me that's missing out, no one else. I can sacrifice one evening of crisps and *Gossip Girl*. I think.

There's another DM asking for my advice. Who are these people and why do they choose to open up to me?

@**LonelyAkon** @Mizzennial My girlfriend passed away and I feel so alone at the moment, like I don't have anyone to talk to. I do have friends, but I feel embarrassed speaking to them about something so intimate. How can I approach talking about death with them? It's not exactly a subject people are keen to discuss.

I think about seeing Julia and how awkward she gets when I mention Adam; I think about Violet and my parents and I start typing.

@**Mizzennial** @LonelyAkon You're not alone! I cannot stress that enough, but I, for one know, exactly how you feel. You felt like part of a tribe before, you felt indestructible, and now you feel the complete opposite. There's a feeling of worthlessness that comes with grief, and it is very hard to shift. I used to feel bad for feeling bad about myself. Your friends are there for you, and they want to be there for you, they just don't know how. If you are struggling, why not try speaking to a counsellor or another third party to make yourself feel more comfortable talking to your friends again? It's strange that the people who are closest to you can often feel the furthest away. X

I still feel alone but maybe I am good at advice? I press 'send'.

I want to be happy again. Not just fleeting happiness, but the kind where it sits embedded in you; it's in the structure of your bones, it flows in the current of your blood. You smile because your lips can't help but curl upwards, you laugh until you become breathless and you cry because you can't laugh any more. The kind of happiness that I once had, the one I yearn for.

@LonelyAkon @Mizzennial Thanks so much, you've nailed it. That's exactly how I feel. I want my tribe back. Take care X

Maybe I shouldn't do myself down so much. I like sharing. I like talking.

Ping.

Friend request from Layla Rose.

I start shaking. I throw my phone onto the duvet as if it had suddenly increased by a hundred degrees in temperature. Not today. Please.

I've been reminded that people's lives are moving on when I'm stuck at ground zero, and now a friend request on Facebook from Layla, someone I specifically chose to unfriend a couple of years ago. I don't want to be reminded about what she's doing.

My life's like a fucking yo-yo.

3 October 2010

I put my skates on by the ring and boldly stand up, only to smash straight down again, leaving half my brow powder on the sticky carpet. My knees are smarting and my whole bum popped out from under my minidress – great start, Milly!

Well, this is fucking fun. Why can't we just drink and dance? Why does it always have to involve an activity that I can't do?

Who's this boy skating over to me? Give me fucking strength, I can't talk right now.

'Wow, you're good at skating! Can I have a lesson?' He grins. He has two cute dimples and piercing blue eyes, but his sarcasm instantly annoys me.

'Do you like bare-bum skating?' I reply, owning my blunder.

'I don't know yet, that's why I'm asking you to teach me.' His eyes flicker and sparkle.

'It's pretty highbrow in terms of skating, and I'm not sure you'd be able to handle it. You go enjoy yourself and I think I'll prop myself up at the bar.' Now fuck off and stop embarrassing me.

'Take my hand.' His palm is outstretched – nice hands, I think to myself. They look strong and caring, not too big, the size of a good side plate.

'Honestly, I'm *fine*,' I emphasise through gritted teeth as I clench onto the side and feel my skates wobbling underneath. 'I'll be at the bar, watching everyone fly around the ring like the winged monkeys in *Wizard of Oz*.'

'How are you going to get to the bar?' He winks at me already knowing my answer, seeing the whiteness in my knuckles.

Why is he talking to me? I look like a complete twat. I hesitate. This could all end in tears, very quickly. I look at the bar. It does seem very far away.

'Fine.' I take his outstretched hand. 'I've been doing a lot of squats recently so I'm pretty proud of my bum that's why I was showing it off – you were lucky you caught a glimpse.'

We hold hands and he encourages me to let go of the railing that's slipping beneath my sweaty palm.

'If you let me fall, I'll fucking kill you!' I screech, nerves suddenly even more apparent. 'I'm keeping my hand near the rail just in case.'

'I wouldn't dream of it.' And he helps/drags me on my tiny wheels towards the bar. 'Do you always skate off with strangers? You haven't even asked me my name!' he asks.

'Well, you came over to me. I didn't ask you to.'

'Nice to meet you, Lady With No Name – I'm Adam. I live in Earling House.'

'It's Milly. Earling? That's where I live. Strange, I haven't seen you before.' I try to concentrate on his words, but the skating is taking its toll.

'Don't think I'm a stalker, but I've seen you around. You walked into me on the stairs and commented on my T-shirt? The one from Bondi Beach. You said you had been there before. You have to actually move your legs to skate, you know.' He looks down at my locked knees.

Oh yes, *that* T-shirt. He's being pretty direct for someone I've never met – borderline rude. His dimples, though. And I kind of like rude.

'I can't do this, I need to hold on.' My hand grips round the metal again – ahh, safety.

I gingerly skate with one hand on the rail and one clenched in his. I can feel myself perspiring from nerves and humiliation, but we keep going. We do a few laps and I do kind of get the hang of it. I try a few skates by myself, but it's two metres before I fall into the metal bar, laughing hysterically, while also crying with embarrassment on the inside.

'Right, shall we get a drink?'

Adam orders two Tango Fango Quaddy Voddys from the bar and we sip enthusiastically on the intensely sugary liquid.

'Cool drink choice.' I laugh.

'I thought you might need something to take the edge off, and you know real men drink Tango – it's the absolute melts that swig beer.'

I smile. He's funny. I take another sip and think about how I might go about reintroducing myself, something more friendly, now my feet aren't all over the place.

II

15 February 2019

'How are you today, Milly?'

Should I do the classic 'I'm fine', or does that make this whole process a waste of money?

'My best friend Julia's pregnant and I'm going to be a godmother,' I reply without the usual happy intonation that should accompany such great news. It was either that or I tell her about my stalker – @LaylaRose.

'Congratulations!' I should take note of Violet's enthusiastic pitch. 'What fantastic news! You don't sound particularly happy about it, though?'

'I'm happy but . . . Oh, I don't know. I want to be happy. I should be happy, she's my best friend.' My words are battling my emotions.

'But . . . ? I feel like there's a *but*.'

'I'm jealous, I guess.' I look into the corner of the screen. What will Violet think? It's such a horrible trait. 'Jealous that she's happy and having a baby. That could have been me.'

'Don't feel bad about having those feelings.' Violet can obviously sense my insecurity. 'There are many sore reminders of our tragic past out there in the universe. You need to try to not dwell on them. Stop thinking "What if? What could have been?" Because you can't change it. Your life will move on, even talking to me is a massive step. If you still want all of those things, then there's no reason why you won't have them – it might just take a bit of time. Try to think how you can use Julia having a baby to your advantage.'

'I can't *use* my best friend.' Maybe Violet mistook my negative reaction to the news.

'I don't mean *use* her, but think how this will positively change your life. Being a godmother, that will give you some purpose again. You're being a guardian angel, and your friend is putting all of her trust in you. I want you to start writing down every day something positive that has happened to you, it could be something as simple as getting a nice message on Facebook. You need to start finding the meaning in the menial. Think of it as talking to someone about your day, telling them one good thing.'

'Yeah, I guess.' I sit, reflecting, before adding. 'I already talk to him though, in my own way.'

'Oh, really? Your husband, you mean?' Violet looks slightly perplexed as I nod. 'And how do you talk to him?'

'Through Facebook mainly.'

I cannot go on like this. I need to listen to Violet and myself; I need to open up more. I need to start living. I need to remember who I once was. Brave, funny, loving.

I think about Layla and one of the last conversations we had together; I was all those things.

I shake my head, trying to retract the memory. I'm in a constant state of flux.

I must seize the day. Coffee, that's what I need, but I want a fancy one, not the Nescafé Gold Blend kind, either. I'm going to treat myself to a Starbucks. Well, I suppose it's not really a treat if I get one most days, but whatever, I deserve it – I haven't had one in weeks! It's still a hassle getting out and about, but I need the fresh air – my skin is starting to fall off. I'm looking more and more like I've been buried alive each day.

@ILikeMyMenHotAndBlack is working – great! She knows exactly how I like my coffee. I used to laugh that people who make hot drinks were given a qualification, but now I've started drinking caffeine on the regular, I've realised just how difficult it is to get the exact balance between milk, froth and coffee. I still don't know what I'm drinking or why I choose a latte over a cappuccino, but no one does! It's one of those things, just like the Big Bang theory, that causes the human mind to explode with the sheer complexity of the scenario.

Adam used to hate coffee until I started making him drink it. He was always a hot chocolate man until I told him it's not very professional to go out for a work meeting and order a hot chocolate with whipped cream and marshmallows when you're supposed to be orchestrating a million-dollar deal – it looks almost psychotic. Thankfully, he switched up his game and became a flat-white man with the odd hot choccie thrown in for good measure.

'Hello!' @ILikeMyMenHotAndBlack, or according to her name badge – Sophie – says cheerily. 'Oh fuck, what happened to you?' She peers over the bar at me doing an iconic representation of a one-legged Hunchback of Notre Dame. 'I haven't seen you in here for ages – thought you'd started seeing another barista!' She chuckles at her own wisecrack.

'Well, I got hit by a car a week and a bit ago . . .' @ILikeMyMenHotAndBlack opens her mouth so wide I feel like I could pop a whole orange in there. '. . . and I've only just worked out how to move around on my crutches more elegantly without inducing a heart attack,' I say jokily; I don't want @ILikeMyMenHotAndBlack to think I'm the most depressed person in the world. I need to take inspiration from nurses: keep my voice upbeat while iterating the depressed script of my life.

'Oh God, you poor thing!' Her eyes are wide and she's basically eating her own hand now. 'I'll tell you what, it isn't very busy, I'll give you this coffee on the house and come and sit with you for a bit.' I smile that I won't have to be drinking a takeaway coffee alone in my own house. 'You're not going to be able to carry a takeaway cup and both those crutches, are you?'

God, Sophie is very clever. Exactly the kind of uplifting spirit and wisdom I need in my life right now. Sophie's also kind. Are some people born with the innate ability to tell when others could do with a friend?

'That would be so kind, thank you very much.' I can't remember the last time I had a coffee in a china cup. You can break my bones, but not my sophistication. My lips are more attuned to sipping boiling hot coffee out of a tiny plastic hole and dribbling it down my chin.

I have a quick scroll on Instagram while I'm waiting to have a coffee with @ILikeMyMenHotAndBlack. (When was the last time I made a real-life friend?!) As much as I want to change my relationship with Instagram, it's hard not to enjoy the occasional scroll. In this particular situation, it's either mindlessly scroll or sit awkwardly looking at the blank wall while someone I barely know makes me a coffee and I make irritating small talk. I pause over @SocialShrink91's latest mantra post and realise that Florry was probably right all those weeks ago – a real-life shrink, like Violet is much better for me.

@SocialShrink91: HEALTH IS WEALTH

Hey Social Shrinkers! You can't photograph healthy. I can tell you everything I eat in a day, how much I exercise, how many hours of mindfulness I do, but how do you really know if I'm healthy? What I put in my body is different to what you put in yours. You need to really listen to your mind and body, become at one with it so you REALLY know how healthy you are. Personally, for my body, I live on a plant-based diet and often do days of raw-food eating, and most days I practise fasting, because that is what my body needs. Some days I wake up and I eat five Quorn chicken nuggets and that's just because my body needs it. You need to really be in tune with what your body needs. I have partnered with @MindfulnessMaggie to produce a series of seminars on how to be at one with yourself for an introductory offer of £40.99 for ONE WEEK ONLY. Check the link in my bio to find out more. X

I contemplate deleting her, but I still quite like knowing what she's up to. There may be some good advice in there. I just don't need to obsess over every little thing she does. Before I can think too hard about the nature of @SocialShrink91's latest post and her advocacy partnership with @MindfulnessMaggie (who can't be that *mindful,* considering she's pushing her latest unqualified seminar series down every Tom, Dick and Harry's meat-eating neck. That's a good idea for a Mizzennial quiz – I'll do that later. 'On a scale of coconut to oat milk, how vegan are you really?') @ILikeMyMenHotAndBlack comes over with two almond-milk lattes and two pain au chocolat. I look up, smile and turn my phone over. I should make sure I take Violet's advice and live in the moment, not be distracted.

'I'm assuming you aren't actually allergic to dairy?' She points to the chocolate croissant.

'Ha no, how did you guess?'

'Because you look roughly the same age as me and I just don't have it in my coffee to save calories for later and' – she puts her right hand on her hip, adding to the performance – 'I think milk smells like a cow's arse even though it came out of its teat.'

I snort with laughter. 'That is exactly what I think! I can't trust anyone who drinks a glass of milk after seeing *Clockwork Orange.* Fucking psychos.' I silently thank Adam for making me watch that film. He was right, it was culturally important.

'Cheers to not drinking butt milk!' We clink our cups and smash our croissants in the air.

We sit and chat for ages, with Sophie, as she formally introduced herself, getting up every so often to serve Croydon's coffee addicts desperate for their next caffeine hit. This must be what it's like to be busy and enjoy life.

'Gosh, you must be popular – your phone hasn't stopped going off!' Sophie points to the steady stream of notifications coming through from Instagram.

How do I say this? No, I'm anything but popular. I can count my friends on one hand and I don't even need to use my thumb. All I have is a dead husband and the beginnings of a social media account to which I currently have no personal association. Maybe I should show Sophie and see what she thinks? If she does think I am a total loser, there's a Costa down the road, even though I think it's run by the baristas who didn't get into Starbucks.

'Well . . . I've been in a bit of a hole recently, and then, I had a sort of wake-up call – well, the car accident – more like someone threw an alarm clock in my face. So, I started this account on Instagram called Mizzennial. Remember *Mizz* magazine? I thought, how funny it would be if we had that exact style of magazine now for the adults who grew up with it. How different it would be. We wouldn't be asking how to put tampons in, we would be asking how to stop being sent dick pics or maybe more serious stuff sometimes too.'

'Wow, that's amazing. I'm a true believer in fate and all that hippy stuff. May I have a look?'

I hesitate.

'It's OK if you want to keep it private,' Sophie says quickly, noticing my hesitation. Oh, the irony of keeping your social media profile under lock and key.

'No, you can look.' I wait nervously, while Sophie opens the Instagram app on her phone and scrolls through my posts. Fuck, what's she thinking? I should never have shared this with her.

'This is truly great, Milly. So raw and funny too. I think you should do more of the agony aunt pages – everyone has problems you know and you seem good at giving advice.' Sophie puts her hand on my shoulder and smiles. Normally, I would think of her as being patronising, but I genuinely feel like she means it. A man in a suit strums his fingers on the counter, glaring at @ILikeMyMenHotAndBlack in her Starbucks T-shirt. She tuts at him and stands up from the tacky brown table. 'Come in again, Milly, this has been really fun!'

We hug and I feel on top of the world. Someone liked me for being me! I didn't scare Sophie off. Is this even possible? Could that happen with love too?

One day, the right person will fall into my lap, be understanding, allow me to wallow in my own self-pity when I need and love me when I'm ready.

New comment:

@ILikeMyMenHotAndBlack You HAVE to follow this girl! **@FrothisDroth @LattetotheShow** This account is Nescafé Gold

This isn't just a fan; this is a real person.

I enjoyed speaking to @ILikeMyMenHotAndBlack. I used to love meeting people, making friends, being the life and soul of the party, but then that part of me got lost, like a forgotten jigsaw puzzle. But it seems like I've just found one of the pieces.

@Mizzennial Someone messaged me the other day, saying they felt so alone. They'd been grieving and pushed all of their friends and family away. I wrote back to her and told her to remember that people are there for you, they just sometimes don't know the right thing to say. I realised that it was easy for me to say this in a message but much harder to do in real life. Does anyone have any tips?

> **@ShelleyFarrell** <heart emoji> You should try and organise a dinner and invite them over. It might feel awkward at first, but it gets better!
> **@Jade1993** You're lucky you even have friends! I just moved to London and I barely have anyone for company.
> **@Mike6969** Come to mine and I'll show you what friends are for :p

I scroll through photos of myself and @LaylaRose, smiling, laughing, partying. I look at the unread DMs. I just don't know if I can do it. Did she do anything wrong? Not really. It's just too much reminiscing. Sometimes when someone dies, you just want to break away from the past. You're not being mean, but everyone deals with grief differently; some people like to be reminded and others don't. I don't want that right now.

I turn off the *Blue Planet* documentary and stare into the empty air. This is getting worse, right? Everything is reminding me of him – even seeing the sea on a television show. And not the big, important memories either. Should it be like this? Is there such a thing as 'should' when it comes to this?

I take a breath and open the Facebook chat with Adam and start typing. I just have this urge to be near him again.

> **Me:** You'll never guess what, you know that girl I always tell you about? @ILikeMyMenHotAndBlack? Well, she's actually called Sophie and she gave me a coffee today. Violet, my counsellor, she told me to . . .

I stop typing, remembering what she said. There's no one typing back, no recurring three dots. Just a minuscule photo of me and him after our university ball and hundreds of blue messages.

I delete what I've written and open up the notes section on my phone instead.

Things That Make Me Happy

1. Today, a girl in Starbucks gave me a coffee for free AND said she enjoyed reading Mizzennial.

I close the notes.

It isn't that I don't want to tell Adam. I desperately do, but now I've thought about it, I don't know if sending him messages on Facebook chat is really making me happy.

14 July 2014

It's one of those days where you wake up knowing that everything's going to be OK. One of those days where the birds are chirping and whistling, the sun's shining, warming the air like a hot bath for the day ahead and the bright green leaves on the trees are gently waving good morning with the aid of a light breeze.

As soon as my eyes open, I turn on my side to face Adam. I like watching him sleep. I'm not a creep, but there's something so magical about being present in a person's blissful slumber, being an outsider to their most secret dreams and desires.

His big, blue eyes slowly open. His lashes framing the windows to his soul.

'Morning, Mills,' he says softly and pulls me in for a hug. I snuggle towards him and rest my head on his chest. It's how we start every morning. That time when it's just us and we're still surrounded by the cloud of happiness that sleep brings with it.

'It's so nice today. Shall we go to the beach?'

We run along the beach, like two puppies that are seeing sand for the first time. Running and jumping along the dunes.

'Come on, Adam! Faster, faster!'

'I'm letting you win *and* I'm carrying the bags.'

I kick my shoes off and throw my shirt on the sand.

'Chuck the bags,' I call behind me.

I run into the sea, Adam merely a second behind me. I duck under the shallow water, feeling every inch a beach babe.

'Fuck, it's freezing. Like actually freezing. Pah, and I've got salt in my mouth.' I spit into the sea.

'Hey, mergirl, you've got something in your locks.'

'Eurgh, what?! Get it off! Adam, help!' I shake my head and flick my hands around my head. Imagining a koi carp hanging firmly by its teeth from my hair.

'It's just seaweed, silly.' He laughs and pulls a clump of brown, leathery vegetation that was hanging limply and slapping around on the top of my back.

He holds my hand and pulls me towards the sea's entrance, where the water gently kisses the beach. He holds out a shell with a perfect finger-sized hole in the middle, places it on my ring finger and loops the seaweed round my neck like some sort of scarf.

'Here's my promise ring, mergirl. I'm knighting you with the power of the sea and the sand. Stay safe out there, Ariel.'

'What an honour, Poseidon. I'll forever be tied to you.' I do a mock bow and take some seaweed from my home-made scarf and drape it over his right wrist.

I lunge forward and push him backwards into the sea.

'Ursula is angry – Poseidon is in her kingdom.'

'Come here, angry traitor!' He kisses me and holds me in his arms. 'You know I'd love you even if you were a fat, wicked half-squid?' he says, kissing me all over my face and neck.

'Would you?'

'Of course. I'll love you forever, no matter what form your limbs take, because you're you.'

'Well, I'd love you too, even if you were an ageing merman with a trident. I'll love you when you are old and grey and the remnants of youth have passed from your body,' I say, putting on an accent as if I'm giving a speech in a movie.

We kiss and go back to splashing each other in the sea.

12

Honk, honk!

Eurgh, go away. I hate those stupid souped-up cars that race up and down the street. I grab my pillow and pull it down over my ears.

Honk, honkkkkkk!

I hop out of bed and angrily push the window up, ready to throw something really offensive, like a toothbrush or a half-dead pot plant from my succulent collection.

'Milly!' Julia's hanging out of her silver Polo with Nicky cheerily waving behind her. 'You've got ten seconds to pack a bag for the weekend and get down here.'

'What? Where are we going?' I'm confused, yet utterly over the moon. A surprise for me? I cannot even find the words to explain how much this means to me.

'Gals' trip! Now, come the fuck on, we haven't got all day!' Nicky gestures towards the car, then makes a running motion with her arms.

I pull down the window and turn and press my back against the cool glass. I feel my eyes smarting slightly – must be the cold air arousing my senses. Someone's doing something nice for me. It's like magic. I wrote that post on Mizzennial a couple of days ago, messaged @LonelyAkon and here I am. Maybe I'm my own fortune teller?

I finish replying to another morning pleasantry from Florry:

I can smell you from Clapham! Have a shower please.

It's her way of checking in and it would annoy me if she was too soppy.

I shove some trackies and a top on and crumple a few clothes from my floordrobe into my holdall. Burst of dry shampoo on my locks and a spritz of refreshing Dove on my pits.

'Ready, Mills?' Julia pops her sunglasses on and puts the little Polo into first.

'Ready,' I respond, buckling myself into the back. 'Where are we off to then?'

'Brighton!'

My eyes smart again at the memories of Adam on the arcade games and fighting off seagulls. Brighton was one of our favourite places, though honestly, I'm starting to think that anywhere I visited with him will be just as painful. How do you overcome grief when you feel like it's already touched every part of the world? Day-to-day life is so menial, but suddenly it becomes so meaningful – every cup of tea, every bacon sandwich, every car drive, songs on the radio, smells in the air – when the person you did it with is gone.

'Who's doing the tunes?' I say, leaning between the two of them in the front. If this is truly a gals' trip, we'd all better get into character – I'm thinking Britney in *Crossroads*.

'Nicky is. We've got noughties R 'n' B – starting with. . .'

The familiar beats cause us to go into some sort of mild hypnosis, where we sing in an untuned unison.

'Tuuune!' Nicky drums her hands on the dashboard. 'Milly, you're Christina. Julia, you're P!nk and I'm Lil Kim – because I'm deffo the sassiest.'

What is it about singing with friends that literally makes your heart sing? I'm so happy it's practically beating out of my T-shirt.

Ping! A DM arrives.

@FauxFighter @Mizzennial My mum died a few months ago and I've pushed everyone away from me. Started fights with my best friends and family. I know they were only trying to help, and it's my fault. What should I do?

I feel a pang of guilt – not everyone is out having fun. That's the place that I used to be in. I think about who I'm with right now and what I'm doing as I settle into the car seat.

@Mizzennial @FauxFighter They'll forgive you, they were never angry in the first place. Be ready to apologise, or explain yourself at least, but chances are, they won't even ask. Reach out to them, invite them for a drink or a meal and start back where you left off. Grief makes people act in different ways and it's impossible to explain yourself. Don't be a stranger. X

I know this is what I should do but I'm not ready to do it with everyone I used to know yet. Thinking about meeting Layla makes the hairs on the back of my neck stand up.

'Right, gals, you grab the bags and I'll get the rosé. Shall we dump our stuff and head straight to the beach? The baby's craving fish and chips.' Julia pats her invisible tummy.

'So funny that everyone always says "the baby's craving . . ." It can't even open its eyes – does it even have eyes, yet? – how does it know what fish and chips tastes like?!' I don't want to question my godchild's taste buds but...

'It literally just said to me, "Mum, can you get me some of those delicious chips from Sid's Fish Bar, and for dessert, can we have some freshly fried doughnuts?" Humans are a clever species.' Julia looks adoringly at her protruding stomach.

We make a little den on the pebbles, hot parcels of freshly battered fish and double-fried chips warming our fingertips.

Nicky lays the rug down and Julia fills the plastic cups with rosé – full to the brim for Nicky and me and a half-glass for her. There's just something about that salty, sour tang which fills the air as we unwrap our golden packages. It makes my eyes sting and my tongue salivate. It's a comfort food in more ways than one.

'Cheers, girls! This is utter fucking bliss. And thank you for doing this for me.' I pause. 'Properly, thank you.'

'We thought you could do with a little cheering up – you've been through it recently.'

I think about @FauxFighter and what I typed to her merely a couple of hours ago.

'I know I haven't been the greatest of friends since Adam died. I've not really been very thoughtful to either of you. I've been a fucking nightmare – I know I have.' Their kindness gives me the confidence to confide.

'Mills, if anyone's been a nightmare, it's us,' Nicky says politely.

'Especially Nicky.' Julia laughs, sticking her tongue out at her. 'Seriously, Mills, it's fine. I'm sure you think the same about us. What happened with Adam was a shock to all of us. None of us have been through it before, so I'm sure we could all learn from our mistakes.' She clicks her nails together – it's awkward talking about death, I get it.

Nicky leans over and hugs my shoulders. She isn't very good at deep, meaningful conversations. We used to joke about her shying away from them, but I've realised, when the conversations are really meaningful, not many people are good at it.

'I just want you to know that I think I'm starting to get back to my old self. I've been seeing that social media counsellor and turns out she's quite nice, and I've started an advice-blog thing.' I pause. 'Called Mizzennial – I'll show you. I've got quite a few followers now, you know.' I pass my phone over.

'Sometimes I do funny posts, like unboxing, that you used to get in *Mizz,* or cringe pages, but mainly people message me, asking for advice. I've started getting loads of other people who need help with a whole range of things – seems like everyone needs to reach out to someone now and then. They DM me and then I anonymously post the questions and answers on the page to see if it can help others. I've even had some messages about friends and loved ones dying. I feel like grieving and death is something everyone feels so awkward about – we're a lost segment of society – it's nice to meet other normal people on it, you know?' I suddenly remember the post I wrote about Julia being pregnant. Fuck. 'Sorry, I didn't mean to tell anyone.' Why am I such a blabbermouth? Julia looks a little confused as I realise she doesn't know what I'm talking about. 'I did a post about a friend being pregnant, but I didn't mean anything sinister. I'm so, so happy for you. It's just sometimes I think that in a past life that could have been me too, you know?' That's the truth, I think.

'Don't worry, I get it. You shouldn't apologise for how you feel, Mills.' Julia squeezes my hand. 'I've started telling people now, anyway. I even wear one of those baby-on-board badges – I need to take advantage of the pregnancy perks – seats on the Tube, no queuing for any toilet or any shop . . . ever.'

'That's OK, Mills. I think, if I was in your shoes, I'd probably think the same. It's our turn to be honest now.' Nicky takes a deep breath and looks at Julia.

'We already saw your Mizzennial account.'

'What? How?' I feel a pang of anxiety. What if other people have seen it? What if people know it's me? I feel my heart start beating uncontrollably.

'It came up on my Explore feed – you know, accounts you might like. I clicked on it and had a read. The posts are so good, so you know, from the heart. It made me think of you and what you've been through. Then I saw the pregnant post and thought what a coincidence it was. Finally, we saw that you followed the account and vice versa. We took a hunch and guessed it was you. So here we are, cheering you up and showing you that we care.'

'Oh, wow,' I say softly. I feel droplets coming from my eyes. 'Thanks, guys. I'm sorry I couldn't talk to you in person. I haven't wanted to admit to people, after all this time, that I'm actually still struggling a bit.'

'You don't need to apologise, Mills. We hadn't realised how much you needed us. Think of this trip as a major apology and a way of proving to you how much you mean to us. You should be proud of who you are, but I get it. You don't want everyone to know how you're feeling all the time. You tell people when you're ready – don't let anyone force you into it.'

'I love you girls.' And we pull in for a massive three-way hug. I know there are tears, but these aren't like the ones I usually have; they are happy ones. As nice as it's been creating my online community and having attention from the masses, there's nothing like real friends. One's with oxygen in their lungs and blood in their veins. You can feel their heart beating through human contact and hold their hands when you need them.

'I bet so many guys prey on grieving women.' Nicky cuts the emotion-filled air.

'Probably!' I laugh. 'Trust you to get back to thinking about guys. Don't start using my page to find potential dates, OK?'

'What do you think of my new lipstick?' she says as she slicks the honey-coloured cream – aptly named 'Orgasm'– across her plump lips, hoping that the marketing team at MAC holds some foresight into her day.

I don't mind that Nicky's changed the conversation. I don't want everything to be about me all the time. I want it to be back to normal. A new normal.

'It looks great. The names of lipsticks are hilarious. Imagine if they were named that way because they were like fortune tellers. Yours is "Orgasm" and mine would be something like, I dunno, "Chastity Belt".'

They both laugh and I imagine myself kidnapped by a superfluity of nuns instead of on a girls' weekend in Brighton.

'Does it feel weird, you know, going on dates now, Mills?' I'm not sure if I'd even call them dates, more of a fucking rampage. Not that I've been on any for ages. The 'fucking rampage' was when I thought that by having sex with people, I could get someone to love me, but it hurt too much.

'Yes, I feel guilty, but I also feel like I'm just having a release. I've fucked guys since Adam, but I don't feel like I've really had sex. There's no emotion there for me yet.'

'You'll get there, as soon as you meet another nice guy.'

I feel my heart twinge. I'm not ready. Adam can't be replaced. He was everything I ever wanted in a life partner – I feel my heart skip a beat at how I was instantly attracted to his dimples and his way of making me feel at ease.

'I fuck emotionless all the time, Mills, literally the best sex. And orgasm? If that's my fortune for tonight, I need to get out there now! I can't keep faking them – my vagina's been teasing me with truth serum.'

I laugh and feel pleased that the conversation's turned. It's just something that people don't seem to understand, that ability to meet someone else, properly meet someone new. I do kind of want to, but sometimes I feel like Adam's still holding my hand.

Everything, one day at a time.

'Are you excited about *Swipe Right*? I think you'll be great and it'll be a laugh!'

'Yeah, I guess. It'll be an experience.' I wouldn't use *excited* as a descriptor. More panicked, apprehensive, anxious. Julia's just trying to be nice to me, and after all, she's planned this weekend for me, so I should do something for her. They just showed me everything I ever wanted: that they care and they're here for me.

19 April 2018

Julia's set me up on a date with one of James's work friends. Like everyone else, Julia thinks it will be good for me to 'get back out there'. No one seems to understand that grief is a long ol' process that some people never get through.

I don't want to date anyone else. I want to be with Adam. It's just a shame he's living six feet under.

I've been putting the dating game off for weeks now, but it's reached a crux, and I've decided that the only way to get people off my back is to get onto mine and meet one of London's eligible bachelors.

This evening's Romeo is called Bartholomew. He works in wealth management, so he's an exact replica of the stereotype you thought he was. Apparently, he's 'super kind, thoughtful and has also been through a "traumatic experience" too' whatever that means.

It will be a great conversation starter. 'Oh, snap! My partner also died! What did yours die of? Cancer? Ooh, another snap!' We'll cheer and laugh about how emotionally damaging it was before fucking against a rubbish bin near the cemetery.

'Do you have a reservation?'

'Yes, under *Bartholomew*?'

'Great, he's already here, over on table nine. Have a lovely evening.'

This is my chance. I could run away now and never put myself through this turmoil. Fuck, he's looking at me. Too late. Is he fit? I can't really see through the dim light. Am I going to go to hell? Is Adam watching me?

Oh fuck!

Smack.

Argh, this is so embarrassing. It's so dark I tripped over in the middle of the restaurant. I couldn't see that stupid little step. Maybe it's the bottle of Dutch courage I drank my way through on the way here. Everyone's staring at me. How long can I lie on the ground for? Can I pretend I'm playing the-floor-is-lava? Save me, Adam.

'Excuse me, can I help?' He offers me a hand.

'Gosh, that was embarrassing! It's so dark, I couldn't see!' I manage a little laugh.

'I'm sure it happens all the time in here – it's like walking round in a bloody blindfold! May I buy you a drink?'

'Yes, needed. Thank you.' I walk towards table nine.

'Should we go to the bar? I'm actually supposed to be meeting someone soon.'

'Yes, it's me! I'm Milly!' Is this what fuckboys do? Date other girls while on a first date?

'Oh my God, I am so sorry. It is so dark in here I couldn't see properly. Of course, let's go straight to the table.'

Should I take this as a compliment or an insult? Barty was prepared to sack off his original date with me for, well, another date with me. It either means he is super attracted to my desirable good looks, or he couldn't give a fuck about who he fucks. Whatever, beggars can't be choosers.

He's quite funny and fit. We're halfway through our second bottle of wine now, so that could be the reason he reminds me of Leonardo DiCaprio. Either way, right now, to me, he still looks like that. Blonde hair, blue eyes and a four-syllable name – the Triple B threat.

'So, Bart, what's your trauma then?'

He coughs on his drink. 'What did Julia tell you?'

'Isn't that how single people introduce themselves nowadays?'

'Ha, it should be.' He takes a long slurp of his gin. 'Well, I may as well divulge everything now.' I lean closer, intrigued.

'I moved in with my girlfriend of six years, Tally, and one day, she told me she had met someone else. That someone else was my sister! Can you believe it?' He finishes his drink and waves the waiter for more, shaking his head. 'Fucking unbelievable,' he says with such force it's as if he's punching me with his words. 'After the education my parents paid for Shelby, I thought she would have learned some fucking manners! You can't steal your sibling's partner – it's bloody unbelievable. We don't talk now – Shelby and I, that is.'

I know my mouth's hanging wide open, but I don't bother to close it – Barty seems to like my reaction, anyway.

I mean, what the actual fuck? What am I supposed to do, sit at the family roast, watching Bartholomew's ex chow down on her roasties and ask her to pass the gravy? No thanks. It's dating 101: don't hang around with the ex.

'It makes me mad every time I think of it! Will she take every girlfriend I bring home?!' He then proceeds to pull out a little white bag from his wallet and takes a bump of cocaine from the table. It's dark, no one would know. 'Want some?' He passes the bag to me. Why the hell not?

I twiddle the ring in my left hand, feeling the cuts of the diamonds with my fingertips, and then proceed to shove his door key up my nose and gulp the last of my 2012 Chardonnay. This is anything but a normal scenario – and it's my first night out in ages, so I may as well make the most of it.

Filled with wine and cocaine, we leave walking on clouds. Bart's looking more and more attractive, and if I squint, exactly like Leo. I'm finally living out my *Wolf of Wall Street* fantasy.

I don't care any more. Who cares if Bart's a total dickwad? I don't need to see him again. This is what young, frivolous, single people do, isn't it? They meet up, go on a date, have outrageous sex and then never see each other again. I can be normal. I can be fun.

We start snogging, and then Bart pulls me behind the side of the restaurant. He pulls my dress up and we start fucking. No amount of alcohol and drugs can take away the fact that this is the first person I have let enter me since Adam. I can't do it. I'm sobbing, fucking sobbing. Bart's crying too, calling out Tally's name. I'm calling out Adam's. I'm not fun, I'm riddled with grief and memories and love for someone who's not here any more.

I pull my dress down and put a hand on his shoulder. 'Sorry.'

Bart looks up. He has snot with white flecks streaming into his mouth. His eyes are red. He's gone from the *Wolf of Wall Street* to full wolf in about sixty seconds.

'I'll be fine in a few minutes.' And he pulls his trousers up and takes the little bag out again.

I'm lonely, but I'm not desperate, and I'm old enough to know I'm not into bestiality.

This night has ended exactly how I thought it would. Two damaged individuals fucking by a rubbish bin.

13

20 February 2019

Sometimes I hate being an adult. There's the day-to-day adulting, which is hard enough. Things like choosing what you are going to have for dinner every night, making your bed, going to work, dealing with a hangover, etc. Then there are the things that creep up on you, and you're suddenly totally fucked. Like whether you need to declare your eBay profits to HMRC, or a husband with a terminal illness.

Today, it's pigeon poop in my window box. I decided to create a makeshift deterrent with cocktail sticks, and like a crazed Ben Fogle, I've just watched the cutest little chaffinch try to fly away, but it's managed to impale cocktail sticks all over its bum. I could be jailed for chaffinch GBH or chaffinch-slaughter.

I message Julia.

> **Me:** My whole life is fucked right now. I think it's karma from Adam for agreeing to *Swipe Right*. Maybe I shouldn't go? I impaled a chaffinch and I can't even seem to change my sheets. How did you become so adult?
> **Julia:** Oh, Milly! I still can't change my sheets and I ask my parents for money every week. I'm not sure what to say about the chaffinch – are they endangered? I don't think you ever become an adult. You MUST go, honestly, you'll be so wonderful.

Me: At least you're married – you have someone who's by your side for ever, it doesn't matter if you can't adult properly. And you're about to be a MUM. I can't even keep my cacti alive. No, they're not endangered, but I still feel awful. What am I going to even wear on *Swipe Right?!*
Julia: Well, that's good. Are they difficult to impale? Just forget about adulting today, think sexy and sultry. Make yourself look insane. I would wear trousers, as your leg does look super scabby.
Me: Turns out not really. Have you ever seen a sexy, sultry, one-legged chaffinch murderer? I guess there are firsts for everything.

I sit and ponder my outfit for *Swipe Right* while editing a cringe post sent in by @LeatherBottle492 – a real shocker.

@Mizzennial I live at home because I can't afford the rent in London, and my dad walked in on me having sex with this guy I'd met online! The thing is, it wasn't just vanilla sex. I'm talking dress-up and a few kinks. What do I tell my dad? I'm 31 – do I have to move out now? #Cringe

'I'm giving out advice on my channel,' I blurt through the microphone.

'Well, that's great, Milly. What are you advising on?'

'Just loads of stuff, I guess. Dating – which is ironic as I haven't even been on that many dates – being young in general, and, err, grief. I posted something on my blog and then a few people messaged me looking for a friend. The advice sort of flowed out of me. I don't know where from. Seems ironic that someone being counselled is giving out advice.' I laugh, while watching Violet to see her response.

'Yes, I can see the irony in the situation.' She doesn't seem to find it hilarious. 'Do you find it easier to give advice than to action what you are telling others to do?'

'Yeah, I mean, I feel a bit like a fraud. I'm telling people to do things that I don't know if I'm capable of doing myself.'

'That's quite normal. Think how many times you've probably given friends advice after a break-up, and then when you and your boyfriend split up, it's much harder to not think about him, move on, stop texting, etc.'

I nod, thinking about it, and Violet continues.

'Think how hard it would have been for those people to message you and how much you would have made their day, taking the time to reply. Being a friend to them. You should use this as a way of them helping you too. Maybe they're showing you that you're not alone? Or maybe they're showing you that you do know what to do? You hold the key to your own lock.'

I twist my face to one side, thinking some more.

'It was weird. I felt a relief telling them what I thought. It was like I'd been harbouring it for so long, it made me feel useful again.'

'I can see that. Well, why don't you start sharing more about what you've learned, build your own little community? Did you start writing down things that made you happy?'

'Yes, I went to my local Starbucks and the girl who works there gave me a coffee and croissant on the house and we had a chat. Free therapy too.' I joke.

'That's great, Milly! Maybe it will be the start of a blossoming friendship.' She clasps her hands together, almost in prayer. 'Did you speak to your husband about it?'

'I started, but then I stopped.'

'And why did you stop?'

'Because . . . because . . . I don't know. I enjoyed talking to Sophie, the girl from Starbucks. But maybe I realised how stupid it was talking to myself on Facebook. Because I'm not crazy, I do know that's what I'm doing – talking to myself.'

'It isn't crazy, Milly. It's perfectly normal to talk to lost ones. It's a comfort, like having a cup of tea on a cold day, getting a hug from a parent. Just from opening up to a random stranger, it is clear to me that you have benefited hugely from it. You'll never forget Adam, but you need to try and separate him from your living life to enable you to enjoy it again and not feel guilty.'

'Milllllllllllyyyy!' Lottie beams at me through her black Stella McCartney frames and over her clipboard. 'We are soooo happy that you could make it.' Is it just me or do people in media always add a million letters into every word? It must get very tiring having to expel breath for such a long time.

My *Swipe Right* interview – I can't believe I made it here. The day where they scrutinise me and see if I would be a good fit for the show. If there's anyone worthy of a widow out there/(more likely) if anyone would want to date me.

'I'm happy to be here! Although a tad nervous.' One lie and one understatement. I'd been worrying about it since Julia told me. Dating's scary. But then I thought about the advice I've given people on Mizzennial, what I spoke about with Julia and Nicky, Violet. And I thought, fuck it, so here I am. I was completely unprepared to meet @ILikeMyMen-HotAndBlack the other day; I went in for a coffee and came back with a friend. I tried something new, I spoke about what happened to me and I felt better, not worse. What if I go on a date and come back in love? Stranger things have happened.

'Don't worry at all, go over to Theo with the camera and he will tell you what to do.'

I walk towards a tall guy, with dark sweeping hair and a Shoreditch layer of stubble. He looks familiar.

'Hi, Milly.'

I panic.

'How do you know my name?'

'Err.' He smiles and waves a piece of paper. 'It's written here on the candidate form,' he replies, slightly confused.

I know him. It's Theo Burmester. Kevin's housemate. Fuck. Kevin, the guy that I told I was engaged, and he thought I wanted a threesome. Holy Mother of God. Fuck. I only know Theo is Kevin's housemate because I felt bad after our date, so did some serious stalking into all facets of his private life.

He continues as if the most embarrassing turn of events of his life hasn't just occurred, because he's standing on the other side of the mirror. I feel like I'm living the dream of standing naked on stage at your school concert.

'If you take a seat in front of the camera, we'll get you warmed up.'

God, I hope I'm not going red – I don't want everyone to see me wincing in embarrassment. I don't want to be made into a meme about tomatoes and fuckboys.

'Are you OK?' Theo asks me. 'Do you need me to open a window?'

Fuck, I've gone red. I should just say I know him, act cool about it.

'No, I'm fine. Hot flush. Early menopause. I don't need warming up.' I laugh awkwardly. Shut up, Milly. That's anything but cool. It's unattractive. You're pawning yourself off as middle-aged. 'Do I know you from somewhere?' I say, studying his face. God, Milly, why did you just throw yourself into the fire?

'I'm not sure,' Theo replies, looking slightly embarrassed himself.

'Yes! That's it,' I suddenly say in a spur-of-the-moment RADA audition. 'You're Kevin's housemate! I went on a date once with Kevin, your housemate, and he told me all about you.' There, now the awkwardness is over, we can chat at ease again. Phew. Good save Mills.

'And did he show you a photo of his housemate on a first date? That seems a bit rogue, what were you doing, thinking of moving in?' He laughs.

I'm feeling sweaty and nervous. Of course, he didn't. You know I stalked you. Why would someone on a first date start going through an online photo album of their housemates? I almost wish Kevin had and then I could have never spoken to him again, instead of pretending I'm engaged. God, does Theo think I'm engaged?

Fuck it, I need to come clean.

'I stalked his Facebook after our date and saw a post about your bromance house-warming.' I feel my face flushing further with embarrassment.

'Well, nice to officially meet you, Milly-the-Stalker.' He smiles. 'There'll be no stalking prior to *Swipe Right* – it's completely anonymous, a blind date – so don't try any of your tricks.' He wags his finger at me, mocking a reprimand.

Now I've got over the embarrassment, I may as well enjoy today – I'm going to be on television! I sit on the bar stool in front of a wooden wall with emojis all over it. A busybody lady comes over, adjusts my hair and pats a bit of powder on my face. I'm starting to feel like a movie star. Then I remember, I'm due my period, my bra's cutting me up and I now have four breasts. The realisation of reality has set in. That fleeting moment of empowerment has well and truly scarpered.

Theo starts chatting with me, trying to make me feel comfortable in front of the camera.

'Honestly, you look great, Milly, there really is no reason to worry. We can show you some of the shots after if you'd like? Try to act really natural, I'll keep the camera rolling so we can see how you come across.' Does he mean that or is he just British and annoyingly good at social etiquette? I'm sweating and giving off an odour of pickled-onion Monster Munch so he must be playing fake flattery.

Theo is fit, all superman shoulders and Beckham legs to match. Exactly my type, but totally off limits now I remember ogling over him on Kevin's Facebook, FFS. Not that he'd fancy me, anyway. God, what's he going to run home and tell Kevin tonight? I role play the possible conversations in my head.

Saw that crazy girl you went on a date with back in January, Kev. You know she stalked our entire house on Facebook – what a nutter.

I shake my head, trying to stop my mad thoughts escalating further and my face turning even redder and spontaneously combusting.

It's that awkward conversation style, where you're over-the-top laughing at things you don't really find funny. I tell him about tripping up on that date with Barty, to which he threw his head back in hysterics, when the real joke was us having sex behind a bin. His head might have come off if I'd told him that. He told me that he once tried to wipe his face with a sanitary pad that he thought was a napkin. It was clean but still gross. Theo is nice enough, but I feel like he's scrutinising my face and every single movement my mouth makes, like he can see behind the smile I've glued on my face. Maybe this is what it feels like to be in porn.

After what seems like an age, Lottie comes back over.

'Right, Milly, all we want to do is ask a few questions about yourself and what kind of guy you are interested in. Maybe tell us a little bit about your past, that sort of thing. We take real pride in who we match our singletons up to on the night, so we like bringing people in to see how they act in person, what they wear, etc.' It is a fine line between Hollywood film and a scientific experiment.

This is crazy.

Lottie asks me a multitude of questions, very in-depth. I don't think I've ever really thought what my type of guy is like. Adam. But I can't think of him, as he's dead and never coming back, no matter how hard I wish. I need to, *must*, move on. She asks me questions like what kind of job would your dream guy have? I mean I don't know, he could be a binman, for all I care. Would he have gone to university? As long as he can read and write, I honestly don't mind. I think I'm speaking for everyone here; at this stage of the game, I'm not going to be too fussy. I admit, looks are much higher on the attributes list than university attendance. When someone is asking you to specifically say what kind of clothes your dream guy would wear, it's hard. I know what I like and don't like, but I don't want to discriminate someone on their outfit! Everyone has bad days. Socks and sandals are a no-go, for sure. But socks and sliders. . . now there's a look. I think the excitement of being on TV has eradicated my nerves about dating.

Then we get on to past relationships . . . Should I mention Adam or is that too much sob story? No, I don't think I am ready to admit that to the British public yet, and I don't want Theo running back to Kevin and telling him my whole life story.

'So why are you here today, Milly?'

I think I'll just have to make something up. I don't want everyone to know on national television that I'm a widow and I don't want to recount one of my handful of dating disasters. The full story, that is, anyway.

'Well.' I look sideways at Theo. 'I've had a few dates recently that my friends or family have set me up on, but they're just not really my type. I want to find someone who I can laugh with, be myself with. I like the tall guy, broad shoulders with dark hair, but looks aren't everything!' I exclaim while suddenly realising that I'm describing Theo's looks. I blush for the third time that day.

Lottie laughs. 'The classic let's-set-our-single-friend-up-with-anything-with-a-pulse move – don't worry, I know it!'

'Exactly!' I laugh.

'On the phone you said you could hula hoop. We brought one in the studio and wanted to see if you could show us your skills?'

Clearly, I am finally feeling comfortable in front of the camera, as I say yes to it. I mean it is a total YOLO experience; it isn't every day that you interview for a TV show, and from my research it's more embarrassing if you come across awkward. I show them my full hula-hooping skills, from the standard spinning round my waist, to a butt spin and finally how I can keep the hoop going around my neck. It looks a bit awkward, like a pecking duck, but I think I probably got away with it – have you ever seen someone hula-hoop on one leg? It's fucking impressive.

I collect my forms from Lottie and Theo, ready to leave, and then Theo smiles at me.

'I've never seen someone hoop like that before. I didn't know people did it any more – you strike me more as a Pilates and yoga type of girl. Impressive,' Theo says, his grin widening from ear to ear.

'Please, hooping is for the more adventurous. Yoga's so yesterday.' I grin back.

'I've never been able to get the hip rhythm right.' Theo laughs, gyrating his hips round in circles.

'Never do that again.' I chuckle. 'The trick is, it's more front to back not in circles. I like to practise to 'All The Single Ladies',' I joke.

Theo hums the song and I jokingly hoop along.

'Now that's not something I see every day.' Theo shakes his left hand doing the 'Single Ladies' dance move and moving his hips from front to back. 'I'd love a lesson in hooping – think I need a bit more practice.'

'Ha, yeah sure, one day,' I reply, maybe a little too quickly.

'Kevin can be such a dick sometimes, can't he? Anyway, see you around, Milly. Was nice to put a face to a name.'

And he walks off.

I smile, and then *what the fuck was Kevin saying about me?!*

I guess it wasn't that bad, quite fun actually. I should be grateful to Julia and James for setting me up. Maybe dating will be good for me.

Everything I've done so far has catapulted me forwards in my quest for happiness.

I love my Mizzennial account, but what if someone else makes the connection Julia and Nicky did? I'm scared that someone might out me and tell me I'm not qualified to advise. I work in healthcare PR not counselling. But then I guess, everyone has life experience and opinions; you don't have to be an expert to advise, you can just be a normal person with a bouquet of experience.

I think I need some support from my community:

@Mizzennial Does anyone else understand what it's like to be a young widow? If anyone else is dealing with love and loss, DM me – it's good to share! X

Ping.

@IAmTheWickedWitch @Mizzennial I used to think of widows as old hunchbacks, like the wicked witch in *Snow White*. I feel so mean and disrespectful ever thinking this. My friend's now a widow and she is only 30, and I've realised that death can impact anyone. It doesn't have any rules or quotas. What can I do to make it up to her?

Maybe this is why everyone's scared of me. I shouldn't judge @IAmTheWickedWitch – I probably thought the same before. Why would I have thought any differently?

After Brighton, it could even be Julia messaging me under a pseudonym.

> **@Mizzennial** @IAmTheWickedWitch Don't beat your-self up about it, I thought the same until I became one myself. Just be yourself with her. Appreciate that she needs time; she may be difficult, she may be upset, but she is still your friend. Her personality hasn't changed, she might just need some time out. Take her for dinner, go to the cinema, go on a weekend away. Try to do nor-mal things with her and show her that life can and will be fun again, even if she isn't ready for it right now. You are not going anywhere. X

6 March 2017

I brush my teeth, spit the toothpaste into the sink and swill my mouth round with water. A mechanical process that I don't need to think about. It's hard trying to be happy all the time. I relish the time with Adam above anything, of course I do, but I also relish time alone. The space where I don't have to smile and pretend everything's normal, put on a brave face and tell everyone that ironic saying: *I'm fine.* It's tiring being fake happy, but that's my job now.

I wipe cleanser over my skin and wash it off with a flannel and water. I put face cream on my fingertips, massaging it *hard* into my parched, dry cheeks.

I switch the light off and get into bed with Adam. Laying there, sometimes he looks dead already. That's the concoction of drugs and the cancer. There's life still in him yet. I don't know about me though. My skin's taken on a grey tinge too, and it's started sagging, as if all my collagen has suddenly dissipated. I need a carer too; I fill Adam up with green smoothies, hide vegetables in pizzas in the hope that the nutrients can fight away the cancer, but I forget to feed myself.

He rolls over and hugs me. It feels like we're suffocating each other. I shut my eyes and try to imprint this moment in my brain forever. That feeling of being loved, of being held, kept safe in the arms of another. A keepsake that I can't capture on video or in a photo. It masks that empty feeling I have when I'm alone, a lost soul.

'Milly?' I look up from his clutches into his soulful, blue eyes. 'I love you so much. So, so much.' I want to record him saying it so I can hear it again and again and again.

'I love you too. Up to the moon and back and round every star in the sky.'

'I've wanted to spend the rest of my life with you ever since we met but . . .' He sighs. 'I always thought that the rest of my life would be a long time.'

'Me too.' Tears start to well as I try to contemplate what a long time actually is.

'Mills, I want you to know that you'll always have my blessing to meet someone else after me. I don't want you to ever feel guilty about it, OK?'

'Adam. I can't, won't, don't want to think about that now, OK?' That's beyond too much. There's no one else in the world for me, only Adam.

'Well, I would normally get down on one knee, but given the circumstances. . . Milly Dayton, will you do me the pleasure of being my wife?' He takes my hand in his and puts the most beautiful ring on my finger.

'Adam . . . Oh my . . . .'

'It was my grandmother's ring. I always knew I would give it to you, and so here it is.'

'Of course, I will.' And I burst into a fresh set of tears – happy, but yet so, so sad. Marriage is forever, and for Adam it will be, but for me it will be over in a flash. I feel like all my happy memories are tinged with sadness.

'The course of true love did never run smooth,' he says, coughing over the side of the bed, trying to manipulate a smile.

From *A Midsummer Night's Dream*. His mum paid for us to watch it at the Globe Theatre only last month. I smile. He remembers everything.

'When were you thinking about getting married?'

'Maybe next week? No time like the present.'

14

I've been sent *three* requests for my advice.

@RedRedRose @Mizzennial I've been messaging this boy for weeks, and we've been on six dates, but since then he's literally stopped replying. Should I keep messaging him or just move on? I've been single for ages now and I really thought he was the one.

@DigiWiz @Mizzennial I want to remove my birthday from Facebook because I find it embarrassing getting random messages and old photos popping up on my wall, but if I delete it, then I'm worried that no one will remember any more.

@Batgirl @Mizzennial I think I'm a vampire, but I only suck dick.

Hmm, not exactly the requests for advice I was hoping for but, I guess you live and learn.

Oh wait, one more.

@SexOrNotToSex @Mizzennial I'm so nervous about sleeping with this guy. It will be the first person since my boyfriend passed away in a car accident. I don't know what to do. What if he doesn't think I'm attractive? What if he thinks I've got too much pubic hair? I was thinking of getting a Hollywood and buying an outfit from Ann Summers.

Now this one has hit home. Another widow like me! I remember this scaring me so much – it still does. I start typing.

> **@Mizzennial** @SexOrNotToSex This can be a scary and daunting experience. I stupidly got myself really drunk and slept with a total dickhead the first time after my husband passed away. I wish I'd waited for the right person again. You need to have confidence in yourself – you're amazing and beautiful! If you want my honest opinion, most guys don't care about that kind of stuff – they will fuck you regardless of what you are panicking about. Trust me, from personal experience. X

Every time I see these DMs come through, I see Layla's blonde halo of hair like a beacon of light on her minuscule profile picture. It's ridiculous. Why can I reply to all these people, but I can't reply to her?

'Shall we get wine? A bottle?' Julia says, peering down at the wine list. She can't get super drunk any more due to the fact that her body is growing a new life form, but it doesn't stop her plying drinks down mine and Nicky's necks.

'Actually, I could do with a pint, but then I'll have wine afterwards.' I'm a known lightweight; two bottles give me a headache.

'I'll have wine, but can you not get the cheapest on the menu again? Last time it tasted like stale piss.' Nicky's right, it was horrible – and Julia didn't even drink it.

'Adam once told me that the cheapest wine on the menu is actually usually quite a good one. It's the second cheapest on the menu you want to worry about. Most people order it because they don't want to buy the cheapest, but that's the one probably made of piss.'

'Do you know what, guys? I'm just going to get myself a drink. You get what you want and then maybe I'll think about ordering a bottle of wine.' Julia turns towards the bar, her dress swirling behind her, adding to the drama.

'Sass pot!' Nicky calls behind her.

Julia turns and winks.

Nicky sits and scrolls on her phone for a minute before pausing on a photo.

'I miss Layla,' she says as I look closer at the photo, seeing that the twiggy blonde girl holding up a tiny Biscoff-coloured dog on the beach is, in fact, someone I know.

'Yeah . . . I miss a lot of things,' I almost hiss back, as if I have a snake tongue. I'm not trying to be rude, but it's not down to Nicky to tell me who to be friends with. 'Sorry,' I say quickly. 'It's just, you know. One step at a time, yeah?'

'Sorry, I didn't mean to say anything. My mouth kind of moved before my brain could catch up.'

Nicky quickly scrolls past the photo and changes the conversation to girls from school and dream holiday destinations.

Our poisons have finally been purchased, and we all take a swig from our respective choices.

'Do you not get bloated drinking all that lager?'

'It's not lager, it's ale.'

'What's the difference?'

'Hmm, one's not as fizzy. Try it.' I hand Nicky my pint. 'Adam was the one who made me first try ale.' I smile.

'Eurgh, it tastes like warm cat's piss. The taste is sticking around my mouth. Yuk. Yuk!'

'I feel like I'm out with my two ugly sisters tonight. Bicker, bicker.' Julia snaps her thumbs and forefingers together like she has two sock puppets on them.

'Ha! That's what happens with besties – you treat each other like siblings.' Since the Brighton trip, that awkward barrier that was still sometimes there between Julia, Nicky and I seems to have vanished. I feel more like myself again – after all, they've read Mizzennial, they know how I'm really feeling.

'Anyway, Nicky, tell me about your dating life. I enjoy living a promiscuous life vicariously through you.'

'Promiscuous? It's the twenty-first century, doll. Well, I had this *terrible* date the other day, and I mean *terrible*. I'd been messaging this guy for ages and he looked super-hot in his Tinder profile – about six foot, six-pack, classic tiger profile shot, you know the drill.'

'Tiger shot?'

'Yeah, tiger shot. On these apps, you need to try and show all sides of your personality through a series of photos. It's quite hard. And you need to look good because no one is swiping based on personality. Most guys tend to choose one of them skiing with mates, a photo of them at some tiger sanctuary in Thailand while they were on their gap yahh, and another of them in some pair of rank chinos and Ralph Lauren shirt that their granny picked out in 1990. I think the tiger is meant to represent their daring, risky side.'

'Oh right. I had no idea that much analysing was done with just a photo.'

'Milly! What have you been playing at? You go on Instagram every day, of *course* you know about analysing photos.' Hmm, guess I did.

'Anyway, I was messaging this guy, and we arranged to meet. I was feeling a bit nervous because, like I said, he was incredibly good-looking. I waxed everything, as I was sure he'd be coming back to mine for some sort of passionate night. I turn up at South Bank, wearing heels, I might add, and I look around. No one that resembles him. I was getting really pissed off by this point as I hate guys who are late – you shouldn't leave a girl waiting, especially not in heels, it's part of dating 101. Then I hear this voice behind me. "Nicky?" Sort of whiny. I turn around and this overweight guy – I'm talking beer belly – about five foot three, in a long sheepskin jacket down to the floor, is waving at me. Long beard – not in a rugged way, in a homeless way. It was the guy from the photos, but not the guy from the photos. Like the same guy, I mean photoshop must work wonders. I was *shook.*'

'So, you were catfished?! What did you do, did you tell him to go fuck himself?'

'Well, no. I was thinking maybe I should give him a chance. I know I can be quite superficial.'

'No, you didn't.' I snort and Julia's eyes widen in disbelief.

'I did. He took me to a bar, but it was his friend's bar. He then explained he didn't have any money, and he only took me there because his friend was giving us free drinks. Anyway, the conversation was also dull as dick – sorry, dick *isn't* dull, but you know what I mean – and at the end he tried to kiss me. Obviously, I declined, but what a waste of fucking *time*. I thought he was going to be dreamy and we'd end up having adventurous, hot, steamy sex.'

'Literally, where do you find these guys? You'll meet someone nice soon, I'm sure of it.'

'I'm not bothered about being in a relationship right now – I enjoy having my freedom, fucking who I please. I'm not ready to settle down like you and James. There's nothing wrong with it, I'm just not there yet.' Amen, Nicky.

We move on to the wine. A nice pale rosé with rocks of ice floating in the crystal-clear pink sea.

'OK, so I have a story, one that my friend told me.' Julia pipes up.

'Which friend? A friend or a "friend". I ask quizzically. I'm wise to the 'friend' tag when you want to disguise your own feelings/thoughts/stories.

'No, an actual friend – Casey, you know my uni friend. She fancied this guy from her home town for ages and when she went back for Christmas, he was single and she was single.

So, they decided to hook up. The sex was great, she said, and then he stayed over. At her parent's house, FYI. Anyway, suddenly he woke up bolt upright in the middle of the night and said, 'Sorry this is really embarrassing, but sometimes I sleep-poo. I've done one tonight but I can't remember where.' I need to note this one down for a Mizzennial #cringe post later.

'What the fuck?' Nicky spits her drink.

'No way?' This must be a real friend.

'What's a sleep-poo? Actually, I don't want to know, that is soooo gross.' Even Nicky finds this gross and she's immune to most things.

'They then spent hours searching high and low for this random poo he had done before her parent's came home.'

'Did they find it?' I'm intrigued.

'Where was it?' Nicky wriggles her nose in disgust.

'The airing cupboard.' Julia answers us triumphantly as if she's just won a TV quiz.

'No. Frigging. Way.' I imagine finding a poo in my Mum and Dad's airing cupboard – gross.

'Did she see him again?' Maybe Nicky's thinking about options.

'Of course not! Such a shame as she said he was really fit, but do you want a guy shitting around your house?' Sometimes Julia really does highlight the obvious.

'That is totally disgusting. I remember when Adam was drunk at uni, sometimes he wet the bed. One time he broke his own PlayStation by urinating on it.' I laugh.

'Ha! Serves him right!'

Funny how I'd give anything to have him wee in my bed now if it meant just having him back. It's weird that everything reminding me of Adam used to be like a stab in the heart with each hot chocolate I drank and biscuit I ate, but these memories are making me happy, remembering him even though I'm still sad he's gone.

'Have you got any dating stories, Milly?'

'You will have soon with your *Swipe Right* experience coming up!' Julia grins.

'Not really.' Kevin? Not even worth telling, to be fair. I think about my reply to @SexOrNotToSex; maybe I should start going out and having sex again. I've done it before.

'Are you on Tinder or anything? I'm not trying to force you,' Nicky adds hurriedly. 'Just asking.'

'I'm not at the moment, but I guess it doesn't hurt to have a profile. I know you're chomping at the bit just thinking about setting me up online. Go on then – do it!'

Nicky and Julia snatch my phone, their eyes eager with glee. One dating profile isn't going to hurt anyone.

'You can never go on too many dates, you know? *Swipe Right* will be good, a bit of fun, but you need *more* fun. I think you need some frivolous one-night stands, you know?' I wish I was as sexually promiscuous as Nicky sometimes.

We gulp our wine – well, Nicky and I do; Julia sips her one glass – and they ask me questions like:

'What's your job title, like your actual job title. . . Not healthcare PR. Make it sound more sexy. Maybe like "Pharmaceutical Secretary"'

'What's your dream date? None of this staying-in-and-watching-a-movie crap, you want a trip to Paris. Remember, the end goal is to get as much out of the date as you possibly can.'

'What's the maximum age range you would accept? . . . Twenty-eight to thirty! That's way too small. I'd probably go for twenty-four to fifty, as there are some silver foxes out there.'

'Height range? You have to mind, Milly. He needs to be at least six foot . . . It doesn't matter if you're only five foot four.'

'OK, eyes, blue. Hair, brown. Height? . . . No, I'm putting you at five foot four— No, I'm not writing five foot three point five – that's unattractive.'

Finally, we're nearly there.

'OK, go on your Facebook or Insta, and choose four of your favourite photos. Remember what I said though, you need to try and show your personality.' Nicky is an old hand at dating apps, unlike me. She seems to know all the tricks.

'All right.' I flick through the years of photos, zooming past his soulful blue eyes, brushing away the guilt. I always knew it was a cliché saying Adam's eyes were sea blue, but they were and sometimes I can't even look at the ocean because of it. *It's not my fault. It's not my fault*, I repeat silently. I'm allowed to move on.

'I'm done. I'm pretty impressed – I think I'm quite a catch.' I pass my phone over to Julia and Nicky, and they snort with laughter.

'Milly, you look deranged in these photos! You need to look the best you've ever looked while also trying to look fun. In this one you've got a Pikachu hat on.'

'I look fun, don't I?'

'No, you look like a dork. Right, I'll do it for you. Clearly you can't be trusted on your own profile right now.'

'I look like a slut in that one, Nicky – I'm in a bikini!'

'Trust me, Milly, I'm a pro. Follow my lead. I take back what I said earlier – guys' photos need to show they have character, in yours you just need to show that you're hot. It's totally double-standard, but the women's rights teams haven't got round to equalizing the dating world yet, so that's how it is. It would be closed down, anyway – too many unsolicited dick pics – anywhere else it would be harassment. Boys seem to think that seeing a photo of their dick is as important as knowing their name – probably more important, in fact.'

After a lot of analysing every single photo on my social profiles, Julia and Nicky's work is complete. We order another bottle of rosé and midway through, my phone starts buzzing across the table.

'You've got a message, Milly!'

My phone flashes provocatively at me.

You've got a match! Why not say hello?

'I don't know what to say.'

'Be yourself, say anything.' Julia smiles at me.

I type . . .

Me: What did the cheese say to itself in the mirror?

And press 'send'.

'Why did you write that?' Julia asks. 'Be yourself means don't be yourself.'

'Why did you say it then? I thought it was a bit of an icebreaker, instead of going through an archived MSN conversation of "How R U? BRB, Mum needs phone".'

'Let's hope he replies. I'll be surprised. Next time, hold off the cheese jokes and think of something attractive, so he's not imagining someone who stinks of Roquefort on the other side of the phone.'

'Well, it's no loss if he doesn't – I don't even know him.'

'That's not the correct attitude to have.'

'He's typing!' I feel my stomach do a somersault. Come on, Milly, like you said, you don't even know him.

David: Halloumi
Me: Correct!
David: Are you a comedian?
Me: No, sadly I'm in PR but I thought it might break the usual "How are you? I'm fine, you?" tradition.

'Congratulations, you've just lost your Tinder virginity. The conversations on here won't all be so pleasant – I count myself lucky if I only see three dicks in a day. Let's stalk him.'

'He could be anywhere between the ages of fifteen and forty-five . . . pre- or post-puberty due to the disparity of facial hair between pictures. I don't want to be dating a fifteen-year-old, but maybe he just has a baby face like me.'

'Let me do some serious stalking – I would be an excellent MI5 agent.' Julia takes the phone.

And she's good, I have to hand it to her. She's found him on LinkedIn – he's a teacher. Hmm, could be cute, but teachers can also be really annoying. Everyone's profession is stressful, OK? You get half the year off! As long as he isn't one of those annoying teachers, then maybe he will be cute, maybe a DILF if he is in fact thirty-plus. He also went to York University so he must be relatively clever. According to Google, he also won an anthology competition once.

'I can't find him on Instagram – people always make stupid names up like DiddlyDum123456. Let's try Facebook. Literally nothing – you have no mutual friends, could be a warning sign. He isn't even on his uni's alumni page. Probably a catfish.' Julia really does know her stuff.

'I bet he's done a classic teacher move and swapped the first letters of his first name and surname' Nicky suggests.

'OK, worth a try.' Julia types furiously. 'Gavid Dubbon, gotcha! I told you I should have be in the intelligence services.'

'Nicky, how did you even know that?' I ask.

'I dated a teacher once, and he told me they all do it.'

'He does look quite fit – not awful.'

'I don't know how you can get into someone so quickly just from a few messages, but thanks for helping me set it all up.' Maybe I should just meet him and get the whole malarkey over and done with. Stop panicking the whole time.

We continue drinking, and then suddenly Julia bursts into tears.

'What's the matter?'

'Sarah's dog died.'

'Who's Sarah?'

'One of Gavid Dubbon's friends.'

'What?!'

'I've been stalking him since I found him. One of his friend's friends once went on *MasterChef* and since series four he has done so much, got his own restaurant in London now. His other friend, Sarah, her dog died a few weeks ago, so sad. Her post was so emotional, it set me off.'

'Oh my God, Julia. Let's get a cab – it's late and your hormones are clearly running wild.'

> **@Mizzennial** What are your top tips for dealing with a break-up? I can't stop looking at their Facebook profile. It's my nicotine. I have such strong urges to scroll, I can barely stop myself.
>
> **@CharlotteRose** I block their number on all messaging platforms and Facebook and I do a little dance in my living room every time I feel the urge to scroll. I even buy myself a present if I manage three weeks.
>
> **@Chloe89** I go on Tinder, respond to the first guy who looks mildly attractive and fuck them.
>
> **@AddisonLeigh** It's perfectly normal to still feel attached – you've shared so much with that person, but realise that stalking won't make them want to get back with you. Concentrate on finding someone else, on the off chance they are stalking you too.

I look at his profile one last time. It's nice to have reminders of him, but I don't need to stalk his Facebook every day. It's not normal. How can I expect to move on or date again if I'm going back every evening and speaking to a dead man on Facebook chat? I love you, Adam. So much. But I need to find myself and I need to do it alone. *Block*. There, now I don't have to worry about messaging him any more.

12 March 2017

I always thought I wanted a big princess wedding; an expensive, sophisticated white gown with a veil down to the floor, bouquets of fresh flowers adorning every spare crevice of the church, hundreds of friends and family and a boozy reception. A big party. A celebration of life.

My wedding will be the complete opposite, but perfect all the same. I'm marrying the person of my childhood dreams, the prince I used to act out with my Ken dolls and Barbies.

Adam's put on a suit and tie – his mum bought him a pale grey one with a cornflower blue tie and waistcoat. He looks handsome, smart, all mine. Skinnier than he used to be, the grey folds of the trousers hanging loosely where they would have been stretched, but there's a smile brightening up his face today, diminishing some of the tiredness. He's still the man of my dreams. I'm wearing an ivory slip from ASOS. I've curled my hair and had a lady come to do my make-up. I wanted to look like the old, happy Milly, the one Adam fell in love with.

'My baby,' Mum says softly, her eyes wet with tears.

'You look stunning, Mills,' Florry says, smiling. Her voice cracks slightly.

'I bought you something.' Layla pulls out a veil and clips it into the back of my hair. 'There, perfect.'

We stand outside the back of our flat on the small rectangle of decking, bouquets of flowers and a cake on the table. Our guests sit on the plastic garden furniture. There are eight guests and a vicar.

I do my own reading – *Winnie the Pooh* by A. A. Milne. It's hard not to cry, but I'm getting much better at putting on a brave face. I hold my breath each time I feel that prickly feeling of tears starting to brew.

'If you live to be a hundred, I hope I live to be a hundred minus one day, so that I never have to live a day without you.'

It might sound ironic, but I mean it. If I could take the cancer away from Adam, I would.

The vicar says his part and then Adam and then back to me again.

'Do you take this man to be your lawful wedded husband in sickness and in health, till death do you part?'

Look at him. Do you need to ask me that?

'I do.'

'I now pronounce you man and wife. You may kiss the bride.'

We kiss. There's more love in this kiss than I ever could have imagined. And hope. Hope that this is all a dream and marriage will solve everything. Make it all back to normal again. I want to remain in this moment for eternity. Capture it in my mind's eye and project it outwards whenever I need to feel loved.

The guests throw confetti over us and cheer. My dad pours us all a glass of champagne.

We clink our glasses together, not needing to make an announcement because 'to health and prosperity' seems jovial right now.

Mr and Mrs Hadfield. We'll say that for now, but legally, I'm still Mrs Dayton. We decided that changing my name would be too much. All the admin, driving licence, passports, documents, just to change it all back again one day. It's a strange feeling, thinking of the time when the marriage will be over before it's even really begun.

We sit on the plastic furniture, holding hands, and bask our faces in the sunshine, taking in every moment the world has to offer.

Sometimes silence says more than words ever can.

15

It's like breaking up with a boyfriend. Worse. Like when you spend every second of every day stalking his profile to ensure he isn't having too much fun since you broke up. Analysing every recently added photo to check for any new women, a new hairstyle, who's been liking the photos – is there a pattern? Any love-heart comments? Any strangers on the scene? Then one day, you finally see a curl of blonde hair creeping into the right of the photo, notice that @Emileeee91 has commented on the last few pictures, put two and two together and send him a message confronting him on the new woman in his life. And he blocks you. You have to politely ask all of your friends to check his profile activity for a few weeks until you finally get over him.

I chose to block Adam and I can easily undo it. I'm stalking someone with no change in activity. It doesn't have to be forever, just for now. You can't move on if you constantly live in the past.

I was in the middle of creating a quiz titled 'Avocados for breakfast, negronis for lunch, OnlyFans for dessert? How Gen Z really are you?' when my morning dose of reality is served.

Florry: Welcome back to the real world, biatch! Have you thought about what you're getting Mum for her birth-

> day? If you want to go halves on something I'll let you, but I'm not doing all the thinking like last year. But I was thinking about getting her something from Decléor. OK, I've just bought it. Transfer me £50. You do the card.

It's been three weeks since my car accident. People say time flies when you are having fun. Work gave me three weeks off, which, to be fair, was pretty generous. Theoretically, I could have sat and typed from home on my laptop, but I wasn't going to let them know that. It was like early maternity leave, without the companion and more sleep. Today, I have to go back to the soulless typing (albeit, thankfully, still from home). No one bothered to message me while I was off because they're not my friends, they're my colleagues, and their pleasantries only take place between four grey walls.

I love writing emails saying 'Sorry, I am WFH today'. It is code for *fuck off*. Whenever I read WFH too quickly, I always mistake it for WTF. *Sorry, I am WTFing all day today and can't make your meeting at 2 p.m., or any time. Ever.*

It's my first day back at work (from home) and my inbox is full to the brim with irrelevant emails such as:

> I know you are off sick, Milly, but Giovanna has gone crazy about the last deck we sent across. We need to discuss the strategy behind this ASAP. As soon as you are better, of course. How are you feeling, btw? OK now?
> URGENT!!!! On the latest video of diabetic patients, one of the boys is eating a chocolate Curly Wurly – he is supposed to have Type 2 diabetes!!! Milly, I need you to start doing the Q&A immediately, the press is going to be all over this!

Have you read a paper recently? The press doesn't give a fuck about pharmaceutical companies miscommunicating, they care whether Kylie Jenner has a new weave and which theme park is next to impale a small child.

@Mizzennial Does anyone else find work infuriating? It's like when you're at work, nothing else matters, nothing is more important than an email. Sometimes, I find it hard to not let people annoy me so much. If you have tips, send them my way!
How do you spend your workday?

a. Chained to your desk, ferociously working from 8 to 6. No task is too big or too small. By 5.59 p.m., your whole to-do list is neatly lined through with a crisp black biro in your expensive Smythson notepad.

b. Working remotely, relaxed, drinking flat whites in your local coffee house, thinking of outside-the-box, crazy, creative ideas.

c. Hiding in the toilet, spending all your money in Pret, scrolling through 'New in' on ASOS and completing BuzzFeed quizzes to find out how best to eat chips.

Mark tried to call me a couple of minutes ago about a presentation I sent through. Just my luck, my stupid phone signal isn't working, so I can't hear him. I live in the capital of the UK; high-speed phone signal's as important as breathing.

'Hey, Mark, sorry about my get-up – didn't realise we'd be on Zoom!'

'No worries, Milly. How are you feeling now?'

There is about a minute of niceties until Mark launches into a very boring conversation about my PowerPoint until he finally hangs up and I can get back to thinking about nothing.

The next thing I know, I have a passive aggressive email from Mark about my 'get-up'.

My loungewear consisted of cashmere jumper, my hair in a ponytail and *shock horror* no make-up. If you've seen the meme about not wasting your make-up on fuckboys, you'll understand my mantra for not wasting it on fuckdays either. I don't earn enough.

Email from Mark:

> Hi Milly,
> Good to chat earlier.
> I wanted to reiterate the office dress code to you: it is smart casual. Obviously smart if you have a client meeting. I know we can be quite relaxed in the office sometimes, but you can't wear your pyjamas to work – what if a client saw you in them?
> Anyway, I hope you get my drift.
> Thanks,
> Mark

Err, I am sorry?

1. I wasn't wearing pyjamas, I was wearing *loungewear*.
2. I'm at home – there are no clients visiting me. Unless I've been inviting them round my house when I'm blackout drunk, the possibility of them knocking on my door unannounced is about as plausible as my mother asking to borrow my Mooncup.
3. I'm at fucking home! I'm not going to wear 'pyjamas/ expensive loungewear' into central London to *work*.
4. I don't want to sit around in a suit in my own (rented) home, looking like a modern-day Miss Havisham.
5. I was *hit by a fucking car*! Does no one care about my welfare?

Honestly, what's wrong with people?

I don't understand why most people seem to have the knack for saying the wrong things. Why couldn't Mark just read the situation for what it was instead of making a mountain out of a molehill.

It reminds me that there are a lot of things people say to you when you're grieving that are totally inappropriate, but no one seems to realise. It's like a nervous twitch – they mean to give you a verbal hug, but they end up punching you in the face instead.

I should probably share them to stop anyone else putting their foot in it.

Five things NOT to say to someone who's grieving:
1. It will get better, don't worry.
2. The only way is up, right?
3. There will be someone else, eventually.
4. How are you?
5. I know what it's like.

Violet and I greet each other with the usual pointless How-are-you?-Good-thanks-you?-Yeah-good tennis before I get to the nitty gritty of what I'm paying her for.

'My friend's set me up on Tinder.'

'Interesting. So, you think you are ready to date again?' Violet questions, clearly surprised based on some of our previous chats.

'I'm unsure. I've dated before slash been on dates and, well, you know.'

'Had sex?' Violet doesn't have the British coyness that I expected her to.

'Yeah.'

'How did you find it?' Am I about to tell my virtual mother the ins and outs of my orgasm diary?

'What the sex? Not great. It was more me forcing myself to do it, in case I forgot how.'

'Do you think it helped?'

'Not really. If you imagine a cross between an angry hulk having sex with an even more emotional Moaning Myrtle, that was me.'

'It does take a while to move on and find someone worth that connection again. There is no point rushing it. Sometimes, it is good just to know that there are other people out there though, even if they aren't quite right.'

'I know. I've been thinking it would be nice to meet someone, but it's a very conflicting set of emotions, you know.'

'Have you spoken to Adam again? It might help if you don't speak to him if you're thinking about going on a date.'

'Actually, Violet, I've beat you to it. I've blocked him,' I say with an air of triumph.

'I do think that it is good to not be so reliant on your conversations with Adam, but I do believe that eventually you will need to say a proper goodbye. You're blocking someone from your life that is essentially already blocked. I think you might have overcompensated slightly, Milly. You don't need to remove all memories of Adam from your life, you just need to get used to the fact that he has gone and not live in the past so much.'

Thanks for signing, sealing and delivering the fact that my husband is dead, Violet. The Grim Reaper should come over when you are at death's door and deliver you with your 'blocked from the game show of life' notice in case you believe in reincarnation and thought you might have a chance of coming back.

Violet must have noticed my face and changes the conversation.

'Have you had a change of heart about being a godmother?'

'I'm trying my hardest to be happy for Julia, but it's really difficult. I'm constantly feeling pangs of jealously when I think about her future family unit. If I'm honest, I don't think I will feel really happy for her until I've moved on myself.'

'That's very astute of you, Milly. Just like people ignore someone grieving because they feel guilty about enjoying their lives, it is a perfectly just reaction for you to feel anger towards others about their happiness.'

We continue for a few more minutes until we both sign off. There was a lot to think about today – a lot of mixed emotions.

I feel like I should message Gavid Dubbon back, but equally I can't be bothered. I'm sure if he's worth it, he will come after me at some point.

Today's been such a non-day. I've given up my life of luxury for a life back at the PR grindstone. The only thing so far that's made me feel like I've achieved something with my day was my conversation with Violet. She does have a natural way of making me feel I have a life well lived.

I sit on my phone looking at my messages and the posts on Mizzennial so far. It does feel pretty amazing to have such a public platform. It makes me feel warm and fuzzy when I see all the likes, comments and messages. In a different way to before. These are people engaging with my content because it really resonates with them. They're not liking a photo of some well-edited eggs on rye so that I comment a love heart on their Ibiza pool pic; these people are liking my posts because I'm helping them. It's giving them confidence and me confidence at the same time.

Ping.

@ShelleyFarrell @Mizzennial Oh my God! I totally love your stuff. I am massively fangirling! You are so brave! Where do you live? I'd love to meet up!

Gosh, @ShelleyFarrell is super forward. What if she is a sixty-year-old-man catfish? If I told Florry, or even my parents, I was meeting someone I met online, they'd have a heart attack. Hmm, what to do?

Fuck it, Milly, you're supposed to be turning over a new leaf.

@Mizzennial @ShelleyFarrell I live in Croydon, bit of a shithole but serves its purpose!

@ShelleyFarrell @Mizzennial Shut the front door. I live in Streatham! So close! We MUST meet up soon!

Have you ever noticed that when you reread your messages, it looks like someone has been sick exclamation marks? It's hard to show your emotion in writing, so an overload of punctuation and emojis does the trick.

Hmm, should I meet @ShelleyFarrell, or shouldn't I? I'm not sure if I'm ready to meet anyone face to face yet. I'll just send her a smiley for now.

How am I considering meeting someone I don't know – who has an equal chance of being a serial rapist as they do a nice person – and I can't drop one incy wincy message to @LaylaRose?

3 October 2010

In the movies, when a girl's about to sleep with a guy for the first time, they start with passionate aggressive kissing, where he starts to pull her clothes off, but then suddenly the girl says, 'Stop, I won't be a minute,' and rushes to the bathroom. In real life, this is where you're looking for any sharp object to shave your legs and bikini line with, usually, his or his flatmate's razor. I have shaved my entire body before with an unknown man's razor, including my armpits. In the movies, this is where the girl comes out of the bathroom in an erotic negligee and heels, and the guy falls over himself trying to get to her in time, as if she was an ice cream and had just started melting.

I'm thinking of this as I try to push a wee out on the toilet. I always panic that I might wee during sex, so I need to get rid of all liquid from my body. I swish some toothpaste round my mouth, give my hair a quick brush, spray deodorant under my arms and wipe eyeliner residue from my cheeks. Ready.

It's starting to feel a little awkward. Do I undress myself straight away, hop into bed and lie there relishing my own naked glory like Rose in *Titanic,* or is that too forward? Do I get half undressed, Calvin Klein-model style, dress half-pulled up and seductive finger in the mouth? Or sit there fully clothed, hoping that he knows exactly which arm to pull out of the dress first to avoid my head being stuck in it? I've only had sex with two guys up until now, and I'm basically still a child so I don't really know what to do. [Note from future Milly: Thankfully, this experience was before *Fifty Shades of Grey* hit the mainstream, so I didn't need to come prepared with handcuffs, a whip and a penis clamp.] Adam starts dressing down to his boxers, so I use this as my cue and peel myself out of my dress like a pig in a blanket, hoping he doesn't notice the mild huffing and puffing as my right elbow gets caught in the seam.

Adam does have a good body. Not a full-on hard-core six-pack but definitely a half one. Delicately tanned too, which sets off his eyes – they're so blue I can imagine little fishies swimming round in there.

We get into bed and joke around a bit about the evening, preamble to sex – basically if you don't want it, speak up now!

We start kissing – Adam's a good kisser. Kissing in sex is a very different capacity to normal day kissing – it's the post-watershed version. Adam removes his boxers and I catch a glimpse of something on his bum.

'Err, what's that?' and I point towards him.

'Oh God, I was hoping you wouldn't notice!' He starts awkwardly laughing. 'It's our university crest. I had it tattooed on my bum so I'd win a bet.'

'Oh my God! That's hilarious!'

Adam gets on top of me and we start having sex. We seem to be quite in sync, as if our bodies have morphed into one. He seems to know my body better than I know myself. He has some slightly obtuse sex faces, but other than that he is up there in the grade A sex chart.

'Erm, Milly. . .'

'Yeah. . . ?' Weird to start having a conversation during sex – I was about to climax.

'Are you OK?'

'Yes, why?' God, have I been making obtuse faces? Does it look like I am having a stroke?

Adam gesticulates to the sheets. Oh, fuckety fuck fuck.

'Adam, I'm so sorry!' and then I start laughing, as I don't know what I would do if I didn't.

'Looks like a massacre! I thought it all felt a bit wet . . .'

My period has leaked everywhere. As if I'd started so violently and suddenly during my first time with a guy I fancy. I thought your body was supposed to be in tune with your emotions?

Adam pulls his penis out and waves it around triumphantly.

'Stop, that's so disgusting!'

'It's kind of killed the mood, hasn't it?'

'Yes, I think so. Sorry.'

16

When we were in Brighton, Nicky used this new app called BeeTrap to meet up with a guy who was in the area. It's supposed to be about limiting the time you spend pointlessly messaging someone, the to-ing and fro-ing about, until finally arranging a date just to realise that you're polar opposites. Anyway, Nicky uses it as a simple way to meet someone for a quickie, as who ever met a guy who turns down sex?

I downloaded it last night and when I was going through the arduous process of logging into my work computer this morning, I decided to have a quick peek.

Quite a strange calibre of men on here.

Atticus JimJam – The lad. Clearly a fake name so there will be no way of contacting him post-fuck. Barrow boy turned trader turned gigolo.

Pierre Potts – Euro-trip central. Again, looking for a quick shag, no strings attached. Roaming different London boroughs to write home about stories of randy English girls.

Bernard Jones – Unsatisfied husband. Doesn't need any explaining; we've seen them all before.

It's easy to see what Nicky finds attractive about it. Anonymity.

Scroll, flick, scroll, flick. William Walker. Hilarious name, sounds like a cousin of Gary Lineker. He looks nice. Brown hair, blue eyes, works in marketing. Pretty vanilla. Maybe I should start liking vanilla. It's so inoffensive.

My finger hovers over his profile.

I've been giving advice out to a whole host of people and the only thing I really feel qualified to talk about is death. Maybe not even grief, as I've only just ventured to the other side of the dark cavern and I'm not sure if I'm even out of it yet. I talk about dating and sex, but my experiences are so inexperienced, it's laughable. I've got my *Swipe Right* appearance coming up, but I didn't even organise that myself – I would've been too scared.

I need to go on a date with a random man, which I've organised myself and get over this barrier I've created between me and the opposite sex. Then maybe I'll also feel less of fraud on Mizzennial.

I type.

Me: Hey William, I'm going on my lunch break in ten minutes, fancy a coffee at Leonardo's on Arbury Street?

I see the three dots.

. . .

Me: And I actually mean a coffee. It's not a code word or anything like that.

Fuck, that was embarrassing. I shouldn't have written that.

. . .

Why is he dotting me? He must think I'm a freak. Maybe I should want to have sex. That's what everyone does.

Me: I mean, we could probably have sex if you want.

Fuck, Milly, pull yourself together. Just delete the app already.

William: Hey Milly, yeah, coffee sounds nice. See you in a bit.

If only I could be more carefree like @Sagittarius89:

@Mizzennial I threw my tampon out somewhere in his living room. I was drunk and horny, k? He messaged me the next day to say his mum found a used tampon in the sofa cushions. I replied – you still live at home? #cringe

I sit down nervously with my oat-milk flat white. My brain starts to have an internal argument. Why do I do it to myself? Because you need to grow up. It doesn't matter, I've got nothing to lose – I don't know him, he doesn't know me. The more people I meet, the more open I'll become. It'll become easier; I'll be less awkward. I was awkward with Adam and it was OK. He humoured me. I mean, he was perfect.

I see Will. Wave. He orders a coffee and walks towards the little wooden table.

'Hi, you must be, err, Milly!'

I stand up and he kisses me on either cheek. He smells of woody aftershave and salt from perspiration.

'Nice to meet you, William. Or should I call you Will?'

'Will is fine. I don't understand why parents go to the trouble of calling their kids long names, just for them to be abbreviated. I mean, what's your real name? Emily?'

Is Will real?

'Amelia.'

'Oh right, makes sense. Milly. Amelia.' Very monosyllabic. Very serious. Very manly.

'Have you done one of these before?' Before he answers, I use the pause to show off my hilarity. 'Congratulations, you've just popped my BeeTrap cherry!'

He sits back. I can hear the creaking of the wooden chair.

'Lunch dates? Yeah, I do them all the time. I find I'm so busy, I don't really have time to sit and type messages out on Tinder yadda yadda. I can go on a date at lunchtime and decide if I want to see them again before the day's even finished.'

'Very efficient. I'm quite busy too.' I lie. There's something off about William, but I can't tell exactly what, like milk on the edge of turning.

'I mean I work in marketing – I'm actually a director at the firm now, one of the youngest to ever be promoted. Pretty chuffed with that. So, combining work with the gym, dates, holidays, pub with the lads, means I really am just rushed off my feet.'

'Wow, very impressive,' I say, not very impressed. William has now officially turned.

'It's quite easy to get dates being averagely good-looking. I know I'm not Brad Pitt or anything like that, but my face is symmetrical so, according to science, I'm good-looking. I feel sorry for people who don't have such a symmetrical face. You're also averagely good-looking, do you find the same thing?'

'Erm . . . I don't know if anyone's ever described me as that before.' It's almost like a compliment, but one that's covered in shit.

'I didn't mean to offend, but it's good to be honest with one's self. You're no supermodel, but you're not ugly either, so you should be happy with what your parents gave you. Life's really tough for people who aren't good-looking.'

'Has anyone ever said your name sounds like a packet of crisps?'

'No, why would they say that?'

I shrug.

'I thought it sounded a bit like someone who worked in the world of fried goods.'

'Hmm, interesting!' He obviously doesn't get my sarcasm. I sit and listen to him talk some more before, thank God, he pipes up with one of his final sentences. 'It's been great meeting you, Milly. Maybe we can do it again sometime?'

'I have to be honest – I'm not really feeling it,' I say. 'At least you didn't waste your evening pulling weights and you've still got time to grab a chicken shawarma from KiKi's.'

'That's a shame. Anyway, no hard feelings.' He stands up, shakes my hand and leaves.

I sit in silence, stirring the last of the milk around my cup.

I start laughing, really laughing. The girl on the table next to me is giving me the what-the-fuck side-eye.

What a fucking weirdo.

Why am I so scared of dating? What was so scary about William Walker? His eyebrows were knitted together, but that was about it.

I stand up, ready to walk back to my home office, shaking my head and smiling.

@Mizzennial I went on a lunchtime date today (my first ever one!) using that new app BeeTrap. Safe to say it was a total farce. One of those guys that loves the sound of his own voice. He told me I was average-looking. But do you know what? I didn't get upset, I laughed! I laughed!

My first ever proper date that I organised by myself. I feel proud. Proud that I didn't get upset, proud that I was able to see the funny side, proud that I am coming closer to the person that everyone on Mizzennial already thinks I am.

Maybe that's it. I want to be the same person I am offline as I am online. Just 100 per cent me.

New DM:

@SoloSister @Mizzennial I've got a friend's party coming up. My boyfriend broke up with me recently and it will be the first one that I'm going to alone. I'm so nervous. What should I do?

Poor @SoloSister. I remember going to my first party solo – it was horrible. I just drank and drank and drank until someone put me in a taxi home. No one told me anything embarrassing that I said, as they felt too bad, so it's just one of those nights that never happened.

@Mizzennial @SoloSister My number one rule is NEVER be the first to turn up to a party alone – you need to be at least half an hour late, if not longer. You probably want an excuse to leave early too – a solid one so people don't flood you with 'Are you OK? Are you sure? Things must be hard, etc.'. My second rule is NEVER speak to someone's partner/boyfriend/husband for too long, because there will always be some sadist who thinks you are having a desperate moment and trying to fuck them. X

24 December 2012

I hear Adam's car crunching on the gravel drive and I swing open the door to greet him.

'Welcome, amigo!' I call.

Our first Christmas together. I've been preparing all morning for his arrival. I'm a preened, perfected, hairless woman.

'You made it – Happy Christmas!'

Adam picks me up and swings me round in his arms. I feel like my man has come home from the war in 1945 and I've got a home-made sherry trifle on the table.

'Happy Christmas Eve, little daff. How's the fam doing? Are the Daytons' festivities in full swing?'

'Of course, we've got a batch of mulled wine on the Aga, and Mum's been making mince pies all morning. It's going to be perfect.' I hold my hands together round the small of his back and look up into those dreamy-as-ever eyes.

I know life isn't a picture-perfect book of fairy tales, but it isn't half nice when it pans out that way.

'Adam, darling, how lovely it is having you here with us this year.' Mum hugs him and gives him a kiss on each cheek while Dad shakes his hand and asks him how the car drove. He says it as if he just bought a new Mercedes straight off the production line, when in fact Adam drives a bashed-up Micra that I'm still convinced he stole straight from a scrapheap.

Mum goes back to her own pastry production line, with sausage rolls next on the agenda and maybe even some cheese twists if we're lucky. Dad heads off into the garden to add the finishing touches to the fairy lights he's artistically thrown over the hedge for the ultimate Santa's grotto experience.

'Are these for me?!' I ask Adam, grappling with a large bag of parcels in the boot. I can't help it; Christmas brings out the child in me.

'Maybe, baby. You'll find out tomorrow, won't you?'

'I'm excited! Put all the presents under the tree. I'll grab us a mince pie and mulled wine and we can watch some festive TV.'

We settle down on the sofa. I rest my head in the nook of Adam's arm and pull the blanket over our knees.

'No, don't change it!' I say hastily. 'I like watching the Christmas cooking shows.'

'How does she do that? Effortlessly combine soft porn and berry pavlovas – titillating.'

'She's just jazzing up the whole experience – it would be so boring otherwise.'

'"Now for my favourite part, a midnight snack! I just pop a bit of cream on each of my nipples, put a cherry in my mouth and rush upstairs to my husband, drowning in diamonds, looking like the voluptuous Black Forest gateau I know I am." Are the BBC sure they haven't started streaming Pornhub in their festive prime time? Shut up, Nigella.'

'I can't watch it if you keep taking the piss out of her. You're ruining the experience.'

'Will Nigella be trialling the edible dildo?'

17

Florry's coming over tonight and I'm cooking for her. She should be cooking for me, I'm the injured party, but it doesn't work like that for older sisters. You're constantly indebted to them, and you don't know why because you can't remember the first three years of your life.

I head to Instagram for some inspiration. Everything and everyone are cutting out animal products at the moment, so cooking a vegan feast seems the only logical thing to do – @TongueWateringlyJemma and @SocialShrink91 are both advocates. Regardless of my new move towards trying to make more of my life off the grid, I can't deny that I occasionally get infatuated with what they have to say, and after all, being vegan is only a good thing – it's saving the planet.

@SocialShrink91 I CAN'T THINK OF ANYTHING BETTER IN THE WORLD THAN TO BE A VEGAN. Morningggggg, social shrinkers! Thanks, @AliciaSilverstone, for being so honest. I get messages every day from people asking how I became vegan and if they should too – read the quote above, ladies! Just to clear the air, I didn't become vegan for health reasons. I did it because I realised the horror of what we are doing to all these animals. How can I cry over a picture of a fluffy chick and then eat 9 chicken nuggets the next day? It just isn't real, and being fake isn't me. Granted, there are health reasons for being vegan, but just like everything, you should sit yourself down and think am I doing this for me? Before I receive a torrent of comments, yes, I do wear a Gucci belt and own a Saint Laurent bag, but I bought these BEFORE I became vegan. I would never buy leather ever again – pleather is perfect for me, gyals! Love y'all xxx

'Mum, I'm cooking a vegan chilli. What are some good spices I can put in?'

'Vegan chilli? Why don't you use beef mince?' She probes. Because every time you cooked it when I was younger, I held a vigil as I thought you were cremating a cow in our kitchen.

'I'm using Quorn mince; you won't be able to tell the difference. Everyone should be a vegan at least a few days a week. It's good for the environment,' I respond, satisfied with my reason.

'I don't think being vegan a few days a week will change the environment,' Mum replies indignantly.

'I think it will. There's so much choice now you wouldn't even notice. You barely used to get enough cow's milk in your ration for a cup of tea – now you can choose between oat, almond and coconut. You can basically milk anything nowadays – it doesn't even need to have an udder.'

'Darling, I don't know how old you think I am, but I wasn't around in World War Two. Next you will be gluten-free, lactose-free, fat-free, maybe even fun-free.'

'No, I won't. I want to be vegan a few days a week. It's called being a flexitarian. It isn't the same as it was fifty years ago, Mum. You don't only eat nuts and seeds – you can eat the same as anyone else.'

'Apart from meat, fish and anything dairy. You won't be able to eat custard, and I know that is your favourite.' Adam used to love Mum's home-made custard. Mum would make huge vats of it when we both came to stay. Creamy custard on a home-made sticky toffee pudding – nothing beats it.

'Mum! I'm making *one* meal that uses Quorn instead of beef mince, please stop,' I shout down the phone. 'I just want to know what your special ingredients are in a chilli.'

'Grated dark chocolate - 90 per cent cacao and ten per cent cow's milk.'

Briiiiinnng.

The queen has arrived! Let dinner be served!

'Hello, shithead! This smells fantastic. I didn't know we had a Fanny Cradock in our midst!'

Fanny Cradock was an insatiable cook from the late fifties. Fanny decided to change her birth name, Phyllis Pechey, for even more of a Freudian Slip – goodness knows why.

'I've even surprised myself! I used one of TongueWateringlyJemma's recipes – have you heard of her?'

'If she's one of your virtual pals who pretends to be a cordon bleu chef, then no.'

'You might alter your opinion about online friends after you've tasted it.'

We sit down on the sofa, craning our necks as we attempt to eat from the bowls on my Ikea coffee table. I didn't have any napkins, so I used toilet roll instead. There's no way Florry hasn't noticed, but she's doing her best to be polite. She's that dicky, annoying older sister most of the time, but she does have manners.

'This chilli is delicious, Milly!' I genuinely think it tastes great, so I cross my fingers in the hope that she's not just being polite. 'How are things, anyway? Going OK?'

'Thanks, Florry!' I beam with pride. There is something overly satisfying about pleasing an elder sibling. 'Well, Julia and James set me up on *Swipe Right*, you know the show? And I'm through to the live shows, which is exciting.' I giggle nervously. 'Oh, and I started back at work – from home, of course – and Julia's pregnant. All in all, things have been pretty crazy.'

'What the fuck? I wasn't expecting all that. *Swipe Right*? That show where you eat in a restaurant with the DILF host? That's amazing! You should probably hide your crutches, or you will be aired on TV as a sob story.' It's a snub to my injury but I wouldn't expect anything else. 'Julia, pregnant! Wow! I remember when you guys used to sneak into my room and steal my lipsticks. How are you feeling about it all?'

It's not often that Florry asks me how I'm feeling. She tends to hide her worry and kindness behind sarcasm or mean comments. She's about as in tune with her emotions as I am.

'Mmm, OK, I guess. I mean, it's crazy. Everyone is moving in with partners, having babies, getting married, and I am starting from the beginning again. I was perfectly happy before – I didn't need a fresh start. But whatever, that's life. Sometimes I feel ready to date, excited even about the prospect of finding love again, and other times I just want to hide in a hole and return to the time when I used to run away with a packet of blackcurrant Frubes and my Beanie Babies.' You can get better and still have bad days, things that make you sad. They just come less frequently, and the sadness gets less crippling.

'It's OK to feel confused, though, Mills. Dating is tough at the best of times without, you know, being plunged in at the deep end. Before I met Chris, I went on some terrible dates, and I mean, *terrible*. Just like guys I'd meet in bars or get with on a night out who I'd meet up with afterwards. At least now you get wined and dined a bit more.' Florry smiles that patronising smile that says, 'life was tough in my day'.

'I still find it so weird that you never had to go on dating apps.' I shake my head. 'You don't know how lucky you were. Wasn't it nerve-racking going up to guys in person?'

'You don't feel lucky when you don't know any different.'

'Yeah, I guess.' It's easy to feel very unfortunate when you had everything ripped from under your feet, like a magician doing a morbid magic trick. 'I did go on a date the other day.'

'With *who*?' Florry's mascaraed eyes are about to pop out of her head.

'I tried out that new app, BeeTrap? It hooks you up with people in the area almost instantaneously. The guy was a real wanker, but it was funny. I'll probs try out dating again, you know,' I say knowingly, as if I'm an expert in love now.

'That's great news!' And she claps her hands together with excitement.

'I do have something else to tell you, but please, please don't tell Mum and Dad, OK? Also, *do not* tell them about *Swipe Right* – if I end up saying anything about sex or kissing a guy on TV, I *don't* want them to watch.'

'Oh my God, what have you done?!'

'Nothing! I basically started an Instagram account called Mizzennial. I was reading the magazines you bought me and thinking about what Violet, my counsellor, said, and it reminded me of how naive we all were in our youth. Remember how much we used to love reading magazines? We would talk about it at school and used to spend time being with our friends, not trying to impress people we don't know through a screen every second of the day.'

'I'm sorry, are you OK? Let's rewind a second here. Your *big* solution to being a social media addict is starting a social media channel?!'

'Ha, yeah, I know what it sounds like.'

'You paid all that money for your social media addict counsellor, or whatever you call her, to tell you to spend *more* time on Instagram? I'm done.' She laughs, crossing her arms and leaning back.

'It's not what you think. Instagram isn't all bad. It's not all truffle pasta and girls in bikinis. It's a ready-made community of people who understand and who've gone through the same as me. You just need to find the right place to look. I've finally found people who get me.'

'Show me this account right now and let me decide!'

Florry almost snatches my phone. She sits and scrolls in complete silence.

Come on, tell me what you think.

To both of our surprise, Florry suddenly exults, 'Milly, this is amazing! I'm so proud of my little sister. I get it. I totally get it.' She leans over the coffee table to give me a hug. Tears prick in my eyes again. Happy tears. I can't show her my weakness. I've always sought her approval. 'You're really nailing the advice; you should become a proper agony aunt. I was thinking the other day, as she popped up on my Facebook, have you spoken to Layla at all?'

'No.'

'Oh, OK. I just thought with the advice you were writing that maybe you thought it might be a good time to meet up? I read some of her statuses, and it looks like she's been through it a bit too.'

'You can't tell anything from Facebook,' I reply, shortly.

We sit in silence for a minute before Florry lights up a Marlboro and tactfully changes the conversation.

'Do you remember in *Mizz* magazine how they always made out that smoking was the worst thing in the entire world?' Florry says, drawing breath on a cigarette, the end crackling as she inhales. She's exactly like those yummy mummies that meet up and share packets of Vogues and drink white wine.

'Hahaha, yes I do, there'd always be a special feature on it every so often to deter everyone from the "cancer sticks",' I say in a ghoulish voice. I hate cancer, but Adam didn't smoke, he was twenty-six and he still got it. I think it's either going to get you or it's not, you do you.

'I wonder how many people listened to it – after all, *Mizz* was a bible.'

Florry and I continue to reminisce about our youth. I don't think I've felt this close to her in ages. Violet was right; as soon as you start opening up to people, they let you in back. I push what Florry said about Layla to the back of my mind.

My sister and I always tease each other – we don't like to show our love. Recently, she was so nice to me, it made me weep. Silently. I don't know how to show her I love her. Do I punch her in the face or give her a bunch of flowers?

20 August 2016

'Milly, you look . . .' Adam starts.

'Glam?'

'I was going to say like you're having some out-of-body experience where you think you are Zoe Ball in 1995 and about to present *Live and Kicking*.'

'That's a pretty in-depth description,' I respond, preening in the mirror one last time. I'm actually happy that Adam thinks that because I was going for a nineties-chick vibe. Hair in two space buns, glitter spray replacing all of my skin cells, Lycra flares and a neon-orange cami. 'You, on the other hand, look way too sensible, like you're in the running for the *Blue Peter* badge at an animal shelter. Do you want some glitter?'

'Yeah, please douse me in glitter, and I'll borrow that tattoo-style neck choker you've got too. Right, come on, the others will be waiting for us.'

I go to spray him with silver glitter.

'Milly! I was being sarcastic. Come on!'

The good thing about London is that seeing someone dressed in sequins, covered in glitter and adorned with two space buns squashed between two men in suits on the Tube is entirely normal. Even if I was having a Zoe Ball out-of-body experience, no one bats an eyelid.

Arabella: Guys, where are you?! The Chainsmokers are on – it's your fave song, 'Roses'!

Leo and Arabella's next message is a really drunk voice note:

Arabella: 'Say you'll never let me go, say you'll never let me gooooo.'

I frantically message back:

Me: We're queuing but don't worry we're drinking!

We queue for what seems an age, drinking vodka and squash out of a water bottle until finally – Lovelost, we have arrived! Luckily for me, there is a whole army of Zoe Balls here and unfortunately for Adam, a lack of *Blue Peter* contestants.

Adam's not made for festivals – it's just not really in his genetic make-up. He comes along to all the festivals, clubs, parties, but he prefers to have some pints down the pub. He does this for me. I'm the one who organises parties, nights out, festivals with our friends. If I didn't do it, he would see people once a year on his birthday. It's not that he's unsociable – he's a boy who, ironically, could organise a piss-up in a brewery, but only if everyone was already there.

'Rosie, Arabella – over here!' I shout, enthusiastically waving my arms in the air. 'Where's Leo?'

'He's gone to buy booze and he said some guy is selling happy pills or something?!' Arabella says while continually jumping on the spot.

'Cool!' I shout back, my face now permanently in a smile. As soon as Leo gets drunk, he goes on the drug hunt. He'll either be passed out in two hours, or awake for the next two days – there's no in-between. It's good to have a mix of personalities in a group – keeps things lively.

Some guy shouts, '*Selfieeeee!*' and his mates run towards him from all angles, shoving their faces against each other, so they can get in the shot.

'Adam, let's do a selfie – this place is magic! And who do you want to see first?'

We put our heads together, smiling. Adam's face static and mine moving around to catch the best of the light.

'Dizzee Rascal – he will be epic. Let's go now so we get a good spot at the front.'

I feel like I'm on top of the world, dancing in the sun to Dizzee. Rosie, Arabella and I jumping and bounding, sneaking sips of vodka and squash. Adam and the boys laughing and rapping, buying us beers. Charlie and Olivia come to join us – let's make it a new tradition. Festival every year. I don't want this day to end.

'Hey, Milly,' Adam whispers in my ear. 'I got us something.' I turn around and he shows me a joint he's rolled. 'Come on, let's smoke it, will be fun.'

'Where did you get that?' I laugh.

'Leo gave it to me.'

'Be careful then,' I joke. 'Could be anything in that and probably not weed.'

The others save our space in the new dance area that we have claimed. Arabella and Rosie are guarding it with their lives – vigorously jumping in front of anyone who dares try to encroach. I love them, I just love our friends.

Adam and I hide behind the side of the circus tent, puffing on the joint.

Adam bursts out laughing, which makes me start to laugh too. 'I've got the giggles.'

'You're high, that's why.'

'I can't stop laughing at you being on *Blue Peter* – I know you always wanted a badge.'

'Literally you would have been the best children's presenter, I can imagine you on there now. "Morning, kids! It's Milly MopaDop. Welcome to Fandango land. Today we're going on a super cool adventure where we'll learn how to wipe our bum bums, here I'll show you."'

'Fuck off.' I nudge him.

'Come on, let's go watch the rest of Dizzee. I feel like a proper lad now.'

'You are the total opposite of a lad, babes, hate to break it to you.'

Adam grabs my arm. 'Milly? There is no one else I'd love to smoke weed with. I'm literally having the best day.'

'Stop being so fucking soppy, mate. Told you, no lad here. You're closer to Mr Darcy – you should be spitting rhymes like Dizzee,' I burst into an off-the-cuff rap.

'You would hate it if I was a proper lad – I'm too soft on you.'

I start feeling a bit dizzy.

'Adam, I think I'm going to be sick.'

'You're about to spew. Come on then, little daff – I'll hold back your hair.'

'I take it back. I like soppy, caring Adam. I don't want you to call me a whore.'

18

Today's my *Swipe Right* meeting – the official date – *arghh-hhhhhh*! I'm supposed to be WFH-ing, but I told Marjorie I had an urgent hospital appointment; my leg had suddenly got infected and they thought I had sepsis. I know this is a bit dramatic, but it limits questioning. I will tell her that it had swollen up due to a mosquito bite or something and it was all worry about nothing – thankfully.

I set a game for my Mizzennial followers:

> **@Mizzennial** How many times can you sneak #GirlBoss into your work emails before your male boss realises that females work in the building too? Comment below with your scores!

'I'm feeling really nervous, Violet. Maybe it's not nerves, more guilty excitement. I feel like I've given a gluten-intolerant person a loaf of bread. I know that the worst thing that will happen is they'll probably just shit themselves, but I'd feel guilty all the same.'

'OK, rogue description there, Milly. Have you given a gluten-intolerant person some bread? That could be considered poisoning, you know?'

'No, of course I haven't! I'm not a psychopath,' I exclaim. 'My friend, Julia, the one that's pregnant, signed me up for *Swipe Right*, the TV show, and it's today.'

'Gosh, this might be my last session before you are famous – I'll have to frame the signature on your waiver.' A total dad joke, but it makes me smile all the same. 'I gather you are feeling nervous because of meeting someone new?'

'Exactly. I've met guys since Adam, had sex with guys since Adam, but I didn't really care for them. My heart wasn't in it. Since Julia told me she's pregnant, I've been thinking that I'd like to meet someone. I do want to be happy again, but it's really hard to leave the past behind. I went on a date the other day actually, a total wanker, but it did the job, broke the ice. On *Swipe Right*, they properly match you up. It's like finding a soulmate over again. How can you have two soulmates?'

'Do you know what, Milly? I think this is exactly what you need. You don't need people to set you up on countless dates when you're not ready – one-night stands causing more pain than pleasure. You need to feel ready yourself and to find someone to ease you in. If you meet the right person, taking it slow won't be an issue. It's possible to have two soulmates because it depends on what you need at the time when you meet them. It's not about replacement but about coexistence.'

I took note of what Florry said and travelled to the meeting point without my crutches. Unfortunate, because I can't remember the last time they showed a crutch on TV with a garter tied around it and it would have done buckets for feminism. I can kind of walk without them if I delicately put my foot down and try not to bear more than 50 per cent of my weight on it. You have to suffer to be beautiful, don't they say? I also took her advice and wore jeans – she's right, my leg is unattractive. I think I pulled off half the scab while I was trying to squeeze my trunk into them, but beggars can't be choosers.

It's a good job I blocked Adam, otherwise I would be doubly nervous. What if the three dots did suddenly start whirring again and he sent me some encrypted message from the grave? I know it sounds crazy, but *you never know*.

I'm ushered to sit in a room with all the other singletons. There's enough alcohol in here to get even the five thousand tipsy, and of course, to make sure we don't act all coy and shy in the background. Ever wanted to know what creates that loud, buzzing atmosphere on a TV show set in a restaurant? Cheap Sauvignon plonk is the answer.

I spent ages doing my make-up, watching a YouTube video so I could get the perfect definition on my brows and outline my lips so neatly it was as if they had been stencilled. Naturally, I take a selfie.

Lottie's here. 'That's my girl, Milly,' she shouts at me, waving as I drink a glass of wine way too quickly and put my phone back in my jean pocket.

I sit at the table waiting for my date. My palms are sweaty. I feel like I'm in an Eminem song. I might even need a nervous poo. My safety ring is burning through my pocket onto my upper thigh. I can't pull the engagement card on a TV show, and I *want* to be here. Fresh starts and all that jazz. *I'm excited. I'm excited. I'm excited.*

Lorenzo (as Florry aptly put it, the DILF host) stands at the front of the room. I look around blearily, the lights are bright, and I've drunk I don't know how much wine. I feel like I'm about to be interrogated. Is that Theo in the corner? He waves at me with a cheeky grin.

'Ciao, ma bellas and bellos! How wonderful to see London's most glamorous singletons!' He grins, a full set of pearly whites, his Daz-white shirt blinding against his bronzed skin. 'Welcome to *Swipe Right* – your favourite dating app in real life. Our team have carefully selected three partners for your three ten-minute slots – one perfect match and two out-the-box. You choose if you want a second date if you . . .' He holds his hands in the air, palms towards the ceiling, encouraging a chorus.

'Swipe Right!' we all shout.

A bell rings, signalling it's finally time for me to meet my match.

'Hi. Liam. Twenty-eight. Live in Kennington with two housemates – Joe and Steven. I've got a pug called Pigme. Work in a fintech start-up. You?' he reels in an Usain Bolt interpretation of a sentence, holding one finger up for every additional fact.

'Hi, Liam.' I smile and stick out my hand. 'Milly.'

'Sorry,' he says, shaking his head, realising that he barely drew breath. 'It's only ten minutes and I panicked. First impressions and everything. You know?'

The awkward to-ing and fro-ing continues. Liam's a sweet guy but that's it – he's like sugar on a bowl of Cinnamon Grahams. He talks about work, his friends, what he's doing at the weekend. I smile because I'm on TV, but I don't laugh.

The bell rings and I swipe left. Fortunately, so Liam does the same. I see a girl with blonde waves, wearing chinos and know she's exactly the girl for Liam – I imagine she has a list of attributes that she can uniformly mentally tick off as Liam reels his introduction.

The bell rings again to signal date number two.

'Edmund.' He holds out a hand to shake – much easier than offering a cheek to kiss for a stranger. 'Milly.' I shake his slightly sweaty palm.

'Shall we?' He passes me a Jäger bomb that he brought to the table from the bar and recites 'One, two, three . . . Bomb squad!' and we down them. The liquorice-and-aniseed mix sits in my stomach, reminding me of university and fun.

Edmund's funny – or I'm drunk. He's a bit toffy, but he's a laugh. He presents himself well, like a sandwich in Marks and Spencer. His parents have a house in Cornwall, and he likes surfing, which is a skill you learn if your parents have money. I learned to run because it's free. I bet

I could have sex with him if I wanted, but I wonder if I'd want to see him again after. Edmund could be my match, but I'm not 100 per cent sure. The conversation seems a bit forced, or maybe it's me. I'm pretending I enjoy running around on a Saturday with activity after activity, but in reality, I prefer hungover days on the sofa, eating pizza and crunching Doritos.

I recoil, thinking about 6 a.m. wake-ups with Edmund, surfing on the beach, hikes in the mountains and him thinking I'm weird for eating fruit on pizza. I swipe left, Edmund swipes right. It's nice to be wanted.

The bell rings again, but this time Lorenzo comes out.

'Ladies, gentlemen – it's starting to feel a little hot and steamy in here.' He winks at the sea of drunk girls and guys – it's not sexy perspiration, it's alcohol sweats and nerves. 'Some of our team will be popping by to freshen you all up a little.'

I look around and see Theo waving at me, beckoning me over. This is the last thing I need: me, a desperate singleton on a lame dating show, and Theo, the cool media guy who gets to watch us all fail miserably and then recount stories to his dickhead friends like Kevin.

A young girl with a name badge that reads, *Hattie*, comes over and pops some powder on my face and gives my hair a little zhuzh.

'How are you finding it?' Theo asks me, smiling, his dimples so deep I wonder if he could pop a Malteser in each one.

'I dunno. It's a bit cringe, but kind of fun, I guess,' I respond, trying to act cool.

'Did you enjoy the tales of Liam's baby called Pigme?' He laughs.

'Ha, did he already tell you about her? Sounded like a real catch. I think I'd rather date her.'

'Yeah, he thinks women are attracted to men with dogs.'

'I think it depends on the dog.' I laugh. 'A little pug called Pigme doesn't scream "sexual magnet" – I imagine it's the kind of dog Ricky Gervais has.'

Theo laughs.

'Milly.' Theo suddenly looks awkward; the right dimple goes skewwhiff. 'Would you want to grab a bite to eat after this? I finish in about twenty minutes, just before the final date – the last chance to "swipe right" with any of your matches. It's OK if you don't!' He suddenly adds. 'But we've got a lot to catch up on, you know, all the housemate stalking, why you chose Kevin, etc?' He winks.

'I'd love to!' I reply, probably a little too quickly.

'Great!' His right dimple goes back to a Malteser-sized cavern. 'Meet me outside in about twenty minutes!'

I walk back to my little table feeling a little giddy. Lorenzo introduces us to our third date and what happens next, the bell rings and another male suitor sits in front of me.

'Hi, I'm Justin!' The most eager beaver I've ever seen sits in front of me. He's grinning like a maniac, like someone's lined his gums with ecstasy. 'How are you finding it all? Good? It's really an amazing experience, isn't it?' He continues talking, so I wouldn't be able to respond even if I wanted to.

I'm pleased I have a chatterbox for a third date. I feel bad, I should give Justin a chance. He could be my match – maybe it wasn't Edmund, but all I can think about is Theo.

'You're a lovely girl, Milly,' Justin says, almost pleading with me like a puppy with a bone as I decide to swipe left and take my date with Theo as fourth-time lucky – a bonus date for the day.

'Thanks, Justin, so are you. I'm just not really in a good place,' I lie. That would have been the case, a standard Milly response, a few weeks ago. The truth is I'm ecstatic about going on a date with Theo.

I meet Theo outside and we walk towards a little Korean restaurant about two minutes away that he said does the best bibimbap in London and I simply must try it.

'Are you OK walking?' Theo asks me as I limp next to him – it's so unattractive. Why did I have to get hit by a car?

'It's better than it was. Don't worry, I can walk normally – you've not been leg-fished. It's still sore, but I need to get used to walking on it.'

'I'm glad to hear you're on the mend. You can tell me more about your fetish for walking in front of moving cars when we sit down for dinner. Just try not to do it tonight, OK? I'm not good with roadkill.'

We laugh and Theo grabs the door of the restaurant.

He pulls my stool out for me at the high wooden table, and we sit pondering the menu.

'I'm not going to be one of those twat guys that orders for you, don't worry. I've had the pork belly and the chicken one. I've never had the beef or the veggie, so I can't comment, but I'm sure it's also incredible.'

'I'll have the pork belly then if you recommend it,' I say, pushing the fact that I'm supposed to be vegetarian to the back of my mind. 'And I'll get an Asahi beer,' I add. Adam's favourite, but also mine.

'Asahi? I love that beer. I'll copy you.' He smiles and goes up to the bar to place our order.

Theo and I chit-chat about everything while we wait for our food – university, his career, my job, where we live, yadda yadda. It's not awkward at all.

'You were right,' I say, my mouth full. 'This pork belly is delicious.'

'Right?' He smiles back, taking a swig of beer before ordering two more bottles.

'Milly, may I ask you something?'

There is only one thing this could be so early on.

'You mean about Kevin?'

'Yes – he told me that he went on a date with you, and you were actually engaged, hence why he never saw you again.'

I wince at the embarrassment.

'It's a bit cringe, but all girls have their tricks. Mine was a fake ring I bought.'

I can't tell him the real story yet – it's too early and I barely know him.

He laughs. 'Running in front of cars, fake diamond rings – who are you, Milly Dayton?'

'You'll have to find out,' I reply, half flirting, half wondering who I really am myself.

Theo pays the bill. I did offer, but he insisted.

We stand outside, waiting for our respective Ubers. Theo is a real gentleman – he didn't even try the we-could-share-a-cab trick.

'You know, I've never really met someone like you before, Milly. You're just so you, and I don't even know who you really are yet.'

I smile inside myself before taking a breath. 'I haven't met someone who's allowed me to be just me, since . . .' I pause. 'For a long time.'

He takes my hand, and we stand in silence for a bit.

'You've got nice hands,' I say, admiring them. 'Like perfect side plates.'

Theo laughs loudly. 'That sounds like something my mother would say.'

'And mine.' I laugh back. I feel something warm inside. Standing in the darkness, holding Theo's hand, I feel safe.

Theo gives my hand a little squeeze as I note the Uber's numberplate, calling it out as if it's in a bingo hall.

Theo starts laughing again. 'See you soon then, Milly' and Theo moves his body towards me and embraces me in a *real-life romantic kiss just like they do in the movies*!

Can you hear someone else's heart beating? If so, mine sounds like that gorilla playing the drums on the Dairy Milk advert but not so rhythmic.

I've kissed boys since Adam, but this one feels different. For the first time in ages, I haven't spent the whole evening thinking about Adam, going to the bathroom to secretly scroll. I enjoyed speaking to Theo, and I enjoyed kissing him too.

@Mizzennial I can't believe it. I met a boy in real life and he wasn't a sixty-year-old man! I feel like Cinderella and I've just met Prince Charming – I've got a bit of a limp at the moment, so I even left the date as if I was wearing only one glass slipper. I kissed him goodbye and departed feeling over the moon. But what now? I'm so confused? Do I text him first? Should I wait for him to text me? Did I dream that we kissed? Are we dating/ seeing each other/night-time frolickers? What next?! I have gone from hero to zero in a matter of convoluted minutes!

@ShelleyFarrell Text him. If he doesn't like you, he isn't worth it.

@ILikeMyMenHotAndBlack No, wait! He should text you – the guy should always make the first move.

@TitsOut4Follows Show me your tits and I'll tell you what to do.

I tipsily message Julia and fall asleep.

Me: You'll never believe it but I ended up kissing one of the guys who works on *Swipe Right* – he's so dreamyyy! Thanks soooo much for setting me up on it. Soooo pleased about my bestie being a mum2be. Love yoooooooo xxxxxx

It's way past midnight – probably 4 a.m. I've been lying awake for hours. Why do I feel so guilty? I've kissed boys since Adam. I've fucked boys since Adam. I enjoyed kissing Theo. I keep tossing and turning and crying. Why did you put me in this situation? What am I supposed to do?! All I want to do is be with you, but I can't. I must move on. Stop making me feel like shit.

All I can see is his face zooming in and out of my consciousness. *Why did you block me? What have I ever done to you? How dare you move on? Why are you leaving me, Milly?*

I'm a horrible person. I don't have any morals. I don't have a soul. I don't have a heart. That's why no one loves me. Violet must have been wrong. You can't have two soulmates.

Am I destined to be alone? Was that what was supposed to happen? Show me what love feels like and then never let me have it again. It's like having sugar for the first time; once you've tasted it, you can't imagine life without it.

I go on Facebook, unblock him and scroll. The pictures become blurry through my tears. I don't fixate on anything, just the need and urge to be near him.

What am I doing?

This isn't really Adam. Just like my Facebook page isn't really me. It's a page of things that he wanted people to see, comments that his friends wanted him to see, photos that I wanted him to see. I know this isn't the real Adam, because I knew him. It's just the cold eeriness of a curated selection of the perfect life of someone who once walked the Earth. But it wasn't perfect, because he got cancer and died. Where's that on the timeline then?

I block him again and throw my phone on the floor.

'I'm sorry I don't understand that,' blurts Siri.

'Neither do fucking I.'

8 August 2017

I drag my heavy feet and heart along the cold, sanitised, life-less floors of the stark white corridor. And stop outside his room, number 334.

I've been here every day, but I knew it was time when his mum called me and told me to come in earlier than usual.

My eyes are constantly puffy from crying myself to sleep and crying myself awake. I want to wake up from this night-mare, but then I remember this is real life, and it's shit. All my zest for life has been zapped away and my body is a walking casket with no soul.

I hold his right hand and he looks me in the eye. I clench his fingers while they hang loosely in mine. His eyes waver and shut again. He mouths, 'I love you, little daff.'

I see Layla holding her brother's hand, crying uncontrollably, Adam's mum, Amanda, squeezing her shoulders. A family unit that I'm not part of.

The monitor goes flat, my mum puts her hand on my shoulder. 'It's time,' she says.

I squeeze the last second of life from his right hand and kiss his dehydrated lips one last time. I think a piece of me, if not the whole of me, just died too.

'Sleep tight, my angel.'

The tears are streaming down my face. I can barely see. My heart is in pieces. I don't know what to do with myself. Do I smash my fists on the floor, run outside, curl in a ball? My mum goes to hold my hand, but I don't want to be near anyone. I don't want any comfort. I want to hurt. I need to be alone.

I run outside the ward and into the car park, light a ciga-rette, tip my head towards the sky and shout, '*Give me cancer then, you fucking cunt.*'

Adam once told me that bad things happen to good people, and that's part of life. It can't be helped. But it should have been me who got sick. I asked for it.

I fall in a ball on the hot tarmac of the car park, tears streaming down my face. Mum runs towards me from the hospital's revolving doors. I want her to hug me and tell me everything will be all right. I want to be loved again. I want Adam back. I miss him already. How can a few minutes without him already seem like a lifetime?

I feel Mum rush beside me, pulling me in for a tight embrace, kissing my head and stroking my hair. I crumple like a baby, softening in her arms. Love me. Just love me.

19

3 March 2019

My eyes are open, but my body is still asleep. I feel like I've run twenty marathons. Nightmares of Adam, night sweats, my thoughts running frantically, trying to get away from whatever it is that was haunting them. I feel like today is a non-day. I can feel the urine in my bladder begging to be let out, but I cannot move from my bed.

Julia's responded to my text, which I now feel annoyed about sending after staying awake half the night regretting the entire evening. I'm so exhausted, I can barely lift my phone to look at her message. The phone light burns my bleary eyes.

Julia: Ooh, tell me all! What was he like? Was he fit? Are you hangy? X

It's these kinds of things that make it clear to me why I can't message Layla. Imagine meeting her after I'd been out snogging random guys. Imagine!

'Morning, Milly! How are you feeling today?'

'Honestly? Terrible.' I look it too; my hair's scraped back into a greasy bun, my face is puffy and my eyes are bleary.

'Did something awful happen on your date?' Violet suddenly looks concerned. 'You know you can tell me anything.'

'No, he was really lovely, and we kissed. That's the problem.' I sigh. Why does life have to be so complicated?

Violet remains silent.

'I felt really good about it until I was lying in bed, and all I could see was Adam's face. I felt so guilty. How can I be out dating when I was supposed to be with him forever?' It feels like I am doing him and us such a dishonour. I should be staying locked inside, not having any fun. Doing penance for his loss. 'I don't think you can have two soulmates,' I add, pondering the words of our previous conversations.

'One of the hardest things with grief is moving on. It's so common that people feel guilty about it. Don't you think that Adam would want you to move on? It sounds like he really loved you. He would want you to do whatever made you happy. You're not devaluing your relationship with him by meeting someone else. Maybe if you tell the person about your past, then they will understand.'

'Of course, he'd want me to happy – he was the most caring person in the world.' I look away from my laptop screen to the ring in my hand.

'Do you think that is part of the reason you've been spending so much time on social media? You've not been allowing yourself to have fun? It sounds like you've been wanting to, watching all the fun that everyone else is having through a screen, but been preventing yourself from having it.'

It's always the same when I have nightmares. You gradually find yourself again as the day moves on and the night-time becomes a distant memory. Violet makes me feel better too, like I'm not going mad and it is 'normal', whatever that may be.

I call Nicky for a welcome distraction.

'Hey, babes.'

'How did *Swipe Right* go?!' she bellows down the phone.

'Well, the guys were all a bit wet, to be honest. One guy had a pug called Pigme, and the other was one of those guys that has to be constantly entertained.'

'Not even worthy of a quick drink and a passionate snog outside the recording studio? I've always fancied myself as a dog mum.'

'Trust me, no. The guy who worked on set was much fitter.'

'Tell me you at least got *his* number?' Nicky pleads.

'Well, actually, we went on a date, and we kissed.'

'*Shut up!*'

'He was a great kisser – not sloppy where it looks like you've eaten a tub of Vaseline, and not that awkward tongue thrust that people sometimes do.'

'Tongue thrust? Vaseline face? What frogs have you been kissing?'

'I can't decide whether to message him or not. Help me! I really liked him, but I don't want to be a keeno. What would you do?' Nicky: the master of dating.

'I think, do whatever you want. Everyone's always playing games these days. Some people must be real. You haven't got anything to lose.'

'Yeah, but what if he thinks I'm a freak for messaging so soon?'

'Well, if you're a freak, you need to find your own freak to match.'

'Yeah, I guess so.'

'I'm so sorry, babes, but I have to go. I'm running really late. I've got a date with this guy who's into axe-throwing. I'm not sure if that's weird or kinky, but I'll soon find out.'

'Oh, OK.'

'Sounds intriguing, doesn't it?'

'I guess in a slightly murderous way. Love you, speak soon.'

Fuck it, I'm going to send Theo a text. I need to move on, and he was a good kisser.

Me: Hey Theo, had so much fun yday, hope you did too! My head is a bit sore today! X

My head isn't sore, but if I did say something embarrassing, he'll think I was drunk. Casual. Hopefully he won't leave me on read too long.

I'm not really the religious type, but desperate times call for desperate measures. I get down on one knee, clasp my hands together and try my hardest to telepathically communicate to an extraterrestrial being, known to some as God.

Please, please, please let Theo message me back.

It'll be so disheartening if he doesn't now. He treated me on a level playing field. He didn't ask me to send a picture of my tits, or insinuate that he wanted to sleep with me. He treated me as an equal, as a human being. But he's probably messaging loads of other girls, anyway. Most boys do.

@Mizzennial I went on a date with someone last night and I had the best time! When I got home, I felt so guilty. It wasn't like other dates where I either wasn't in the mood or the guy was a dick; he was too nice – that was the problem. I lay awake half the night worrying, but I woke up and spoke to my counsellor and she said, 'I'm not devaluing my relationship by meeting someone else' and it really stuck. So, I wanted to share that advice with anyone who is feeling the same. X

I feel like I've always been different. That said, being a widow is the ultimate differentiation factor in the entirety of life. All girls nowadays have fillers, Botox, hair extensions, microblading, dermaplaning, blah, blah, blah. As soon as I was in a relationship, I didn't care about that kind of stuff. Sometimes I wouldn't shave my legs for weeks – Adam didn't mind. I wouldn't dare let Theo or any other boy for that matter, stroke my stubble. Embarrassing. That's a delight for six months in; the gradual evolution of dolphin to gorilla. When

I was dating, I'd have less body hair than a Barbie; now I'm a widow, I'm lucky if I even use deodorant. Waxing is a thing of the past, and if I saw a pair of tweezers nowadays, I'd probably eat them.

Anyway, I know now that if I'm back in the dating game, I cannot let myself go. It's imperative that I make an effort. I'm having a DIY pamper night. It'll be like an episode of *Stars in Their Eyes* – 'Tonight, Matthew, I'm going to be. . . beautiful. Hopefully.'

I open up KimLeFaye's YouTube 'Warming Oat Facemask For Baby-soft Skin' and get to work. Her skin's already gleaming like a mirror. I'm sure the weekly microdermabrasions and Botox play a part, but clearly Quaker's Oats do too.

I get to work, smashing avocado and mixing it with almond milk, honey and oats before slathering it over my face. It sounds like something the Kardashians would eat for lunch, but I'm so fat I put it on my face instead. I even chop two slices of cucumber to give my eyes a little *je ne sais quoi*.

Ahh, time to sit back and relax. A little me time.

Dum di dum. I twiddle my fingers. I tap them on my legs. Dum di dum.

Fuck it. I'm not made for relaxing. I rip off the two pieces of cucumber and shove them in my mouth.

I carefully wax around the two slithery slug trails I call eyebrows and pop some dark brown dye on them. Leave for five minutes – much more my kind of timescale. Adam always said I was terrible at relaxing. He said, and I quote, '*Every time you say you are going to have a night of relaxing, I feel like I'm teetering on a cliff edge, waiting for you to realise for the hundredth time that you hate relaxing and break down in some sort of fit of rage.*'

Five minutes to catch up with my Mizzennial crew. I 'press' post on my new questionnaire: 'How millennial are you? You chose mostly *A*s) You're so bacon; mostly *B*s) Total frozé hosé; mostly *C*s) You're a placid pizza'

New DM:

@KonundrumKate @Mizzennial We all know that the only certainty in life is death, so why is it so hard?

I sit and ponder. Why is it?

@Mizzennial @KonundrumKate There's nothing easy about death. If we spent our whole life thinking about it, we wouldn't do any living. We all speak about life so much, everyone's afraid of death. I think it needs to be spoken about more, or we need to share more stories to help people come to terms with it, or at least, not feel so embarrassed speaking about it. I don't have an answer for you, I'm afraid. It's never going to be easy but there are people around to speak to. X

Fuck, my brows!

Dark brown dye had bled all over my skin, joining my two brows – I look like Frida Kahlo but angrier.

I frantically type, 'How do you get eyebrow dye off your skin?'

Mumsnet has the answer to everything, and I cover my forehead in toothpaste until I smell like a Mentos factory.

Adam was right. I'm terrible at pampering and relaxing.

I need coffee or even one of Adam's hot chocolates with all the trimmings and enough whipped cream so I can dip my nose in it.

'What the fuck happened to you?' This seems to be a standard greeting from @ILikeMyMenHotAndBlack.

'Honestly, don't ask. I was dying my eyebrows and I forgot about the dye.'

'Pahahahahaha.' She guffaws. 'You should be a walking advertisement for Veet!' She peers closer at my new look. 'Funny how eyebrows really make your face.'

'I look permanently angry – I'll never be happy again!' I joke.

She puts a coffee down in front of me and waives the charge.

'Won't you get in trouble for this?' I point towards the bucket of coffee.

'That? No. Do you think Starbucks have time to do an inventory on milk levels and coffee beans? They don't care – just another conglomerate with oodles of cash.' She busies herself with retying her hair up into a ponytail. 'Anyway, tell me how Mizzennial's been going. I was thinking maybe you should do a meet-up or something?'

'Yeah, I know, but that would involve me telling everyone I'm behind it.' I've been widow Milly for so long, being something else takes me one step further away from Adam. It's confusing. I want to be the new Milly, but I don't want to forget Adam. People know me as Milly the grieving widow; if I'm not that, people might think I don't care any more.

'Yes, but that isn't a bad thing. You're very talented. You should be proud of who you are. It doesn't need to be a big thing, just slip it into one of the posts – you need to take credit for your work!'

'Hmm, OK, I'll think about.' I take a sip of my coffee and spill it all down my front and over my chin.

I return to some comments on my latest post:

@**Rouge6879** Never feel guilty for being who you are! Nothing was your fault, you are just learning to deal with it

@**LeafMeOutOfIt** Why don't you talk to this new guy about it, tell him how you feel? There are some nice men out there. . . #needleinahaystack

Grief is one of those unchartered territories that we all know we will one day discover, but we don't know when, or how, or why.

Before I met Violet, I never spoke about Adam, not really. I was nervous that people would expect me to forget him and move on with my life. I didn't want to burden others with my grief, or even share it with them. He was all mine. No one can be more upset than me. No one can even imagine what I was going through.

But I was wrong. Everyone who I've spoken to has been so understanding.

@ILikeMyMenHotAndBlack had some good advice. Maybe I should do a meet-up. I could meet @ShelleyFarrell and see if she's who she says she is. It would give me a taste of who's really behind the Instagram handles I engage with every day.

@ShelleyFarrell Keen for that meet-up – name your day!

I scroll on Layla's Instagram, suddenly caught up in the past. I see photos of us together, of Adam, of her friends, people I met at lunches, dinners, parties. It all seems so alien now that we used to share that life. Nicky said she missed her. I think I miss her too but there are some people who being around makes it feel like reliving his death all over again.

It's hard to break down the barrier that I've created for myself. It's so much easier to disassociate myself with that life, remove all the shared friends we had, his family and just focus on progressing myself.

Maybe I'll decide to let her back in, maybe I won't, but it's up to me.

2 February 2018

I came into work today, as everyone says it's important to keep yourself busy. Today's an important day for me, but for everyone else around me, it's just another fucking Wednesday. The world's passing me by, and no one cares what is going on inside my head or what is happening to me. They care about new handbags, shopping and which Instagrammable location they are going to drink dry tonight.

I want to take some time and remember Adam and his last birthday, but I can't. If I want to move on and be happy then I cannot, *must not*, remember the past. As soon as his smiling face starts to seep into my subconscious, I bash it away with swearing and screaming. It's impossible to be happy and remember; if anyone tells you otherwise, then they're a liar.

My Instagram feed is filled with girls promoting Chanel bags, friends of friends getting engaged, planning weddings, holidays to far-flung places and açai bowls. Nothing important. Most days, it feels like escapism, but today it feels like the devil's teasing me.

No messages from friends because even though his eerie page still exists on Facebook, Adam deleted his birthday from it a long time ago. People didn't remember it when he was alive, let alone now he's dead.

'Milly, I need you to write up the minutes from the Albanian country toolkit meeting. Didn't I ask you to do that last week? Remember your review is coming up soon.'

Fuck off, Marjorie. It is the anniversary of my dead husband's birthday. Give me some space.

'Yep. Will get that done.'

Ping.

Jemima: It's the final day for the money pool for Hayley's moving to New York gift. Milly, you are still left to pay. Can you send me this today?

Me: Sure.

What's more important than money? Nothing.
Ping.

Mum: Thinking of you today, darling. If it is today, you know what I'm like with birthdays.

Yes, it's *today*, Mum. It's fucking today.

I get up from my desk and go outside. I'm instantly hit by the smell of London pollution, the beep of horns and sirens, the hustle and bustle of life.

I start walking, one foot in front of the other. I can't stop. I know I will get in trouble at work, but who cares? My mind seems unaware of the destination, but my legs seem sure of it.

Finally, I stand at the entrance to the London Eye, where we spent last year's birthday together, unaware of what the future held.

The memories of that day flood my mind, I can't stop them. My eyes overflow with tears, my body contorting with the pain, my arms shaking, my legs jelly. This isn't one of my nightmares, it's real life.

I can't lay flowers on his grave because it's in Hampshire, where his family's from, not in London, where we lived together.

I want a spot to remember him by. A place of love and happiness, not a grave with worms crawling out of his eyes and maggots in his ears. I walk over to the riverbank, take off one of my rings and throw it into the Thames. I would make a wish, but they clearly don't come true.

20

4 March 2019

Theo has responded to my message – *finally*. He wants to go on another date tonight. I still look like, now merely slightly annoyed, Frida Kahlo. I've delayed it by four days, hopefully my brows have calmed by then.

I'm currently lying on my bed, with my phone at arm's length in the air.

Homies & Hoes is pinging off this morning!

Julia: Oh my gawdddd! She's kicking!

Julia sends a video of her moving tummy.

Nicky: adorable!
Me: Does it hurt? It looks like an alien's squirming around in there!
Julia: It does hurt a little bit.
Me: How do you know it's a girl?
Julia: I paid shit tons of money to get an early blood test.
Nicky: How are you having a baby when I'm still drunk from last night?

She sends a snapshot of herself in bed with a random guy. How's Nicky so carefree?

Me: Guess what? I'm seeing Theo again!

Julia: YASSS, Milly! Do you know where he's taking you?
Me: No, not yet. I've asked him to surprise me.
Nicky: You better get a wax in case you shag.
Me: I don't know if I'm ready for sex yet, but you're right, I do need a wax.
Nicky: It's better to just stay waxed – you never know when it's going to creep up on you. Anyway, I've got to go. José's pestering me for round two. Love ya!

I click off WhatsApp and head straight to Instagram to help other people who also don't have a handsome stranger in their bed.

God, @JanieJane35 you poor thing. I type back, trying to be as consoling as possible about her forwarding a dick pic to her granny #cringe.

Apart from this morning, I've barely looked at my phone today. What's up with me? By *barely*, I mean one and a half hours down on my five-hour screen time – I'm no nun yet. It's finally time for me to meet the mysterious @ShelleyFarrell at my local caffeine addiction centre.

@ILikeMyMenHotAndBlack props me up in a window seat and pops my usual down in front of me.

'You look better, almost happy again, apart from a dark shadow.'

'Ha! I did put some concealer on to cover the dye.'

'I said better not perfect.'

A girl comes ploughing through the front door, darting her eyes round the room. I look towards the commotion; that must be @ShelleyFarrell. At least I hope so – it's weird having a blind-friend-date.

I cautiously put my hand in the air, trying to capture her attention. Her eyes lock with my hand, and she gingerly waves back.

'Are you . . . ?'

'Yes, Milly.' I stand up, smiling with my hand out. Adam always said that shaking hands shows confidence.

'Phew. Shelley,' she replies, although by this point it's pretty obvious who she is. 'It does make you nervous, doesn't it? Meeting someone for the first time.' We both sit down.

'I know shaking hands is a bit formal, but I didn't really know what else to do.'

She laughs. 'I didn't know if you were the kissing type, and waving across the table seems a bit kindergarten.'

'Well, nice to meet you!' I exclaim. 'I can't believe I'm meeting someone who follows my account – totally surreal!'

'I love it – I just knew we would be really similar!'

@ShelleyFarrell orders a coffee and @ILikeMyMen-HotAndBlack brings them over.

'I feel like you're doing something so new on Instagram.' @ShelleyFarrell sips her coffee and licks her lips. 'Unboxing designer bags, boasting about your wealth, your holidays and giving advice about gifts for your boyfriend – it's so . . .' She waves her hand in the air before exploding. '*Boring!* Everyone else's Instagram is all about how they look, and yours is about how you feel. It's iconic. You must feel so special, helping so many people about real things, not waxing lyrical about how important an oatmeal blazer is for summer – give me fucking strength!'

I snort with laughter – I like @ShelleyFarrell. She's funny.

'Thanks!' I beam. 'It's nice receiving compliments from strangers, not that you're a complete stranger, but you know. It's so crazy to think we met on Instagram and now here you are, exactly as you described yourself.'

'Compliments from strangers are a rare thing, I'll have you know!' She nods knowingly.

'At least you weren't a catfish.' That would have really fucked me up.

'Per-lease, the biggest catfishes online are influencers. I stopped following them all a few months ago. I kept trying to look like them all the time, and then I found that as I was getting more and more "modern-day beautiful", I began getting trolled. Started receiving negative comments – it was horrible. I tried getting rid of Instagram entirely, but I couldn't – I enjoy keeping up with all my friends and seeing what they were doing.' I nod in agreement; I know what she means. 'I made a pact to myself, so now I only follow friends and accounts that make me laugh. I wanted to see if you were a real, nice person. I stopped having Botox, even stopped going to the gym every day, and you know what? I feel EVEN better!' She grabs a roll of fat on her stomach and shakes it, laughing.

'Oh wow. That takes some commitment. I'm sorry you were trolled – that can't be nice for anyone. I kind of forgot about that side of social media. Don't worry, I'm not a troll, although sometimes I look like one after a night out!'

'Ha, don't we all! Please tell me *everything* about Mizzennial – I absolutely love it.' She leans in and slaps her hands on the table.

We sit and chat for at least an hour. It's like @ShelleyFarrell has just walked out of my phone screen as a ready-made friend; she's exactly how I imagined but, a few months ago, I'd never have had the guts to speak to her normally.

I told @ShelleyFarrell about Adam. I already told her what happened anonymously through a screen and now I'm just backing it up in person. I guess I feel like if she had already judged me, she wouldn't have turned up here today.

'I am really sorry to hear about Adam, Milly. I can't even imagine how tough that must have been for you, and I thought my trolling was bad.'

'No, you shouldn't compare problems. Everyone's problems are important in their own way – that's something important I've learned. But thank you, I appreciate it,' I say, smiling. There's nothing truer than that.

'I run a podcast, you know, called *Talk Thirty To Me*. I speak to girls in their late twenties, early thirties about issues they face. It would be wonderful if you felt up to coming on the show and speaking about your experiences?'

I feel my heart skip a beat and a wave of anxiety bubbling in my throat.

'Thanks, Shelley, but I'm not sure if I'm ready for that yet. Maybe one day, but not right now.'

Telling @ShelleyFarrell is no different to telling everyone that follows me on Mizzennial or doing a podcast, I suppose, but that still feels too scary. To tell everyone it's me, the widow of Adam Hadfield, still riddled with grief but gradually coming into her own, feels odd. I haven't come to terms with it yet, so I don't expect anyone else to. People might judge me, troll me, because they don't really know me, they just know a voice behind a screen. I feel like I'm able to trust @ShelleyFarrell, her telling me that she was trolled felt like her big secret, so I was able to share mine.

That's what I'm like for everyone who sends in their problems: the big secret keeper. Maybe everyone has demons.

'Do you know what, Milly? I think this is the first time I've seen you properly smiling! Tell me *everything*!' Violet's eyes widen and her face is beaming, mirroring mine.

'Well, I met up with a girl who I'd been speaking to on my channel, and she was exactly as I expected. *And* a guy came up to me and said I was beautiful. That hasn't happened for years, if ever. *And* I have a second date.' I reel off my list of positivity, not stopping for breath.

'Well, I never, Milly. There's definitely something different about you, your aura maybe. Positivity attracts positivity.'

'I did also have a pamper night.' Glowing skin and a glowing mind, it's a match made in heaven.

When we're done, I close the chat and break into a rendition of 'Don't Stop Me Now', complete with Roger Taylor on the drums.

18 October 2017

It's been over a month since Adam passed away. I mean died. Adam died. *Passed away* makes it sound like it was something relaxing, like he decided to have a long sleep in a bed of flowers. There was nothing therapeutic about Adam's death; it was ugly. It involved him puking every day, not being able to keep liquids down, dehydration so bad he could only drink through a drip. In the end, he couldn't even go to the toilet by himself – he shat in a bag in his bed – something that I thought was only acceptable after doing fifty shots of sambuca. It involved crying, distress, starvation. The love was there but hidden under sagging skin, thinning blood and changing bags. We didn't make love, but I know it was there. I still feel it now, aching in my bones.

Sometimes I feel relief. Adam's in a much better place, one where he doesn't feel embarrassed about what happened to him, one where he has his dignity back. Then I feel angry. How can I feel relieved that the love of my life has died? I'm a disgusting person.

Julia organised a night out for Nicky and I. She wants me to get back to feeling myself again. After all, Adam's been dead six weeks now – I should be well on my way to being married and my womb should be filled with another man's sperm.

Julia feels awkward around me. Everyone does. Julia's stopped mentioning James. I'm not stupid. I know that just because my husband died doesn't mean everyone else's did, but I appreciate her thinking about me. Let's pretend that my life has stopped so everyone else's has to too. I know going out with me is a drag because I don't have anything fun to say. All I can do is ask everyone pressing questions about all the exciting things they've been up to while I've been drowning in my own tears, wearing one of Adam's jumpers for the last six weeks.

Come on, Milly, get that fake smile plastered on and have a wash so you don't stink of metabolised white wine and BO.

'You look fan-bloody-tastic, Milly!'

'Darling, your hair? How did you get it looking so shiny?'

Fake niceties. There is no amount of showering and scrubbing that can wash away the grey cloud of grief hanging over my heavy head. Do I appreciate it? I'm not sure if I do. Why do we live in a society where the only way to be socially acceptable is to lie? Even to your best friends.

'Thanks, guys. Tell me everything that has been going on. I want to know it all!' I exclaim, my smile already hurting my taut cheeks.

Julia and Nicky take it in turns to update me on their upbeat, young lives. I laugh in all the right places, but they could have been swearing and shouting in my face for the past half an hour and I would still react in the same way.

'So, err, what about you, Milly? You know, if there is anything we can do . . . ?'

Yes, you could dig to the bottom of Adam's grave, pull him out with your bare hands, clean him up and perform voodoo on him until his lungs fill with oxygen again. Sing happy songs into my ear every night so I stop having nightmares of cancer taking over my body and waking up in a cold sweat. Kiss me, hug me, hold me and tell me that it is going to be really hard, but one day it will improve while wiping away the salty tears that are sticking to my face every night. Stop me from wanting to stab my heart with a bread knife to ease the pain of heartache.

'Honestly, I am absolutely fine.' I smile towards them. 'Get us some shots, Nicky. I feel like getting fucked up.'

I don't remember the rest of the night. I wake up on Nicky's sofa, with sick in my hair. I look in the mirror and see my puffy face is black and blue. My back all bruised. Oh, and part of my tooth has vanished. When you are down, the world likes to make you really down. Never say 'it could be worse', because it always can be.

'You tried to run in front of a car last night, but you tripped over the pavement and knocked part of your tooth out instead,' Nicky says nonchalantly as she stands in the doorway in her pants with her breasts dangling down.

I poke my tongue through the black hole where my tooth used to be. Nostalgia can come in the strangest forms. I'm instantly transported back to being ten years old and waiting for the tooth fairy. Fleeting happiness.

'Fuck. Why didn't you try to stop me?'

'You seemed pretty set on it. You've never been good at aiming, anyway. You look hideous. Never stop going to the dentist.'

At least Adam isn't here to see me with a toothless grin. Ouch, I think the pavement's given me whiplash.

21

8 March 2019

I'm really enjoying our dedicated Zoom chats.

Violet has her hair piled up into some sort of bird's nest creeping down to her forehead and she has a lime-green plastic clip on the right of her head which says *Parrot*. Her style's eccentric, to say the least.

'I've been thinking about what you said to me last time – positivity breeds positivity! Before I met you, I could count on one hand the number of positive things that happened to me over the last *two years*! Now, I would need about ten hands for the last couple of weeks!'

Violet laughs knowingly.

'You pay me, Milly, not the other way around. You are completely in control of what you do. I'm just guiding you and here for moral support. Sounds like your happiness list must be getting rather long!'

'It's weird. If I had known therapy would have had these sorts of results, maybe I would have done it sooner. I kind of stopped doing the list – there's just too much to be happy about. The more that happens, the more I believe in myself again.'

'That's wonderful. It's all about timing, Milly. You need to be ready to open up, ready for change. I don't think you would have been before.'

'True.'

'Have you spoken to Adam much recently?'

'Not really. I've been speaking to lots of different people instead – it's quite nice, actually. Loads of people, in fact.'

'And have you found that you've been relying on social media less as well?'

'Yeah, I guess, I haven't really been thinking about it. Maybe I rely on it in a different way – I've been using it more for my Mizzennial channel, but I haven't been doing so much green-eyed stalking. There are loads of people out there who have problems – it's giving me confidence with my own. I've been giving out advice, and others have been advising me back. I know loads about death and grief, but nothing about dating boys. It's a win-win.'

'It seems to me like you are making progress, Milly. Social media was filling a void that was filled with real-life family and friends eighteen months ago. You didn't want to go out and see people any more – maybe you didn't know what to say to people?'

'I felt embarrassed. Embarrassed that I was still upset. I thought everyone expected me to be over his death. I've realised that although everyone else wasn't very good at knowing what to say, I wasn't either. Maybe I was to blame as much as them. I think a lot of it was in my head.'

'Have you been able to share more on your Mizzennial channel, you know, open up? Show people the real you?'

'I've definitely opened up more, but I haven't done the big reveal. Sometimes I don't feel like it's me giving the advice – it's like I'm having an out-of-body experience. Like we spoke about before, it's easy to say things and much harder to do.' I pause. 'It's joining the dots that I can be a widow and still be happy.'

'Everyone has a past. It shapes you, but it doesn't have to define you.' She's right, and it might be one of the wisest things she's ever said.

'True.'

'I wouldn't put too much pressure on yourself, Milly. Influencers show the world photos of themselves all the time, but they don't really show what's in the heart. You're showing people what's in the heart but not acquainting them with you yet. It's OK, you're not devaluing yourself, but it may be good to set yourself a goal of showing your true identity, one day, when you're ready.'

@DeathPeeve97 @Mizzennial I lost my dad a couple of weeks ago, and all anyone says to me is it will get better. There is nothing I find more annoying. How can it get better? He's dead.

I know exactly where she's coming from – there's nothing more annoying when you can't bear to see the light at the end of the tunnel. But it does get better. I'm living proof.

@Mizzennial @DeathPeeve97 I'm so sorry to hear that. I know what losing someone is like. I've learned that people find death awkward, and the only thing they know what to say is a promise that it will get better. I remember the sensations of losing a loved one: you feel like a stranger to yourself, every emotion you experience is new. Just allow yourself to feel like that until you feel able to feel something new again. Don't rush yourself. X

The more I think about tonight, the more I panic. I don't know how I should greet Theo. Should I kiss him straight away? Pull him in for a hug, or is that immediately friend-zoning him? Recite 'Sonnet 114'? Lie my naked, broken body in a bed of rose petals and ask him to eat sushi off me? Ahh, the perils and torment of dating in the twenty-first century.

Handshake? Guess that's too formal. But I think shoving my tongue down his throat is also way too much. I've only met him once. Well, technically twice, but the first time wasn't a date.

Hopefully, I'll be able to read his body language and mirror whatever he does.

Should I transfer money from my Premium Bonds in case he goes all Dutch on me? I like to think I'm all righteous and feminist and we should split the bill like equals, however, I don't have any money and am not in a position to have views like this.

I've made a list of conversation starters, in case things get awkward. Julia said that guys like talking about themselves and I don't want him to think I am self-obsessed or anything. I don't even know if I have anything interesting to talk about – I don't do anything that exciting. I could explain who is who on the most recent season of *Love Island*, the conspiracy behind the death of President Kennedy that I learned from Channel 5's new blockbuster documentary, or who I really think the killer in the latest *Silent Witness* is. Fuck. Come on, Milly, you're not seriously this tragic.

Hmm, what about some new content?

'I saw that Leeds made the premiership. Who do you support?' All boys like football and he won't feel threatened that I'm about to ruin all his future Saturdays by requesting brunch dates not chips and gravy at the stadium.

'Did you watch the latest tell-all Charlie-Brooker-style documentary on Netflix? The one where it demonstrates that everything we do as a human species is going to either a) cause us all to die, b) kill the planet, or c) make our children so fucked up we might as well have killed everyone, anyway?' We can debate the topic and Theo will think I'm all cool and opinionated.

'Wow, your job's so cool! How did you get into it?' Theo will feel really good about himself and proud that I admire his achievements, and everyone loves showing off.

'My favourite movie is *Layer Cake*, what's yours?' It isn't, but this is a guy's movie, and then Theo will start imagining cosy nights in watching action movies and eating pizza.

I can't decide whether to go for an edgy or a sexy outfit. Heels and mom jeans with a tight body, or trainers, teddy coat and ripped jeans? I can't fully remember his style. Oh shit, I can't wear heels, trainers will do. Fuck it, I will go for sexy, I guess – Soho sleek with sunglasses. Then maybe on the second date, I'll go more Croydon chic.

As if on cue, to ease my worried mind, Theo texts me.

Theo: Hey Milly, still up for tonight? I was thinking we could go to CandleLight for drinks and then I booked a table at Maïa for dinner at 8 – that sound OK? X

Has God come down to Earth for a day? That sounds like the best night of my life. I've been in a relationship before, clearly. I'm fully aware that it isn't all dinners, drinks, hot passionate evenings under the stars and PDA to the point of resuscitation – after six months, you're lucky if you get a finger in you before the pizza arrives from Sloppy Joe's. I don't care, I'm all here for a bit of wining and dining.

Sounds beaut. Look forward to seeing you later X

I've been waiting for this kind of treatment for a while. I scream and punch my hands in the air. And then it hits me. The reminders. Adam, again. How we used to go on dates to Pizza Express at university and eventually transitioned to fancy restaurants when we first moved to London on our graduate salaries, and even just the nights on the sofa at home eating takeaway and watching movies. All that love, all the learning about each other's lives, all those pivotal moments we shared that I have to repeat all over again with someone new. Not even a replacement love, an additional love.

@Mizzennial Is it possible to love two people at the same time? I am still infatuated with my past lover; I wasn't ready for it to end. I thought it would continue forever and ever, but then he died. Now I feel as if I am starting to like someone else, but how is that possible, when I am so deeply in love with my first love?

@TwoisBetterthanOne Take inspiration from everything around you. People get divorced when they still love their partner and eventually move on. Give yourself time to heal and one day you will be ready. Don't feel guilty, you're allowed to love again.

@LadyValentine This happened to me. Write down all the things you loved about him, the memories, your life, like a Valentine's card every day. You will never forget him, but he would want you to be happy.

'Hey Milly! You look beautiful,' Theo says as he stands up from the table and kisses me gently on my right cheek. I blush, suddenly flooded with emotion.

'Thanks, Theo, you don't look too bad yourself!' I don't want to sound too cringey, but he looks divine; if I was a cannibal, I'd eat him there and then. I struggle to slide onto the bench in an elegant fashion, before just giving up and slumping down. My jeans are a bit tight already and I haven't started eating. I feel like I'm getting an anxious bloat. Stop worrying, Milly! 'This place is amazing!'

'We came here once for work and not that many people seem to have heard of it. There are so many cool cocktails – I'm making it my mission to sample every one.'

A waiter heads over to our table, with two cocktail glasses of candyfloss perched on a silver tray. He places them onto the table and then pours a pink liquid over them both, disintegrating the perfect pink cloud.

'I hope you like candyfloss.' The old Milly would squeal and instantly whip out a phone to film the whole process, post it and wait for the affirmations from people she didn't know that this was cool. The new Milly sits and relishes the moment. Candyfloss cocktails with an attractive man – delicious.

Theo is one of the nicest guys I've ever met. Bar Adam, of course. He's attractive, funny, cool. I feel guilty when I squeak with glee as he tells me that his favourite movie is *Legally Blonde* – Adam never wanted to watch that with me. Everything I've always thought I wanted and . . . I think he likes me! I hope it's not too good to be true. We finish our drinks and I haven't even needed to use any of my conversation starters, which is great, as I don't even know if he supports Leeds, which he probably doesn't, as he lives in London. How stupid of me.

'You are really funny, Milly. I don't know why Kevin was being such a dick about you.'

'Some boys are just dicks. Has he been weird about you seeing me tonight?'

'Not really. I mean, he hasn't been overly happy about it, but I think it's just a bit strange. He is still under the impression that you are engaged, or some sort of deluded psychopath – like in one of those BBC drama series.'

I cough on my drink. 'Eurgh, what a wanker. I know he's your friend and everything, but I think he's a massive dickhead. And I'm not engaged – you can check my marital status in the Croydon town hall, or however you would do it. I'm as single as they come.' It's not a complete lie. I don't think you can get more single than your ex being dead.

'I thought that was probably the case.'

'Anyway, we don't want to spend the entire night talking about past conquests! Shall we go get some food?'

'Yes please – I'm fricking starving!'

He takes my hand and helps me squeeze out of my seat. What a gentleman.

'Stop!' I laugh, wiping tears away from eyes with my hundred-thread Egyptian cotton napkin – softer than my bed sheets.

'Ha! My friends always ask me to do impressions, and Anne Robinson is an old favourite.'

'How can you do a woman's voice so well?'

'My mum said I should have been an actor, but I got swept away with everyone at uni and followed the golden path of money to London.'

'I think everyone did that and then realised the path is made of golden nuggets and not gold.'

'Cheers to that!' and we both clink our cut-glass tumblers, mine filled with fifteen pounds' worth of gin & tonic and Theo's a twenty-pound-plus Old Fashioned. That was what Adam drank. I can taste it on his breath now. Spiced, malted barley. Talisker was his poison of choice.

The Uber drops me outside my flat and Theo gets out to say bye. He pulls me in for a hug.

'I had such a great evening.'

'Me too.'

We stand and stare at each other for what seems like an eternity, then I move my head towards him in a quick, jolty fashion and kiss him. He kisses me back!

I don't invite him in, as the Uber's engine's still running. I cannot sleep with him on a first date – it will give off the wrong impression. I really like him, and he paid for the whole dinner, so I would feel like a prostitute.

I slam the door behind me. I'm grinning so much. I haven't been on my phone all evening! I've been captivated by Theo. For once, my home seems welcoming. It's starting to look and smell of comfort again. I've a torrent of WhatsApps filled with kiss faces and aubergine emojis from Julia and Nicky.

I feel like I've stepped off the set of a Hollywood romance movie. I miss Adam, but he isn't here, and he isn't coming back. Maybe it is possible to like and love at the same time.

I don't think I've gone to sleep this contented in a long while.

10 August 2017

Human contact's a funny thing. There's a fine line and you never know when you are going to cross it. Like the 250ml-of-Sauvignon-Blanc-difference between being tipsy and telling your boss you want to fuck him.

Ping. Notification. *Ping.* Notification.

> Thinking of you X
> I promise it will get better X
> I wish I could make everything OK again for you, hun X

I turn my phone on silent, but it doesn't stop me from constantly turning it over and peeking, like a pervert outside the changing rooms in Ann Summers. Tears are streaming down my face. Messages. I want more messages. I want more love. Fuck it, leave me alone. Fuck off everyone. Why me? Why did this have to happen to me? I'm not strong enough for this. I'm weak. Pathetic.

There are so many messages. Everyone wants to make sure I'm OK. They can't message me enough. But no four-word message and an *X* is going to bring Adam back, so what's the point?

It isn't acceptable to reply: 'Thanks for the message, Linda, but I'm not going to start fucking my phone at night.' *Nothing will ever be ok again. What* are you thinking about me?! I know 100 per cent that you are not sitting at home crying and screaming and smashing things. It's Tuesday, you've got Pilates.

I've had enough.

Ten sweaty minutes later, heavily breathing, I'm on the Underground. Not that I'm travelling anywhere special, but I've found it's a good hiding place when you want to ride

out a particularly bad day. I'm a state I know that. I need ref-
uge. Somewhere where people can't contact me. I'm wearing
sweatpants, Adam's sweatpants. A strap top and a sweatshirt.
I'm not wearing a bra, which is unusual for someone with
D-cup breasts, but nothing matters any more. I want someone to look at me, notice me the way Adam used to. He could
spot me across the tracks of the Northern Line even in rush
hour. I could smell his cologne, his love, miles away. Maybe
having my nipples out will be a new pulling technique. Are
burger nips still attractive? I have half a bottle of wine with
me. I don't want to get drunk, as it makes me emotional. I
don't know what I want. I want to be numb. The acidic liquid
burns my throat as I swig and mix it with the salt of my tears
and snot that seem to have lodged themselves halfway down
my gullet. '*Ugly crier*'. That's what Adam would say, while
wiping my tears.

Why are some seats so clean? What happened on those
seats that made Transport for London decide to replace that
fabric and not the others? People are getting up and down,
puffs of brown dust being released into the carriage. Air filled
with skin cells, human hair. Life.

A couple opposite me kiss, and the lady looks at me, puz-
zled, intrigued, concerned. I think my mouth has given up on
smiling; I snarl at her like a dog, not the mutt kind, a cross-
breed. One of those teacup pugs that should have the best
life, living in Kensington with his rich parents, but in fact his
joints hurt because it isn't right to breed pugs with teacups.
Even dogs have a story to tell.

That's how I feel. I look like I'm one of those Clapham
mums, drunk on white wine, ready to go out with Cosima and
Maria to Raoul's birthday party opposite the green, but my
insides are dead because the love of my life was taken too soon,
and that just isn't right. That isn't what's supposed to happen.

22

11 March 2019

'Hello, shithead, everything OK? I'm just getting my nails done. Do you think pink or nude?'

'Hey, Florry. Erm, nude – pink I find is always a bit Miss Piggy-esque. I need your help.'

'Hit me up!' I hear her eagerly shuffling closer to the phone – this is any older sister's dream. 'What is it you need my expert advice on? Boy trouble? Financial advice? Ooh, do you want me to give you a makeover?'

'No, unfortunately, none of the above.'

'What then? The suspense is killing me.'

'You know, after, erm, after, Adam died . . .' I clear my throat and am welcomed by a sombre silence.

'Yes Mills.' Her voice is soft and caring, the jovial atmosphere has dissipated. I can't remember the last time I mentioned that four-letter word in the vicinity of any family member by choice. 'Well, I stopped going out and replying to all my friends. Julia and Nicky were the only two that stayed by my side. I watch all my uni friends on Instagram going to parties, weekends away – all things that I don't get invited to any more. It makes me so sad.' I feel the beginning of a lump in my throat. 'I've made so many steps in the right direction. I've spoken to Julia and Nicky about how I behaved, and they forgive me. I speak to Violet, I help people on my Mizzennial channel but . . . I still feel embarrassed about reaching out to my other friends again. I thought about what you said about Layla too – I feel like I should message her again, but I feel so nervous about everything. I think I'm scared of rejection after all this time.'

'Oh, Mills. I'm so sorry life's been so tough on you, I really am. You and Layla used to be so close – I just have a feeling that if you messaged her, everything would be OK between you both and you'd feel able to message other people too. Do you want me to come over?'

'No, it's OK. I want your advice. You've known my friends as long as I have. And I know at the time you were encouraging me to see people, but I just couldn't. Do you think if I message them, they might let me back in?'

'I think you should choose one person and ask them for a drink or something. Make the first move. You don't have anything to be sorry about, but people can be ignorant sometimes. I got on really well with Adam – I thought he was a great guy, you know that. But he wasn't my husband or my twin brother. Layla might be the one person you've been seeking this whole time, the one person who can help you get through it all and vice versa.'

'I have been thinking about her a lot. I don't know what it is that's made me create such a barrier.'

'It's probably just the fact that she was so close to Adam. It's hard to get to the point where you're able to move on and be reminded at the same time.'

'Yeah, maybe you're right. Thanks, Florry. I'll do that.'

'This is your final step in moving your life off the grid – you'll start telegramming the Queen next.' I smile. She can't resist the sarcasm.

'Love you, Florry.'

'You too, Mills.'

@ThamesWaterWorks @Mizzennial I cry all the time, like every day. I miss her. I just want someone to tell me it's normal to cry.

Of course, it's normal, we all cry. You shouldn't keep emotions pent up.

> **@Mizzennial** @ThamesWaterWorks People always think crying is bad – I think it's good. If you're feeling sad, you should let it out. Harbouring emotions is never good. It's normal to cry, you're only human. X

Text from Theo:

> **Theo:** Did you ever watch *I'm a Celebrity*? I swear I just saw Joey Essex in the work café. Nowhere near as orange in real life. Kind of a shame really – the lighting would have had him glowing (I'm from Essex, so it's OK coming from me) X

It's so strange having that message tennis with a boy again. I used to message Adam all the time, not afraid to send a stream of messages if he wasn't replying fast enough for my liking. There was never anything that exciting to send, not after we'd been going out for so long. Things like; *What do you fancy for dinner? Did you see that Molly's pregnant? What was that show again?*

It feels nice having someone want to speak to me. Someone who wants me to be the first person to hear about their day. Theo could be the first person I tell things to, like Adam used to be, but something about that doesn't feel quite right yet. Unjust, like the universe isn't balanced.

3 July 2016

'Do you have to read every single plaque?'

'Why not?'

'It takes soooo long. I've already been round this room once already, and you're only on the third thing. No one else is reading it all.' I know I sound like a petulant child, but it's genuinely how I feel.

'Do I need to be a sheep? Do you copy what the rest of England does? Answer this question and I'll let you off acting like a little baby. Who did Caesar have a baby with?'

'That's easy.' I scoff. 'Cleopatra.' Lucky escape for me.

'Ha. How did you know that?' Adam retorts, knowing full well that I hate history and museums.

'Secrets. Riddle me that, Einstein. It was the first plaque, and I always read the first one in every room – it's by the third one that I'm bored.'

'We paid to come in. Surely you want to get your money's worth?'

'I like looking around and reading some bits I find interesting, but not all of it. Why do I need to know every single detail about Julius Caesar? He's already lived his life, he doesn't need you to live it as well.'

'That's basically blasphemy. Well, you don't have to wait for me, you go around by yourself and then grab a coffee and meet me at the exit, OK?'

'Whoop! Thanks, Dad.'

'See ya loser.'

Finally, I see Adam walking out of the pillar-guarded exit.

'You're alive!'

'How long have you been waiting here?'

'About an hour?' I reply, slurping my coffee and finishing the last of my chocolate brownie.

'An hour?! We only got here at four p.m. and it shuts at five thirty. I'd have stayed longer, but I didn't realise it was closing. I'll have to come back another day and read more about Caesar's promiscuity and how he was kidnapped by pirates.'

'Are you joking? An hour and a half wasn't long enough? Just so you know, I'm *never* going to a museum with you again – I think it's slowly killing me. Want to know a secret?'

'I will teach you to love history one day, Ms Dayton. You wait. What secret?'

'Don't call me *Ms* – it makes me sound old. Hurry up and propose to me so I can be a *Mrs*. Well, there was a slot at eleven this morning, but I purposefully booked the four p.m. one so I didn't physically die of boredom. And that has happened before, in America. I watched a documentary about it.'

'It's impossible to die of boredom in the presence of Julius, but just to check, I'm going to lock you in the museum overnight.' Adam suddenly runs at me, grabbing me by the waist and swinging me in his arms.

I squeal and laugh, enjoying the role play. When we stop laughing and play-fighting, I pipe up. 'Shall we have a wander round Hyde Park? The weather's still nice and I want to try and catch some rays.'

'Sure!' Adam takes my hand in his. 'Oh, and Milly?'

'What?'

'I'll propose to you when you start enjoying history. Once I'm happy with your base-level knowledge of Roman history, I'll propose. That's the deal.'

'Whatever, mate. I know you'll give in before that. You don't want to lose a catch like me.' I grin and poke him in the ribs.

23

13 March 2019

Theo texts me:

Theo: When can I see you again? What are you wearing? X

Eurgh, why do all boys have to sext? It's so cringe. I'm nowhere near ready for sexting yet. At least that confirms that Theo is 100 per cent not perfect.

I reply:

Me: Sudocrem, an old Spice Girls T-shirt and some moccasins. You? X

I'm not a prude but I'm not ready to have sex with someone I actually like yet, and I can confirm, sex is something that is much better in person than through a screen. Look at that, Violet – growth.

A picture message from Theo. Please, God, no, don't be a dick pic.

Phew, it's him pulling a face at work. Thank the bloody Lord. That would have been the end of a blossoming relationship.

Penises are not as attractive as men think. Would anyone want to eat raw sausage meat being pushed out of the plastic sheath?

@AubergineAddict @Mizzennial I've seen people say they struggle to meet someone after they've lost a partner. I'm the complete opposite. I've been out having one-night stands all over the place. I think I slept with five people last week. It's like a release, but I know it's not healthy.

I think about my own sex rampage all those months ago. It didn't help me in any way. I should have just spoken to a counsellor.

@Mizzennial @AubergineAddict There's no normal when it comes to dealing with grief. Everyone deals with it in their own way. I've also slept with random people, and I think I did it because I was seeking some sort of comfort, love, but I realised I wasn't getting it from sex with strangers. Why not sit down and really think about what you're looking for, or speak to someone about it? That said, if you want to go out and sleep with five people, then do it! X

All this penis talk's making me hungry. Not.

Violet's in the middle of telling me about a news story regarding millennials and purchasing experiences, not things. I interrupt; it's time.

'I think I want to tell you about Adam.'

'And what do you want to tell me about him?'

'He was supportive, the voice of reason, funny. Everyone loved him. He loved the elegance and strength of history. He liked watching films, reading, particularly about Roman history – he loved Julius Caesar. And he loved me. He loved me.' My voice cracks with the thought that someone loved me for being me.

'He sounds like a lovely person. Julius Caesar, hey . . .' She pauses and laughs lightly to herself. 'That's a fun one. How did he . . . ?'

'Cancer. Terminal, obviously. We thought it was just a lump in his balls, but it was a tumour.'

'I'm sorry, Milly, that's awful.' I can see the sadness in her eyes. It's the way everyone looks when I tell them. They imagine themselves losing a partner, but they can't. It's unimaginable.

'Adam.' I cough. 'He was a twin.'

'And what happened to his twin? Does he live near you?'

'She, and I don't know. I was horrible to her, Violet. She reminds me of Adam. She's closer to Adam than me – she's his twin! But he was the love of my life and no one knew how I felt. No one.' I feel breathless.

'It's hard, Milly. Adam was your husband, no one else's. Everyone's relationship with him was different, special in its own unique way. It doesn't need to be competitive – Adam's twin isn't trying to take away your grief, or special moments. Have you thought that maybe you might be able to help each other?'

'Oh, I don't know any more, Violet. Sometimes I'm fine, sometimes I'm scared. Sometimes I think I did the right thing, other days I hate myself. I have more going on with my emotions than my social life.'

'Why don't you try to meet up with her and put this whole thing to rest? Remove all the negativity and worry from your life? Take a step back and see how far you've come. Everything you've achieved has seemed impossible at points and now it looks like a walk in the park. You need more confidence in yourself, Milly.'

I'm being the most inactive I've ever been, yet sweat is pouring down the small of my back. I told Violet I was going to do it yesterday, so why am I so nervous? I know full well that life isn't a straight path of good fortune. I'm aware that there are setbacks, or in my case, boulders of destruction. I'm scared that I'm nearly ready to get to the other side of the hill, but this could push me to the bottom again.

I open Instagram on my phone, click into my DMs. My hand's shaking. I scroll down until I see @LaylaRose's halo of blonde hair in her profile picture and open the messages. I can see at least ten unread messages from her, but I don't read them. I cannot dwell on the past. History has already printed its facts.

@Milly.Dayton24 @LaylaRose I think I'm ready to meet you now, if you are. M X

10 May 2011

'Why are you acting like that?' Adam asks.

'Acting like what?'

'You're fidgeting so much, and you keep flipping the radio stations.'

'I'm nervous.'

'Nervous about what?'

'Meeting your family, especially your twin.'

'Why are you so scared about meeting Layla? She'll love you!'

'Do you think so?'

'Milly, she's basically me in female form, and I love you, so why wouldn't she?'

'I don't know. I just want to make a good impression, that's all.'

'And you will.' He moves my hand to his lips and kisses it, just before he tries to crunch the tinny little Micra into fourth gear to do the slowest overtake the motorway has ever seen. I shut my eyes in case he doesn't make it.

'Darlingggggg!' Adam's mum pulls him in for a tight hug and kisses him enthusiastically. He emerges with two pale pink smears on each cheek.

I smile.

'And you must be Milly?'

'Lovely to meet you, Amanda.' I hold out my hand. Amanda's shoulder-length hair is blow-dried into soft waves that sit neatly on her shoulders. Her face is minimally dressed in neutral shades of Clinique's finest, but from the earlobes to collarbone, Amanda's gone for a maximalist look – thick, gold hoops with tiny diamonds and art-deco-style gold necklaces. On a younger person, it would be too much, but on her it only adds to the glamour.

'No need to be so formal, darling. Come here! Adam's told me so much about you.' She pulls me in for my own hug and kiss.

'All good things, I hope!' I hate that response, but I can't think of anything wittier right now.

'Tank!' Adam shouts as the smallest Yorkshire terrier bounds towards him. 'Milly, Tank would like to welcome you to his humble abode.' He holds out a paw, which I shake.

'Where's Dad and Layla?'

'Your dad's out playing golf with Ed, and Layla should be back any second, I think. She just nipped to the shops.'

Just as Amanda sweeps a blow-dried blonde wave from one of her perfectly mascaraed lashes, I hear the gravel crunch.

'Come on, Milly!' Adam rushes towards the door and runs outside. Layla swings the car door open with the engine still running and leaps into his arms.

'Baby bro!' Layla was born two minutes before Adam. She swings her arms around his neck, and he swings her. I've seen photos of her on Adam's phone, but it's strange seeing people so similar in real life. It's not that they look more similar than any two siblings, it's just their mannerisms, the intonations in their sentences. Like two peas in a pod.

I stand on the sideline, observing their interactions. I don't know why, but I feel a pang of jealousy. Someone Adam loves more than me.

Layla hops down from Adam.

'And you must be Milly. I've been dying to meet you!' She pulls me in for a hug that's so tight and warm I immediately feel stupid for feeling jealous. 'Come on, guys. Let's go inside. I bought some gin for cocktails.'

'I just put the kettle on though, sweetie.'

'Come on, Mum – they don't want tea. We're celebrating!'

'What are we celebrating?'

'Milly, of course! A new member to the Hadfield gang.'

'Lally!' He nudges her. 'We're not married yet!'

'Well, I can already tell that she's perfect. Come on.' Layla grabs my hand and drags me inside.

Maybe I'll have a new best friend as well as a boyfriend.

24

17 March 2019

I must be open-minded; you can't eat an ice cream nowadays without seeing someone downward dog in your face. The more I'm putting myself out there, the more I'm getting back. Maybe after this session, I'll also be one of those people that swears by their morning sun salutation and despite needing oxygen for every millisecond of my existence thus far, have now, in my late twenties, realised the importance of breathing.

'Ready, Milly?'

@ILikeMyMenHotAndBlack has done this before, matching crop-top and leggings accentuating her toned thighs and abs. I've always thought, if pheromones were clothes, they would be Lycra. All that caffeine must do wonders for her metabolism.

I don't look too bad myself – I know that wearing an old T-shirt and shorts to work out in is so 2000. My Lululemon ensemble cost half my rent – the thought of dirtying it makes me sweat more than working out.

I send a selfie of myself pouting to Theo. It's cringe, but it always is at the start.

'I love your outfit!' I say to @ILikeMyMenHotAndBlack as she plucks at the seamless Lycra. 'Very *The Hills*,' I add, remembering the trash TV show which I hate to love.

'Thanks, I got it from Skimmed Milk. Everything is made from recycled plastic bottles. I'm really trying to do everything I can for the environment now.' She waves a reusable water bottle as emphasis.

'At least that makes up for all the coffee cups.' I wink at her, laughing.

'Shut up.' She gently shoves me. 'I'm thinking about the turtles.'

'All I can think about is that surfer turtle from *Finding Nemo*.' I laugh. 'What was his name?!'

'Crush! Oh my God, I used to love him. I had a boyfriend once who sounded like him and he called me Little Blue,' Shelley says dreamily.

I take a selfie of the three of us. 'I'll caption it "Nemo, Dory & Crush".'

I pause for a second, this isn't how I planned on doing my Mizzennial reveal, I'm not ready. I upload to @Milly.Dayton24 instead.

'I hope you're not going to make anyone on Insta feel guilty for eating a pack of doughnuts instead of bending bones in ways that should be illegal because, when I get home, that's exactly what I'm going to do,' Shelley says checking out the picture.

'Don't worry, I'm not into guilt-tripping. Anyway, this is supposed to be *fun* – let's get flexi.'

The three of us, from *very different* walks of life, head towards our 'enlightening'.

Theo replies:

Theo: You look great! Don't come out being some super hippie yogi please. Can't wait to see you again soon X

The tent is utterly majestic. A giant tepee-style construction, with brightly coloured cushions all around the edges, pieces of fabric pinned to the inside walls, huge feather dreamcatchers. There's so much incense burning that I'm feeling slightly hedonistic.

It isn't really a yoga class as such – there are loads of mats and people are coming and going. You can join in as soon as there is a free mat. The lady at the front is speaking about her karmic alignment and ridding her body of negative energy. This is a yoga *festival* on the common, and @ILikeMyMen-HotAndBlack suggested I try it because it's amazing for mindfulness. I've never really been a yogi, mainly because I don't want to turn into one of those people who spouts on about how a headstand has led to their karmic awakening and a downward dog has brought them at one with the Earth. But maybe I'm being too negative. I do need to find myself. I'm yet to meet a yogi who hasn't found themselves, so there must be some truth in it.

This lady is incredible – she must not have any bones. Her body is so flexible, it's as if she's made from reinforced rubber. When she stands up, her body is pure muscle: rows and rows of abs. A total dream machine.

'Can you feel the negative energy leaving your body, Mills?' @ILikeMyMenHotAndBlack calls over to me as she bends like the rubber-paperclip-sibling of the instructor. @ShelleyFarrell's already in a heap on the mat next to me. I don't think she's worked out in a very long time. She looks how I feel.

'Hmm, not yet, I'm still mastering the art of bending.' One of the helpers tries to assist me reach my toes by gently pushing my back down – she genuinely looks shocked as I bounce back up and then fall into a ball on the floor. Hopefully, I'm able to improve on my flexibility, but I'm coming to the shocking realisation that my arms and calves may be stunted and there will be no hope for my yoga career.

After thirty minutes of intense downward-dogging and sun salutations, it's time for us to meditate. More incense is lit around the tent and we're all instructed to sit cross-legged on our little foam mats with our eyes shut. This 'mind cleansing' involves tapping pieces of quartz, smoking sage sticks, but, unfortunately, no hash. Gwyneth Paltrow and her LA coven must be making a frickin' fortune!

'Close your eyes, feel the negative energy leaving your soul, cleanse your mind. Let the impurities flow out of your body. You can feel them gradually departing from your fingertips, your toes. Breathe in. Let this new, cleansed air dissipate around you. Your body is merely an empty shell, encasing the energy inside you. Let it ignite a fire within and charge you for the day ahead. You can achieve anything you set your mind to. You never thought your body could bend in the ways it has this morning – surprise yourself with your achievements.'

I open my eyes in a trance-like state. All I was thinking about were her dulcet, soft tones. For once, I didn't think about my life, just the words she was saying. Maybe there is some truth to this meditation malarkey.

'Wasn't that *amazing*! I feel so invigorated.' @ILike-MyMenHotAndBlack genuinely looks like she's just been cleansed. @ShelleyFarrell on the other hand, looks as if she has woken from a very long nap; she has the imprint of the wooden yoga block on her right cheek.

'I'll go and fetch us some chai before the next session.' I say to the others, needing a little break from all the bending and stretching.

The milky, spicy warmness is exactly what I needed. I step away to take a minute to myself before I am rudely interrupted.

'Excuse me, are you here alone?' a girl asks me so intensely I fear she might abduct me. She has thick, mid-length brown hair and wispy, thin tattoos all over her arms.

'Err, at the moment, but I'm waiting for my friends.'

'Ohhhh, cool!' I think maybe she's from Texas. 'I'm here with my boyfriend' and she points to a guy with long hair, standing behind her in the shadows. This is all very weird.

'Well, nice to meet you.' And I start to gradually turn to walk away, holding my three chai teas.

She puts a hand on my shoulder. 'I know this sounds a bit forward, but my boyfriend and I were wondering if you wanted to hang with us?'

'Well, erm, my friends are waiting for me, so I should probably go back to them, as they'll be wondering where I am.' *Are* they trying to abduct me?

'OK, no worries, doll. Well, I'm going to put it out there, if you are into it, and not everyone is, which is fine. But we were wondering if you wanted to join us for a play date?'

'A play date?'

'Sex, darling. We're looking for someone to join us and you looked really sweet and you're British, which is one on our tick list.'

I stand with my mouth open. 'No, sorry.' And I walk away. Why did I say sorry?

I message Theo:

Me: OMG, you'll never guess what just happened to me! X

He was the first person I thought of telling. I think he'll find it funny. Whenever anything exciting or funny or shocking or just anything happens to me, the first person I always think of is Adam. Adam, Adam, Adam. Even though he's died, I haven't been able to shift that innate reaction. We told each other everything when he was alive; we shared everything: the happiness, the laughs, the sadness.

It's the same feeling when you used to win a prize at primary school and couldn't wait to rush home and tell your parents.

That's what's been the hardest, the one person I want to talk to. Gone. I can talk to Julia and Nicky, and they will always be there for me, but it's not the same. And suddenly, it's not Adam, it's Theo.

Maybe it was because I was already in the throes of messaging him. It doesn't mean anything, apart from maybe betrayal.

It feels like betrayal.

Traitor.

I shake my head. This is all part of moving on. Violet said it would be tough. *Nothing good comes easy*. I repeat the mantra in my head as my thoughts go from Theo to Adam, Adam to Theo, and back to Adam again.

I rush back to tell @ShelleyFarrell and @ILikeMyMen-HotAndBlack, who I really should start calling Sophie, but it just doesn't have the same ring to it. I recount the threesome story to 'Oh my God!', 'No way!', 'Wait, is that them? Totally gross!'

Both the girls help me edit the situation into a hilarious #cringe post, and we leave chit-chatting away. I don't have to rely on one person to support me – I can have support all around me!

Violet cleans her glasses on the hem of her fuzzy pink cardigan.

'I messaged her, and she hasn't replied. It's been three days now, and I know she's read it.'

'Milly, these things take time. I'm not a mind reader, but I'm guessing it has been a while since you made contact with Layla?'

'Nearly two years.'

'If you received a message out of the blue from someone after two years, would you buy them a bunch of flowers and propose to them on the London Eye?'

'No, of course not.'

'Exactly, point made.'

I'm reluctant to admit she does indeed have a point, so I change the topic. 'I tried yoga to help with mindfulness, and then someone asked if I wanted to have a threesome with them.'

'The gods of flexibility can do strange things to us all.'

@Mizzennial Quote of The Day: Time is a healer and death is the epitome of awkward in British society. 'Help' is a verb we all need to share.

Ping. New DM:

@AtomicBomb @Mizzennial I had a nice life before. A good job, loving girlfriend, I had fun. I feel like I've been in self-destruct mode since Elise died. I've been going out getting really drunk, paralytic almost. I look at myself in the mirror and I look shit. I don't know how to get back on the straight and narrow.

@Mizzennial @AtomicBomb It's the feeling of worthlessness that gets you down. That feeling that nothing is worth as much as it was before, that you are not worthy of this life. Well, you are MORE than worthy. This is your life and you need to seize it. You've had your blow-out, now you need to work out how to get back to the new you before you blow up. There are loads of good support links on griefguidance.com X

25 August 2017

I stand up behind the brown wooden lectern. I rub my hands across the polished wood. Shiny, smooth. It looks new. Strange how a church can mix new and old life so seamlessly. One out, one in. The joys of christenings, the birth of a baby girl on the same day we lay one of God's children to rest. You shouldn't swear in a church, but I wonder who makes these rules? The same person who decides who dies of cancer and who doesn't? Life roulette. What a wonderful job that must be.

I keep looking down at the eulogy, but God must have taken away my power to read, courtesy of a lifetime of profanity. All I can see in front of me is a page of scribbles. Hieroglyphs are jumping out from the page. Eyes, mouths, screaming faces. Everyone's staring at me. The vicar looks like he's contemplating laying me to rest in the casket next to Adam. I'd like that, I think.

'Come on, Milly! Remember what I always tell you to do? Imagine everyone naked. Look at fat Aunty Cressida. Her boobs would be jangling all over the place. And Miranda, I've always wondered what she looks like without the cloak of clothes. Tell me some jokes. Go on, it's boring inside here. Make me laugh. I want everyone to remember me how you do. Leave me a legacy that no one will forget!'

I smile at him, sitting cross-legged on top of his coffin, puffing jovially on a cigar. You shouldn't smoke inside a church.

I look down at the pieces of paper, take a huge breath, sniff in a gulp of snot and read as if my life depends on it, because it does.

'"Which death is preferable to every other. The unexpected."' From there, the words come, if not easily, at least manageably.

That was Adam's quote. Plagiarised, of course, from the great Julius Caesar.

I sit back down next to my mum, who puts her arm around me and gives me a little squeeze.

'That was so brave, Milly,' she whispers in my ear.

That wasn't brave. Bravery is lying trapped inside a wooden box on a conveyor belt towards an impending inferno, never wondering about an afterlife and blasphemously cursing 'cunt' once inside your village church. He didn't mean to, but Leo had told him a 'foolproof' bet on fantasy football and he lost all his Christmas money from his grandma. Still, you don't know who's watching.

25

Ping.

> **@LaylaRose** @Milly.Dayton24, I can't believe it's you.
> Yes, I would love to meet. Name your place. Layla X

I message Florry:

> **Me:** Layla replied!!!
> **Florry:** Told you! Big sisters always know best X

Theo and I have been trying to arrange a day to meet up, but it's so much harder now I have more social engagements. Julia and Nicky said it's good to keep a guy waiting, so you don't look too keen. I don't want to rush into anything; Theo is a great guy, but I'm aware that my emotions are still precariously perched on a cliff edge.

The other evening, we had a 'Netflix and Chill', but the pre-watershed version – it involved a movie, pizza and cuddling. We made the decision to stay in rather than go out for drinks. It made me realise that maybe we'd crossed the boundary of casually dating and moved into relationship territory. I haven't had anything more than terrible sex with anyone since Adam died. Cosying up on the sofa with a movie and a man isn't what's advertised on Tinder – am I ready for that?

It's my first day in the office, but I've been 'allowed' to travel in non-rush hour due to the fact that if my leg gets bashed, I'll be returning home immediately. I mean, I was doing yoga a few days ago, but that involved careful adjustment, like a dog cocking his leg up a tree.

I thought I'd have people swarming around my desk, checking if I was OK, maybe even some flowers. But then I remembered this is an office and people only speak through Outlook. I have emails saying, *You look great, we're so happy you've returned to work,* from people who are sitting opposite me. They give me a quick smile and then get back to furiously typing and listening to music through their AirPods.

Marjorie decided to say I look better on email before barking orders at me in person. I wish she'd done it the other way around.

'What are you doing, Milly? It looks like you only have one eyebrow on.'

'I'm prepping for the meeting at 11, like you asked me to.' Come on, Marjorie, I'm not an imbecile, but also fuck, I must have forgotten to draw the other one on.

'I was just wondering, as usual, when you are waiting for your computer to turn on – you are scrolling on Instagram.'

'I think my *car accident* altered my brain slightly.'

Some people.

I forgot how much I hate it here. I was starting to feel better about my life and as soon as I stepped over the grate into SugarPharmers, I realised what a shambles it actually is. I work with a group of people who hate me and do their best to remind me of it on a daily basis.

The depression of this office is making me think. Overthink. I like Theo, but I don't know if I'm ready for a full-on relationship again. But then he was the first person I thought of telling about the whole yoga-sex scenario. And that's a whole conflict of emotions of its own. My brain can't decide whether that was a good or a bad thing. It feels like I'm having an affair.

Maybe it's not that I've been too busy, but that I've been unintentionally putting off a fourth date with Theo. Just because you think of texting someone first or enjoy watching movies together doesn't mean you're ready to get married, does it?

Maybe I should start getting to know myself again? Maybe it's not any of that, and maybe it's that I'm scared to officially cut the cord with Adam, to allow another being to be the main subject of my emotions.

Eurgh, so many thoughts – it's exhausting.

'Milly . . .'

I turn to Marjorie. Her voice sounds weird. Different to the abrupt, flat tone it was earlier. Crackly, almost.

'Are you OK, Marjorie? You look like you have been . . . err . . . crying?'

'Yes, I'm fine,' she says, hurriedly wiping away a fresh tear that's started to drop from her right eye. I don't think she wants me to notice, but I know what 'I'm fine' means all too well.

'Do you want to go and grab a coffee from downstairs?' I hate seeing people cry, but even after she was a total bitch to me, I don't wish her bad vibes.

'That would be great. I'll grab my bag.'

I order two flat whites, soya milk for me and full-on cow milk for Marjorie. We sit in silence as we stir the foam around in our respective coffees.

'Do you want to talk about it?' I crack the silence.

Turns out, Marjorie's husband cheated on her a few years ago and he's done it again. She's finally found the courage to ask him for a divorce. That's why she's been stuck in this job, begging for a promotion – money and men. I feel bad for her. Why have I been such a bitch to everyone? Blaming my behaviour on everyone else.

'I'm sorry for being such a bitch to you this morning, Milly. It all got a bit much for me.'

'That's OK. I know what it's like when things get too much. I'm sorry too. It's good to talk to people about your problems, and life's tough. No one can blame you for having an outburst.'

Finally, I'm using my words to make someone feel good about themselves – it's like Mizzennial but in real life.

'John's been a dick to me for such a long time now. I don't know why I put up with it. After, err, after your husband died, Milly, it made me really think about how awful it must have been and still is for you. And with John, I thought, why fix a marriage if it's not 100 per cent broken? Life is difficult enough as it is. I know I said it at the time, but I am so sorry for you, Milly. I don't know if I ever truly realised what it must have been like for you, that the outbursts came from a place of grief, not nastiness. The last few months with John, I feel like they've made me become more compassionate and resilient at the same time.'

'Honestly, please don't worry about it.' I put my hand on hers – not 100 per cent sure if it's office appropriate, but I feel like we're friends now so I'm going with yes. 'I don't think I ever really understood what was happening myself.' And I give her a smile.

'I think I can see some of the old Milly coming through. One of your best features is your smile.'

Would this be classified as inter-colleague flirting?

24 November 2016

'Milly, Adam, over here!' I look over and see Julia and James waving their arms frantically above the crowds.

We shove our way through the hordes of people drunkenly singing 'Sweet Caroline' and spilling their beers onto people's heads as they swing their arms in an uncoordinated unison.

'You made it!' Julia pulls me in for a hug while Adam and James shake hands, say, 'Fuck it,' and go all for it with a man hug.

'It's packed! We had to queue for ages – they're only allowing one in one out, it's a nightmare!'

'Here, we got you a beer.' They thrust two steins in our sweaty mitts.

'I fucking love Winter Wonderland – I think it's my favourite place.'

'Don't start her on this, Julia – she's been on about it the whole way here.' Adam winks at me.

'Shut up, Scrooge. Cheers, guys!'

We clink our litres of beer and join in a chorus of 'All I Want For Christmas', which is the universe's signal that the festive period has begun.

'What did you guys do this morning, then?'

'Not much, really. Went for a walk round the common, had a coffee and some scrambled eggs at that place, you know, on the corner? You know they serve the eggs with salmon sashimi now?'

'God, you two on your morning walks and Saturday breakfast dates. So middle class, makes me feel sick.' Julia puts two fingers down her throat.

'What did you lovebirds do, then?'

'Went for breakfast and saw James's mum.'

'Sickening,' Adam says deadpan. 'When's the wedding going to be then, James?'

'Well, if you hurry up and propose, mate, we could share the cost! Bloody expensive, you wait.'

'It won't be that expensive. I think we'll get married here, in the beer tent. I'll stand on the stage and you can be my backing singers to "I Will Survive".' I say, doing my best Gloria Gaynor impression.

'There's no way we are getting married in a fake German beer tent with an old man singing covers from the eighties on stage. I'm putting my foot down.' Adam stamps jovially. 'Unless you want me to propose here, and I'll put your ring in a hot dog or string it on a fried onion. Forget the magical proposal on Table Mountain or anything like that.' He pretends to start getting down on one knee.

'Ha, whatever. I think you forget how low-maintenance I really am. You've got it good.' I give him a playful kiss on the cheek.

'Who else is coming today then?' Adam asks me.

'Erm, Nicky, Olivia. I think they might bring some work friends with them. Nicky said she might bring this guy she is supposed to be going on a date with tonight. Seems a bit forward to make him meet all of us, but what do I know.' I shrug my shoulders.

'She makes me die. There's no way I would be that confident. I honestly feel so thankful that I don't have to be out there dating. Nicky's out there holding the feminist flag – evening out the ratio of fuckboys to fuckgirls. I even feel sorry for some of the boys.' Julia laughs, shaking her head.

'Nicky? She's an animal – she'd eat me alive,' Adam says.

'How do you think you boys would fare then in the modern dating world? I wonder what kind of daters you would be. Dick pics? Ghosters? Awkward profile picture – the family photo where you've cut out your family?' Julia's finding herself hilarious.

'Definitely the awkward-profile-picture type – I've seen some of Adam's!'

We all laugh and swig our beers.

'Adam, is that Layla?' I say pointing at a girl with blonde hair who's chanting, 'Is this the way to Amarillo' on a table-top, swinging her beer.

'Oh my God! *Lally!*' he shouts.

Julia and I also yell her name at the top of our lungs – since Julia and Nicky became friends with Layla, she's kind of inte-grated into the group, joining us for casual drinks in the pub and espresso martinis on nights out.

Layla turns, jumps off the table and runs towards us.

She's super drunk, but who cares?!

'I can't believe you guys are here!' Layla's always ecstatic to see everyone – she instantly puts you at ease with her smile. 'Let's dance!'

'No,' Adam says abruptly.

'I wasn't talking to you.' Layla cocks her head to one side. 'Dad-dancing embarrasses me.' She grins at Adam sticking his tongue out. 'Come on, Milly, *you* dance with me!' She grabs my hand and tries to pull me up on the table.

'No, I can't.' I suddenly feel all coy and shy.

'Come on, party pooper! You had no trouble last week-end at Fisher's.' And she leaps up, still holding her arm out-stretched.

I sigh and grab it. Layla gives me confidence; it's like she's the other part of me when I'm not with Adam. She brings out my sassy, confident side. I've never really had a friend like her before. Layla's the sort of person who buys a round of tequilas to liven up a party, persuades you onto an empty dancefloor and thinks that having fun is more important than being embarrassed, regardless of the situation.

Adam smiles at us both and we do silly poses while he takes snaps of us. Julia joins us next and then finally, all the boys, and we stand on the table, stamping our feet and screaming the words to every song until we sound hoarse and security start heading over.

26

Violet looks like she's been in combat with my grandma's curtains and got some of the rings caught up in the bird's nest on top of her head. If I looked like that in my Tinder profile, people would say I was deranged, but it kind of suits her. Elegant eccentricity.

'Layla replied, and I'm meeting her on Thursday.'

'That's good news. Have you had a chance to think about what you might say to her?'

'No. I guess, sorry should be quite high on the list.'

'I obviously don't know the ins and outs of your relationship with Layla, but the fact she replied to you is probably a sign that she wants to ignite your friendship again. Keep an open mind when you see her – you don't know what she's been going through. I would imagine it's a similar cycle of hurt and anger to your own. Grief is a very cyclical emotion.'

'I'll try my hardest. I was so scared about associating myself with the past again and the life I had with Adam, but now I know in order to move on, I need to make peace with everything. Remove all the ghosts from my closet.'

'You've come a long way, Milly.'

'Thanks, but I also keep hitting hurdles.'

'Hurdles are a good thing. Before, you didn't have any hurdles to hit because everything was negative. Now you have good days, new experiences and every so often a hurdle comes along – it shows you're progressing, Milly.'

'Yeah, I guess. I've been seeing this boy; you know the one from *Swipe Right*? But I don't know how I feel about him any more. I liked him, then I felt guilty, then I liked him again.'

'In what way? You've loved before, Milly. It is possible to love again. It's perfectly normal to feel confused. Am I right in thinking that this is the first person you have really felt something for since Adam?'

'Correct. What if I'm just using him for comfort, though? Shouldn't I learn to love myself again before I think about loving other people?'

'Well, only you know that, Milly.'

@Mizzennial What happens if you've already found the man of your dreams and he's now gone? Is there ever going to be another man like that out there – I thought I'd already caught him? Why can't people be tagged from birth so it's easier to find your soulmate, and a backup in case one goes awry.

Everyone keeps telling me that I'll find the man of my dreams one day. Every time I go to the park or a disco, I look but I can't find him. I took a step back from the situation and decided to look at it literally. 'Man of my dreams' . . . . oh, that's what it means! The next time I went out, I tied dreamcatchers all over me, to my clothes, in my ponytail – I need to physically catch the man of my dreams. My eNeRgY has been all off. I was right, it worked. The son of God showed me his lava lamp.

Theo and I grabbed a coffee yesterday. He came all the way over to Croydon and I introduced him to Sophie aka @ ILikeMyMenHotAndBlack. It was a lovely date, but it made me feel all weird. The last time I introduced a boy to my friends was when I brought Adam back to Norfolk for the first time.

Even after all my negative thoughts at work the other day, I decided to give him one last chance. It's not him, it's me, however clichéd that sounds.

But I just couldn't shake the thought that I felt like I was having an affair. I was kidding myself; I'm not ready for this at all. Why do I always get myself into situations that are a real pain to get out of?

When I first took Adam home – rather he took me home in his banged-up old car – all my Norfolk friends were shocked at how I had managed to grab myself such a hunk when I had gained about two stone through a diet of sugar, carbs and crisps. He was shocked at how beautiful the bump of England was. I think he was expecting me to live in a sewer with my parents and sister as three inbred monsters.

I visualise all those moments vividly in my head; I try to shake them off at every opportunity, but it's hard this time. It's distressing.

How can I be dating Theo and still be in love with Adam? I'm cheating myself, I'm cheating everyone around me. Thinking of messaging him first, nights in eating pizza and now introducing Theo to my friends – it's relationship territory. I can't be ready for that yet.

Me: Hey Theo, it was great seeing you yesterday, but I've been thinking, I don't think it's really going to work. Sorry x

Done. Now I can move on with my life. I'll probably stay single forever, but that's OK. I'll learn to be happy on my own. I feel instinctively better, like a weight's been lifted from my shoulders.

Right, now to get on with my day.

It's a Saturday, the sun's shining and I've got no plans. Kind of the way I like it. It's always nice to have a day every so often with no itinerary. I was a planner, I planned everything, wrote lists, used calendars on my phone and on the wall, then I went to having no plans. Ever. Now I think a balance is best. It's great to be busy, and it's great to be quiet. Life's an equilibrium.

I've created a graphic for Mizzennial that depicts exactly how much avocado toast you would need to buy in order to have wasted an entire house deposit. I don't think it's feasible to eat that much – you'd have a terribly upset stomach.

I'm going to get a coffee in Clapham, walk round the common, maybe get a sandwich from the nice deli on the corner, maybe sit on the grass and read my book. I'll be spontaneous. I have a new podcast about that con artist in New York that I want to listen to on the way and some responses I need to draft for Mizzennial.

Adam and I used to go for walks in the morning around the common, get piping-hot coffees and eat scrambled eggs in our favourite brunch spot. It was on our doorstep, so it never seemed special, just pleasant, part of a routine.

I take the bus this morning; I like watching everyone scurry about their Saturday-morning routines, like a fly on the wall. It's peaceful.

@HappyIsMoreThanASmile @Mizzennial My wife's been diagnosed with terminal cancer. I want to make her last few months amazing. I don't want to get lost in the grief – I have plenty of time for that after she's gone. How do I make the most of now?

This is one that feels raw. I might not be ready to have a proper relationship, but I definitely think I've come on leaps and bounds in terms of dealing with death. Talking about it doesn't scare me any more.

@Mizzennial @HappyIsMoreThanASmile I'm so sorry to hear this. This is a very difficult situation and one I battled with myself. Firstly, you are allowed to be upset, allow yourself that. Secondly, be very conscious that your wife's ability to do certain things will change over time. Remember to take time to just be you two and share the present. And finally, what about adapting things you used to do together? Like creating a restaurant at home, going for a drive instead of a walk? Singing to your favourite songs? Remember, you're never alone.

25 August 2017

My parents and Florry insisted that I stay with them after the funeral, but I wanted to be alone.

The wake was held in a pub nearby, one of Adam's favourites, the Hawthorne. Family members stood chatting, expressing their condolences, while stuffing their pie holes with plastic-cheese sandwiches and cheap sausage rolls made with pig bone. It makes me feel sick.

Adam came with me once to my aunt's funeral. We sat in the corner, drank a bottle of wine and I told him stories about how she used to look after us when we were younger and once popped a whoopee cushion so loud, I thought she was going to die, ten years before the cancer decided it was time. The *real* God of this world.

I don't have anyone to talk to now. No one knew Adam how I did. No one knows the way he used to kiss me or play with my hair. No one knows our secret wink or our in-jokes. No one.

Some people had decided to give me money. Get me back on my feet again. White envelopes filled with cash. I ripped them all open when I got home. Money is useless. What a benign object. It can't bring people back, it can't love, it can't cry. It's a life sapper. It makes people die; it breaks people up; it makes people cry. Money is a cunt.

Money only deserves to be spent on worthless things. There's a guy on the corner, outside Sainsbury's Local, who's a drug dealer. His mouth moves like he's constantly chewing half a gobstopper and his sweat smells sweet from the metabolising drugs perspiring out of his body. His name is B. Conspicuous. He used to work in the Sainsbury's and his name badge read *Barry*. He got fired because he tried to sell drugs to the off-duty manager once.

B is a constant. I buy two bags of cocaine from him with the £150 and tell him to keep the change.

I return to him for a tenner, as I need something to snort the white powder with. Adam wasn't really into drugs. We did it a few times at parties, but we weren't part of the snow brigade.

Line after line after line. I want to feel numb. I feel high as fuck. I do voice note after voice note after voice note to Adam. I have so much to tell him about the day. I have so many funny stories to remind him of. Line. Remember that time when we were out, and I basically got with a seagull? Line. Oh my God, you won't believe what the vicar said? He said you were a keen sportsman! He must have been sarcastic. Line. Where are you, Adam? Line. What the fuck? How can you leave me like this? What am I supposed to do?

Line. Line. Line.

I want to cry myself to sleep, but it's next to impossible when your eyes are as big as your head and your heart is about to beat straight out of your chest and lie pumping erratically on the living room floor.

I cry. Really cry. Tears tumbling out of my gecko eyes. I scream. I smash. I kick. It's 6 a.m.

11 a.m. Heart still beating. I don't actually want to die. I don't know how to live alone, though. My mouth is dry. My eyes are dry. My insides are dry. I'm a shell. I need to rebuild.

'Good night?' B asks me inquisitively as I stand outside Sainsbury's the next morning looking like a pile of shit, if I say so myself. 'Got another delivery in if you fancy a big one again tonight?'

That could be me. Standing on the corner, selling drugs to grief victims to pay for my own dirty habit.

'I think I'll abstain for now.'

I purchase orange juice with bits, fresh coffee beans and a croissant and go back to my middle-class, respectful life that I'm expected to lead. The one where you are supposed to wipe away the grief as if it were a ring on a coffee table and carry on. After all, the only way is up, right?

27

I got up early this morning. I've never been very good at sleeping when I'm nervous and decided to draft a tongue-in-cheek unboxing for Mizzennial to take my mind off later today:

> . . . I found THE perfect eyeshadow – a shiny, cream baby blue. I used my grubby fingers to rub it all the way up to the arches of my pencil-thin brows and it looked soooo good! Then I used the clear mascara to do my lashes, and it really made them look greasy, which was exactly the look I was going for. See the selfie I took on my disposal camera for inspo.
>
> My next favourite thing was an Impulse White Musk. I sprayed it all over me, several times. My mum said she couldn't breathe and was about to have an asthma attack, so I knew it was the perfect amount . . .

I start tagging Theo in a meme on Instagram – @*TheoIsMyName90 This is what I meant by beer tower. . .* – but stop before I post. Oh yeah, we're not dating any more. I haven't even read his latest message, I couldn't face it. I message Florry instead to take my mind off the impending meeting.

Florry: STOP WORRYING! Remember, you've known Layla for years, and you've done nothing wrong. Be

YOURSELF (Don't be yourself – sometimes you're really weird). Love you X

I decided to meet @LaylaRose in the Starbucks when @ILikeMyMenHotAndBlack was working. It's becoming my usual meeting place. What if something bad happens? What if @LaylaRose wants to murder me? This day has been giving me nightmares for almost two years – it's like resurrecting the dead. Although, in fairness, it can't be worse than telling Theo it's over. I need to get rid of everything holding me back, address all my fears. Remove all my shackles.

'You OK, Milly? Your face is the colour of a babycino.'

'Yeah. I'm meeting someone who I haven't seen for a long time.' I wring my sweaty hands together, twisting the fingers of my right hand in my left. My mouth has gone dry. I have his ring in my pocket, a lucky charm. I feel like Golem.

'Is it a ghost?!' @ILikeMyMenHotAndBlack peers at me over the counter. 'Are you sure you're OK? Do you want a chocolate bar or something? I can't have you passing out on me.'

'It's a ghost from the past. No thanks, I've lost my appetite.'

'I should start hiring Starbucks out as a meeting place for lost souls – you know this is the third person you've brought here? I'm not complaining, just saying. Maybe you should branch out – it's not exactly Soho House,' she continues, making jokes to herself.

I was contemplating telling Sophie about @LaylaRose until I saw her. Flicking her soft blonde waves away from her face, the way Adam used to do to me, the earnest look in her piercing blue eyes as Layla realises she's at the door of our meeting place. My breathing turns frantic.

As she pushes the door open, I feel a rush of adrenaline. What to say? How do I greet her? Layla scans the coffee shop before her eyes lock with mine. The corners of her lips curl up into a confused smile and she gives me an awkward wave.

I stand up, not sure how to greet her. Awaiting my instruction.

'Err, hi, Layla. I didn't get you a coffee because I wasn't sure what you, err, wanted. Sorry, that was rude of me. Here, let me get you something now—' The words stumble awkwardly out of my mouth. I'm now half-sitting, half-standing in a solo game of hokey-cokey.

'Come here!' She cuts me short and pulls me in for a hug. My eyes prick with tears as I recall the last time I was hugged so hard I couldn't breathe. Adam.

I'm not sure how long we were hugging, but eventually we both decide to come up for air and wipe our cheeks from the years of pent-up emotion.

'I'm sorry,' I say again, wondering why I didn't message her before.

'You don't need to apologise, Mills. I'm sorry too.' Layla wipes my face with a napkin. 'Your mascara's gone everywhere!'

'Thank you.' I sniff, wiping my eyes. 'Thanks for not making me sit here like a distraught panda.'

Layla chuckles. 'I've missed your little jokes.' She laughs again.

'It's been so long, Milly! How the bloody hell are you?!'

'I'm OK, I've been better.'

'Haven't we all!'

Layla orders her non-dairy coffee as I relay in detail the whole being-hit-by-a-car incident with interruptions like, 'Oh my God', 'I'm so glad you're OK', 'Why didn't you tell me?!'

'. . . and then I started the Mizzennial account, but I guess you saw it, as you messaged me on Instagram and then the Facebook friend request. I meant—'

Layla interrupts me.

'Oh my God, Mills, that account is so good! It's funny, heartbreaking. It's all the questions I wanted to ask about

Adam, but I had no one who really understood me to talk with.'

I sit and stir my coffee. 'No, I didn't either.'

'And you've always been so creative – remember that gorgeous photo album you made me?'

'The one for your twenty-fifth? With the photo of us all in the turkey hats at Christmas?'

'Ha yes! And Adam made us all Singapore Slings. Ah, that was a good Christmas.'

I look up to Layla, who also appears to be thinking about the last couple of years and the intense trauma that binds us '. . . And what about you?'

'Not good to be honest, Milly.' I see her eyes brewing with tears and I put my hand on hers. 'After Adam died, I went into a hole.' She squeezes my hand.

'Yeah, me too,' I respond.

'I lost my twin – I felt like I had lost half of my soul.' I feel the hairs on the back of my neck tingle as I remember that emotion.

'I stopped turning up to work and started drinking instead. Work were good to begin with, but eventually they had to let me go, which I totally understand. Mum sent me to an AA group, and then remember Oliver?'

'Yes, of course!' Who doesn't remember tall, brash Oliver – Adam never really liked him.

'Well, he dumped me. So, all in all, a bit of a bloody mare!'

'What a dickhead!' I respond, but I know Adam would be happy about that – Layla always deserved someone better, he used to say. 'He had a horrible laugh,' I add to make her feel better.

'Didn't he just? And he couldn't even be bothered to come to your wedding – that should have been a red flag to me then, but I couldn't be bothered to deal with a break-up in, you know, that time.'

'It was the right thing.' I nod, knowing that I wouldn't have been able to deal with my brother dying and breaking up with a boyfriend, even if he was a dick. 'Sorry I wasn't there for you. Julia and Nicky would have taken you out on one of their drink-till-you-pass-out nights to cheer you up.'

'I'm glad they didn't – I was a loose cannon on drink.' She rolls her eyes at her own addiction. 'Anyway, I've been living with Mum for about eight months now—'

'How is Amanda?' I interrupt. I lost my husband, Layla lost her twin, but Amanda lost her son. We send each other the odd message, limited to birthdays or death days, but I know neither of us is honest in our replies – neither of us wants to let the other down.

'I think, to begin with, I was being such a nightmare that it kept her occupied and as I started to improve, I think her own grief settled in. Vicious cycle.'

We both sigh.

'I've got a new job now. Living with Mum and Dad isn't ideal, but it keeps me on the straight and narrow. Although, I brought a guy home the other night and Mum walked in. Cringe!'

I almost spit out my coffee, thinking of the embarrassment.

'You could add it to one of your Mizzennial posts if you like, Mills?' She smiles, appreciating my reaction. It's odd how you can be so sad yet find things funny at the same time.

'Gosh, Layla, I'm so sorry.' Why wasn't I nicer to her before? We could have supported each other. Of course, I wasn't the only one in the world feeling grief. 'I went through a bad patch as well. I feel so guilty all the time. I pushed everyone away including most of my friends and went into a very angry place.' I look down at the little wooden table.

'Ahh, grief, what a wonderful emotion.' Layla raises her eyebrows as she sighs. 'I miss him so much, Mills. Everyone says it gets easier – I'm less angry but I'm still sad. So, so sad.'

Her face droops and tears begin to build up in her eyes, the same ocean blue as Adam's. She sniffs to clear herself.

'Me too. It makes me feel like my heart is breaking into pieces all over again. There seems to be only a very elite club of people who know what it's like to experience death.'

We hold hands again for a minute, silent, sharing our sadness.

'My counsellor says it's because people feel awkward. They don't know what to say, so they don't say anything at all. It's just like you point out on your Mizzennial channel. Do you have a counsellor, Mills?'

I think about my sessions with Violet, the social media addict counsellor, but she's so much more than that.

'Yes, kind of. My counsellor's amazing, kind of a friend now too, even if I am still paying her to chat with me. I need people to be patient with me. It's almost like I needed to be given a get-out-of-jail-free card from society for eighteen months and then I can join back in when I'm ready.'

'Amen, sister.'

'Do you hate me, Layla?'

'Of course not!' she exclaims, coffee particles spraying.

'But you know, for pushing you away. For ignoring all your messages about wanting to speak to me? I'm sorry, really, I am.' I need to make my peace. 'You're Adam's twin and you remind me of him so much. The way your lips curl up when you smile, your eyes, your mannerisms, your laugh. I, couldn't be reminded of him, but now I've realised reminders are good. You didn't do anything wrong, I just wasn't ready to bring a part of him back in again – scared of being reminded about what I'd lost.' I sniff, suddenly having a flashback to the roller disco all those years ago and then him lying on the bed with his eyes closed and then me remembering how much I love him again.

'No, Milly, I don't hate you. I wanted to see you desperately because I wanted someone to share my grief with.

You remind me of happy memories with Adam. I wanted to sit up, drink wine and reminisce about my brother because I felt so alone. But everyone's different.'

'We can do that now.' I smile and hold her hand.

'We can – although maybe not the wine.' She winks. 'Grief makes you act out of character. You can't explain it. I've done my fair share of acting-out, so no, I don't judge; you weren't ready and that's fine. I promise. I've learned not to judge people, as you really never know what's going on behind closed doors.' She smiles and continues. 'Tell me more about your life, it's so boring at home!'

We drink more coffee, we chat, we laugh, we reminisce about our old friendship, Adam, our past lives. It's in moments like this that it's almost possible to forget that we're conjoined twins in death. Life seems almost normal, or what we all become attuned to thinking is normal, anyway.

We grab our bags and give each other a hug. Layla says bye and walks left, and I turn to walk right. But I can't leave it like this; it sounds like Layla needs someone right now. We all do.

'Layla!' I call and she turns round.

'Let's go for a coffee or something again soon, maybe grab lunch? It's been so nice seeing you again.'

'Oh, Milly, I'd love that!' She runs towards me and hugs me again. I feel suddenly elated that I've made someone's day, like I used to when Adam was alive. 'I've missed our friendship. I know we had Adam binding us together before, but we were such good friends.'

'We still are.' I smile. 'We needed to deal with things in our own way. Nicky and Julia have missed you too.'

'Have they? I've missed you all so much! How are they?'

'Nicky's still Nicky, you know, boys.'

'Doesn't change! And Julia?'

'Pregnant!' I exclaim, keeping things short, it's awkward reliving the last two years on a pavement. I hesitate, but she'll know soon enough. 'My friend actually set me up on that show *Swipe Right*, you know the one?'

'Of course! The one with Lorenzo the total DILF!'

'Well, you can come to the viewing party if you like, at mine? I've got some friends coming to watch me make a fool of myself – Julia, Nicky and a couple of others. I mean, if you don't think it's too awkward,' I quickly add. 'You know with me being married to Adam before.' God, I was married, it's so hard to believe now.

'Milly, I'd love to. Adam always said he wanted you to be able to have a life after him. You really should never feel guilty – nothing was your fault, you know that.'

We hug again and this time say goodbye.

I feel tears start to stream down my face. I know it wasn't my fault, but I've wanted someone to say that for so long. Reassure me. But I can't help but still feel guilty about Theo. It's not easy trying to love again.

It's so weird. I always felt like you were supposed to get better and not look back. Keep going up. But it seems that the most uncertain thing about grief is wondering when you are going to fall back down again. The reason why it's so hard is that it's so up and down, it makes you feel seasick. You can have good and bad days – Layla's reassured me of that – at least now I have a companion in grief, someone who really does understand.

I couldn't face reading Theo's reply before. I've fucked it all.

Really, Milly? I thought we had a great time the other day, and you introduced me to your friends – that nearly holds as much gravitas as being Facebook official ;P Can we maybe meet up for a drink? X

I'm so confused. Theo is lovely and I feel like I really like him. I shouldn't feel guilty. Then why are my emotions so conflicted? I don't need a life coach; I need a life manager.

@RedRagToABull @Mizzennial I know I'm not a naturally angry person, but there is a rage inside me I can't control. Every time I see or hear someone talking about their mum, I snap. Mother's Day wasn't that long ago and I couldn't control myself. Every time someone told me what their plans were, I flipped. I don't want to be like this. It's no one's fault, I know that.

I think about the rage that sometimes starts bubbling up inside of me. Anger at what's happened. Why me? Why Adam? I get angry at myself for being angry, for hating the world, but it's not my fault, it's just part of grief. I can't expect everything to be smooth all the time.

@Mizzennial @RedRagToABull It's totally normal to feel rage at the world. You can't comprehend what happened and you feel angry at everyone else for their life being so perfect. You need to find a release, have you tried writing? X

2 February 2017

'Morning, sunshine!' I bound on the bed with a tray of presents, cup of tea and scrambled eggs. I made the eggs with cream and loads of pepper – Adam's favourite. Indulgent but celebrations of life deserve it. 'Happy birthday!'

'Ha, Milly, you didn't need to do this, thank you so much.' He kisses me. 'OK, OK. My favourite eggs made by my favourite person – stop being so sweet.'

'Open your presents, then!' I shove a tower of badly wrapped squishy gifts on his lap. I chose navy-blue wrapping paper, as I'd guess that's his favourite colour. But favourite colours, animals and shapes don't tend to dominate conversations like they did when you were ten.

'Do you hate the way I dress or something?' Adam asks jokingly as he pulls out another T-shirt.

'Just think of me as a personal fashion advisor.' What else do you buy guys? And yes, I do hate his fashion sense, but that's part of being a girlfriend – teach your boyfriend how to dress. I got him an entire new outfit because he never buys his own clothes. Adam hates shopping but is fussy, so I have to be careful with my choices.

'What do you have in store for me today, then?' Adam asks as he dresses in his new clothes. It reminds me of when I was younger, and if you ever had any new clothes, it was imperative that you wore them all out at once, regardless of the weather. Hailstorm outside? Why I must wear my new Havaianas – everyone will be begging to see my birthday toes.

'Well, you've always said that you wanted to go on the London Eye, so we're having a tourist adventure in London – I even got you a selfie stick for the day!'

'You are so thoughtful, Mills.'

'You can even wear your sunglasses on the Tube and ask me for a photo in front of any major entrance or exit.'

'Ha! Yes, I'll hold an umbrella up so you know where to find me if I get lost.'

'Oh, I did get you another present.'

'Stop it, you're spoiling me.' He fakes coyness as he rips open the wrapping paper, gazes into his hands for a minute and leans over to kiss me.

'I remember that day like it was yesterday. Look at my hair, I look awful! I think we've grown more beautiful with age.'

'I'll say – I look like I ate all my university housemates.'

He props the photo on his bedside table. Adam and I, smiling, dressed in bin bags and salad leaves – a very accurate representation of the Slug and Lettuce.

'Oh my God – I just noticed something awful!'

'What?' Adam looks intrigued as I pick up the photo from his bedside table.

'I thought that was part of your leg, but it's actually your ball sack hanging out of that dress!'

'Shut up! That photo's been on Facebook for years! Go online immediately and delete it – what if my colleagues see?'

28

29 March 2019

Tonight, my episode of *Swipe Right* airs, and I'm pleased that I've got the girls coming round to take my mind off the fact that I'm about to hugely embarrass myself and that Theo is probably watching.

I was going to cook but I can't be bothered, so I decided to order pizzas; with everyone's dietary requirements, any culinary creation would have been such a hassle. What can you make that is vegan, gluten-free, sugar-free, lactose-free and doesn't taste of dust?

Julia and Nicky arrive first, Nicky with a big bottle of prosecco and Julia with a box of chocolates – which I think accurately demonstrates the different stages of their lives. One stays in, eating chocolates and the other goes out, downing prosecco. Whatever, we all have our weaknesses – I quite like both.

Next to arrive is @ShelleyFarrell, also with a bottle of alcohol, quickly followed by @ILikeMyMenHotAndBlack, who brings a reusable Starbucks cup she stole from the till.

Then finally Layla. She gives me a huge bunch of flowers, which I shove into a vase, and then Julia, being the mum she is, takes them out and snips all the ends off so they last longer. I've never been good at flower arranging, even though my flat did resemble a florist's those immediate weeks after Adam died.

I introduce the two sets of friends. I was feeling nervous about it before, but it seems like they get on like a house on fire. I know

Layla felt awkward at first, but then Nicky and Julia poured her a big glass of prosecco, which she respectfully declined, but drank an orange juice and had a chocolate instead and they seem to be getting on simply fine. Like old times.

We start our pizzas, ready for my television debut. I was going to order my favourite Hawaiian, but Adam and I shared our love of fruit on pizza, and it would feel almost blasphemous eating that while I watched myself date other men, so I ordered a pepperoni instead.

I've made it into the introduction credits with my hula-hooping – thank God they chose the clip of my hooping round my waist as opposed to my pecking-deck interpretation. I cringe thinking of Theo watching, his dimples burning from laughing so much at my embarrassment.

'You look great, Milly! Your hooping skills are insane,' @ShelleyFarrell kindly points out while taking a massive swig of wine.

'Is it too much to Insta story my hooping on the TV?'

'I think wait until we see how the rest of the show pans out first – you don't want to draw attention to it if they are showing embarrassing clips.' @ILikeMyMenHotAndBlack seems to be the fountain of knowledge.

'True.'

I ended it with Theo, but he hasn't technically ended it with me yet. Will it spark something in him, seeing me on TV again? What's he thinking? Maybe that I'm a real catch, or thankful that I blew him off.

We watch the whole first part, having only seen the back of my hair.

'At least your hair looks good,' Nicky comments while an advert for alopecia treatments plays in the background.

'So far, you've done nothing but look good, you are acing TV,' Julia says, trying to be positive, but I can sense an air of sarcasm. 'You look really . . . nice.'

'You do realise that saying someone looks nice is not a compliment – you're making me sound vanilla.' You wouldn't want the vicar reading your eulogy describing you as 'nice' and then thanking everyone for coming.

The next fifteen minutes aren't much better. There is a snip of me coughing into my hand, which Nicky has realised that if you slow it down, it looks like I'm giving a blow job.

WTF. Why are they not showing more shots of me looking glamorous and sexy?

'They're clearly concentrating on the other two dates for the first half – I'm sure you'll be in the next slot. Did you not tell them about your car accident? If you didn't then, that's probably why you haven't featured yet. You're too vanilla, too boring for TV.'

I should have told them I was a widow, then I would have had 90 per cent of the airtime.

Finally, in the last fifteen minutes, they share some clips of me with accelerator-voice Liam and eager-beaver Justin. God, is this what dating's like? I remember how awkward the dates were and how happy I was having dinner with Theo after. There's nothing wrong with him – he's perfect. Almost.

'You look great, Milly; your contouring is incredible! Did you use Kim Kardashian's new kit? I would date you just based on your new cheekbones!' Layla's always been someone that makes me feel good about myself.

The camera focuses in on Liam and I chatting about our jobs. Hope no one at work watches me slating the entire company on national TV. Hopefully Mizzennial will take off soon and I can leave with my head held high.

Ping.

Theo: Are you watching *Swipe Right*? Looks like Liam really likes you. I can pass you his number if you like ;p x

It's Theo. He's watching.

> **Me:** That's OK. Was it you who edited the coughing scene? Looks a bit X-rated for a pre-watershed TV show! X
> **Theo:** Ha ha, no. Anyway, hope you have a nice evening x

He is thinking about me. Someone who cares about me and makes me laugh. I pop my phone back into my pocket, feeling all fizzy, like a refresher in a glass of water.

After the show, Julia gives me a quick low-down on how they've been preparing for the imminent arrival of their new mini-me – I can't believe that's so soon. I can't think about it. It makes me nervous for her. Then she has to say her goodbyes because she's pregnant and the days of getting blackout drunk are behind her. You must feel so good when you're pregnant. Literally no more embarrassing nights out ever again!

If you stopped having hangovers and scrolling on Instagram, it would probably be like having a fourteen-day week. I can't do it all at once – that can be for next year.

Layla also says her goodbyes – she's not really into clubbing these days. We vow to do a lunch soon, with Julia and Nicky too.

Nicky goes outside for a cigarette and returns absolutely wasted.

'Millllllly! Heyyyyyyy, do you wanna be my lover?' Nicky drools while trying to do a sexy pose in the doorway.

Rushing towards me, she trips over nothing and falls flat on her face.

'God, what was that? I am not even drunk!' says every drunk person ever.

'Come on.' I pull her up on the sofa next to me.

'God I'm feeling so sick, really sick.'

'You know where the toilet is. Stop retching like that – go to the loo! Nicky! Go now!'

Nicky stands up, sways and throws up on my floor.

'God, I'm so sorry Milly. I don't know where that came from.' As she's sick again through her fingers. She looks like a monster, red-wine sick splaying through her fingers. It stinks. It's like her insides have fallen out all over my room. It's a good job she's my friend.

I put Nicky in an Uber, and @ShelleyFarrell and @ILikeMyMenHotAndBlack start cleaning my room. The putrid smell of red wine that has already gone halfway through the digestive system is about to set me off.

'Right, girls – let's go out! I know a really cool club in Chelsea that'll let us in, probably even get us a table if you want,' Shelley says, rapidly texting one of her club promoter friends. When you get older, you realise that the term 'club promoter' is a synonym for pervert.

After a quick touch-up, burst of dry shampoo and downing the remnants of our wine, we all clamber into an Uber and head to Chelsea.

'ID please?'

'Really, I'm twenty-eight!' @ILikeMyMenHotAndBlack exclaims.

'Well, you look eighteen,' the guy on reception jokes.

'I'll take that as a compliment,' she says, snatching her ID and holding it up to her face, smirking.

I thought he was giving @ILikeMyMenHotAndBlack her entry ticket, but in fact it was his number! What have I been doing stuck inside for so long? There's so much life to be lived!

'What do you want to drink?!' @ShelleyFarrell shouts in my face as some of her saliva goes into my mouth.

'I don't mind!' I shout back. I can't hear her over the latest remix of P!nk's 'Get the Party Started'. There isn't any new music nowadays. We just take all the old songs and cut them up with car horn sounds and someone having a stroke on the decks, and voila! Vintage.

@ShelleyFarrell's at the bar and @ILikeMyMenHotAnd-Black and I are standing around pretending to dance but just shifting our weight from one foot to the other. How have we forgotten how to dance? Are we too old to go out? Everyone else is out in crop tops and we decided to cover our midriffs this evening, making us look the oldest people in here. Apart from the mum and daughter having dinner while ten-year-olds get down and dirty in front of them. She must have read the website incorrectly; this is not a dinner establishment.

All that wine has gone straight through me. As I'm jostling my way through the hordes of girls anxiously waiting for the toilet, I see something. I must be really drunk. I walk closer, as I can't really believe my eyes. Gosh, it isn't any old mum and daughter – it's @SocialShrink91!

I thought that if I ever met her in person, we would become the best of friends and she'd help me on my path to becoming a successful blogger. Not that I even need her for that any more. I get sent daily DMs from people asking me to post about teeth whitening or workout gear, but I'd prefer to promote things my followers actually want.

She's eating a full-fat, full-meat burger! What the fuck? She's supposed to be a vegan, promoting healthy living and a clean lifestyle. This can't be her. My eyes must be playing tricks on me.

It's definitely her. Tousled locks framing her face and her bronzed, elegant, lean frame.

'Erm, hi, are you Social Shrink? I, erm, am a big fan.'

'Yes, I am, do you want a selfie?' she says, trying to hide her burger behind her back.

'I thought you were a vegan,' I say, pointing to the burger.

'Oh, err, it's a jackfruit burger!'

'No, it isn't, I can smell cow, and isn't that a new season Gucci?' I nod towards her bag that is 100 per cent not pleather.

@SocialShrink91's mum is sitting there, slurping her drink as if she's watching her favourite blockbuster movie, not her daughter being outed for being a fake vegan. She looks exactly like @SocialShrink91, as if someone had taken a twenty-something's face and added a couple of lines for good measure.

'God! Does it even matter?' She turns looking to her mum for support, but she's still slurping, almost egging her daughter on for more entertainment. 'Do you want a selfie or not? Get me back to the Rose Garden asap!' She starts to look really pissed off. Her mum turns her wrist to check her Gucci watch for added drama.

'What's the Rose Garden?'

'It's the VIP area – you wouldn't know it. I only came here for a fucking burger with my mum, and as soon as I do, someone like you pounces on me and basically starts bullying me. You must be one of those social media trolls!' @SocialShrink91's mum looks shocked that she has met a real-life troll, almost choking on the last few slurps of drink.

I've never really been a mean person, not intentionally, anyway. Since Adam died, sometimes it feels like I don't know how else to express my emotions. I guess even those that are successful on social media can still be trapped by its expectations – just like I was.

'Sorry.' I look down at my shoes, shaking my head. 'I know what it's like. I don't know what happened there, I got caught up in seeing someone I loved so much on Instagram and realising that not everything you see online is real. I know that already,' I say, thinking of everything I've learned over the last few months. 'Please, just have your burger and enjoy your evening with your mum – everyone needs a break sometimes.' I smile.

She smiles gingerly back, not sure whether to believe me.

'I have an account called Mizzennial . . .' I pipe up.

@SocialShrink91 rolls her eyes slightly; I assume she thinks I'm as fame hungry as everyone else out there.

'It's a bit like the *Mizz* magazines – not sure if you remember, the ones with the cringe pages, agony aunts, you know?'

'Oh, you used to love those!' @SocialShrink91's mum stops slurping and pipes up. 'Remember, when you started thinking of cringe stories to send in and . . .'

'Shut up, Mum!' @SocialShrink91's eyes glare towards her fifty-going-on-twenty mother.

'Well.' I swallow. 'It's more than that, it's a place where you can anonymously disclose how you feel, advice for young people from young people. A ready-made community of people who really care and make you feel better about yourself.' I swallow again, a little harder this time. 'Sorry if I was a bit abrupt earlier. I started my Mizzennial account because my husband died and I realised I could help others deal with problems too. I've been in a bad place for such a long time, sometimes I forget how to act. I'm still learning.' @SocialShrink91's mum's eyes look slightly pained at my past and @SocialShrink91 reaches out a hand.

'I'm sorry for not being the person you thought I was. It's hard keeping up with everyone's expectations of you online. Sometimes I want to go back to the old me, but that's not the person I've told my followers I am.' She looks up. 'And I miss burgers, real juicy meat burgers.' She grins.

'Me too – I'm Milly, by the way.'

'Finley. It's not all cool and gender-neutral; my mum wanted a boy.' Finley's mum raises her eyebrows in shock. 'Nice to meet you.' Her eyes light up and she takes a big bite of her burger.

'Maybe see you on the 'gram!' I smile and walk away.

I walk back over to my girls as my phone buzzes and I see Mizzennial has a new follower – @SocialShrink91. There is such a thing as karma!

'It was three for two! What a bargain!' @ShelleyFarrell exclaims, carrying three bottles of white wine towards me as I walk back to the group. Basically, one for each of us.

'Have you had any thoughts about coming on the podcast, Milly? After seeing you on *Swipe Right*, you're a natural media personality,' @ShelleyFarrell says drunkenly while filling my wine glass right to the brim.

'That's kind of you, Shelley, but I'm really not sure. Can I have a think about it? Let's just get drunk and enjoy tonight.'

'Cheers to that!' We clink our plastic wine glasses, spilling the fluorescent liquid into each other's drinks. We're like three wine sisters.

2 May 2017

'How are you feeling about today?' I ask Adam while I grip the steering wheel tighter. My palms are sweaty; I feel nervous and today isn't even about me.

'Apprehensive but OK. It's not something I thought I would be doing, but one to tick off the bucket list, I guess.'

'Yeah, I guess,' I say absentmindedly.

We drive for about ten more minutes in silence. It doesn't seem appropriate to listen to music or to make mindless conversation. I pull into the concrete car park. Grey, grey, grey. You'd think they would make a funeral director's a little less depressing than it already is.

Adam gets out of the car; I rush round to check if he needs any help. I know I'm probably being annoying, and he doesn't want to feel like a charity case, but I can't help it. He grabs my hand.

'I know this feels weird, Milly. It does for me too. I just couldn't leave this for you to do alone. I'm going to die, there's nothing I can do, so let me make sure that it's not any more stressful for you once I'm gone.' He kisses me. It's funny, at the beginning I would have been broken by a conversation like this, but now we talk about death at every corner, over breakfast, dinner, cups of tea, in bed. It's still sad, but it's inevitable. I still cry, but all the connotations surrounding the word *death* have, ironically, become part of life.

'Ahh, you must be Adam Hadfield. Lovely to meet you, sir, come right this way.' The chubby, red-faced funeral director named Chester greets us. He looks like Santa's brother; maybe that's on purpose to cheer people up.

We make our way through to his little office and sit at the circular wooden table. Chester brings us both a glass of iced water.

'How can I be of assistance today then, sir?'

'I'd like to plan my funeral, please, Chester, and let's make it a good 'un!' Adam says smiling.

Chester looks slightly taken aback.

'Oh right. I'm sorry to hear that, young man. We don't get many like this in here. May I ask when, erm . . .'

'When the big day will be? Hmm, well, they said about six months from the diagnosis, give or take, so probably around August or September, something like that.'

I can't help but smile. It's not funny. Nothing about this is funny, but it's still him. My Adam, cheering me up. Doing his best to make light of a situation.

Chester asks him a few more questions and then gives us a brochure of headstones and coffins; Like an extremely morbid Argos catalogue, but one where you don't have to worry about whether or not you're in to receive the parcel.

'I'd like a marble headstone, please, an engraved one, and I want to be buried with space so that if my wife wants to be' – he looks at me – 'she can be there next to me, but hopefully not for a few decades yet. And her new family too. I want space for everyone. I also want one of these shiny pine coffins, but I don't want to be buried. I want to be cremated. I don't fancy the thought of turning into a zombie if there was a zombie apocalypse. *But*, I am a bit scared of the burning part. Can you just check I'm well and truly gone before you send me into the flames? I am a little ticklish, so if you could give me a quick tickle under the arms for good measure, I'd appreciate it.'

I squeeze his hand tight. I know he's nervous, scared. I am too.

'Ok, sir, all noted.' Chester smiles at me. 'And, my darling girl, will you be in charge on the day?'

'Actually, no, I think Adam's mother, Amanda, will be. I think it's her wish, although I'll be on hand to help if she needs me at all.'

'I'd like the wake to be in the Hawthorne pub, my favourite, and I want an open bar. I want people to celebrate my life. For the music, nothing sad – it won't be a nice day for anyone. I'd like some rock music, perhaps T-Rex.'

All of Adam's requests are noted down, we pay the deposit and walk out to the car.

'Are you OK, Mills?'

'Yes, I'm fine. Are you OK? I can't imagine, you know . . .'

'I am nervous. I don't know what's waiting for me on the other side, but I have my granny and grandpa waiting for me there, so they can look after me. I just want to make things as easy as possible for you, Mills. I'll do anything I can to make this easier.'

'I know you will.'

We embrace in the car park, just as a hearse is pulling in. Nothing's ever seemed so poignant.

29

30 March 2019

There's a parcel on my doorstep, something I didn't order on ASOS. Inside is a box of chocolates – my favourite, those fancy chocolate shells that Adam used to buy me; a set of face masks; a book – *Life Is What You Make It;* and a card:

> *I'm so proud of you and how far you've come, Mills. Love Florry X*

I told Florry about @ShelleyFarrell's podcast and she insisted that I do it. She said I would be amazing and it would be so helpful for others going through grief to hear my side of the story. This must be a gift to say well done – I've never really had someone send me something before.

I smile. How kind and unexpected.

I laugh. The last time I received a parcel in the post, it wasn't for me but for a neighbour that I'd accidentally opened in my eagerness, thinking that someone would want to send me something. Luckily, it was a boring old cookery book, not something embarrassing like sex toys from Love Honey that I'd have to hastily rewrap and give back alongside a batch of home-made cookies, because I felt so morbidly embarrassed about the whole thing.

Great content for Mizzennial – I find a meme about neighbours and dildos and post onto the grid.

I think about how far I've come on my journey to being myself again and the unexpected kindness of strangers and even my own sister. How all these people have unknowingly helped me so much. I told Florry I would do it and now she's sent me chocolates, so I have to, I'd be a fraud if I didn't.

@Mizzennial @ShelleyFarrell OK, I'll come on your podcast, but I am a bit nervous. Can I still stay anonymous for now? X

'Gosh, Violet, are you OK?'

'Don't ask, Milly.' Her forehead looks like it's been stuck in a beehive for a week. 'I am going through a midlife crisis.' Depressing when you define your existence as at the midpoint; at what age do you decide that's it, you only have half your life to go? Adam's would have been at fourteen. 'I've had an allergic reaction to Botox.'

'I'd say! It'll go down in a few days – don't worry about it. You don't look *that* bad.' My eyebrows furrow in that way people do to hide the fact they are lying.

'Thanks, Milly. I am aware I look hideous, sweet of you to protect my feelings. I have a date on Saturday, so let's hope I look less blow-up doll by then.' There are so many things I don't know about her yet.

'Think positive and maybe take some antihistamines?'

'Don't worry, I've already had two today.' She absent-mindedly rubs her forehead, as if by saying the medication out loud it may have shrunk a couple of millimetres. 'Anyway, how can I help?'

'One of my friends has a podcast. She asked me to go on it and speak about my relationship with grief. I think I'm ready, but I don't know if I'll regret it. I've been opening up gradually, but on my own terms, not on anyone else's. This makes it seem more real.'

'Only you know if you're ready or not, Milly. It might be good to speak about Adam and what you've been through. Why don't you give it a go, and if you change your mind, you can always release it at a later date? It might be good to record how you feel.'

'I guess, it's only what I'm doing on Mizzennial, but in real life. I did say to myself that I wanted to become the same person I am offline as I am online.'

'This is your chance, Milly. You can give it a go without going too far, and if you aren't happy, no one has to know it's you. If you're able to unite your online profile with the real emotions you feel offline, well, you'll be doing what we all wish we were brave enough to do ourselves.'

'Today on *Talk Thirty To Me*, we have the mastermind behind the Instagram handle Mizzennial here with us to talk about her experiences. If this is your first time tuning in, *Talk Thirty To Me* is the podcast where we discuss issues that affect all of us in our late twenties and early thirties.'

@ShelleyFarrell's so confident in front of the microphone. It feels weird, recording it in her bedroom, but also strangely nostalgic, like I'm in a Lizzie McGuire movie.

'Mizzennial, tell us a little bit about who you are and why you started the channel.'

'I remember being so excited to receive my magazine subscription when I was younger. Which freebie would I get this week? I couldn't wait to read the embarrassing stories section, get a new poster for my wall and read about other girls' problems, which were eerily similar to my own. It was like Instagram but in paper format, and people asked questions because they were curious and not because they wanted likes,' I say with a sudden ooze of confidence. What was I so worried about?

'Was it this that made you start Mizzennial – which, guys, if you aren't following you really should!'

'I've experienced some trauma in my life, and I was in a bit of a hole. I find that when life gets you down, it likes to give you another kick just to make sure you're still there! I was reading some magazines one day and it made me reminisce about them when I was younger. I wanted to create a platform to discuss serious issues and make people laugh too!' I've practised these lines; they are flowing easily, like the water in the little brook near my parents' house.

'Would you mind telling our audience about your trauma?'

I gulp. It's OK.

'I, erm, I.' I feel balls of anxiety, agony and sick rising and bubbling in my throat. 'I can't do it.' There it is. The confidence knocker. Speaking with raw truth and in detail about what happened to my love, my life, me, that's when the gates to the castle come crashing down.

@ShelleyFarrell presses pause.

'It's OK, Milly. We don't have to talk about it, we can save it for when you are ready.'

What's the matter with me? I've spoken about this with Violet, I've told @ShelleyFarrell before, I've even told my entire Mizzennial following. I've reached out to old friends, I've apologised, I've met Layla. Maybe it's that final essence of vulnerability. It would be linking it all together.

'I want to do it, but I don't know if I can form the words.'

'Let's take some deep breaths. I'll make us a cup of tea.'

The magical powers of tea leaves come into play yet again.

'I don't know why I can't speak about him. I know he's dead. Gone. Nothing's going to happen if I say his name – I'm acting like he is Voldemort. I've told Violet, my counsellor, about him. I stopped messaging him on Facebook chat, stopped stalking him every day, pretending he's there. It feels like this is the last hurdle, and once I finally rip the plaster off and tell the world, that part of my life will be over.'

@ShelleyFarrell remains quiet. 'That was so raw, so honest, Milly. You can speak about him. I was recording, but I'll delete it if you want me to.'

There we have it: my feelings, recorded for eternity. Do I want them deleted? It's the only proof I have that I am a caring person, not a total stone-cold bitch.

'No, keep it.' I say softly. 'I'll try again.'

'Tell me how you and your husband met?'

'We met at a roller disco in freshers' week at university. I can't skate and he offered to help me.' I laugh, remembering how bad I was. 'I was rude to him because I felt embarrassed – I mean, I literally couldn't stand – but he persevered and I liked that. He had these eyes that were so blue sometimes I swear I could see my own reflection. And he was funny.'

@ShelleyFarrell laughs. 'Oh dear! Do you think you can tell me a little more about your relationship and then what happened?'

Can I?

'We were together for nearly seven years; we knew everything about each other. He loved history, but would sit and watch *Gossip Girl* with me. I knew the exact amount of milk he had in his tea and how he liked tomatoes in a salad, but not in a sandwich. His family were my family and mine were his. We shared the same friends, spent every evening and weekend together – you know how it is.' I look to @ShelleyFarrell, who's nodding knowingly in agreement. 'And then one day.' Gulp. 'He came to collect me from work, in London, and we went for a drink. I thought it was a normal day. We would have a drink and then go home, cook dinner and bicker about whether to watch a murder mystery or historical drama. Then he told me he had testicular cancer.

Stage Four. Nothing they could do.' I start to cry, thinking about it. I feel shivers down my spine remembering him say those words. C-A-N-C-E-R. Remembering when life slowed down, and it felt as if Adam was talking in slow motion. When was the last time I really remembered that fateful day?

'That must have been so awful.' @ShelleyFarrell says in one of the sincerest voices I think I've ever heard. If I'm not mistaken, there are tears rolling down her cheeks.

'I don't remember the rest. It's a blur.' I'm trying to remember, but I can feel the resistance of my memory pushing back. 'It was awful. He was the love of my life. I thought we were going to buy a big house together, have children, create the perfect fairy-tale life. I used to wake up in the arms of someone I loved, get sent cheeky texts saying "I love you", flowers on Valentine's Day. It all suddenly changed, and I started to wake up alone, crying, wondering if I'll ever love again.'

I hear @ShelleyFarrell press the 'stop' button. I'm crying, really crying, and she's hugging me.

Eventually I come up for air.

'Let's stop, it must be so hard for you.' @ShelleyFarrell says, holding my hand.

'No, I want to continue.'

'OK, only if you are a 100 per cent sure.' @ShelleyFarrell sorts out her recording again. 'How do you feel now about love and dating in the millennial world? I'm assuming you never went on dating apps before?'

'No, I didn't. It's a bloody minefield of liars and dicks and people who lie about their dicks, haha. I've been on both sides of the love coin. Feeling super smug that you're in a relationship, and then seeing people with partners that they're clearly just settling for and you know they could do better. I've lived vicariously through single friends, thinking it's all fancy dates and hot sex, to find it's just a barrage of dick pics. I can't keep up with everyone else any more. Sometimes, I fantasise about being a homemaker but that's not even a choice I can make, because I don't have a boyfriend or kids. I'm trapped in this world that wants me to be independent and successful, and I just want to lean my head on someone else's shoulder for once. My life would've been over in the olden days because no boys would have fancied me, so I would probably have been the only female in the world still working at twenty-eight. A barren beast selling insulin injections from the boot of a Ford Thunderbird. I have nothing to celebrate. I have no life achievements and no career ones either. And when I scroll on Instagram, I'm constantly reminded about how irrelevant my twenty-eight-year-old life really is. If I wanted to meet your baby, I would've come over already, OK?!' Wow. That was a lot of suppressed anger.

'Do you know what? I totally understand! Dating's so rubbish nowadays. My granny met my grandpa at a dance and then travelled to Manila to marry him after a year of love letters. There is no way you could do that now. Time moves so fast; by the time Royal Mail had sent your letter, he would have probably fucked half the girls across the Atlantic!'

'Very true. Recently, my friends set me up with an online dating profile. I didn't realise, but there are some rules for dating profiles. It's really hard to try and get people to fancy you in four photos. I thought my photo choices were really fun, showed that I had a bit of personality, but my friends said they made me look deranged. Due to the disparity of my hairstyles, I looked like four different people, and my friend Julia said unless I wanted to look like I was advertising an orgy, I should probably find some photos where I look more consistent.'

'Are you dating now, then? How do you feel about introducing someone new into your life? Are they understanding?'

'I was dating, but I ended it. I felt like it was all a little too soon. I did really like him, but I was battling with the love of my past too. Sometimes I have up days and others down. It is a long process and one that only time can heal.' Violet would be proud of me for saying that.

'Thank you, err, Mizzennial. It has been extremely enlightening, and I hope to have you on the show again soon.'

Maybe it's finally time I show everyone the real me.

'It's Milly. And his name was Adam. He was called Adam.'

28 April 2017

'Are you sure you're up for it?'

'Yes, I'm not an invalid, Mills, I'm fine.' I look deadpan, but in my head I'm rolling my eyes. I know it's hard for him to admit that he needs to be looked after now, but I don't think you can get much more invalided than terminal cancer.

'Have you got everything? Remember if you suddenly don't feel well, please tell me immediately.' I plead with him. This is not the time for pretending to be all macho.

I triple-check my rucksack to ensure we have everything and pop it in the boot. I open the passenger door for Adam, and he sits himself down. Chivalry isn't dead yet.

I turn on Kisstory, and we sit in happy silence, punctuated by the odd sing-a-long to Kid Cudi or All Saints, and the satnav telling me to go left or right, or Adam shouting that I just drove through a red.

'I see the sea, little daff!' Adam suddenly calls.

I turn and grin at him. Hearing the upbeat notion to his voice brings a smile to my face; it's like old times.

We park a little way from the pier and the beachfront.

'Who knew one of the perks of cancer would be free parking?' Adam jokes. He still has it in him.

'They should add it to the NHS website,' I try to joke back, but the pain riddles my words. It's not that having cancer is a joke, but you can't get upset about it every time it's mentioned. What's the point? 'Do you want beach and chips, or arcade and doughnuts first?'

'Arcade. I want to beat you on the dance mat, and I fancy winning myself a treasure chest of pennies. You can't take it with you.'

I slow my pace considerably; I don't want Adam to feel like he has to keep up with me. We hold hands, tight. When you know there is only so much of something left, you don't take anything for granted. It's like your senses suddenly come alive. The salt from the sea is so sharp it pierces my nose, punctuated with woody, spicy wafts of Adam's aftershave; my tongue salivates at the concoction of fried goods in the air; my eardrums vibrate and take supersonic impressions of the tone of Adam's voice, the way the syllables rise up and down, the way he says my name; my fingertips caress the soft skin on the back of his hand and tickle the tips of his; and my eyes take vivid snapshots of everything in their vision – Adam and I holding hands, the way his mouth moves when he talks, the way it curls when he smiles. Him. Just him.

'Charlie? Olivia?' Adam calls to a tall guy, head and shoulders above the crowd, and a girl with a short blonde bob who are smiling and waving in our direction.

'Surprise!' I say to Adam's smiling face.

It's one of those weird situations. We've always had a busy social calendar, a strong cohort of university friends, work friends, home friends, but what do you do with your weekends when you don't know how many of them you'll have left? Everyone wants to see Adam, but they don't want to overwhelm him. I know deep down Adam wants to see his friends, but he also feels a bit awkward. He doesn't want everyone to feel sorry for him, he doesn't want to say bye for what could be the last time. But if I don't organise these things for him, he might never see them again and I know that would make everyone sad, including Adam.

Olivia and Charlie hug Adam tight. I briefed them before they arrived. They saw him about a month ago, but I warned them that he's deteriorated. 'Act normal,' I told them.

'Mate!' Charlie says, giving Adam a little nudge on the shoulder. 'Let's get some food I'm bloody starving!'

Olivia purchases a bag of freshly cooked doughnuts from the man on the pavilion and hands it to me. I see a seagull in my periphery.

'Shall we get a Slush Puppie, Adam? Blue raspberry, your favourite! Remember when you made Slush Puppie cocktails, and Charlie was sick everywhere?'

'Don't remind me.' Charlie laughs.

'You made a right twat of yourself.' Adam laughs. 'In front of Tilly – you were trying to impress her, and you looked like you'd eaten Papa Smurf!' He laughs more. It's good seeing him laugh.

Seagulls suddenly start swarming around us on the pier.

'Not again, Mills!' Adam throws the bag of doughnuts on the wooden slats just before a group of seagulls swoop down and peck them to death. 'I can't have a winged creature stealing yet another kiss from my girl. Last time we came to Brighton, Milly basically got with a seagull.' Adam kindly reminds us. 'He took a doughnut right out of her mouth. Don't start dating seagulls when I'm gone.' He winks at me.

Olivia and Charlie look slightly awkward, not sure whether to laugh or not.

'You saved my life,' I joke back, trying to alleviate the situation. I feel a tear in my eye; not out of sadness, out of remembering how carefree we were the last time we came here. What I would do to turn back time. Olivia grabs my hand reassuringly.

We decide to give the doughnuts a miss and head straight to the arcade for the ultimate dance mat competition. Adam slots two pounds in the machine and gets to it, on expert level, of course.

'I'm going to thrash you, mate.' Charlie grins at him.

He's good, but not as good as me. 'Come on, slowcoach, what you playing at?' I joke to him as Charlie lets him win. I love him so much, my dancing partner. He finishes, and I get on for my turn. I know I could beat him, but I decide this isn't the time for competitiveness.

30

2 April 2019

I feel different after the podcast recording. The anxiety, grief, worry has been bottled up inside me for so long, but speaking out loud to @ShelleyFarrell was a powerful release, like the popping of a cork on a champagne bottle.

I've been thinking about Theo more and more since the airing of *Swipe Right* and our banterous messaging. I felt compelled to tell him about my interview on *Talk Thirty To Me,* but then I remembered that he knows nothing about me. If he knew about my history, he'd probably swipe left quicker than an Aldi cashier.

Ping.

Message from Theo.

My heart pulses. I feel a buzz every time he messages, even though he's my own forbidden fruit.

Theo: Have you got hordes of people messaging you after your *Swipe Right* debut? I knew I should have kept one of the Asahi bottles to sell on eBay in case you became famous!

Me: TBH I'm struggling to get through the throngs of messages from hot boys. That would have been creepy, but I'll send you my autograph on a napkin, if you like?

Theo: Or you could give it to me in person?

I probably do owe Theo the courtesy of explaining that there's a lot more to me than my goofball exterior.

> **Me:** Can you meet me at The Sheldon after work tonight? Like 6 p.m.? There'll be a black Hummer outside and the *Daily Mail* paps, so you can't miss me ;p

Theo agrees immediately. Why's he being so nice? Boys aren't like this normally. What if he's in fact a serial killer? I've spent the last eighteen or so months filling my mind with conspiracy documentaries on Netflix, so sometimes I think everyone's out to get me.

Everyone has their own devils with grief. I think mine's been about letting go. If I keep focusing on the past, how can I ever expect to move on? I always felt like I was cheating on Adam emotionally and physically. He's always there but in a different way to before. I'm allowed to have other relationships; I'm not doing anything wrong.

I order a pint of beer, as I need some alcohol to numb me and I'm not trying to be sophisticated or impress anyone by choosing some ridiculous gin-and-egg-yolk cocktail. Adam liked me even though I drank beer, and Theo and I already shared some Asahi.

I see his head bobbing past the window. This pub is inconspicuous; no one would normally come here from work because they're not fat, bald fish farmers. I got some funny looks when I walked in. One man jeered, 'How much do you charge, love?' Before cheersing his other slimy eel mates. I'm not being big-headed, but based on the appearance and the smell, I must easily be the fittest girl they've ever seen. That's right, Milly – power to women.

Theo looks quite confused when he walks through the door. Maybe he thinks I've pranked him.

'Not another pompadomp!' one of the men shouts. I think that must mean *posh person* but I'm unsure.

I wave to Theo so he doesn't immediately run back outside, wondering whether I'm somehow associated with the Kray twins.

'Hey, Milly, you OK?' He leans over to kiss me on the face. I contemplate moving my head away, but think twice about it. I offer my cheek as an alternative.

I do really like him, but I'm scared.

'Yes, fine. How are you?' It wasn't supposed to sound so flat and awkward, that's my guard coming up.

We sit and have mindless conversation for a few minutes, the type of chat that you're both doing to fill a void of silence because you don't want to get to the awkward part that you both came here to address. The dry conversation finally peters to a silence.

'So . . . are you going to tell me why you ended it? I know it might seem weird, Milly, or too soon, but I really like you. There's a connection between us. I can be myself, natural.'

He likes me?

'It's just. Erm. Just. Look, we're obviously at different points in our lives and I know we're not going to work out, so I wanted to end it now.' I can't put him through the bad days that I will inevitably have, the crying, the inferior feeling that my heart will always belong to someone else.

'How can you possibly know that? I thought we got on? I respect your decision, but I'm going to need more to go on than that. Has something happened?'

'Nothing has happened, Theo. I don't want to hurt you, that's all.' I can feel tears pricking in my eyes. Why am I crying? Please don't say my period has decided to start right at this moment. I twist the ring in my right palm, thinking. Part of my heart does belong to Adam, but I've been getting that feeling that the other part may open up to love again.

'I know you're feeling a bit down at the moment with the car accident and everything, and I'll give you all the space you need, but I do really like you.' Theo puts his hand on mine. His eyes look pained suddenly, like he really wants me to understand.

There's real sincerity in his voice. I take a deep breath.

'There's something I haven't told you, Theo. I told you that I'd broken up with my ex-boyfriend because of differences. Well, that isn't true.' My eyes well up again. 'Well, actually he was my husband and he, err. He died. Nearly two years ago now. It was a shock.'

He closes his eyes briefly, chews his bottom lip slightly and bows his head down to the table, as if he's praying. Finally, he looks up.

'I am so sorry. I had no idea. How do you . . . ? How does anyone get through something like that?'

'It's OK. It was ages ago now, I should probably have got over it.' I wipe away the tears; no one will ever understand me and my complicated back story. I should probably scrap all the fake things I write on my Tinder bio and replace it with *inconsolable widow*.

'It doesn't matter how long ago something like that happens, it always has a place in your heart. I'm sorry, Milly.'

'Thank you.' And I look up into his eyes, mine now brimming with tears. 'I'm not sure if I'm ready. I do really like you too, Theo – you're the first person I have liked since Adam. But I'm so scared. I don't want to get hurt again. I feel guilty. What happens if I get upset?'

'I understand, Milly. Look, I'll be with you, give you space, whatever it is that you need. I won't pressure you to do anything. I just want to tell you that I really like you, and I'm happy to take things slowly, you know? We can look at the path as it comes; if it's too difficult, we will end things. But I'd like you to give me a chance?'

'You say slow – at a snail's pace?' I look up, smiling. I know what my friends, Violet would say – I shouldn't let Theo go.

'Ha, yes, a snail's pace.' He grins back, his dimples almost grinning by themselves.

I smile and he takes my hand. I lean across the table to kiss him. There's something that seems so familiar about him.

Maybe I can give this thing called love a chance again? Life, love, relationships, it all has a very funny way of working sometimes.

'Why don't you tell me all about him?'

'Who?' I look confused.

'Adam, of course!'

No one has ever asked me that. Before I know it, I've launched into a story about how we first met, what we used to do together, his funny habits and mine too. Theo listens patiently, laughing in all right the places and genuinely looks interested in my real-life story.

I struggle sometimes, feeling guilty about being happy. Good things can happen. The past is not the present.

@Mizzennial I can't believe it. I just did the one thing I think I was most afraid of. Telling someone I really like about my deceased husband. He didn't brush me away or make me feel stupid. He made me feel better than ever! #TheseMouthsAreMadeForTalking

8 June 2017

'What are you doing?' I ask Adam as I walk into the bedroom.

'I'm sorting out my things. I remember my dad doing it for my grandpa and it made him really upset, a horrible job. I'm putting the things I don't want or need in a bin bag. Can you take them to the charity shop for me? Over in that bag, the one I've marked "Big Day", that's what I want to wear in the coffin. I chose my All Saints shirt, black jeans and my new Nikes, the ones you bought me. Do you think that's OK? It needs to be a day-to-night outfit, really. As I'm not sure if you get to change your clothes in heaven, or do you have to wear the same thing every day?'

It's all too much. I burst into tears on the bed.

'Oh, little daff. Come here.' He rushes over to me and pulls me into his arms. 'I'm sorry, I'm just trying to be helpful. I want everything to be easy for you.'

'I know, I know. Just you in here chucking out your clothes because you're going to die – it's all so macabre. I just can't do it. I don't want to think about it any more. It's all so unfair. I want to pretend it's not happening, that it's a practical joke and the doctors will turn around and say the cancer's all gone.'

'I know, darling Mills, but that isn't true. I feel useless just sitting around waiting to die.'

We hug and cry on each other's shoulders before I break the silence.

'Can you not throw everything out? I want to keep some of your clothes, maybe your navy woollen jumper. Keep wearing it though and don't wash it, I want it to smell of you.'

'Of course, anything you want.' He kisses me on the forehead. I want it to imprint on my soul so I can feel him kiss me forever. 'I've written you a letter, here. I just want to give it to you now, so I know you have it. I want you to know just how much I love you and what a special person you are. It's not the last letter by any means, but I want you to have this one now.'

He stands up and goes into the kitchen to make a cup of tea, and I open the little piece of white parchment.

Little Daff,

I want you to know how truly special you are. You're a wonder woman, brave, loving, charismatic. There's no one in the world I'd rather be going through this process with. There's no one in the world who would be as strong as you're being.

Every morning, when I turn and look at you sleeping in bed, I am thankful that we met all those years ago roller-skating at uni. I'm so pleased you gave in to my bad jokes and let me take your hand in mine.

You will make the most incredible partner to someone else one day and I never want you to feel bad about moving on – it feels so important to me letting you know that. You have my blessing.

I wanted to tell you some of your little quirks that I love so much so you can feel special in everything you do:

I love the way that when you sing, it sounds like a cat screeching down a blackboard.

I love the way you nuzzle into my shoulder in the morning.

I love the way we are totally opposite yet the same all at once – you watch the Kardashians and I love Julius Caesar, yet we share our love of fruit on pizza.

I love the way we can poke fun at each other – you're no comedian, but you make me laugh every day.

I love the way you pretend you're a good cook, when we both know I'm the best.

I love the way your four moles form on your back and you say it's your star sign.

I love the way you find people falling over on YouTube literally the funniest thing.

I love the way you're you.

All my love, forever and always,
Adam X

31

3 April 2019

I live about ten minutes' walk from the station. It isn't a particularly scenic route, as you can imagine – Croydon isn't known for its haven of green patches and unusual bird species. The pavements are delicately scattered with chicken bones and cigarette butts, not manicured green hedges and pots of geraniums. You have to walk with your head down to stop people asking you for money, (they wouldn't waste their time on me if they could see inside my bank account), but also to ensure you don't step on faeces (probably human), sick (again probably human), mushed-up doner kebab, or a drunk person.

Normally, when I walk (drag my feet) to work, I have my AirPods in and am completely unaware of my surroundings. Not today.

The weight of secrets, lies, grief has been lifted from my shoulders. I feel liberated. Able to show off to everyone about Adam as if he was a trophy in my cabinet. Not hide him away like a naughty secret.

I was so caught up in myself that I nearly smashed straight into the glass door of the tax-avoiding conglomerate I love to support.

'Hey girl!' @ILikeMyMenHotAndBlack beams at me over the counter. 'One oat-milk flat white coming your way!'

'Thanks, Sophie! What happened to you the other night?'

'Oh, ha.' She looks sheepish. 'I went home with the bouncer!'

'No fucking way! Did you sleep with him?'

'Milly, I'm twenty-eight. Do you think he plaited my hair before we played fire trucks? Yes, we had sex, and he was insane!'

'What do you mean "insane"?!' I try to remember the last time I described sex with a stranger as insane. God, I can't even think about having sex with Theo yet; it'll be like losing my virginity all over again.

'I'm not trying to be crass, but his penis was like the head of a snake. He had a towel on – I thought I had been dick-fished for a second – but it was 100 per cent real. Never seen anything like it!' It makes me shudder; I hope Theo hasn't been taking growth hormones. I'm barely ready to have sex, let alone mate with Medusa.

'Are you seeing him again?'

'Tonight, actually – I can't wait!' and she hands me the coffee, and I depart, wincing a little as I walk.

Ping.

@ILikeMyMenHotAndBlack has sent me a picture. *Gross!* Before you send anyone a picture, you should say to yourself, 'Would I be embarrassed if my mum saw this?'

This one's for you @LlikeMyMenHotAndBlack.

How do you know what type of shoal you are messaging? Did you answer mainly As, Bs or Cs?

a. Hatfish. I'm sorry but all those photos of him standing at the back of the squad, the close-up selfie of him from about ten years ago, the images you have spent hours scrutinising over where you think it looks like he has swept his hair forward. They are trying to tell you something – he has a receding hairline. You are being hatfished. There's nothing wrong with it, but you need to grab the bull by the horns before he starts wearing a Rod Stewart wig to your first date.

b. Catfish. You think you've seen him before somewhere. The rock-solid six-pack abs, the arms of steel, teeth as white as snow. He is probably from the television, a Columbian model they never thought you would recognise. You, my friend, are being catfished by the polar opposite of a model. Possibly even a polar bear. Run. Run as fast as you can before you get mauled to death.

c. Dickfish. You've been sent pictures that make you recoil in agonising horror. The thought of the first date is making you wince in pain. Tens of photos of phallic objects about three feet long being shoved under towels at varying angles but not a photo in the flesh – he is 'saving that for later'. I'm afraid to throw a spanner in the works, but these are the contents of his dad's toolbox. Under there? Well, who knows? Probably a merkin and a cornichon.

Ping!

> **Julia:** Girls, I wanted to let you know that James and I have decided on the name Saffron – Saffy for short. I wanted you to be the first to know! If you don't like it/ know anyone who has that name, just pretend, OK? I'm not going back to the drawing board on this one.
> **Nicky:** Welcome to the gang, Saffy! I'll have the prosecco on ice <heart emoji>
> **Me:** Jules, I LOVE it! Hurry up, baby Saffy, I can't wait to meet you!

I'm seeing Theo tonight and we're doing an 'activity'. It's not that sitting in a bar and drinking gin after gin isn't fun – it's bloody fantastic. However, I've relied on alcohol, drugs and an electronic square with a microchip for a brain to fuel conversations for too long. And hangovers aren't what they used to be. I only have to suck on a grape to induce a migraine and a two-day onslaught of hang-xiety.

We're going to NuttyPutters – it's one of those nouveau London places that's been created for dates. It used to always be 'movie and dinner', but then everyone realised that sitting in the dark, in silence, with a stranger doesn't exactly scream romance, more awkward torture. You can infiltrate the silence by hitting balls off target into spinning ice creams, and it doesn't even matter if you are good at golf or not, because outside these adult toy towns shooting plastic balls into the eye of a giant windmill isn't a life skill anyone really needs.

We give our names and shoe size at the front desk, and in return we each receive a hideous pair of brown-and-white-striped shoes and a tweed flat cap.

'What,' I say, looking down at the pair of shoes hanging from my hand, 'are these?!'

'Golf shoes.'

'That was rhetorical.' I grin. 'It looks like my grandad has dressed me for a date with one of his cronies.'

'They're not exactly Church's, but, I mean, you can pull them off. In a couple of years, they'll be high fashion.' Theo does his up and prances around me like he's on a catwalk, creasing with laughter at his own joke.

'Hope you don't want the deposit back – I might nick them.' I do the left shoe up. 'Do they really think people are going to be stealing these? They shouldn't waste the paperwork.'

'Come on!' he exclaims, raising his eyebrows. 'You can give them some fashion advice later – I've got some golf to beat you at.'

We grab a Diet Coke each at the bar and walk over to the first hole. I can see why it's so hard to get a slot – NuttyPutters is always fully booked – the bright lights and loud music are caressing every button in my brain. All activities nowadays are designed around adults wanting to be kids again – mega ball pits for grown men and women to drown themselves in, soft-play areas to practise our crawling, unicorn bottomless brunches, or even dress up as a wizard and play fight in your local park for the day.

A giant hippo with inviting cartoon eyes and a lolling tongue awaits us.

'You've got to get the ball through his tooth, I think,' Theo says, lining up his ball for the perfect putt and showing me the hole where Mr Hippo appears to have severe decay.

'Who even designs these? It would be such a fun job.' I momentarily imagine myself at NuttyPutters' design HQ before Theo shoots, and the ball bounces off the little plastic wall and boomerangs itself back to the starting position.

'I thought you were supposed to be good at golf?' I joke.

'No one's good at crazy golf – you can't practise it. It would be pretty mortifying admitting that you come to NuttyPutters every Saturday to practise your swing.'

'I might become the first woman champion of crazy golf.'

Theo swings again and this time manages to hit the other wall. 'Why is this one so hard?'

'It's because you've got a stunning girl here, distracting you.' I wink.

He has two more swings and finally gets it through the laughing hippo's tooth.

'My turn!' I rush forward and take a hit without doing any of the measuring up or working out the right angle.

'Oh my God! *Hole in one!*' Theo cheers and we high-five.

'Told you I would be a champion.'

'Beginner's luck, more like.' He marks our score in the little book.

We stroll over to hole two: a giant helter-skelter – this one looks hard even for a reigning champion like myself.

'What's that weird term in golf again? A buzzard?'

'Ha ha, do you mean a birdie?' Theo laughs.

'Yeah, that's it! Why does such a serious, emotionless sport have such hilarious names for things?'

'It's when you hit one under par on a hole. So, if the average was five, and you got four, then it would be a birdie. Two under par is called an eagle, and three under par is called an albatross.'

'Great mansplaining.' I giggle. 'Wow, so technically, I'm an albatross.'

'I'm not sure it works like that in crazy golf, but if you want – yes, you're an albatross.'

Theo goes to take his swing and slips on the artificial green. I lunge to catch him but in the process release my golf club up into the air. He falls backwards, laughing hysterically, while I watch my club land with a clatter in the helter-skelter.

The surrounding couples, presumably also on dates, look at us horrified and, I assume, seem thankful that their other half is better on the green than us two first-timers.

'Theo, are you OK?' I say, concerned, although his aching cheeks are already telling me the answer.

'I'm fine. I'm fine!' he replies, bashing away my helping hand. 'Please tell me that's not your club?!' He points to the lone stick hanging lost out of the little window at the top.

'Now you know I'm a keeper – I'd do anything to save you. Even lose my albatross status.'

One of the NuttyPutters employees starts walking towards us to find out what's led to this unusual scenario. He appears kind of stern despite Theo and I wetting ourselves with hysterics.

We try to explain what's led to my golf club smashing through the helter-skelter, with Theo cleverly adding that his slip should be recorded in the accident book but Mr-I-Live-For-Days-When-I-Can-Show-My-Authority assumes we're drunk and forces us to leave. We were laughing so much I nearly forgot to go and collect my own shoes – at least now I can see why they ask for the deposit.

'Stop!' My breathing's so erratic it's causing me to hiccup. I haven't laughed like this in years. 'We weren't even drunk!'

'No, go on tell me. How much of a twat did I look?' Theo's laughing too. So much that he spills his iced-tea mocktail all down his front.

It was quite an ordeal at NuttyPutters. Really embarrassing, no, hilarious. But I don't feel embarrassed in front of Theo. I feel closer to him. When I first met Adam, I stacked it at a roller disco, like Bambi on ice – I clearly have a history of literally falling for someone. It's these comical moments that we share that become the intermissions in our story. We share grief, anger, love, friendship, so many emotions with the people close to us, but as long as we can laugh about it, everything will be OK.

25 July 2017

'Milly?' Adam says as we lie on the bed next to each other. We do this quite often now. He gets tired and I enjoy purely being still with him. We used to lie in bed together a lot at uni; we've always just enjoyed each other's company.

I turn on my side to look at him.

'I want to admit something.'

I nod, allowing him the space to speak.

'I'm a bit afraid of dying.'

I clasp his hands, feeling a sudden rush of emotions. This is my time to step up. Be the rock he needs. I can't admit that I would be scared too, I think everyone is.

'Don't be afraid of death. It's peaceful. When I close my eyes, I imagine it to be everything that I always wanted the Earth to be. Think of it as everything positive and nothing negative. It's the dream world you create in your imagination.' I smile. 'It's all PlayStation and Hawaiian pizza for you.'

'And you, Mills, you'd be there every second of every day. It seems silly to be afraid of something that's the only certainty in life. I think it's just the unknown of it all. I just wanted to tell you because we never have any secrets.'

'I know.' I clasp his hands tighter. 'It's OK to be afraid of things, though. It's nothing to be ashamed of.'

'I just wanted you to know that I am a bit afraid, but I never want you to be afraid of it. Because I'll already be there waiting for you with open arms. So, you should never be afraid of anything because whatever is there in this new world, you'll still always have me.'

We look at each other, our eyes wet with tears, and continue lying next to each other in silence, holding hands. He strokes the top of mine and I stroke his palm.

32

This day is all about me. I'm being selfish, but for all the right reasons.

My episode of *Talk Thirty To Me* is ready to be released to the public. @ShelleyFarrell sent me the recording for approval. I thought I wouldn't be able to press play, there's nothing more excruciating than hearing your own voice back. Especially listening to it talk about a pain I've harboured for so long, but I listened to the whole thing. I found it therapeutic. Hearing a familiar voice speak about grief, everything I feel, everything I've experienced, made it feel as if I was listening to a well-versed friend who had also loved and lost. The part of my soul that has been in hiding for so long is finally being released from captivity. The part of me that's been responding to all those people on Mizzennial for the last few weeks.

I sent the link to Theo, Layla and Florry – I wanted their approval. They said I was amazing and should be proud of myself, but I still feel nervous. It's my biggest secret, admitting that I'm still sad sometimes.

Violet looks younger today. Her hair's tamed, as if she's employed Alan Titchmarsh for some last-minute pruning. Her eyelashes are coated in a thick, black mascara and her skin's glowing. I would say she's been on holiday, but I've been speaking to her nearly every day, so I know this isn't true.

'You look different today, Violet?'

'Do I?' She smiles and looks over the moon with the half-compliment.

'Yes, the Botox reaction must've been worth it.' Maybe I should contemplate some minor facial enhancements myself?

'If you must know, I met someone. At a social media conference. I know it is totally hypocritical of me, but I cannot stop going on his social media. I'm suddenly addicted to my phone!' She laughs, and I laugh too.

'See, Violet, love makes us do crazy things! My podcast's coming out today – you can listen to it if you like.'

'I will! How do you feel about that, Milly?'

'I listened to the whole thing, and I found it therapeutic. Hearing my own voice was like being reunited with an old friend.'

'Why don't you try recording how you feel occasionally? It might be good therapy for you, now ours has come to an end. Obviously, I am always here for you, but I don't think you need me any more.'

'I might start a podcast you know – a millennial group-therapy type thing. Very of the moment.'

'You will be giving me a run for my money soon, Milly! I better up my game.'

'Ha. Thank you for everything, Violet, you've switched my life upside down.'

'You've made me revaluate mine too, at points.'

'Are you still OK for me to call you on Sunday?'

'Of course, Milly, like I said, whenever you need me, but you're doing pretty well by yourself these days.'

I smile, she smiles and I log-off.

I send Layla a message:

Me: Still OK for Sunday? X

I turn my phone over and get back to reading my book. I've started this new thing, where instead of scrolling incessantly online, I read for ten minutes. It can be anything, but my latest literature is *The Success of a Sunderland Life Coach*. I want to help people that don't know they need help.

My phone buzzes across the sofa.

Layla: Of course! I'll meet you at The Hampshire at 10am. X

I'm feeling strong today. Empowered by my ability to change my life around. I've been in a dark place for so long, it's refreshing to see how quickly, with a bit of determination and the right people surrounding me, I was able to scramble out of it. And I did it myself. I can be alone.

I open Instagram and scroll. I flick my thumb up and down really fast, the little nine-square grid populating as I go; nights out with friends, holidays around the world, family dinners, birthdays, selfies, puppies, Christmases. I need to get back to where it all began – 21 April 2013. My first ever photo on Instagram. A lilac macaroon – I was trying to be artsy, back when people envisaged the app would be for budding photographers not bragging and soft porn. I photographed things, not people, all complete with a highly overexposed filter and taken very poorly on an iPhone 4.

As I slowly scroll upwards, the quality of my photos starts to improve. I start to see all the significant moments in my life that I chose to capture. Flooding my mind with memories. I didn't used to use the platform to brag to the world but for myself. My life, my friends, my memories. It's like someone unlocking the vault of hidden memories inside your brain, ones that are often clouded by more significant ones, but don't lack importance on the happiness scale.

However nostalgic I'm choosing to be, that's not what I'm here for.

And suddenly there he is, in all his glory. His debut on the grid. Adam, smiling into the camera eating an ice cream. And he features again and again and again. Selfies of us on Brighton Pier, sunbathing on holiday, candid shots of us at Florry's wedding, him walking around the common, brunches we shared, nights out we enjoyed, Adam with his friends, me with mine. Memories. Happy memories.

Tears are falling down my face, but I'm not sad. All these moments that I locked away in my steel casket of grief have come back, but not to haunt me, to enlighten me, invigorate my soul once more.

I don't know how long I've been sitting here. At least a few hours. I have successfully ordered all the photos of Adam and I. *Memories are Forever*, that's what I'll call the album. It's meant to sound like a greatest hits album, because it is – the crème de la crème of our time together, what we'd been working our entire lives for.

I click onto Adam's Facebook. I take a few deep breaths and I unfriend. I don't need to absorb myself in an online profile; Adam didn't really care for it when he was alive, so he wouldn't be bothered about it now he's dead. I have all the memories I need and I have the people to share them with. Adam has died. His online profile doesn't make him any more alive. In fact, I think it makes him even more dead.

I've been gradually psyching myself up to today's last bombshell move. The candid openness of complete strangers, trusting me with their problems, has finally given me the courage I need.

@Mizzennial Dear Mizzennial crew, as you probably guessed from some of my previous posts, my husband died nearly two years ago now and I've been struggling to come to terms with it. I want to thank every single one of you, because your comments and messages have enabled me to see the light. I recently did a podcast on *Talk Thirty To Me,* where I discuss my experience with death. Link in bio – please listen and leave your comments below. Milly X

I walk the few steps from the sofa to the kitchen, boil the kettle and make myself a soothing cup of tea. I take a few deep breaths; consider the mountain I've climbed and allow my mind and body to reset. I can hear my phone pinging and buzzing. I need a few more moments without it, to prepare myself for the onslaught.

@ILikeMyMenHotAndBlack HUGE love, Mills! x
@ShelleyFarrell You star x
@FlorryMarie That's my sister! x
@AvaisFashun Inspirational – you go, girl! x
@Nicky666 I think you need to start your own podcast! x
@JuliaKnight I'm so proud of you x
@BlueisMyMood Bravery doesn't even cut it x
@FrothisDroth I want to hear more from you – so real x

A tear forms in my right eye. The corners of my mouth start to twitch. My heart starts to beat faster. I smile. I'm smiling. I'm fucking smiling! People do love me. People do care! I just hadn't known how to let them in.

I call Theo, grab my bag, and go out for dinner.

That happiness that I yearned for, aching in my bones, flowing in my blood. I've finally got it.

1 March 2017

We walk in silence for a few minutes. It's a beautiful day, pale blue sky, barely any clouds, but cold. The daffodils are out in force on the common, I wonder how I'll feel when I see the little yellow trumpets waving in the breeze after he's gone. Happy memories or will it make me too sad to look at.

'How are you feeling about it all, Milly?' Layla asks keeping pace with me.

How am I feeling? What a question. I don't even know if words can describe it.

'Actually, stupid question, don't answer it. I don't know how I'm feeling myself.' Layla answers her own question for me – thank God.

'Oh, Layla, I'm so sad. I don't know what to do. I feel like more and more pieces of my heart are breaking off every single day.'

'Me too, Mills. You've been amazing for Adam – you know that, don't you? He really loves you.'

'I love him so much too. I don't really know what I'll do, you know, after he's gone.'

'Me neither.' Her eyes well and mine mirror hers.

'I keep trying not to cry, as there's so much time after it's all happened for that. I want everything to be enjoyable, perfect for him.' I say, looking at all the bursts of yellow against the green grass, I want everything to be perfect.

'It's OK to be upset, though. I'm always here. Just a train ride or a phone call away. It's so depressing at home – Mum and Dad are in bits. I try and be strong for them, but no one's really strong when it comes to death, are they?'

'No, I guess there's no point trying to cover a sadness that everyone's eventually succumbed to. Pointless.'

'What a fucking shitter, eh? Why is he always so bloody positive too? He's like a fucking angel!' Layla laughs.

'What a wanker. A glorious wanker!' I laugh too.

We smile at each other through the tears.

'Thanks for always being here, Mills. Things are going to be tough, but at least we have each other.'

'Love you, sis.'

'Love you too!'

We embrace for what seems like a lifetime but probably was only a few seconds. I bend down and pick a few daffodils to take back to Adam.

33

Despite the unusual luxury of a duck down pillow, I thought I wouldn't be able to sleep last night. Mum and Dad paid for me to stay in a five-star hotel to ensure this trip was memorable for all the right reasons. I thought my mind would be wandering and my thoughts frantic, but my sleep was so deep, so comforting, when I woke, I had totally forgotten where I was.

Layla will be here soon. I brush my hair out and look at myself long and hard in the mirror, trying to stare away any last-minute nerves.

I want to look nice, of course. Who wouldn't? But I want to make sure I look exactly like myself. My cheeks look plumper, no thanks to being unable to properly exercise for weeks, but my face looks fuller. Full of life. Happiness really does take years off you.

Layla: Running a tad late, be there in five. L X

Enough time for me to get one last piece of moral support.

'Milly, don't you look lovely!'

'Do you think? I want to look exactly how he would remember me.'

'You look beautiful, Milly, and happy. You look happy!'

'Thanks, Violet, I am happy. And I wanted to say, thank you so much for everything you have done for me. You won't ever know how much I appreciate it.'

'You did this all yourself. I was just there to give you a gentle nudge now and again. Remember, this isn't goodbye, but hello, to the new you.'

I end the call. I didn't even pay her for that one.

I see her golden hair from the lobby, surrounding her like a halo. My angel.

'Milly!' Layla beams and pulls me into a huge bear hug. I feel my eyes stinging with tears. I can hear him next to me – *'You've only just done your make-up, silly! Think of something funny like that time you told the interviewer at your old job you were reading* Fifty Shades of Grey.'

'Let's go, shall we? No point in hanging round here.'

She has the same piercing blue eyes as Adam, the ones that make you think she has peeled back your skin and is reading your soul. That happy-go-lucky attitude, where you don't dwell on the past but only look to the future. They still remind me of the ocean, but I can look at it now.

We walk in silence, not an awkward one, just comfortable quiet. There was nothing that needed to be said. Nothing significant enough. Finally, we stop. I put my hand on the top of the heavy wooden gate and push it open.

'Stop,' Layla says immediately. Her voice cracking, tears tumbling down her face. 'I can't do it.'

'You can, I promise.' I pull her towards me and grab her bony little shoulders. 'I know the pain feels debilitating at times – dealing with his loss is so hard. There are good days and bad days. Sometimes I don't want to get out of bed and other days I have this weird energy to take back control of my life.'

Layla looks down at the floor, nodding in agreement. 'But you always seem so knowledgeable on Mizzennial. I'm not like that. You're brave, Milly.'

'I'm not brave!' I snort. 'Every day is a battle for me, just as much as it is for you. I'm just learning to live with grief and not keep putting myself down for not getting over it. He was special, to both of us – it will never be easy.' I take her hand in mine. 'I can't do it without you, anyway.'

We fill our lungs with the fresh country air. It feels like bragging, taking in so much oxygen in a graveyard, but I know it isn't. We can't help being alive.

Fresh flowers are already present in front of the gravestone.

'Mum,' Layla whispers. 'She puts them there every week.'

We both stand in silence. Crying.

Adam Michael Hadfield
2 February 1990 – 8 August 2017
Loving grandson, son, brother and husband.
Taken too soon. Rest in Peace.

I lay a copy of *Caesar, Life of a Colossus* by his grave. It must be boring for him up there. And then I start to read aloud.

'Adam, I want to tell you I'm sorry. I want to apologise for not being my best self after you were diagnosed.

'Ever since you died, I've felt guilty. It should have been me – I haven't made the best of my life in the way that you would have done if it was the other way around. I haven't done your life justice. I can't bear to remember you; it makes my stomach churn and coil. I haven't forgotten you, far from it, but the memories we shared together were so fun, so buoyant, so full of life and that is far from what I've been.

'Every day, something reminds me of you. A smell, an advert, a note of music. I walk in the street and I smell a man wearing your aftershave. I laugh at silly adverts and turn to my right on the sofa where you used to sit next to me. Songs play on the radio that we used to sing together.

'I wince every time I see tomatoes in a BLT, as you'd always pick them out. I cry at pickles in Big Macs. I throw Bourbons at the wall in rage.

'I've been so angry at everyone, at you. I want to apologise. You completed me, made me into a better person than I was alone. I've been acting out over the last two years; I've been horrible. I used your loss as a scapegoat for everything else in my life. I don't want to remember you like that.

'I know you told me to move on with my life and never feel guilty, but it's so hard. I wanted to write this letter to you, to tell you that I love you and I always will. Regardless of what happens in my life, my heart remains yours. I've realised that I can't spend my life feeling guilty and scared. I have to move on, but I want you to know that you will never be forgotten.

'I think you'd be proud of me now. I've started this Instagram account and I've made loads of new friends. I've even started having the odd hot chocolate again because it reminds me of you, in a good way.

'It's really hard grief, but it does get better. You never forget what has happened, but you learn to live with it. I'm glad you never had to go through it.

'Love you forever and always,

Little Daff x.'

As the intense weight of grief is lifted from my shoulders, I cry. I can't stop. It's everything. Emotion, relief, love. I should have done this years ago. Who knew it would take this long.

'I love you. I love you so much,' I whisper to the sky.

'That was beautiful, Milly.' Layla turns to me, her eyes and cheeks wet, still holding my hand.

Finally, we hug goodbye. Layla goes back to her parents and I head on the train back to London. I'm not quite ready to see Adam's parents again yet, but I will be. Things take time. Layla and I are meeting for coffee next week when she's in London for work. I don't know why I victimised her so much – after all, she was going through the same tragic loss as me. Layla was the only person that really understood.

Theo: Get home safely, Mills. I can get a pizza for us tonight if you like. Hawaiian, your favourite? X

Theo is nice. Really nice. I think I like him, but it's too early to tell. He won't ever be Adam, but that's OK. He can be wonderful in a different way. There can't ever be two of anyone.

There's one last thing I need to do before I can indulge in a pizza and a huge glass of wine. I purchase flowers from the local Waitrose – yellow daffodils, my favourite. *Our* favourite. I hated them after he died, but I love them again now. They make me remember. I walk to the nearly fatal spot all those weeks ago and contemplate how far I've come. I'm finally the girl I used to be. I'm back to the charismatic, zest-for-life Milly Dayton. I have an edge of darkness, but doesn't everyone?

I lay the flowers on the pavement, where the Toyota Yaris once ravaged me. There isn't always a silver lining and it's nigh on impossible to see the positive in the love of your life being diagnosed with a terminal illness, but some things do happen for a reason. And I guess, being hit by a car was the lesson I needed.

Reaching rock bottom catapulted me to the top again. I've learned to walk and to love again. I can smile without faking it and be happy without trying.

I needed to make my peace with Adam's passing, to make peace with myself and everyone else again.

Welcome back, me.

Acknowledgements

Thank you to my friends and family and to the following people:

Victoria Hughes-Williams, the first person other than my mum to read the initial draft - I wouldn't be here without you.

My incredible agent, Hayley Steed at Madeleine Milburn, for believing in me, shaping and cultivating my ideas into my first novel.

My editor, Bea Fitzgerald, for your encouragement and enthusiasm throughout the editorial process. Your meticulous insight and wit has made *Love Loss and Little White Lies* better than I ever could have imagined.

To my husband, for his unfaltering support through all of my drafts and for always lending an ear to my many ideas.

My mum, thank you for reading every single draft possible and for just being the greatest.

Finally, thank you to my friends and family once more for believing in me, for reading snippets, for childcare and for being the most supportive group of people I could wish for.

About the Author

Born in North Norfolk, India grew up along its picturesque coastline before leaving to study Cell Biology at Durham University and embark on a career in Marketing.

Expanding from the tiny towns of East Anglia to the hustle and bustle of the big city made her see the world for all its wonders and faults — it's a big place to try and change yourself but India wants to give muted societal issues a voice and give scary topics a friendly face.

She believes all good ideas come from a spicy Bloody Mary, a niche documentary and over-hearing conversations in cafes.

India lives in South West London, with her husband and Crocodile Rock obsessed one-year-old, Archie.

Love Loss and Little White Lies is her first novel.